FIRST
CUT

FIRST CUT

Also by Judy Melinek and T.J. Mitchell

Working Stiff: Two Years, 262 Bodies, and the Making of a Medical Examiner

FIRST CUT

A NOVEL

JUDY MELINEK
AND T.J. MITCHELL

HANOVER
SQUARE
PRESS

HANOVER
SQUARE
PRESS™

Recycling programs
for this product may
not exist in your area.

ISBN-13: 978-1-335-08133-9

First Cut

First published in 2020. This edition published in 2021.

This edition published by arrangement with Harlequin Books S.A.

Hanover Square Press
22 Adelaide St. West, 40th Floor
Toronto, Ontario M5H 4E3, Canada
HanoverSqPress.com
BookClubbish.com

Printed in U.S.A.

For both our moms, who love a good detective.
In memory of Eric Lundstedt.

FIRST
CUT

PROLOGUE

LOS ANGELES

MAY

The dead woman on my table had pale blue eyes, long lashes, no mascara. She wore a thin rim of black liner on her lower lids but none on the upper. I inserted the twelve gauge needle just far enough that I could see its beveled tip through the pupil, then pulled the syringe plunger to aspirate a sample of vitreous fluid. That was the first intrusion I made on her corpse during Mary Catherine Walsh's perfectly ordinary autopsy.

The external examination had been unremarkable. The decedent appeared to be in her midthirties, blond hair with dun roots, five foot four, 144 pounds. After checking her over and noting identifying marks (monochromatic professional tattoo of a Celtic knot on lower left flank, appendectomy scar on abdomen, well-healed stellate scar on right knee), I picked up a scalpel and sliced from each shoulder to the breastbone, and then all the way down her belly. I peeled back the layers of skin and fat on her torso—an ordinary amount, maybe a little on the chubby side—and opened the woman's chest like a book.

I had made similar Y-incisions on 256 other bodies during

my ten months as a forensic pathologist at the Los Angeles County Medical Examiner-Coroner's Office, and this one was easy. No sign of trauma. Normal liver. Healthy lungs. There was nothing wrong with her heart. The only significant finding was the white, granular material of the gastric contents. In her stomach was a mass of semidigested pills.

When I opened her uterus, I found she'd been pregnant. I measured the fetus's foot length and estimated its age at twelve weeks. The fetus appeared to have been viable. It was too young to determine sex.

I deposited the organs one by one at the end of the stainless-steel table, and started working on the head.

"Howdy, ladies."

"Howdy back," I said, without looking up from cutting into the dead woman's scalp. It was Matt, the forensic investigator who had collected the body the day before. We were alone in the autopsy suite. Matt was prone to bad jokes.

"Clean scene," he reported, depositing the paperwork on my station. "Suicide."

I asked him where he was going for lunch. Yogurt and a damn salad at his desk, he told me: bad cholesterol and a worried wife. I extended my condolences as he headed back out of the autopsy suite.

I scanned through Matt's handwriting on the intake sheet and learned that the body had been found, stiff and cold, in a locked and secure room at the Los Angeles Omni Hotel. The cleaning staff called the police. The ID came from the name on the credit card used to pay for the room, and was confirmed by fingerprint comparison with her driver's license thumbprint. A handwritten note lay on the bed stand, a pill bottle in the trash. Nothing else. Matt was right: There was no mystery to the way Mary Walsh had died.

I hit the dictaphone's toe trigger and pointed my mouth

toward the microphone dangling over the table. "The body is identified by a Los Angeles County Medical Examiner's tag attached to the right great toe, inscribed LACD-03226, Walsh, Mary Catherine…"

I broke the seal on the plastic evidence bag and pulled out the pill bottle. It was labeled *OxyContin*, and it was empty.

"Accompanying the body is a sealed plastic bag with an empty prescription medication bottle. The name on the prescription label…"

I read the name but didn't speak it. The hair started standing up on my neck. I looked down at my morning's work—the splayed body, flecked with gore, the dissected womb tossed on a heap of other organs.

That can't be, I told myself. *It can't.*

On the clipboard underneath the case intake sheet I found a piece of hotel stationery sealed in another evidence bag. It was the suicide note, written in blue ink with a steady feminine hand. I skimmed it—then stopped, and went back.

I read it again.

I heard the clipboard land at my feet. I gripped the raised lip of my autopsy table. I held tight while the floor fell away.

PART ONE

SAN FRANCISCO

JULY

CHAPTER ONE

The summer fog in my new neighborhood doesn't burn off, it doesn't lift, and it doesn't fade away: It sits, clammy and stifling. I was underdressed and had to turn on the heat in my car. Cranking up the heater in July. What the hell is wrong with this place?

"It's a green arrow!" I hollered at the silver Prius in front of me. *"Rusz się—!"*

When me and my brother Tommy were growing up, our immigrant mom spoke to us only in Polish. The mother tongue lashes out of me sometimes. Sitting in my growling BMW 235i at the bottleneck left turn off of Stanyan Street by Golden Gate Park was one of those times.

"Light not green enough for you? *Rusz się,* already!" The driver didn't move. I hit the horn. He glowered into his rearview. He had an ironic waxed mustache and a goatee and a little peaked hat like a fucking goatherd.

I got to the Hall of Justice with barely five minutes to spare. The Hall is a fossil, a crumbling ash-gray concrete box squatting over a bleak city block at 850 Bryant Street. It houses

JUDY MELINEK & T.J. MITCHELL

most of the police department, a courthouse, the city jail—
and, tucked into the back like a dirty secret, my new place of
employ, the San Francisco Office of Chief Medical Examiner. With its honeycomb of identical undersized windows
and a three-sided staircase leading into oversized doorways,
the Hall was built on a scale calculated to intimidate. It does.

I made it past the line of double-parked police vehicles and
cut down the alley to the loading dock, where I'd been instructed to park. It was full: two morgue vans and a bunch of
cars. One was a hearse with a black-clad man standing over
an empty gurney, writing something on a clipboard. I took a
chance and rolled down my window.

"Hey, excuse me—you're in my space there."

The mortician looked up. "Who're you?"

"Dr. Jessie Teska."

He peered at my dashboard. "Where's your placard?"

The parking pass! It was on top of an unopened moving box
on my kitchen table, along with a pile of insurance paperwork
and other bullshit I still needed to read and sign.

"It's my first day, I don't have one yet," I lied.

"Gonna need a placard, ma'am," the mortician said, and
rolled his gurney toward the loading dock at the end of the
cramped lot.

"Wait, wait—" I pleaded, but my voice vanished in the
roar of a highway viaduct directly overhead. The mortician
pushed up the ramp to a pair of gray metal doors, then stood
aside as they slid open. A figure came out—an Asian woman
with thick black hair and long hard legs. In one hand she carried a pair of textbooks.

In the other? Car keys.

"Excuse me!" I yelled through a stinking cloud of dust off
the freeway.

"You're in luck," the woman said before I could even ask. "I'm in the Subaru, just up the block."

I could've kissed her, and said so. She smiled brightly and pointed her chin to the curb, at a cobalt blue sports car, the supercharged type of thing that frat boys at UCLA like to drive. I swung out of the loading dock and swooped my Beemer into the space as she left it.

First day of work and five minutes late. When I entered the conference room, that was the verdict on every face. Every face but one.

———

Deputy Chief Medical Examiner Michael Stone offered an effusive welcome and crossed the room to usher me in. I had first run across Mike five or six years earlier, when I was a pathology resident at UCLA. He was directing a research project, and had flown down from San Francisco to Los Angeles to collect some specimens. I was struck by his exuberance about his vocation: He tried to recruit me as a forensic pathologist on the spot. "Lab pathology will bore you to death," he pitched. "You want to sit in a basement all day, staring through a microscope, slowly going blind? No—you do not."

Dr. Stone struck me as an overgrown nerd, brilliant and opinionated and completely unfiltered. I like nerds, and I've been told many times—many times—that I could use a stronger filter myself. He was tall and ropy, rugged but not handsome, with big features all around—a bulbous nose, long face, bushy animated eyebrows, blocky crooked teeth. He had gigantic muscled hands, more like a welder's than a doctor's. His Adam's apple pursued its own berserk notions of what it should be doing. He spoke too loudly anytime he was in charge of a group, especially if there were students.

Half the room wore white coats, one guy had green hospital scrubs, and the rest were in business attire. A lifeless oil painting of some past chief medical examiner glared down like a god in judgment, a reminder of better days, decades back, when the office was flush with funds and well staffed. Now it was falling apart and shorthanded. I took in the scarred tabletop, the mismatched chairs, the half-assed lighting.

Nicks and scratches don't bother me. I need this job.

Dr. Stone went around the conference table and introduced everyone. One name rang a bell: Dr. Ted Nguyen, the other assistant medical examiner, in the green scrubs and looking bored. The medical students from UCSF, the local teaching hospital, were wearing their lab coats. At the head of the table sat a fireplug of a man and a brick house of a woman. He was bald, with a pinkish oval face. She had hawkish features under short curly hair with frosted tips. Stone introduced them as Cameron Blake and Donna Griello, "our night shift two-five-seven-eights"—the city's administrative code for medical examiner investigators.

Stone had been saving a chair for me and there weren't enough to go around, so most of the students stood along the walls. They looked excited, and I knew why. When you are learning medicine in a teaching hospital, you spend a lot of time lurking over sickbeds while clinicians talk at you. When I was a med student, I had hated it, all that gabbing without doing. One thing you can say about your rotation at the city morgue: There's never a dull moment.

"Please join me in welcoming our new assistant medical examiner, Dr. Jessie Teska," Dr. Stone said. Everyone muttered in greeting, and I mustered a suitable expression of thanks. Stone then swiveled to the medical students and resumed the spiel I'd interrupted.

"Today you are going to see your first forensic autopsy.

It is not at all like the anatomy lab. There will be blood and fecal material. You may be working on trauma cases involving the evisceration of organs or disarticulation of limbs. Some of you might get a little light-headed. That is not an unusual response, especially because you will be wearing a lot of personal protective equipment, and the PPEs get hot and stuffy. So if you feel woozy, do not be afraid to excuse yourself and step out of the autopsy suite. I would rather you do that than make me interrupt my work to peel you off the floor."

Stone waited for the inevitable nervous tittering to subside, then took his seat at the head of the conference table.

"All right. Let's get to work." He turned to the investigators. "Cam…?"

Cameron Blake the 2578 flipped open a manila file and started his presentation without prelude.

"Case SFME-0727 is a twenty-four-year-old female, found unresponsive by staff members at the Bodwell House detox center. Our investigation found the decedent supine in bed with vomitus around her nose and mouth. A search of the sparse residence revealed a half-empty box of cigarettes, within it a small bindle containing powdery white material. There were no syringes, cookers, or other signs of drug abuse at the scene. The body was still warm, with no rigidity, and lividity was unfixed and consistent with the found position. There was no evidence of trauma."

"Okay," Stone said. "Next."

Cam put aside the folder and opened another. "Case SFME-0728 is an eighty-six-year-old man with a history of congestive heart failure, coronary artery disease and hypertension, status post bypass in 2002. His wife called nine-one-one when he choked on his breakfast. Paramedics arrived and intubated him. He remained unconscious and—"

"Did they find anything in his windpipe?"

"They didn't note anything on the EMS run sheet. He survived ten hours at the hospital and expired yesterday at eighteen hundred hours. A CT scan showed anoxic brain injury."

"Next."

Cameron continued rattling off the case list, describing San Francisco's sudden, violent, and unexpected deaths of the preceding twenty-four hours. In the end there were plenty to go around. Dr. Nguyen signed up for a hanging and a motor vehicle fatality. Stone took the old man and the day's only homicide, a single gunshot wound in the back. He instructed me to ease myself into my new job with 0727, the halfway house slam-dunk probable-overdose.

———

Donna Griello was in the women's locker room, lacing up a pair of high-gloss Doc Martens. She and Cam were coming off the night shift, and she had changed out of her polyester work outfit into jeans and a leather jacket that said *RocketDyke* across the back, with a kind of motorcycle missile launching in a blaze of silver studs. She pointed me to the locker full of personal protective equipment, proffered a jaunty grinning salute, and wished me luck.

I wiggled into a Tyvek PPE jumpsuit, a blue plastic apron with sleeve covers, paper booties up to my shins, three different pairs of gloves and liners, and an N-95 respirator mask. I had to wrestle my hair under a bouffant cap, and topped that with a claustrophobic face shield. I was already sweating into this moon suit by the time I shuffled to the autopsy suite. A quick look around didn't help settle my first-day-of-school jitters. My new workplace was a museum piece.

In the Los Angeles morgue I had trained and worked at they had stainless-steel surgical stations. San Francisco had embalming tables of dingy, chipped porcelain. They looked like toilets and operated on the same principle, with a pedal for flushing fluids and stray bits of flesh off the work surface into a floor sump. A pair of brown glass—*glass!*—specimen jars perched at the foot of my table, just waiting to be filled with fresh human tissue and shattered on the floor in a spectacular workplace biohazard. I was horrified.

A middle-aged woman barely five feet tall, cloaked like me in PPEs, approached and introduced herself as Yarina Marchenko, the morgue technician. The single and only morgue technician. There are supposed to be three, she complained, but only money for one. Yarina the tech also managed to mention within thirty seconds that she was a fully accredited medical doctor herself in her native Ukraine. The eyes over her N-95 mask looked me up and down, gauged my age, and reckoned I barely met that standard.

The students were clumped around Dr. Stone's station in the far corner of the room, where he was teaching—loudly—while he cut his case. Dr. Nguyen worked quickly and in silence at the next station. I could see from the tangled mess of limbs on his table that Nguyen had chosen to start with the pedestrian versus panel truck accident. My tools were piled next to the brown glass jars. I did a quick inventory and found everything I required, with one critical exception.

"I need a number twenty-two scalpel," I said to Yarina. She nodded gravely, then reached into her pocket and presented a box that looked like it might hold a fancy pen. She pronounced that it was her personal gift to me.

Inside the box was a pink scalpel handle and a packet of #22 blades.

"It's pink," I observed.

"For the lady doctor," Yarina said.

I hate the color pink. Really do. I don't much like being

called a lady doctor, either. But if it is bad luck, as my *mamusia* always told me, to offer a knife as a gift, it's certainly worse luck to refuse that gift from the coworker who is about to help you cut up a dead body.

"Thank you, Yarina," I said, and may have detected a tiny twitch of a smile in return. I loaded a blank body diagram on a clipboard, and we got to work.

The pale naked corpse was already laid out on the porcelain table. I looked overhead for the dictaphone mic. Yarina scoffed when I asked where it was. No money for dictaphones. So I jotted notes, pen on paper, and drew into the body diagram the elaborate tattoos—trees and swirls and fragments from Rumi—inking over both the woman's arms. A couple of students took an interest, and pretty soon the whole herd had migrated to my table.

"You know what these are for, right?" I said, but only got blank looks in reply. "They camouflage the track marks." I told one of them to fetch the magnifying glass from my pile of tools. It was an antler and brass antique, a gift from my boss in Los Angeles, Dr. Emil Kashiman, when I'd passed the anatomic pathology board exam.

"Use that to take a close look at the antecubital fossa." One student came in close and I flipped the corpse's inner elbow toward the light. The kid jerked back.

"You can handle the body," I said. "It won't bite."

The student took the hand from me, but gingerly. I didn't blame him. You need months of training before holding a fish-cold hand no longer causes every fiber in your body to recoil.

Stone lifted the heart out of the homicide victim he was cutting, dropped it into his grocer's scale, and said, "If you want to see some good track marks, I've got something to show you after we de-gown."

What the hell did he mean by that? I wondered. Judging from the looks they exchanged, so did his medical students.

"I am blood type O-negative, a rare privilege which makes me a universal donor," the deputy chief continued. "When I was a pathology resident, the hospital blood bank called me every fifty-six days like clockwork, and like clockwork I obliged. They award you a pin when you reach a gallon of donations. By the time I completed my residency I had—"

"...a shoebox full of them," Ted Nguyen said, and didn't pause in cutting his motor vehicle accident. "And a T-shirt..."

"...and big towel for beach," muttered Yarina.

Stone erupted in a loud, raw laugh. "Dr. Nguyen and the rest of the staff have heard this story too many times. I'm proud of that shoebox. The only downside of producing all those pints is the scars—I don't heal up well, so I've got some track marks, and no tattoos to hide them. But it's worth it."

The students took turns crowding over my table, passing Dr. Kashiman's magnifier from hand to hand and peering at the camouflaged drug injection scars on my first San Francisco stiff. I smiled behind my N-95 mask. There I was again in a medical examiner morgue, in my element, doing what I did best—taking apart a human body and scrutinizing every single thing in it and on it. Finding answers. Barely two months ago, I had thought I might never lift a scalpel again.

Things are looking up.

"All right, people, Y-incision time—make some room," I said, and shooed the medical students back from the autopsy table. Then, with my new pink scalpel, I pressed into the dead woman's right clavicle and made the first cut.

CHAPTER TWO

I heard Bea going apeshit before I reached the gate at 892 41st Avenue. There's no natural noise so urgent as the baying of an antsy beagle.

"Bea! Enough, Bee-Bee! For Chrissake…"

Back in May when I was house-hunting over the internet from Los Angeles, I'd noticed that the farther west you go—the higher into San Francisco's numbered avenues—the cheaper the listed rents get. Cheaper was what I needed, with a pile of student loan creditors breathing down my neck. The cheapest place I found that included a yard for my dog was on 41st Avenue in the Outer Richmond District.

"The Avenues go into the forties?" Tommy quipped when I called to ask if he would check it out. My tech-serf little brother had left our hometown of Lynn, Massachusetts, years before and had gone native in Northern California just as I had done in Los Angeles, and he was willing to do the apartment-search legwork for me as I prepared for the move to San Francisco.

He called me back that same night. "You have *got* to rent that place."

Tommy is a man of few words. Infernally few, sometimes.

"*Why* do I got to rent it, Tomasz?"

"It's a cable car!"

"What?"

"A cable car! It got dumped out in the sand dunes like a hundred years ago."

"But it's listed as a house."

"Somebody jacked the thing up and built a foundation, then added a kitchen and toilet."

"A cable car house...?"

"Fucken-A!"

Send pictures, I told him.

The place was hidden in the backyard of a dumpy beige two-story building. Tomasz and his smartphone camera entered through a sidewalk gate in a weathered wooden fence. The landlord had painted the inside planks in alternating blue and yellow, and nailed up a line of abalone shells. Spindly trees straight out of Dr. Seuss towered over a haphazard garden—weedy, wild and lush—and a low building, mustard yellow with white trim, fought to emerge from it. The wooden car's loading platform served as a snug porch, its grip rails framing the door.

The interior pictures showed me a pew of bench seats under the vault of the slatted ceiling with its gabled skylights. Tommy had taken a close-up of a brass plate fitted to the molding:

Mahoney Brothers.

#45

1887

Beyond this narrow parlor were two additions—a shoebox of a bedroom and a galley kitchen. The pastel-green fridge had a chrome handle, and the gas range looked to be an old match-lit monster. I didn't see a tub or shower, only a toilet in a water closet off the kitchen. But then I clicked on the final picture in the collection my brother had emailed me. He'd saved the best for last. In the back of the cabin someone had installed a hinged trapdoor into the floor. Hidden underneath the dining room of Mahoney Brothers #45, sunk into the foundation's crawlspace like a shallow grave, was a tiled box with plumbing fixtures and a cast-iron bathtub.

The cable-car cottage at 892 41st Avenue, all 372 square feet of it, lay only half a mile from the beach and cost only $1,900 a month—a steal, everyone assured me, in the country's single most expensive housing market. At that rent I could keep making my crippling student loan payments and not have to lose the BMW. Mahoney Brothers #45 was the one and only thing about San Francisco that I loved at first sight.

Bea the beagle tackled me at the door. I wound my way through moving boxes to grab the leash. We'd only lived in the Richmond District four days, but Bea already had a favorite route. She dragged me across the garden, out the gate, across Fulton Street, and into Golden Gate Park.

My stretch of Golden Gate Park is not the tourist's. It's an overgrown thicket of yew tangles and thorny blackberry. Bea's stubby legs worked like mad, past the Chain of Lakes and all the way down the hill to the Dutch Windmill. And there, just past the tulip garden, she bolted around a blind corner and cut off a runner on the paved path.

"Whoa!" the runner yelped, and I braced for impact.

He didn't slam into me, though, and didn't fall on my dog, either. He landed sideways in a squat, hands splayed out and a startled expression on his face. The runner was an Indian or

Pakistani guy, very dark-skinned, with huge eyes and lashes to match, a long thin nose and a strong chin. The runner pulled himself up and I started to apologize, but he just scowled and took off down the path without even removing his earbuds. He had hard legs and a damned fine ass, and looked altogether fit, with the sort of nonsteroidal athleticism I usually find irresistible. Usually.

"What an asshole," I said to my dog. She seemed to agree.

I unleashed her on Ocean Beach and off she went, bounding into the sand and rotting seaweed and pounding surf, the happiest dog on earth. I jogged down the end of the beach to the rocks underneath the Cliff House, where waterlogged bodies come ashore sometimes. The fog had cleared, but it lurked on the horizon.

"Come on, Bea," I said, clicking the snap hook on the leash until she came to heel. Pulling up stakes was so easy when I was twenty-two and left college for medical school in Los Angeles. Now, at thirty-one, the move from LA to San Francisco had wiped me out.

"Let's get us old ladies home to dinner and bed."

I only realized the phone was ringing when Bea's barking interrupted my dream.

It was Mike Stone. "Want to visit a one-eighty-seven in the Tenderloin? It's late and you're not on call, so you can say no, of course…"

Right. I stumbled around the cable car in search of a pen. One-eighty-seven meant a homicide. No way in hell I could say no to on-the-job murder-scene training from the boss himself.

It was 10:45 p.m. when I turned left off O'Farrell onto

Polk. A solitary patrol cop at a yellow-tape cordon waved her flashlight back and forth and pointed me away from it. When I slowed to a stop instead, she aimed the Maglite's beam in my eyes.

"Polk is closed. Go down to Larkin."

"I'm with the ME," I said.

She swept the light across my dashboard.

"Where's your pass?"

Shit. It was on my goddamn kitchen table, in the same envelope as my parking placard.

"I'm new. They haven't given me one yet."

Cops know when you're lying.

"Show me your badge."

"Same deal."

"Wait," the cop said, and keyed her radio. I put the car in Park. She shined her light around the front of my BMW 235i and wrote something in a fat notepad.

I wasn't waiting long before a big man lit from the knees up by my headlights stormed past the DO NOT CROSS tape. It was Michael Stone, holding his gold ME shield at arm's length. The look on his face made the cop take half a step back.

"Why are you stopping Dr. Teska?" Stone demanded.

"This woman doesn't have a police pass or a badge."

"You're delaying the processing of this one-eighty-seven, Officer."

"I'm sorry, Dr. Stone, but regulations—"

"Regulations allow me to take anyone I want onto a crime scene."

The patrol officer stared down the deputy chief medical examiner for a moment, a finger resting on the key to her shoulder mic. Then she removed her hand.

"Yes, Dr. Stone," the cop said. She held the yellow tape up and told me to drive on through, slowly.

Stone's head shot around to my window. "Don't move, Dr. Teska." He turned back to the patrol officer. "Did you record her VIN and plate?"

"Yes."

"Give me that note."

Now the cop's face showed real anger. "You know I can't do that."

"Did you log it?"

"Excuse me?"

"Did you record Dr. Teska's vehicle identification number and license plate in the crime scene log?"

"No, not yet…"

"It's just in your notebook?"

"Yes."

"Then tear out that page and hand it to me right now, Officer, or I'll have Captain Waters over here faster than you can say shitcanned."

Even under the sickly street lamp, even under the shadow of her billed cap, I saw the patrol officer turn red. Without a word she ripped the page out of her notebook and handed it to Stone. He took it and climbed into my car. I put the Beemer in Drive and crept forward under the yellow tape as the police officer held it up. She glared at us with venom.

When we were past the cordon, Stone said, "Where is your scene pass?"

"On my kitchen table."

"Put it in the glove compartment when you get home."

"Okay. I will… Thanks." He pointed me to park next to the medical examiner van. "Sorry," I added.

Dr. Stone whipped around at me, angry again—even angrier.

"What are you sorry for? That's a beat cop! You are her superior. Don't forget it. We do not take shit from cops—

33

from any cops! They'll never respect you if you buckle, and if they don't respect you, you'll never get what you need out of them when it's down to a muddy death investigation they don't want to take on."

We got out of the Beemer and wound our way through the clot of patrol cars parked every which way on the closed block of Polk Street.

"Do you know why I pulled rank for this?" Stone asked, holding up the note he had confiscated.

"No."

"One of the reasons to have a scene pass is so that the cops don't record your VIN and plate when you arrive at the crime scene, and then feed that data into the system." He folded the note in half and handed it to me. "If they do, a detective might stumble across it and come up with the bright idea that you were involved in the crime."

The streets around us were lined with once-grand four-and five-story buildings, wood trim blurred by decades of grime and chipped paint, scarred marble still lining entrance lobbies, busted teak screens over the upper windows. On the ground floor were nail salons, massage parlors, auto body shops. Laundry hung off the balconies, and the gutters were black with greasy debris. We walked past a tarp-and-cardboard homeless camp in the alcove of one boarded-up edifice.

"The Tenderloin," Mike Stone said.

The fog had pushed all the way in from the beach, and swirled through a tiny parking lot lit by the neon of a rundown hotel called the Somerville. A gust lifted my collar and sent a chill down my back. A chill, on a July night. I wondered, again, if I had made the right choice in coming to San Francisco. Then again, I had to remind myself, there hadn't been any choice involved.

Stone steered me toward a corner coffee shop on the south-east side of the intersection. It was called Café Oui-Fi. The place had big picture windows looking out in two directions. Some of them had been shot through, and from the cones of force beveled into the glass, I could tell the direction was from the inside out. A couple of tables and a few chairs had been overturned. Evidence markers sectioned off drops of blood near the door. There was more, a thin spattered mist, on one window. Uniformed police guarded the perimeter against the inevitable crowd, and plainclothes officers were interviewing people at tables and booths. A bald man in a blazer the color of a day-old bruise nodded to Stone while he went about his work, interviewing a young man in dreadlocks.

"...just popped right up after him and pulled out a gun and started spraying..." The witness imitated the shooter, swiveling around like something out of an action movie. "Fuck, man—why he do that?"

"Could you identify him?" the cop in the brown suit asked as Mike Stone led me out of earshot.

"Up this way," Stone said, and went out to Geary Street. It was closed off, the entire block between Polk and Larkin one giant crime scene. Stone led us to a midblock restaurant called Kim Son 88. A uniformed officer holding a clipboard stood post in the doorway.

"Doctors Michael Stone and Jessie Teska, San Francisco Medical Examiner's Office star one-oh-two, call number zero-charlie-seven," Stone rattled off. The cop checked his watch, wrote in his pad, and stood aside for us without a word.

Kim Son 88 was a takeout joint. There were four or five tables, a cashier counter, and a pass-through to the kitchen. The owners had installed their ancestor shrine in a corner alcove—a gold Buddha with a couple of pieces of fruit and a brimming shot glass. The fruit was starting to rot.

The dead man lay on his back just shy of the kitchen doorway. He was young, Asian, with a round ruddy face, brown eyes and short black hair, full lips on a wide mouth stalled in a half-hinged grimace. Short: body length maybe five foot four or five. I couldn't eyeball his weight because he was wearing clothes too bulky for the weather, even with the fog wind blowing down Geary. There was a red hole in the middle of his forehead. Blood stained the white tile floor—a neat pool under his hair and a separate splotch a couple of feet to the left of it.

"Hey, Keith." Stone addressed a husky black man in a turtleneck and sports coat. He was leaning over a bullet casing by a numbered marker.

"Hello, Doc—nine-mil shells," the man said, then cocked his head and examined me aslant. He was about Stone's age, with deadpan brown eyes under boxy brows and a mustache like a scowl. He wore round, black-rimmed eyeglasses and a beaver-felt fedora, and moved around the crime scene more nimbly than his size suggested he should.

Stone said, "Inspector Keith Jones, this is our new assistant medical examiner, Dr. Jessie Teska." I offered a collegial smile, and the detective nodded back, his eyes thawing a little. "Do you have a presumptive ID?"

"Eugene Chen, aka Lumpy. System has him as a petty thief. He last went down, couple of months, for breaking into cars out by Lincoln Park. Got out three weeks ago."

We gathered over the corpse of Eugene "Lumpy" Chen. "This time he tried to boost a laptop. Witnesses report Lumpy coming into the coffee shop on the corner there, looking around like he's meeting a friend. He stops in front of a man working on his laptop. Lumpy grabs the computer and runs for the door—but the laptop's owner pulls a pistol and fires several shots. He chases Lumpy out onto the street, and Lumpy ducks in here. That's where the guy gets him."

The detective had a miniature flashlight in his hand. He used it to point around. "After the shooter drops Lumpy, he walks over to him, picks up the laptop, puts it in his bag, and takes off." The penlight flashed to the four corners of the room. "Security cameras all over the place, and on the street, too. If they were recording, we should have multiple angles."

"How many rounds?" Stone asked.

The detective grinned. "That's your job to tell me, ain't it?"

It seemed a harmless enough jab to me—but Stone bristled. "How many casings and bullets has CSI recovered?"

"Eleven casings and one slug so far, in the wall by the register," Inspector Jones said. "I'd like to know what you can tell me right now."

Mike Stone pulled a pair of purple exam gloves from his pocket, and, to my shock, handed them to me.

"Dr. Teska, would you please oblige Inspector Jones?" He was glaring at the detective.

The nitrile gloves were sized for Mike's enormous hands, and left flappy stems at the tips of my fingers, like condoms. My new boss wanted me to perform a field test as part of some interdivisional pissing contest? Okay.

I bent to examine Lumpy Chen's body, starting with the visible wound. It was a semicircular defect in the midline forehead with no visible soot or stippling. When I pinched the edges of the torn skin together, the margins meshed in a ragged line.

"Exit wound on the forehead," I told Jones. Chen was wearing a leather letterman jacket from a chain store over a dark hooded sweatshirt. "I need a light."

Jones handed me his penlight. I used it to nudge aside the edge of the hoodie at the dead man's collar. The flashlight's beam revealed at least three other layers of shirts. With almost all his skin covered, I couldn't assess whether there were track marks or gang tattoos. I unzipped the jacket, eased the shirts aside, and stuck the penlight under there. It lit up two red, star-shaped wounds in the dead man's chest. I found another next to his belly button.

"At least three to the back, all exiting out the front torso."

Keith Jones was eagerly jotting these physical findings into his notebook. Something else occurred to me as I looked at Lumpy Chen's eyes, which stared out, lopsided, in two directions.

"Who flipped him?"

The detective glanced at Stone before he answered me. "Witnesses report Lumpy fell on his face after the shot to the head, with the laptop underneath him. The shooter turned him over to get it back."

I nodded and pointed out the small crimson blob to the left of Chen's head. "That's where he landed. He wasn't prone for long. Your gunman didn't waste any time worrying about shooting a man in the head before he took that laptop back."

I stood carefully and stepped away from the body and the bloodstains.

"Okay, Inspector Jones. I'm going to give you four perforating gunshot wounds right now—three to the torso and one to the head. But understand that this is my ballpark estimate. We won't know the final number until we get him back to the morgue."

"Matches what the witnesses are saying," Inspector Jones said. "We'll see if we can retrieve video, too."

Dr. Stone was smirking. I had passed his test. I handed Jones's penlight back to him. The detective leaped away from it in mock horror, seeing as I had just used the thing to poke at a corpse. I laughed out loud—but then my eye fell on the open door. At the corner of Larkin, hemmed in by police tape, stood a clutch of news vans and cameras on tripods. That was the last thing I needed: My laughing mug, live from the scene of a brutal murder, all over the eleven-o'clock news on my first day of work.

That should have been the end of my association with the late Eugene "Lumpy" Chen. Chen's homicide wasn't supposed to be my case, after all—Stone was the doctor on call. But when I crawled back into bed with Bea shortly after midnight, I had one of the few full nights of sleep I would enjoy in San Francisco that summer. All because of Lumpy Chen and his stupid, final mistake.

CHAPTER THREE

One coffee barely got me into the car for the drive to work, so I slipped across Bryant Street to a café called Zeffiro for another before heading to the OCME conference room. Dr. Stone was absent. He was still the doctor on call, and he had been called—to the Tenderloin again, this time for a dead body in a hotel room. Dr. Nguyen took responsibility for running the morning meeting.

Ted Nguyen has a long face and wide-set eyes under a patch of weedy black hair. He's a couple of years older than me, a slight man with a slight accent of the Upper Midwest. He drooped in his chair and mumbled when he spoke, and never made eye contact. He complained a lot. He struck me as a sour and aloof loner.

"At least it's a light day," Dr. Nguyen muttered, after Cam the 2578 presented our three cases: a hanging in a locked, secure room with a suicide note, a middle-aged Canadian in town on business found dead in his hotel room, and the homicide of Eugene Chen. "We can hold the homicide for tomorrow, but then the cops will be pissed off, and the press will start breathing down our necks."

It was an easy decision.

"I'll take the homicide."

Ted Nguyen looked up at me in surprise.

"I was there last night," I continued. "I already know the case. And besides, I might as well do my first homicide on a light day."

"Fine by me. I'll take the others." He held out his hand to Cam, who put two file folders in it—and then, without a word of adjournment, Dr. Nguyen got up and left the conference table. The small herd of medical students rustled in confusion.

"I'll have my scene report for you before I go off shift," Cameron said in a low voice, his eyes following our colleague out the door. "Dr. Nguyen doesn't like to work high-profile cases, so thanks for making that easy for us, Doc. If you hadn't stepped up, we'd never hear the end of it."

He handed me case file SFME-0734. The Lumpy Chen homicide belonged to me.

"What do you mean there's no radiology tech?" I demanded.

Yarina shrugged. "Budget."

We were standing over a gurney. On it lay Chen's shot-up body in all its bloodstained clothes. I couldn't go digging for bullets until I had an X-ray study to guide me.

"Who's going to do the X-rays?" I asked Yarina.

"You do."

She wheeled the gurney to the corner of the morgue, parked it in the door of the radiology room, handed me the instruction manual, and left.

The X-ray machine looked like secondhand surplus from

a mothballed army field hospital. It was crusted in buttons and dials, with an alarming collection of exclamation points and DANGER: RADIATION labels. I wrestled Chen's gurney into place. After some running back and forth, I managed to flip the right switches. The X-ray equipment made a thud, emitted an ominously sci-fi whine, and then thudded again.

The computer screen showed two bullets for me to recover inside the body, one in the chest and one in the right forearm. I managed to maneuver the gurney out of the cramped radiology room without bashing any of the equipment, and found the medical students gathered at my autopsy station; they weren't interested in Dr. Nguyen's two mundane cases if there was a murder in the house.

I opened Eugene Chen's letterman jacket carefully. The three exit wounds I had noted on his chest and belly at the crime scene had left only two bloody holes in the jacket's leather front. There was a puckered divot where the third hole should be, and inside that I found the chest bullet from the X-ray.

"Well, that was easy," a student remarked.

"Bullets will sometimes perforate the body but get trapped in clothing, especially in leather," I said, and instructed that kid and another one to hold the gurney steady while I yanked at a jacket sleeve. When I did, a whole pile of mail fell out of an inside pocket and scattered on the floor. So much for demonstrating strictly professional evidence collection standards for the medical students.

We gathered the envelopes. Most held bills and account statements, some blackened with blood, a couple with bullet holes. They were addressed to six different people. I pulled the other sleeve off and went through Chen's pockets. He had a lot of pockets. In one I found a handful of broken gold chains. In another, a wallet with an ID belonging to another man.

It looked like Eugene Chen had been a busy young fellow—stealing mail, picking pockets, snatching jewelry off tourists. In his pants he carried a bunch of change and a single spark plug. A student asked me if that meant he had been fencing car parts.

"No—it's a burglary tool. They use it to smash a car's window."

Beneath his leather jacket Chen wore a dark gray San Francisco 49ers sweatshirt, still sticky with blood. Under that, five layers of T-shirts. I told the students it was not uncommon for homeless decedents to come into the morgue wearing everything they possessed, but that wasn't the case with Lumpy Chen. His shirts looked new and clean, apart from the blood. The top two had price tags on them: likely shoplifted from a dressing room. I enlisted the help of two of the meatier students to flip Chen's naked body off the gurney, face-down onto the autopsy table. The three entrance wounds formed a tight grouping on his back. I demonstrated the hole that remained in the middle of each when I tried to force the wound margins together with my fingers.

"Can't do it, see? Round defects, no matter which direction I squish them. A typical entrance wound is punched into the skin by the bullet. An exit wound will leave torn flaps, and you can reapproximate the margins."

With the dead man now in a prone position, I located the spot I wanted to examine on the back of his head, checked it for soot, then lathered up a patch of bloody hair and shaved it with my scalpel. The entrance wound was right where I expected it would be, in a slanted line opposite the exit in his forehead. I found two bullet holes in Chen's left arm and two in his right. One was an entrance without an exit in the inner right forearm. The bullet I had seen on X-ray should be in there.

The other hole on the right arm left me puzzled. It was a doughnut-shaped entrance wound near the elbow—but there was no exit wound, and I hadn't seen a bullet in that arm on the X-ray. So where was it?

"How's it goin'?" demanded a gravelly voice from the far end of the autopsy suite. All eyes turned to the swinging doors. I was about to face my first Howezit Goin' rounds.

San Francisco Chief Medical Examiner James Howe was a slender bald man in a neat suit covered with a surgical apron. He didn't wear a mask. He was old but not frail, with toilworn features and claw hands with knotty knuckles. His eyes were forty years younger than the rest of him. We traded courteous nods; no one shakes hands in the morgue.

"Dr. Teska…! I can't tell you how pleased I was to hear you had taken the initiative this morning to tackle your first homicide. You have big shoes to fill, you know."

"So I've heard," I lied. In fact, nobody seemed to want to talk about the abrupt departure of my predecessor, Dr. Brian Sutcliffe. All I knew was that he had taken a job in Maine and essentially disappeared.

"Emil Kashiman sent such glowing reports of your work in Los Angeles," Howe continued.

Now he was the one lying. I knew, because I had personally faced the shock and contempt on my mentor's face when I told him why I was quitting. I felt I owed the truth to Dr. Kashiman, and it had cost me. I hardly knew Dr. Howe, and owed him, as far as I could see, nothing. I had left my job and needed another, and he had lost an employee and needed another. With Kashiman it was different.

Howe looked down at the mortal remains of Eugene "Lumpy" Chen.

"Who do we have here?"

"Twenty-three-year-old Asian male, status post multiple

gunshot wounds. He grabbed a laptop off the wrong guy, who shot him several times, witnessed, in a restaurant. So far I've mapped three on his back, two in each arm, and one to the head."

Dr. Howe strolled around the table, never taking his eyes off the body. I pointed to the dead-end defect near the right elbow. "This one has me stymied. It's a penetrating entrance wound, but no bullet shows up on radiology. I'm going to dissect the wound track and dig it out once I start cutting."

"Have you probed the trajectories?"

"Not yet."

Howe went to my tools, picked out a pencil-width stainless-steel probe, and poked it into the mystery wound. He eased it down the bullet track, squinting one eye like a golfer lining up a putt. The chief medical examiner left the wound probe dangling from the cadaver's arm and turned to the computer monitor where I had opened the X-ray image. He pointed.

"There."

He was right. Tucked into the pectoral girdle was a sliver of metal, just a tiny bit brighter than the bone thicket surrounding it. The rest of the bullet was obscured by the metal teeth of the jacket's open zipper, and the hoodie's drawstring grommet. Camouflaged.

Dr. James Howe had a reputation as a shrewd and cold-hearted bureaucrat; but I learned at that moment that he was certainly no figurehead. My new chief had a superb eye for the essential details of our branch of medicine.

"Looks like a good case for your first homicide," he said, and started toward Dr. Nguyen's table. Then he spun back. "Be sure to stop by my office this afternoon, after you type up your case. I will have the honor of swearing you in as a peace officer—and presenting you with your badge."

I told the chief I was looking forward to it. That was no

lie. Handing my badge across Dr. Kashiman's desk when I quit had been one of the hardest things to bear on that bad day in Los Angeles. I knew full well how lucky I was that Howe had taken Mike Stone's recommendation to hire me. If he was as calculating as everyone said, and if he had figured that I would prove a loyal employee, then Dr. James Howe had figured right.

Since Chen was my first homicide on the new job, I took it slow and careful. I diagrammed the defects on the outside of the body, then cut down to retrieve the bullets. The slug embedded in the bone of the right shoulder took a good deal of wrestling to extricate, but it came out in one piece. The other bullet, the one I had seen on X-ray in Chen's right forearm, was deformed but not fragmented. Inside that penetrating wound I also teased out two pieces of foreign matter that looked like metal and plastic. Given the amount of stolen whatnot Chen had been carrying around in his jacket pockets, I was not surprised to find random debris carried through a wound track.

I didn't find anything noteworthy inside Chen once Yarina and I opened him up. The bullets had missed his spine and aorta, corroborating the witness statements that he kept running after the first volley of shots. The only immediately incapacitating wound on Lumpy Chen's body was the last one: the head shot. I made an incision across the top of his head from ear to ear, and peeled the scalp off the skull. Yarina fired up a handheld bone saw with a worrying rattle—another piece of morgue equipment past its prime—and scored an equatorial line around the calvarium. When I pried the cap off Chen's skull and peeled back the membranes covering the brain, I found a subarachnoid hemorrhage. I hooked my fingers under the brain behind the eyes and lifted it right out. The force of the exiting bullet had fractured the orbital plates and pulped a section of frontal lobe. A class one brain lesion, immediately fatal.

By the time we finished, Yarina and I were the only living people left in the autopsy suite, and I was starving. I washed up and changed and hustled across Bryant Street to the Bear Flag Deli, where the 2578s had told me I could get a half-decent sandwich. Meter maids and messengers, clerks and lawyers and cops formed a line out the door. Same for Caffè Zeffiro, the only other place in sight that wasn't a bail bonds or a mechanic. I wasn't yet desperate enough for McDonald's.

"Try the taco truck," said a voice from beyond the open door of a place called Baby Mike Bail Bonds.

The busybody was a light-skinned black woman about my age, sitting behind a desk. She was slight, with fine features and a dancer's careful posture to her neck and shoulders. She wore a white blouse offset by a gold brooch on a daring purple suede jacket, her hair pulled tight and tucked under a matching newsboy hat.

"El Herrador, right up the next corner," she said. "They're good, and the line moves fast."

The office was small and spare—two phones, a coffee cup, two computers, a fingerprint machine, and a spray of fresh flowers. Framed certificates and licenses were mounted on the walls, none of them even a fraction off the plumb and level.

The bondswoman rose to shake my hand and said, "I'm Sparkle."

"Sparkle...?"

"Mmm-hmm."

"I'm Jessie."

"Pleasure."

"How much does El Herrador kick you back to watch that sandwich line and advertise for them, Sparkle?"

The corners of Sparkle's eyes crinkled her meticulous

makeup, but no hint of the smile came to her lips. "God's honest truth, those are damn fine fish tacos at that roach coach down there."

"All right—but if they aren't, I'm coming back here."

"I'll alert Baby Mike," she replied, nodding to a photograph on the wall. Baby Mike was a mountain of African American man, head shaved and arms crossed across a tight black eponymous T-shirt.

I asked Sparkle if she cared to join me, but she said she was waiting for a client to come back from the Hall.

"Next time."

"Only if they're good tacos," I said.

"You'll see."

Sparkle wasn't kidding. El Herrador made some damn fine fish tacos; so I was in a good mood as I made my way to Dr. Howe's office for my official swearing in.

The office sat in the rear of the Ops Shop. That's what everyone called the Operations and Investigation Dispatch Communications Center, where the 2578s worked the phones and computers when they weren't out on a call. On first glance the Ops Shop looked like a Depression-era bank lobby, a maze of desks—half of them empty—clustered in cubicles clad, like everything else there, in dusky gumwood paneling. A huge map of San Francisco covered the wall, and a chimney column in the middle of the room held an old green chalkboard. *Chen, E.* was up there, with the notation *CPB 21:45 7/1, Geary b/n Polk & Larkin, 187/mult GSW,* along with at least a dozen other cases, the day's open calls, scrawled likewise in shorthand gibberish.

Dr. Howe's door was open, and he hollered for me to enter. The chief's spacious private office was a study in organization by pile. Legal boxes with files tumbling out littered the floor and covered three armchairs and a leather sofa. A double-barreled long gun was propped in the corner by the sofa, a toe tag tied to its trigger guard. Howe sat behind an enormous carved-oak desk piled with papers, more boxes, books, an ancient brass microscope, two computer monitors, and random objects that were either pieces of evidence or paperweights— a revolver cylinder, the spent probes of a Taser preserved in a plastic block, the petrified skull of some toothy mammal.

This seemed to be the only room in the inner-office complex that had windows—huge filthy wooden-sash windows that looked through chicken-wire glass onto an ashen alley. Over the sofa hung a bunch of diplomas, a city declaration extolling our office, and a slew of crooked pictures of Dr. Howe with assorted dignitaries, including a procession of mayors that, judging from the hair and wardrobe, stretched back to the early '80s. Mounted among these frames was a four-foot-long opium pipe stained with use and age, and a dusty mounted swordfish.

Chief Medical Examiner James Howe ruled over this unholy mess from behind the desk. He rose. "Dr. Teska," he declaimed with exaggerated officiousness, "it is time for your investiture." He rattled through a key chain, unlocked a desk drawer, and pulled out a leather wallet. It held a convex seven-pointed star, gleaming gold and elaborately embossed with laurel leaves. The words MEDICAL EXAMINER SAN FRANCISCO curved around the city's emblem.

"What's your middle name?" Howe asked.

"Gladys," I said. Howe raised an eyebrow. "Really. It's Gladys."

"Very well. Jessica Gladys Teska, raise your right hand…"

I did so, but felt the need to balk. "Dr. Howe?"

"What?"

"My name isn't Jessica."

"Then what is it?"

I told him.

"Come again?"

I repeated my proper name; then, in the mantra I had chanted since the first grade, spelled it out.

"*C* as in cat, *Z* as in zebra, *E, S* as in Sam, *L* as in Larry, *A-W-A*, and the *L* has a line through it."

Dr. Howe assumed the exact same expression my first-grade teacher, Mrs. Gail Guimond, had shown at Sacred Heart Elementary School on our first day there: *You poor, poor dear.*

"Chess-swah-vah," he said.

"That's what's on my birth certificate."

"Chess-swah-vah," Howe repeated.

"Right."

And he began again:

"Czesława Gladys Teska, do you solemnly swear or affirm that you will support and defend the Constitution of the United States and the Constitution of the State of California against all enemies, foreign and domestic?"

I swore I did, and Dr. Howe went on with the rest of the oath, requiring me to confirm I had no mental reservations, and promise to faithfully discharge my duties.

I swore I would do those things, too. And I meant it.

"Dr. Chest—" said Howe, then stopped. "Chest...?"

"Chess-swah-vah."

"Dr. Czesława Gladys Teska, you are now officially an assistant medical examiner for the City and County of San Francisco."

He handed me the gold shield. It bore the number 207.

My eyes teared up. When I walked out on Dr. Kashiman in LA two months ago, I thought I might never carry a badge again, never practice my profession again; yet here I am, a sworn and salaried peace officer. I stroked a thumb over its surface.

"Number two-oh-seven," Dr. James Howe said, beaming at me like I was high school valedictorian. "Brian Sutcliffe was the last one to carry this badge. He's a fine doctor. It's a lucky charm."

Maybe that was true. I can't say. If it was, the luck didn't linger.

The office I shared with Dr. Nguyen was depressingly spare. I resolved it wouldn't stay that way, and hauled in three boxes of the certificates, diplomas, and knickknacks I had accumulated over a decade in Los Angeles. While stowing some textbooks in the cabinets, I found a handle that wouldn't budge. There was no key in the desk drawers—nothing but old paper clips. So I used those.

"What are you doing?"

Ted Nguyen had come in while I was wrenching the cabinet lock's cylinder with one bent paper clip and raking the pins with another.

"*Lynn, Lynn, the city of sin… You never come out the way you went in.*"

"What?"

"It's a place back East where a girl can suffer a misspent youth, and learn…"

The lock popped and the latch released.

"Aha! *Świetnie*—!"

I threw open the cabinet door.

A gun barrel glared back at me. It belonged to the business end of a semiautomatic pistol with an evidence tag tied to its trigger guard.

Ted Nguyen grunted in something like amusement. "Figures," he said. "You better make that safe."

No shit. At least the magazine was out, and the safety on. I opened the firing chamber. Empty; a relief.

"Brian was always worried someone was messing with his high-profile cases—he didn't like sending evidence to the lab." And with that cryptic statement, Ted vanished behind the cubicle divider. Locked up with the pistol I found a syringe and a burnt spoon, three small envelopes of fingernail clippings, and a baggie of bullets. The back of the cabinet was crammed full of case files and autopsy reports. I sat down at the desk I'd inherited from Dr. Brian Sutcliffe and leafed through the old files.

A skateboarder in the Mission District got creamed by a semi turning a corner. His family sued the trucking company.

A defective pacemaker failed and the decedent's survivors joined a class action against the manufacturer.

A man stabbed his wife multiple times, then went to the police and turned himself in. He'd generated a dispiriting pile of mental-status paperwork.

A floater got wrapped up in a crab crew's lines. The decomposed corpse was missing his head, both hands and one leg below the knee, and had a horizontal ligature mark around the remaining stump of neck. Dr. Sutcliffe determined that this injury was not the result of a postmortem tangle with crab traps—it was evidence of assault. The floater was eventually identified as a missing person named Robert Falmouth. Sutcliffe ruled the manner of death as homicide.

The homicide detective's report was in the file. The fishermen who pulled the body up had no connection to the dead man. Falmouth was known to be a low-level drug dealer, but none of the usual threats and enticements yielded any useful information about him from confidential informants or anyone else. The case had gone nowhere.

Maybe Dr. Sutcliffe kept the Falmouth file around because it bugged him, and he liked to open it up from time to time to rehash. I had done that with one or two of my own dead-end cases back in LA.

"Ted," I hollered over the divider, "what should I do with this stuff?"

He told me to ask Stone. So I piled everything in a box and headed down the hall to the deputy chief's office.

"You keep doing this even though it never gets you any-where! Are you nuts…? I mean it—are you fucking *insane?*"

My boss's voice was booming right through his closed door.

"No…! *No*, I did not. You are fabricating all of this shit, and you know that's… We've been over this… Well, if you can behave like an adult, we'll talk about it when I get home. I'm hanging up now."

I'd frozen. I grew up with fights like that; playing the dor-mouse becomes a reflex. I performed a thirty-second count-down, then knocked.

Dr. Stone looked flustered, but no more so than any man-ager in a city bureau might look at four o'clock on a Thursday. I showed him the box. He asked me if the pistol was made safe. I told him it was. He hefted it.

"How kind of Dr. Sutcliffe," he said. "The perfect teach-ing moment."

Stone instructed me to seal and label all the other evidence in individual bags, and sign the seal tape. Then we piled the stuff back in the box and headed out the door. I had to trot to keep up with his gangling strides down the corridor to the toxicology lab. When we got there, he told me to shove each one through the mail slot in the door.

"That's it?"

"That's our evidence drop. Tomorrow they'll log them in. If you have any packages bigger than the drop slot allows, try the doorbell."

Stone reached for two bare copper wires sticking out of a

broken switch. He touched them together and I heard a bell ring. Footsteps; then a lab tech opened the door, and Stone asked her for a gun box.

"This place is such a pit," he said, then sighed as he transcribed the case number from the pistol's trigger tag to the cardboard carton.

"I hadn't noticed," I said. "I think the antique porcelain tables with their twee toilet sinks are charming as can be."

Mike Stone's eyes brightened, and he laughed. I was relieved. Maybe he had family problems. They were none of my business as long as he could leave them at home.

You're one to talk, said someone in my head.

Stone asked me to follow him back to his office. "How'd the post on that Tenderloin shooting go?"

"Seven wound paths, the last one fatal. Nothing I haven't done before."

"Still, you did me a favor." He scrawled something on a sticky pad. "Let me make it up to you. Saturday night my wife is throwing a Fourth of July potluck at our house. She has a bunch of musician friends. A 'salon,' she calls it. I'd love to see you there…"

He held out the note. It was an address.

"Mike, it is my policy never to pass up an opportunity to meet fascinating artistic types as long as there is also free food."

I called my brother as soon as I got home. "What the hell do I bring to a potluck? I haven't even unpacked my kitchen!"

"Premyslaus."

"Goddamn it, Tomasz, couldn't you rub together two words for a change—?"

"Premyslaus Deli. On Geary in the Avenues, somewhere

in the twenties. Old-world Polack runs the place. He'll remind you of Jerry the meat man back in Lynn. Get a pot of bigos or some pierogies, and you'll impress everyone with how multi-culti you are."

I asked my brother to come to the party as my wingman, and assured him there would be single women there. With Tommy along, I could relax.

The fog on Geary Boulevard was so thick under the streetlights that it felt like Boston in a night blizzard when the snow is blowing in fast and dry—I half expected the Beemer to skid at each stop sign. I crept along until I spotted the old-world lettering of Premyslaus European Delicatessen and Meat Market. The man behind the counter was meaty himself: six-four, three hundred pounds, kielbasa fingers on ham-hock hands. He lit up when I greeted him in Polish, and when I left he wrapped a hunk of farmer cheese, on the house, with the bigos.

"Miłego wieczoru," he said as I left. An old-fashioned farewell. People don't much use it anymore. He was locked in time, the sausage man, a long way from home.

Locked in the past.

Back in my car, I sat in the driver's seat, alone in the phone's pale glow. I opened the voice-mail app and scrolled down, back more than two months, until I found it again. I hit Play.

"Hey, it's Barry. I got the Catalina ferry tickets, and booked the tram tour to look at the bison. Bison! The hotel's all set. Let me know when you'll be home on Friday so I can pick you up and we'll head straight down. Can't wait!"

Once again I counted off through the background hiss—one-Mississippi, two-Mississippi, three…until the voice came back.

"I love you, Doctor."

The message ended. My thumb trembled as it stood over the words *Call Back* on the screen.

I closed the voice-mail app.

I could never call Barry Taylor, not ever again. He, too, was locked in the past—and in the past he would have to stay.

The fog was even worse going home—home to my slobbery dog and lonely back garden absurdity of a rental.

CHAPTER FOUR

A mezzo-soprano rattled the windows of Casa Piedra.

I was surprised to find that Deputy Chief Medical Examiner Michael Stone lived less than a mile away from my beaten block of surf-bum renters and elderly homesteaders. Dr. Stone's neighborhood was called Sea Cliff—and I recognized as soon as I walked through the carved granite gateposts into Sea Cliff that we lived in the same zip code but on different worlds. His world featured stately homes with green lawns and architectural rigor. Mine had dumpy duplexes with peeling paint and jerry-built backyard shacks.

Casa Piedra. They had engraved it into the lintel. The House of Stone was stucco—and enormous. The art on the walls was real. The furniture glowed with the kind of finish that only time and labor can evoke. The grandfather clock in the far corner of the entrance hall might have belonged to a French count. Somewhere in the place there was a real opera singer.

Tommy leaned in close. "Why aren't you living this way, Doctor?" he whispered.

"Two hundred grand in student loans, *głupek*."

"*Głupek?* Who're you calling a—"

He was stopped by the approach of a woman, smiling brightly, welcoming us. She was tall, in her midforties, with chestnut hair and olive skin, high breasts, high heels, diamond earrings. I envied her dress more than any piece of wardrobe I had ever seen in my life.

"Can I take that for you?" she said.

I am way out of my league here, I realized as I handed the dazzling woman my potluck offering. Sauerkraut juice was leaking into a sad pouchy puddle on the bottom of the takeout bag.

"Sophia Kalogeras," the woman said.

"Jessie Teska." We shook. Her hand was soft and warm and bore four rings with a dozen gems shared between them.

"Dr. Teska!" Sophia Kalogeras exclaimed, and clasped my arm with her other bejeweled hand. "Such a pleasure! Thank you for coming." I must have looked dumbstruck, because she had to add, "I'm Michael's wife."

My boss, who worked a city job near the bottom of the civil-professional totem pole, lived with a trophy wife in a mansion full of antiques and fine art.

"Oh my!" I blurted. Michael Stone's wife laughed merrily, and I forced myself to mirror her, and our awkward moment was put out of its misery as she turned her attention to Tommy. He stared in wonder and mumbled something polite. Sophia Kalogeras thanked me for the bigos and told us to make ourselves at home, then took her lyrical hips off through the crowd, meeting and greeting.

Tommy and I parted ways immediately, our usual habit at parties. I followed the sound of the mezzo-soprano. Her voice was climbing a set of stairs—heavenly, soaring, passionate. It led me to a basement music room with an audience in folding chairs ranged around a grand piano. Next to the piano stood the singer, a middle-aged woman in a simple dress and expensive shoes. A man at the far end of the room watched me come in, though he tried not to show it. His tailored cream suit flattered a trim build on wide shoulders. He was strawberry blond going gray at the temples, with pale eyes set in an unlined face.

I made my way out after the applause, when the mezzo-soprano ceded the piano to a shaggy man tinkling away at Bach. Tommy and I crossed paths again by the French doors that led out to the backyard. He asked me if I'd come across anyone from work yet.

"*O wilku mowa...*" I said.

Speak of the devil. Dr. Michael Stone, in a parrot-print Hawaiian shirt, jeans, and flip-flops, weaved across the yard in our direction. Behind him the Golden Gate Bridge blazed its legendary fire-red in the low sun. The hills on either side glowed green and gold.

"The sundown tease," Mike Stone said as he reached us. "This time of year the fog likes to lift half an hour before sunset. Then it comes back in, overnight." He stretched out an arm melodramatically, and the slanting sunlight lit up those type O-negative blood-donation scars he had bragged about in the autopsy suite. "Enjoy it, because this is the best you can expect in the Avenues in July—half an hour of dying sun."

He offered my brother his gigantic hand. "Mike Stone."

"Tommy Teska."

"Tommy!" Mike exclaimed, and held his grip too long. My boss was tipsy. He asked us if we were having a good time. We assured him we were.

"Have you met Callie yet?"

"Callie...?"

"My daughter. Calliope."

"Oh! No. I met your wife—"

"Ah. Well." Stone was looking around in a vague way.

"You'll meet Callie. Thank you for coming, both of you. My wife works in the start-up world, so I don't…" He trailed off, then lifted his glass. "Let's just say that it's refreshing to have someone here from the groom's side."

Mike Stone spotted something across the yard and his smile fell off. I glanced over my shoulder but only saw the crowd, milling and chatting. Mike steered us toward the bar.

"Now—doctor's orders—get yourselves a drink. I'm needed inside…"

"Is that Dr. Teska?" boomed a man's voice from behind us. We all turned.

He wore an expensive suit, patent shoes, and the sort of haircut you see on network anchormen. His teeth were too white, his skin tanned too evenly and wrinkled beyond his years. He zeroed in and came right at us.

"Well, Mickey…? Is it?"

"Yes," Mike Stone said. Then he regained his host face and introduced us to Jackson Heffernan.

"Call me Jack," the man said, and extended his hand—cuff links and a gold watch, a college ring and a tight wedding band. He kept his murky green alligator eyes locked on mine.

"Jack is an old friend," Stone said, the fake smile fighting his skittish body language.

"Oh, much more than friends, Mickey, much more!"

Heffernan was a criminal defense attorney; a prominent one, he bragged, largely thanks to the hard work Stone had done for him over the years as a paid consultant.

"Dr. Stone here is my best expert witness. If it has to do with death investigation, he will neutralize *anyone* the other side puts up. Time and again." Heffernan patted my boss on the cheek with aggressive affability. "You're my golden goose, Mickey."

A business card materialized between his fingers, and he

pressed it into my palm. "And you, Dr. Teska…" He scanned me up and down. "You are a lot easier on the eyes than most of the old farts I put on the stand!" He laughed uproariously. Stone forced a similar response. I wasn't laughing and neither was Tommy.

Heffernan switched gears to unctuous sincerity. "Dr. Stone tells me he recruited you from the Los Angeles coroner. That Dr. Kashiman runs a hell of an operation down there. I crossed him once in court. Tough nut—I was impressed."

Jackson Heffernan leaned in sideways, close enough that I could smell his expensive cologne and count the hairs curling out of his ear.

"You're going to learn a lot working with Mickey. So let me know when you're ready to get in the game. I want to be top of your list. You'd be amazed how much someone with your expertise can make working with my firm…"

Mike Stone took Heffernan by the arm. "Jack, I think if we hurry—"

Heffernan glared at Stone's hand on his elbow.

"—if we hurry, you can join me to hear Callie. On the piano. I'm sure she'd love for you to be there…"

Heffernan said nothing. No one did, for what seemed like a long time. Then the venom vanished and he nodded amiably.

"I'd love to, Mickey," the lawyer said. As Mike Stone led him toward the house, Jackson Heffernan reached out and tapped a manicured finger on the card he'd planted in my palm.

"I'll be waiting for your call," he said.

———

While the tuxedoed bartender shook martinis, I explained Jackson Heffernan's spiel to Tommy. "Forensic expert wit-

JUDY MELINEK & T.J. MITCHELL

nesses can be crucial in both criminal and civil cases where there's been a death. They get paid a lot of money."

"How much?"

I pointed to a bronze sculpture: "This much, apparently."

"But you don't want to?"

"Maybe someday. Not now."

"What do you owe in loans, Doctor?"

"Two hundred grand."

"You'd pay it down."

"I don't know how thrilled my new chief would be about his junior ME working a side hustle."

"He lets Stone do it."

"Stone has been Dr. Howe's deputy for more than ten years. He's earned his expertise."

My teetotaler brother took his Coke with a squeeze of lemon and handed me my two-olive martini.

"Don't sell yourself short, *siostrzyczko*."

I brandished Jackson Heffernan's business card. "*Braciszku*— would you do business with this man?"

He conceded he wouldn't.

"*Na zdrowie.*"

"*Sto lat.*"

We clinked glasses and sipped. The martini was excellent.

Tommy surveyed the crowd. "Hot damn, Jess—where does your boss's wife work?"

"You got me."

"He wasn't kidding about her friends. This place is a who's who of high tech."

My brother is an inveterate risk-taker, destined for Silicon Valley if anyone ever was. Either Silicon Valley, or identity theft and corporate espionage...maybe even sabotage. There was a time I had worried about his inclining toward the latter.

"You look like a kid in a candy store."

"A fox in the henhouse. Let's mingle…"

In another corner of the yard, a party clown was twisting balloon animals. Not the ordinary poodle dogs and hearts and swans, but huge, multicolored fantasy creatures. A line of fidgety kids waited. I decided I was going to have to come back for one later. Something with horns, to hang from the rafters of Mahoney Brothers #45. A talisman.

Tommy found an old colleague from some start-up or other, who he introduced as "a rockstar UX designer." The rockstar UX designer started jabbering about how he was going to disrupt online gaming and disintermediate something something about a responsive HTML5 something. I smiled and nodded. Tommy asked him about click-through, and the guy turned back to Tommy and I made my escape, backing away and melting into the crowd.

I found the buffet inside, in the opulent dining room. My sad pot of bigos clung to a corner of a table piled with Greek appetizers, noodle dishes, pot stickers, shish kebab, tapas. Someone had brought a humongous platter of sushi. I froze, plate in hand, unsure where to begin.

"The lumpia," said a man behind me.

I turned. It was Mr. Cream Suit from the music room. "Don't miss the lumpia."

"Of course not. I never do. What's a lumpia?"

He smiled and pointed.

"Egg rolls," I observed.

"Not just any egg rolls! Tiny, scrumptious Filipino egg rolls." He had a perfectly charming accent, Australia or New Zealand. "No San Francisco potluck is complete without them."

I took one. "Take three," Mr. Aussie Cream Suit insisted. I complied.

"Arnie Spitz."

I took his hand.

"What did you bring?" I asked Arnie Spitz.

His blond eyebrows popped up. "Wine. Beautiful wine. Do you know the Chateau St. Abbo cabernet?"

"I don't drink wine."

"You mean you don't drink?"

"Oh, I drink. I'll have a vodka gimlet, a martini, any old smoky scotch. Beer. You bring any beers?"

He looked a little offended. "No…"

"Pity." I pointed to the bigos. "Try my bigos. It's home-made. Family recipe."

Arnie Spitz eyed the bigos with undisguised skepticism. "What's in it?"

"Sauerkraut, ham, smoked sausage, dried fruit, bunch of herbs and spices. Goes well with beer."

He scooped a respectable spoonful and said, "This is… what, German?"

"Polish."

"Apologies."

"Think nothing of it."

"And your name is?"

"Czesława."

Why did I do that? Why did I drop the Chess-wabomb on the poor man? He reacted with class.

"It's a lovely name."

"You can call me Jessie."

"I shall, Jessie."

"You shall. I'll bet you say that to all the girls."

"I do, Jessie."

Arnie Spitz and I piled up our plates and sat down together in a quiet corner. We made small talk until he asked me what I did for a living. When I told him—he really lit up. Turns out Arnie Spitz is one of those laymen who goes nuts for forensics.

Nearly an hour later our plates were clean and he was working toward the bottom third of his fine bottle of wine—and I had put away a couple of fine IPAs—and he was still peppering me with questions about autopsy, ballistics, decomposed bodies, and weird suicides.

"You must get tired of talking about all this."

"Not at all," I lied, and brushed his fingers as I reached for his wine. I sipped. Then I wrinkled my nose, and spoke frankly.

"That's nasty."

"Bite your tongue."

I said nothing at all to that suggestion, though I was sorely tempted to. I reminded myself of what Barry Taylor had done to me. I reminded myself I had sworn off men until I was sure I had a solid footing in San Francisco. But this man Arnie Spitz was hard to resist. I hadn't been the subject of such skilled attention in a long while.

My brother stumbled unwittingly to my rescue as he always does.

"Lumpia!" Tommy enthused, brandishing a bunch and flopping down beside me. He introduced himself to Arnie. They knew each other by reputation—and immediately launched into another technobabble conversation, comparing notes about companies with gibberish names that produced digital widgets. I took the opportunity to wander outside and get another excellent martini. The little kids had cleared away from the balloon clown, so I hit him up for one of his fantasy creations before rejoining my brother and the attractive man in the cream suit.

"Lookit," I said, thrusting the balloon animal right under Arnie's chin.

"What the hell is that?" Tommy said, annoyed.

"It's a phoenix," I said. "Symbol of our fair city. It's going to keep my new abode safe and secure."

Arnie considered my balloon phoenix. "It's a corker," he decided.

"Seriously?"

"A corker. Spiffy. That's an ace phoenix."

I gestured outside. "You can go get your own, you know."

"I believe I shall. I could do with a mascot."

"Whatcha gonna get?"

"Hmm?"

"What animal?"

"Oh." Arnie thought about it. "Nessie," he said.

"Come again?"

"Nessie. You know…" He swam an arm out, wrist making a sine wave. "The Loch Ness Monster."

"Ah!" I said.

"Why?" asked Tommy.

"Because," Arnie Spitz said, "everyone knows she doesn't exist."

His eyes narrowed in practiced mischief.

"Even though she does, and everyone knows it."

The fireworks made me homesick.

I grew up on Boston's North Shore, where the Fourth of July is a big deal. We used to go watch the fireworks out on a beach the next town over. The rockets' red glare—and blue glare and green glare and all the gaudy glares—lit up the sea. Even as the years wore on, and Dad drank and *Mamusia* shrank, and Tomasz got beat up and I got run down—even then, we never failed to get out to Short Beach in Nahant for the fireworks on the Fourth.

So I parked myself on a lawn chair in Casa Piedra's backyard with its postcard view of the Golden Gate and waited, eagerly, for the show to start.

Except there was no show.

The fog snuck under the bridge in the dying sun, and spread as twilight went purple until I couldn't see the palm fronds ten feet overhead. I knew when the fireworks started because I could hear them echo off the house, but there wasn't so much as a tinted glimmer in the gloom above. The other guests retreated inside as the temperature dropped and the damp soaked in, but I stayed on the lawn till the bitter end. And a bitter end it was, too.

"Why are you out here?" a small voice asked.

It was a girl. Her features were delicate; an almost perfectly round face with cream skin and dark eyes. She had a ballet student's stiff dignity. She also had Sophia Kalogeras's chestnut-colored hair.

"You must be Callie," I said. She nodded. "I guess I was too optimistic about the fireworks."

Callie Stone looked puzzled. "But we can't see the fireworks from here."

"What...?"

"The Presidio's in the way." She pointed. "Those hills."

I had assumed the fireworks would be launched over the Golden Gate Bridge. "Wishful thinking," I said.

"Fourth of July is always the first week of hella thick fog anyway," Callie said in the helpfully condescending manner of precocious preteen girls. "Always."

I followed her back inside. The party was drunker now, and louder. A clot of medical students tried to pull me in for gossip, but I drifted past with a distracted hi while I searched for Arnie Spitz. He was nowhere to be found. I did find Tommy, who wanted to leave; he's never been a night person. I decided we could slip away without making goodbyes and I'd thank Dr. Stone in the morgue on Monday.

I pointed out to my brother how beautiful the neighborhood around Casa Piedra had become in the fluid night fog; but Tommy fixated on the prosaic, as usual. He was studying the streetlights.

"LED lamps out here," he said.

"Tell me about that Aussie guy."

"Arnie Spitz?"

"Right."

"Serial entrepreneur."

"What's that?"

"Comes up with some brilliant idea, starts a company, watches it get on its feet and go operational, and then he leaves that company and starts another."

"Why the hell would anyone do that?"

"They're risk-takers who bore easy. Spitz has started a dozen companies, and I know of at least two or three that have gone supernova. That's an excellent record in the internet start-up world. But then he fell on his face with…"

Tommy stopped. He was peering across the street, at a parked car.

"Is that woman crying?"

I looked. From the driver's seat, a young woman watched Stone's bright, noisy party. The cold light of the street lamps showed her weeping. The sight shook me—because I had done the same. That was me, on an afternoon in May, sitting in the employee parking lot of the Los Angeles County Department of Medical Examiner-Coroner, ignoring the worried stares of coworkers until the shock wore off and my new reality settled in enough that I could put the Beemer in Drive and leave that place for good.

"Should we…ask her if she needs help?" Tommy said.

"No. We'd better leave her alone."

"How come?"

The car was a souped-up Subaru, the supercharged type of thing that frat boys at UCLA like to drive. It was cobalt blue. I had seen it before. I had seen the young woman before, too.

"It's none of our business," I said.

———

Tommy had parked by my place, so while we walked back through the deserted Avenues I told him about the Asian woman with an armful of textbooks who had emerged from the morgue loading dock to give me her parking spot on my first day of work. And Tommy told me about Arnie Spitz the serial entrepreneur.

"He made a fortune in enterprise storage solutions, with a software fix for a hardware challenge having to do with heat sinks. He built banks of virtual machines to increase the efficiency of... Well, trust me—it was a big deal." After that Spitz helped finance a company that invented earbud speaker diaphragms with a novel, and much-improved, shape profile.

"He had a couple of other decent ventures," Tommy said. "Then he struck out." We had reached the edge of a golf course. It was a stunning sight, the moonlit fog blowing over the tops of cypress trees, the empty fairway rolling away from us. "With gaming, of all things. Arnie Spitz may be the only entrepreneur to start a failed online gaming company. It's low-hanging fruit."

Our feet whispered in the short wet grass and bats wheeled overhead, hunting bugs. The fairway had narrowed to a canyon with thick woods on either side. I asked Tommy if he wanted to crash at my apartment instead of driving back to Menlo Park.

"Where? In that trapdoor bathtub?"

"You'd be welcome," I said. "Anytime. Under any roof of mine."

I meant it, and Tomasz knew I did, too.

Our moment of sibling tenderness was ruptured by an animal sound—loud, close, and horrible.

"What the Christ was that…!"

Tommy had stopped dead in his tracks. "I don't know."

"It sounds like a freaking baboon!"

The thing wailed again.

"Coyote."

"That *cannot* be a coyote! Coyotes…well, they yip, right? In LA they yip…"

Tommy moved slowly toward a break in the golf course fence. He pulled something out of his pocket and aimed it, waiting. The sound came again, and, the moment it did, a brilliant white light flashed from Tommy's hand into the trees. It cut a beam through the fog and settled on an enormous animal.

It was a coyote, all right—but one hell of a big one. It considered us from its perch atop a hillock maybe ten yards away and flinched but didn't retreat. It snarled. Tommy backed away but kept the light on target. The coyote lowered its snout. Its neck muscles strained under the fur as it tugged at something on the ground. Then its head came up again.

"Is that…?" Tommy said. "Is that…real?"

I pulled out my phone. I dialed 911.

The coyote had a bloody rag in its jaws and was gnawing at it. The rag had four fingers and a thumb.

It was real, all right.

CHAPTER FIVE

A couple of students had gone pale, and one was wobbling in a way that made me worry he might take a header right across my autopsy table—and John Doe #58.

"See the jagged edges and puncture marks on these facial wounds? Textbook canine depredation." I was trying to find a teaching point in the mangled horror on the table. "And no vital reaction. That's a salient finding: The heart wasn't pumping when these injuries occurred."

The coyote had eaten the dead man's face. Scavenging animals eat the lips and eyeballs first. They'll go for the nose, the ears, anything they can tear off. I had spotted the first cops bushwhacking up the golf course hill and remembered in the nick of time to pull out my new badge. White bone gleamed under their flashlights—empty eye sockets and a rictus of teeth in naked gums, tan and pink flesh torn to ribbons beneath a grotesque mop of perfectly intact hair. The cops turned their lights away and beamed them through the trees, hands on their holsters.

I instructed them to call off the ambulance. Then I phoned

my own office and told Cameron what was going on, and that he shouldn't bother Dr. Nguyen on call. After a while a homicide detective came crashing through the brush. He was young, slight, and twitchy, with pasty skin and red hair that blazed like a torch in the Maglite beams. I had to talk him down from his feverish theory that someone had cut off the dead man's face.

"What if it's a serial killer?"

"I can't tell you in the woods under a flashlight what this is or isn't, Inspector. I'll know after the autopsy if it's a homicide, okay?"

It wasn't a homicide. I stood over my morgue station and pressed a triple-gloved finger into John Doe's liver. The organ was bright yellow and dense as a leather saddle.

"End stage liver disease," I told the students. "Terminal cirrhosis in a chronic alcoholic. Scar tissue through and through. Give it a poke and remember what it feels like." But most of them wouldn't go anywhere near the disfigured body on my autopsy table, and I didn't force them.

"He drank himself to death," one said.

"Plenty of people do."

"Didn't he have ID on him?"

"Yes, a VA medical card."

"So why is he still a John Doe?"

"They couldn't match the picture to his face."

The student put a hand to his mouth and made a croaky sound.

I didn't dwell on John Doe #58. It was a busy Monday morning at the San Francisco Office of Chief Medical Examiner—fifteen deaths over the holiday weekend. I was finishing the coyote guy when Stone called all the students to his table. He was starting the day's headline case.

Graciela Natividad was in her late teens; Hispanic, small

and dark-skinned. She was made up and dressed like a prostitute. Her white blouse was torn in half. Well, it wasn't torn, exactly. It had been cut. She had been cut. Her belly had been cut wide open from the pubic arch to the breastbone.

Several guests at the dodgy Hotel Somerville on Geary Street in the Tenderloin called the desk to complain of a sewage reek in the top-floor hallway. The stench got worse as the night went on. Around eight in the morning the hotel manager started knocking on the door of the room where it seemed to be coming from. When no one answered, he let himself in. He expected to find a clogged toilet. He didn't.

We all saw the scene photos at morning meeting. They showed the girl spread-eagled on the floor, her belly torn open and her viscera spilling onto the carpet in a heap. A vinyl purse that matched her boots lay on the other side of the room. Four KFC takeout bags and a bucket of fried chicken sat on the desk. Next to those stood a box of Ex-Lax. The bed was covered in blood, shit, and bits of flesh.

"This is not a homicide," Dr. Stone said to the students around his table. "How do I know?" He was met with a ring of blank stares. "Take a look at her arms, hands. Her neck and face. See any injury?"

A couple of them leaned in, but most kept their distance.

"No defensive wounds," Stone continued. "No bullets on X-ray and no visible gunshot wounds, either. Take a look at her eyes." He lifted the dead woman's lids with his purple-gloved fingers. "What do you see?"

He pointed at a student who was hanging back. "You."

The kid was forced to come stand over the mangled girl and peer into her blind eyes.

"Nothing."

"Right. No petechiae. If she'd been strangled, you'd see burst blood vessels in there. I can't rule it out until I open up her neck and check the strap muscles for injury, but so far I'm not seeing any evidence of trauma apart from this single, long, vertically oriented incised wound along her abdomen."

The kid retreated. Some of the others did, too. Stone's clinically detached description of the gash made it even more obscene.

"Do you notice anything about the wound margins?"

There was a pause, then someone said, "No vital reaction?"

"Excellent! Who was that?" Stone boomed. One of the students who had just watched me autopsy the animal-depredation case raised her hand. Stone pointed out that the scene photos from the hotel room weren't very bloody. "If this woman had been alive when she was cut open, the floor and walls would have spatter all over the place. I've seen arterial blood leave an arc across the ceiling of homicide scenes. She was dead when this incision was made. So now we come to the question I'm sure you are all eager to hear answered—why the hell would someone mutilate a dead hooker like this?"

I knew why but didn't want to spoil Stone's lesson. He aimed a bloody finger at the abdominal X-ray hanging over his table. A line of lumpy white blobs stood out in the black-and-gray field of the dead woman's gut.

"Those things don't look like they belong. What are they?"

The students stared. Then one said, "Hematoma?"

"Wrong."

"Tumors?" ventured another.

"Good guess, but they're too dense and the margins are too sharp."

"Is it something she swallowed?"

Stone returned his attention to the corpse.

"Time to find out."

The gash had made a mess of Graciela Natividad's abdominal organs. Coiled intestines spilled over the severed belly muscles. Her stomach and duodenum were laid open, leaving chewed bits of her last meal visible. Nicks and slashes criss-crossed the small intestines, and an incision split the transverse colon. The spilled contents of the digestive tract generated a sickening stench of stomach acid and feces.

Yarina shouldered aside the closest students and assisted Dr. Stone. It only took him a couple of minutes to slice through some twenty feet of small intestines, where he reached the juncture of the cecum and the ascending colon. The large intestine drooped heavily in his hand—we could see a line of bulges running through it. He paused to request a photo from Yarina, then pushed the surgical scissors with practiced care along the bluish elastic tissue of the dead girl's bowel.

"How's it goin'?"

Dr. Howe stood in the door to the autopsy suite. "What you got?"

Stone opened Graciela Natividad's cecum and revealed an oblong white balloon the size of a strawberry. He pushed the scissors and uncovered another. A third looked deflated. There were more behind it.

Howe pointed to a student. "What are those?"

"I don't know," she confessed.

"Anyone?"

Another student said, "Drug condoms. She's a smuggler."

"She's a mule," said Dr. Stone. "Not the smuggler. She's just his transport. The smuggler got her to swallow these bindles in exchange for some money and a plane ticket. It's called body packing."

"But," one of the students said, "why...why are the drugs still there if they cut her open?"

"They tried to retrieve them but failed and gave up," Dr. Howe said. "I've seen it happen many times. Harder than it looks, dissecting the human alimentary canal. Intestines slither around. Not a job for an amateur."

Dr. Stone removed the first condom and placed it on a cutting board. He retrieved the second, then stopped. The third bindle in the body packer's cecum was torn. Dr. Stone coaxed it open with a surgical probe and revealed crumbs of white powder inside.

"One of them broke. If it turns out to be cocaine or meth, she went into a fatal cardiac arrhythmia. If it's heroin, respiratory arrest. Death in minutes at the most."

Michael Stone had lost his professional dispassion. He looked heartsick and worn; a father, not an ME.

"See the chunks of undigested food in the stomach?" Dr. Howe said. "We often find that smugglers feed the mule a greasy fast-food meal when it's time to pass the product."

"You'll recall the KFC bags and laxatives in the scene photos," Stone added.

No jokes from the medical students. No more teaching points from the doctors. Even Ted Nguyen stopped what he was doing. We all stood there in silence, a city morgue stunned for a moment by the shit-smeared death and brutal desecration of a nameless young woman.

"How many are in there?" someone asked.

"We'll see. Most I've ever found is eighty," replied Stone, to gasps from the students. "Dr. Howe?"

"Ninety-six."

Yarina had finished stitching closed my John Doe and was hosing the body down. I did an external exam on my second case, an Alzheimer's patient, while Yarina wheeled in the third, a profoundly decomposed probable-overdose found in a house. I could smell the bloated corpse from across the room, even through the sewage stench at Stone's table where he was rinsing fecal material off the collected drug bindles before photographing them. I muttered the mantra I recite before I tackle every stinker.

This is why they pay me the big bucks, this is why they pay me the big bucks, this is why they pay me the big bucks...

I changed gloves, grabbed a second hairnet, and took up my pretty pink #22 scalpel.

"There are bad decomps and there are bad decomps. And *that* was a bad decomp."

"Lot of juice," agreed Yarina. She was closing the Y-incision, or trying to. The flesh, slimy brown and yellow and coming apart in tatters, didn't want to hold together under the heavy twine. The 2578 report described the corpse melting into a cloth couch in an Ingleside house littered with drug paraphernalia. I had spent nearly an hour sloshing through a fetid soup of decomposition fluid and liquefied organs on the autopsy table, and was desperate to scrub out the stench. So I hustled for the locker room, stripped down, and tugged hard on the shower's ancient handle.

It squeaked. There was a shuddering groan but no water. I tried again. Something the color and temperature of day-old tea dribbled out of the showerhead onto my feet.

Son of a bitch. Now the handle wouldn't budge. I grabbed the thing with both hands and wrenched at it. Nothing. I let go.

When I did, the entire handle assembly exploded out of its fitting and slammed into the stall's opposite wall, smashing shards of shower tile at me. Ice-cold water gushed from the flange. I used my palms to angle it down while I stepped over porcelain shrapnel, and treated the empty locker room to some choice Polish obscenities. I found a cobwebby utility closet behind the shower stall and yanked the main valves closed.

So. No shower today.

I dressed in my street clothes and doused myself in perfume, but nothing was going to hide the reek. I pulled a hank of my own hair to my nostrils for a test sniff, and gagged. Then I went stomping off to the lobby, to find Mike Stone and make it clear to him that, budget cuts or no, nonexploding showers had to be a priority in a workplace where people plunge their arms elbows-deep into stinking cadavers all morning long.

"Hey, Doc…" It was Keith Jones, the detective on the Eugene Chen case, coming out of the conference room and donning his brown fedora. When he got close enough to smell me, he stopped dead.

Another cop-looking character came through the doors. Jones pushed him forward. "My partner, Daniel Ramirez."

Homicide Inspector Daniel Ramirez recoiled and grunted a howdya do. I recognized him as the bald man conducting interviews at the Café Oui-Fi. He wore the same ugly bruise-puce blazer.

A dark-skinned man in a sharp suit followed the detectives out of the conference room. He saw me and his jaw dropped. I felt mine do the same. It was the hot Indian guy from Ocean Beach, the one Bea tangled up in her leash.

Jones said, "You two know each other?"

"No…" Hot Indian Guy said. His eyes were even deeper and darker than I'd remembered. They were like scorched driftwood. They drilled right through me. Prosecutor. Got to be a prosecutor.

"My dog tried to kill him," I said. Hot Indian Guy didn't take the cue to joke it off or even to smile. He just kept drilling. I didn't like it.

Jones and Ramirez exchanged a look. Then Jones said,

"Anup Banerjee, from the district attorney's office. This is Dr. Jessie Teska, the new ME."

"My pleasure, Dr. Teska," Assistant District Attorney Anup Banerjee said without conviction, and held out his hand.

I squeezed it. Hard. Autopsy is manual labor and builds hand strength.

Jones told me they had managed to collect videotape from the shooting scene in the Tenderloin. They wanted to review it with me. "We've got it upstairs, but maybe it would be better to look at it in your office. Ours is…crowded."

"Noisy, too," added his partner, helpfully.

I found the key to open the morgue door.

"After you."

I held the door for the cops and glanced back at Anup Banerjee.

"Small world," I said. ADA Banerjee nodded politely and turned away.

The detectives had a flash drive. I tried to fire up the video software on my computer, but it didn't want to work. The three of us stared at the monitor and watched it tell us it was loading, loading, loading…

"I hope this thing doesn't explode, too."

"What?"

"Never mind. I sense you've noticed my new fragrance. It's called Eau de Comp."

Daniel Ramirez looked at his shoes, but Keith Jones grinned wickedly. "It sure is distinctive."

"Don't get me started."

A video window finally popped up. "Here we go," said Ramirez, and reached past me for the mouse. The footage came off a camera across the street from Café Oui-Fi. It centered on the parking lot of Hotel Somerville.

"Isn't that the place where Stone picked up his drug mule on Thursday morning?"

"Yeah."

"Two bodies on one street corner, twelve hours apart?"

"Not unusual around there."

We watched the video. A woman walked a small dog along the sidewalk. A tattered figure in a wheelchair took the same path in the opposite direction. A stocky man with dark hair entered the café. A hipster woman crossed the street at Polk and Geary and nearly got creamed by a car squeezing the yellow light. I thought of the morning's three cadavers in the morgue cooler patiently waiting for me.

"Detective, today I autopsied a military veteran with his face chewed off by a wild animal on federal property. Can you imagine the paperwork I'm going to—"

"Here we go."

On the silent computer screen, the door to the Café Oui-Fi swung wide, and the stocky man with dark hair who had just entered came bursting back out with something under his arm. He stumbled to the curb and then was up again, sprinting past the corner. Another man, in a short black jacket, with a bag over his shoulder and a gun in his hand, followed out the door. He lurched toward the corner with a pronounced limp, and raised the gun. Muzzle flashes came out as he ran off-screen in the same direction.

"Okay," I said. "That was Eugene Chen with the stolen laptop and the other man is your suspect."

"Right. Did you see his limp?"

"Hard to miss."

"Here's what we want to know—do you think he got injured in there, in the café, before he came out?"

"What do you mean?"

"In your medical opinion."

"In my medical opinion, what?"

"Does that limp look like someone who's just sustained an injury."

I looked from one detective to the other, waiting for a punch line. It didn't come.

"Was the guy limping when he went *into* the café?" I asked, fighting the urge to add *"you knuckleheads?"*

"It's hard to tell."

"Let's take a look."

Jones fiddled with the video. "This wasn't our idea, Doc. The sergeant is on our ass."

"What does he expect me to tell you?"

"We had our seventy-two-hour meeting today," Ramirez said, "and CSI brought in four pages of biological evidence, bloodstains from the restaurant, the café…"

"Out on the sidewalk," added Jones.

"The sarge noticed the shooter's limp on the video, and wondered if some of that biological material inside the café could come from him."

"Like maybe he shot himself pulling his gun out?"

"Yeah."

"So why don't you run DNA on all the blood and compare it to Chen's?"

"Resource management," growled Jones. "CSI doesn't want to run fifty different lab specimens and find out it all comes back to the victim. So the sarge says if the doctor watches the tape and tells us the suspect was injured, *then* we'll run the DNA. Otherwise, it's not likely to yield useful information."

"His exact words," added Ramirez.

"All right then," I said. "Show me the suspect entering the café."

Ramirez checked his notebook, then fiddled with the video and ran the tape from 19:12, two hours before the shooting. It was still plenty light out. A taxi double-parked on Polk with its hazards flashing. A woman with a long ponytail bummed a cigarette from the parking attendant. At 19:15 the suspect—short jacket, shoulder bag—entered the top of the frame. A jaywalker carrying a bunch of plastic bags came from the same direction, then cut across the Hotel Somerville parking lot. A couple got into the taxi and it pulled away.

The man who killed Lumpy Chen over a laptop appeared at the top of the monitor screen and walked toward the bottom. He had an erect, military bearing. I guessed his age to be in the mid to late thirties. I could see why the detectives weren't able to decide about his limp. It was subtle.

"Yeah, he favors his right leg with a minor falter," I told them.

"How minor?"

"He doesn't need a cane."

"Could it be that he hurt himself recently?"

"I doubt it. Looks to me like he's used to walking that way."

"It's a lot worse when he comes out shooting, though. Couldn't he have shot himself?"

"No. Or not necessarily. Running with a mobility deficit is a lot harder than walking with it. A small limp turns into a big one."

We watched while the suspect went into the Café Oui-Fi.

"Does he do anything else?"

Jones consulted his notes. "He steps out to call somebody."

"Let me see that."

Ramirez fast-forwarded the video at 4x. The shadows leaned over and butterscotch street lamps came on. At time stamp 20:45, the suspect stepped out the door with his phone held to his ear and the laptop bag slung over his shoulder. He looked up as though gazing at the treetops while he talked. The conversation lasted a minute and a half, and then he put his phone away and went back into the Café Oui-Fi.

"That's it?"

"That's it until the shooting," Ramirez said. "One witness at a table near him said the guy looked nervous."

Jones consulted his notebook. "Nervous, maybe frustrated. She said he was working on his laptop and kept running one hand through his hair. He was texting on his cell phone when Lumpy grabbed the computer."

"And the shit hit the fan," Ramirez added.

"What about computer forensics?" I said. "Can you figure out if his laptop was connected to the internet, or who he was calling on his cell phone?"

The detectives guffawed in stereo.

"Doc," Ramirez said, "we're lucky they managed to lift the footage from that security camera."

Inspector Keith Jones sighed and slapped Inspector Daniel Ramirez on the knee. "Let's get out of Dr. Teska's hair."

"Yeah. Good luck with the face-eating thing."

"All in a day's work," I said.

After the detectives left, I really should have typed up the coyote depredation case—if that one hit the press, it would be best to have a report, even a pending one, rather than feeding the speculation machine with a statement that the investigation was "ongoing." The message light on my phone was blinking. I didn't want to check it for fear that it might be the family of the dead Alzheimer's patient—or, worse, their lawyer. I probably should have started a report on the Ingleside stinker while the autopsy was fresh in my mind and the odor still clung to my skin.

Instead I rewound the video to watch Lumpy Chen again, stumbling out of the Café Oui-Fi moments before he died and became my problem. I watched the man with the limp charging murderously after him, the muzzle of his gun flashing. I remembered counting four beveled bullet holes in the plate-glass windows when I visited the crime scene. The man with the limp shot first and chased Lumpy after. He shot up a café full of people, and hit at least two cars outside. Then he sprayed bullets across a city street corner.

He wanted that laptop back at any cost.

I rewound to the footage from 19:15 to watch the killer enter the scene and sit near the window of the café. Nothing unusual about him. He sipped, typed, read, typed, texted. He ran his fingers through his hair. When he stepped outside to talk on the phone an hour and a half later, I could just make out his chin in the streetlight as he pointed his face skyward. He kept it pointed there and hardly moved it during the conversation.

What was so interesting up in those trees?

A number I didn't recognize came up on my phone while I was squeezing the Beemer past an accordion bus on Fulton Street. I ignored it and continued fighting into the outer Avenues, barely ever breaking my high-performance marvel of German engineering out of second gear. I wanted to get home and scrub out the stench of decomp; candles, bath salts, and a bottle of quality scotch were waiting.

I had just settled into the trapdoor tub in Mahoney Brothers #45 when the phone buzzed again, the same number. This time I answered.

"Hello, Jessie. Please tell me you don't have plans for Saturday."

Arnie Spitz. Much as I didn't want to admit it, he had me at hello.

"Arnie. What a pleasure to hear from you. Did I give you my number? Because I don't recall giving you my number."

"I have my ways," he said without a hint of jest. I sat up and must have sloshed, because he added, rather too eagerly, "Are you in the bath?"

"Washing off a long day."

"Come with me Saturday. I'll take you over the bridge. To the woods. On an excursion."

In his Aussie accent the word came in four syllables with a lascivious curl in the middle. I splashed one knee loudly over the other to give him a wee thrill. I heard him suck in his breath.

"Well, Arnie," I said, taking my time and splishing around some more, "I don't know about that. Do you call many single women while they're indisposed in the bath, and ask them out for a mystery drive?"

"No. But unless I've fully misjudged, you are not just any single woman indisposed in the bath."

I sipped my scotch. Bea wandered over and peered down. Her eyes admonished me to say no. *Play hard to get*, my beagle advised, the crafty bitch.

"Well, Arnie," I said again, "it so happens I have no plans for Saturday, and I'm not on call this weekend, either."

I could hear him smile from the other end of the line. "Please tell me when I may arrive to fetch you."

———

Crossing the Golden Gate Bridge in a convertible, even bundled up against the wind, made for a thrilling start to our Saturday excursion. Arnie's ride was a low, wide-bodied electric roadster—a test prototype, he said, from a company that was seeking his advice about "the optimal approach to securing venture capital."

"They're wooing you."

He looked over, flashed his perfect teeth in honest pleasure. "You are a bold and direct person, Czesława."

"Good memory," I said. "But call me Jessie."

He glanced at me again, probing from behind his tortoiseshell sunglasses. "What does your mother call you?"

I said, "I'll tell if you will."

"Pookie."

"No!"

"No. She calls me Arnold."

"Very funny. Well, my mother calls me Czesia."

"That's right lovely."

"It is, yes."

"No one else does, though?"

"Only my brother when he's being ironic."

"Ah." We had reached the midpoint of the bridge, where the main cables dip to their lowest ebb.

"Then I shall call you Pookie," declared Arnie Spitz.

The highway beyond the bridge arced up and over a green crest. We went through a tunnel with a rainbow painted on its arch, and when we emerged we were in another world. Midsummer sun blazed down. Timber replaced grass, and the convertible hugged curves through woods thick with the scent of eucalyptus.

"How did you know I love a good road trip?"

"Perhaps you mentioned it the other night."

"Did I?"

I didn't. And that reminded me of something.

"You never explained how you got my phone number."

"I have my ways."

"So you said. Enlighten me."

He glanced sideways.

"Jessie. Nothing is secret nowadays. Everything is data. Everything. We float in a sea of data. Some are better at fishing it than others."

"My number isn't listed."

"You're right."

"I switched carriers when I moved. I've only had that number a couple of weeks."

"Ah!" he said, and eased out of a curve. "Time does not exist in cyberspace. Data is instant and eternal. Once it joins the sea, it is equal to all other data that swims there. I know the internet in its depths, in ways that few people do. They—you—skim along the surface of the sea. I dive in." He turned and looked at me from over his sunglasses. "And I know where the trenches lie."

"Eyes on the road, Captain Nemo."

We twisted down an especially crazy set of switchbacks, and then, quite suddenly, emerged in a breathtaking evergreen forest.

"Muir Woods," Arnie said as he slid the humming car to a stop. He took my hand and caressed the tops of my knuckles with his thumb. My fingers tingled.

"Let us stroll through the most beautiful forest in the world."

———

When I was seven years old, a hurricane scoured its way up the coast of New England and passed right over Pinkham Street in Lynn. The rain pounded against the side of our house like it was aimed from a fire hose. The street trees bent over backwards from right to left, and branches snapped off. Sheets of aluminum siding skittered down the sidewalk. When it stopped, my father took me and Tomasz outside. The air was thrumming but there was not a breath of wind. Dad pointed up. The clouds swirled around a patch of blue sky right over our heads. We were standing in the eye of the storm.

Then, out of nowhere, the wind started to gust again, and Dad hustled us inside. We stayed well behind the windows with their masking tape Xs and watched while the neighborhood trees bent over backwards again, this time from left to right. The aluminum siding slid back up the street. The rain pounded the windows on the opposite side of the house. When the hurricane was all over, a willow tree had ripped right out of the ground and landed on Mr. Benfiglio's car just up the block.

I felt the same awe at Muir Woods as I had that day in 1994. Arnie Spitz and I stood under the sighing redwoods that reached to the heavens in a helix of branches, each a giant feathered in green. We strolled through the most beautiful forest in the world hand in hand, and talked quietly about other beautiful places we had known, and about storms we had weathered.

We continued up the coast. The road ran along the edge of a marsh that looked a lot like Essex or Ipswich at low tide—except for the sea lions. Arnie pointed them out, lolling in the mudflats, logs with eyes. I leaned back and enjoyed the salt wind blowing over the convertible. I hadn't been anywhere that smelled of seagrass and ebb tide decay since I'd left Massachusetts nine years before. Seaside cliffs and windblown trees gave way to a ribbon of road running through a pasture with cows taking shade under scattered oaks. We passed a couple of crossroads towns, then reached an oyster farm with a roadhouse restaurant. A steam trough piled with crabs greeted us on the porch.

We had a wonderful dinner—candlelight, rope and tackle, an old net draped from the ceiling. Arnie wanted to hear about autopsies, but I demurred for the sake of our fellow diners. Instead I told him how I fell in love with my field.

"I started college as a nursing student. I commuted an hour there and back and waited tables on weekends, but still money was tight—my dad was out of the picture and my mother was barely getting by. I took on one loan after another, serious debt."

Through the restaurant's picture window, the sun was setting over a man out in a dory checking the oyster racks. We watched him.

"I was working nights at Mass General, the big hospital, cleaning bedpans, that kind of thing. Hated it. Come summer I needed a full-time job, and the college aid office got me into the city morgue, doing paperwork and filing. One of the medical examiners there kind of took me under her wing. Monica Dealey. Monica was the best. She started bringing me into the autopsy suite, asking me to scribe."

"Scribe?"

"Take dictation while the doctor does the cutting. By the end of the summer, she was letting me assist in the autopsies if they were naturals or easy accidents. Sophomore year I started filling premed requirements. I kept working at the medical examiner's office whenever I could. I was hooked."

Arnie held up his wineglass. "To Monica Dealey." I joined the toast.

The oysterman rowed in and the clouds faded to violet. It was getting chilly by the time we left. Arnie put up the convertible's roof. In the dark, the tree-crowded road became a path through a haunted forest. Arnie drove with concentration and care, and we fell silent for the first time since he'd picked me up. The fog returned. I couldn't see the tops of the Golden

Gate Bridge's towers when we were right underneath them. Arnie negotiated ever thicker pea soup through the Presidio to get back to my neighborhood.

We said good-night at the garden gate. He asked if he could see me again. I told him yes.

"I'm afraid it'll be a while—I'm off soon, overseas on business for nearly a month. But when I return…?"

"Let me know."

We kissed. We kissed again. He slid a hand into my hair and I put one on his chest. I was aching to take him into the cable car and rock it around.

But I didn't.

Arnie Spitz hummed off in his roadster, and I turned the house key while hushing Bea and then it hit me again. It hit me like a brick, the harm Barry had done. Barry Taylor, badge 2784 of the Los Angeles Police Department Detective Bureau, Robbery Special Section. That lying son of a bitch.

PART TWO

SAN FRANCISCO

AUGUST

CHAPTER SIX

"They're paying you a doctor's salary to type?" Sparkle said. She led me along a littered alley to a park a couple of blocks from the Hall of Justice, where we settled down and unwrapped our fish tacos.

"Not they. *You*, my dear taxpayer of the City and County of San Francisco."

It was early August. I hadn't even been on the job a full month, but the honeymoon was long over.

"No budget for transcriptionists or even for recording equipment. So I take notes in the morgue, bloody gloves and all, and then type up my findings afterwards. And, believe me, I am one crappy typist."

The park had its share of shady characters, but it also had picnic tables and a lovely garden. Sparkle and I had a standing Friday lunch date there.

"There's only one morgue tech for the three doctors. That means on a busy day I have to package the evidence by myself."

Sparkle bit into her taco. She's a vocationally good listener.

"I did a case yesterday, a homeless man found dead on the

street. Everything the poor guy owned was in his pockets. Half a dozen of the little toiletry bottles they give out in shelters, three disposable lighters, a folding knife. Wads of aluminum foil, couple of dirty needles, a cook spoon. Documenting the evidence took me half an hour. That's half an hour that I'm not doing another autopsy, or clearing the paperwork on two or three old reports."

"Somebody killed him?"

"Don't know yet. His only trauma was a scalp contusion, and that could have come from a fall. But when I popped his skull, I didn't find any blood in the brain, so he didn't die of a head injury…"

Sparkle put down the fish taco and pressed a napkin to her lips.

"Sorry," I said.

A pickup basketball game started across the park—a bunch of weatherworn, aging men in cutoffs, the ball gray with use. One of them recognized Sparkle and waved.

She blew him a kiss. "Repeat customer. His brother's got a habit, gone down twice, burglary and armed robbery."

"He seems fond of you."

"I'm a sweetheart. In my business it pays to be a sweetheart."

A pack of motorcycles idled at a red light on Folsom Street, halting all conversation. After they blustered off, Sparkle asked if I was involved in the RICO trial. It was all over the news.

"No, those are old cases. I haven't been here long enough. My boss is down there today."

"They called Chief Howe?"

"No, Mike Stone, the deputy chief. He got subpoenaed on one of his homicides from a couple of years ago. He's not pleased about it. And Ted Nguyen is sick and tired of taking more morgue work with Mike off testifying. Everybody in the office is cranky. I mean *everybody*, Sparkle."

"That's why I work alone."

"Yeah, well—I might as well be. Keeping my head down and doing my job."

"Be grateful you don't have to go into the RICO trial."

RICO is a federal prosecution under the Racketeer Influenced and Corrupt Organizations Act. It's usually invoked as a way for the feds to lock up the leaders of organized criminal enterprises. If they can connect a crime boss to a homicide, even if some foot soldier pulled the actual trigger, the feds can put that boss away for conspiracy. Sparkle told me that the usual alphabet soup of law-enforcement agencies were working the San Francisco RICO case, and that it comprised more than a dozen criminal cases anywhere from a year to a decade old. The news accounts listed drug smuggling, extortion, kidnapping, obstruction of justice, human trafficking...

"And murder. I saw the name of an old client in the paper on a federal conspiracy charge. I bailed him on a drug charge couple years ago, when he was a juvenile."

She picked something out of her fish taco and flicked it into the grass.

"This was a county charge. His lawyer wouldn't take a deal from the DA. Big gamble, but he got the boy off. Acquitted at trial."

"And now he's all grown up and a murderer."

"Allegedly."

"Guess he didn't come back to you for bond this time."

Sparkle used a napkin to brush the taco bits onto the ground, where the boldest of the sparrows stalked them.

"I hope he never darkens my door again. I don't want that kind of business. His lawyer's a big shot now. I hear he's on the RICO defense team. Name of Jackson Heffernan."

I almost choked on my horchata.

"Ethel Sofronas, eighty-six, found unresponsive in a skilled nursing facility. Long cardiac history includes a remote MI and CABG."

It was Donna Griello's turn to present the cases at Monday's morning meeting. Judging from the slender few folders in front of her, San Francisco had not had a terribly deadly weekend. This was a relief; the federal attorney running the RICO trial had gone behind schedule on Friday, so Mike Stone was stuck in court again and wasn't going to be cutting any autopsies.

"Why is Ethel our problem?" Ted Nguyen asked testily.

Donna scanned the top sheet on the pile. "The doctor covering that shift says he doesn't know this patient, so he refused to sign the death certificate. You can probably external her."

"Okay," grumbled Nguyen. "What else we got?"

Donna went on to present a decomp found in McLaren Park, an asthmatic respiratory arrest in the ER, and, finally, a probable-overdose in a locked home. "SFME-0955, Rebecca Corchero, age twenty-four. Roommate found her cold and stiff Sunday morning, with a tourniquet around her arm and a syringe nearby."

"Was the residence locked and secure?" I asked.

"Locked but not secure. Roommate says the door was slam-locked but the dead bolt wasn't set."

"Was it usually?"

"Yes. She opened it and found the body in a chair, then called nine-one-one from her cell phone."

"Did the decedent have a history of drug use?"

"None documented. She was until recently a childcare provider and had just started nursing school. Her family's in the Philippines and have requested to talk to the investigating physician as soon as possible. They're Catholic and want an open-casket funeral—whoever does this one, remember to fill out a letter of noncontagion so the body can be transported internationally."

"I'll take her," I said. It looked like a routine OD, and I knew Nguyen would be reluctant to volunteer for a case with overseas next of kin to talk to, plus extra paperwork. I could claim Ethel the geriatric external, too, and Ted would have to deal with the stinker from the park along with the asthma death.

A bargain, I reckoned.

I made quick work of Ethel Sofronas—a cachectic corpse with no trauma and a single healed scar from a coronary artery bypass graft. Natural death by heart disease; one down, one to go.

Before I started on 0955 Corchero, I logged into the autopsy suite's poky computer to look over the death scene photos. The first showed a trio of drab two-story houses leaning shoulder to shoulder on an incline. They were identical except for paint and trim, each with a bay window over a garage door and a metal entrance gate at the top of a brick staircase. There are thousands of this type of house in the Avenues, the untouristed San Francisco neighborhoods that never had architecture that could be described as Victorian or Edwardian, or anything other than utilitarian. The specimens in the scene photo were variations in gray, the only splash of color a blue car parked in the driveway of the center house. I checked Donna's 2578 report. That was the scene, 1461 30th Avenue.

I clicked to the next picture. It showed the open doorway and front hall with a handful of cops, one in a CSI windbreaker. Before I could click further, the unmistakable sound of a body bag zipper stole my attention.

"We start?" demanded Yarina. She is not a patient woman.

I began with a quick walk-around. Rebecca Corchero was

still clothed, in a V-neck shirt and khakis, and barefoot, with pedicured, glossy red toenails. Her hands were clean and soft, no fingertip scars. She wore fake fingernails, missing one on her right index finger. The exposed nail bed was irregular and abraded, and still tacky from the beauty shop adhesive. Her skin was unmarked and tanned, except for the pale round outline of a watch on the back of her left wrist. In the crook of her left elbow I found a single puncture wound with some crusted blood and a large, fresh ecchymosis—the bruise left behind by a sloppy needle stick. There was a band-like indentation on her upper left arm. A knotted nylon stocking lay in the folds of the body bag. The knots corresponded to marks on the indentation. There were no scars on her left arm. No track marks.

None on her right arm, either, though she did have an odd injury on her wrist. It was a fresh bruise, an irregular ring of contused abrasions—small cuts that looked like the petals of a daisy. A thread of dried blood led away from it, past her knuckles and down between her fingers.

Rebecca Corchero had Asian features, thick black hair gathered in a loose ponytail, and a single piercing with a simple gold ball in each earlobe. Her face showed some purple congestion, typical of an OD. Her eyes were open, the corneas clouded from postmortem drying; but they were not yet opaque, and I noted their color as brown. The whites were bloodshot, with bright red spots of scleral petechiae. I took a forceps and flipped her lower left eyelid inside out. Spidery blood vessels and more red spots: conjunctival petechiae. I peered up her nostrils but didn't see any damage at all.

If this woman was a junkie, she was taking better care of herself than most. Hot crack pipes leave scarred fingertips. Needle addicts have track marks on their arms, or tattoos to cover them. Snorted cocaine corrodes the cartilage inside the nose, leaving telltale holes. She was an athlete—great muscle tone, especially in her legs. And her watch tan... Cell phones tell time. Who wears a watch anymore, except for runners?

Of course, she might have been a naive user. There's a first time for everything, including shooting up. The orbital petechiae could have come through passive congestion. The body was found in full rigor mortis, seated, head slumped down. Full rigor means she'd been dead for at least ten, twelve hours, plenty of time for the pressure of pooling blood to burst the delicate vessels in the eyes.

On the other hand—those petechiae could also be a sign of strangulation. I didn't see any throat trauma on the outside, but I would be sure to do a layered neck dissection when I cut into her. I everted her lips to look for more petechiae. There weren't any—but I did find something else. The thin bridge of tissue attaching the lower lip to the gums was torn, and blood coated the teeth next to it.

How'd she end up with a lacerated frenulum? She hadn't been punched—I would see a contusion on her mouth. Same with a fall, unless she landed on a soft surface. That was a possibility. Junkies fall down all the time, onto all kinds of stuff.

The drug paraphernalia, the facial congestion, and the single needle stick pointed to an overdose. The fresh daisy-shaped abrasions on the right wrist, the damage to the inside of her lower lip, and the petechiae pointed to an assault. A lot of could-be's. Sometimes the external examination raises more questions than it settles.

I photographed the full body, then took close-ups of the torso and lower extremities, the bruise injuries, the knotted stocking tourniquet. I leaned in for a head shot.

Something was bugging me. I couldn't put my finger on it.

"Undress her?" Yarina said.

"Hold open her lips for me first..."

She did, and I got a good flash photo, showing the torn pink frenulum of Rebecca Corchero's lower lip, the light film of still-red blood in the gaps of her teeth. Yarina removed the clothing and placed a rubber block under the corpse's shoulder blades. I lifted the camera again.

"Oh shit!" someone yelped from across the autopsy suite. Medical students were scattering back from Ted Nguyen's table. A buttery fluid was spilling off it, pooling on the floor in a clotted mess. The McLaren Park drug dump had been harboring a bellyful of decomposition ascites. The stench punched me from across the room. Yarina muttered something in Ukrainian and went to gather a mop bucket, and Dr. Nguyen started baling the stinking goo out of the dead man's abdomen with a soup ladle.

When I returned my attention to Rebecca Corchero and looked through the camera again, I caught my breath in déjà vu. I lifted her head off the neck block so she was looking at me.

I knew this woman. I had seen her before. Where…?

The morgue computer still showed the scene photo I'd left off with—the loitering cops, the girl's body slumped in a yellow chair behind them. I clicked to the next one, and two more. Each brought the camera closer to Rebecca Corchero in her death pose. She was barefoot, in the same clothes Yarina had just stripped off her body. Her chin was on her chest. The knotted stocking was wrapped around her left arm. The right hung down. A syringe lay on a side table, drops of rusty fluid under the needle's tip.

The last picture in the sequence was a close-up of the corpse's congested, purple face. Her pupils were dilated, her expression cockeyed and vacant. One corner of her mouth crimped down and the other ticked up. I clicked again. The computer went to a thumbnail screen of the entire photo set from the death scene. And there it was: the single flash of color. The blue car parked in Rebecca Corchero's driveway.

Cobalt blue.

I turned away from the computer and back to my autopsy table. The déjà vu lifted as soon as I looked at her face again.

Rebecca Corchero was the mysterious sobbing onlooker to Dr. Michael Stone's Fourth of July party. My parking spot guardian angel. My Monday morning autopsy.

Yarina rejoined me.

"We cut now?" she said.

CHAPTER SEVEN

I wanted to be alone.

I wanted to be alone from the moment I cut into Rebecca Corchero's uterus and felt its thickness against my scissors. Inside was a two-inch-long fetus: knobby head, hunched body, spindly curled limbs.

Rebecca didn't look like a junkie on the inside any more than she did on the outside. Her liver was pristine. Normal lymph nodes. No pulmonary edema or visceral congestion. No trauma, either: The strap muscles of her neck were clean and firm and the hyoid bone intact. She had been a perfectly healthy twenty-four-year-old woman in the first trimester of pregnancy.

The students had gravitated to my table after Ted burst his stinker, so I assumed a professorial mien and taught the future doctors how to remove a dead fetus from its dead mother and how to measure the length of its foot to calculate gestational age. This specimen charted out at twelve weeks. Same age as the fetus I had removed from the dead body of Mary Catherine Walsh during my last autopsy in Los Angeles.

My hands were trembling. One of the students noticed. Her eyes asked me what was wrong. I ignored her.

And what *was* wrong? Last month I had exchanged a few pleasant words and a parking spot with this stranger on my porcelain table. A couple of days later I happened to see her in a parked car, alone, crying. These were not reasons to recuse myself from an autopsy. We weren't related. She wasn't a friend.

So why were my hands shaking?

I went over to the cold closet and placed the fetal specimen in the drawer marked *Teska*. It would get logged at the end of the day. Then I returned to the table, where the students were watching Yarina cram the red biohazard bag that contained Rebecca Corchero's organs into her empty torso, and then stitch closed the Y-incision with white twine. Yarina hosed her off, put her in a new nylon pouch, and laid her to rest in the morgue's storage locker.

I could have signed up for the gushing stinker and let Dr. Nguyen take case number SFME-0955. But that hadn't happened. Rebecca Corchero was my case. I resolved to close it quick.

I started with the investigators' findings. They listed the personal effects on the body as a syringe, a crucifix pendant on a gold chain, and a bracelet. The next of kin page gave me her family's phone number in the Philippines. Middle of the night there, though. I'd try the roommate first.

Melodie Ortiz swore up and down there was no way that Rebecca could have been using drugs. "I can't believe she's dead," she said at least three times.

"You two kept different schedules, right?"

"Yes, but it's not like we never saw each other. We had dinner at home together on Saturday night before I went out."

"Where did you go?"

"To my boyfriend's."

"What time was that?"

"About eight thirty."

"And you returned in the morning?"

A slight pause. "Yeah."

"That's when you found her."

"Yes," she whispered.

"Rebecca didn't have plans?"

"No... I mean, I don't know. She didn't seem like she was expecting her boyfriend. And she said she had a ton of studying to do."

"You know her boyfriend?"

"No. I only know he's a medical student."

"At UCSF?"

"I don't know. I never met him."

"What's his name?"

"She just called him 'my *bato*.'"

"*Bato?*"

"Spanish for 'homeboy.'"

"You mean boyfriend?"

"Not exactly. Boyfriend is different, *mi chulo* or *mi amor*."

"Why'd she call him her *bato?*"

"Beats me. Rebecca didn't talk about her love life a lot—but you could tell she was really into this guy. He's this, like, superstar student, lent her books and stuff, and gave her lots of school advice. He even helped her get into the nursing program..."

She faded out. I said nothing.

"She was so psyched about it..."

Melodie started crying. I delivered the usual soothing lines about unexpected deaths being the hardest kind. I meant every word, too.

Medical students have access to needles and narcotics. I had come across Rebecca Corchero outside the Hall of Justice carrying textbooks under her arm, and again outside Dr. Stone's Fourth of July potluck. Maybe her boyfriend was one of the students who had rotated through the morgue. Maybe he'd been a guest at the party.

I found Mike Stone in his office. He looked worn-out.

"Tough time in court?"

"No. It's a simple case. Single gunshot wound to the head."

"But this is the RICO trial, right? I heard there's like a dozen rabid lawyers in there."

He grimaced. "Yeah, but there was nothing for them to work with. The shooting was close range at the midline to the back of the head. Defense kept trying to get me to say the exit wound was the entrance... It's their theory that the decedent was charging at the defendant, and the defendant shot him in the forehead in self-defense. But during the autopsy I took photos of the beveling in the skull, with a classic cone-shaped exit wound in the frontal bone. There is no way I could say it was front to back." He shook his head. "No way."

"Well, let me ask you something. It's about my new case."

"Busy around here this morning?"

"About average. No homicides. I picked up a twenty-four-year-old woman, probable OD."

I told Stone about the roommate and the unnamed medical student boyfriend, and asked if he had invited any of our rotating UCSF students to that Fourth of July party.

"There were a handful. Can I see your findings?"

I handed him my autopsy notes—and Mike Stone stiffened. His finger was on the top of the sheet, under *Name of Decedent.*

"Rebecca Corchero," he said. Then he rasped, "Let me see the photos."

I went to his computer and logged in. While I did, he scrutinized the body diagram and my notes.

"She was pregnant?"

"Twelve weeks."

I got the thumbnail photos up on the screen. Stone stared at them, then grabbed the mouse from me and clicked on the decedent's face. He turned white. He said, "Oh God, no," and turned away.

Stone slumped over his office chair until his color came back. Then he said, "Rebecca was a dear family friend. She was my daughter Callie's nanny for...oh, for years."

The room was silent but for the hum of the computer's fan.

"I'm sorry... I'm so sorry, Mike. I didn't know, or I wouldn't have..."

Dr. Stone stood up and paced across his narrow office. Then he returned to the desk and pounced on my autopsy notes.

"It's an overdose?"

I clicked to the scene photo of the body slumped in the chair, with the tourniquet on her arm and a dripping hypodermic on the table.

"I'm pending it for tox."

Stone's eyes got small, and started darting. "When did she die?"

"Sometime Saturday night."

"You said a roommate found her?"

"Sunday morning. In full rigor." His eyes hadn't stopped moving. "Are you sure you want to discuss this right now, Mike? Maybe I should leave you alone."

"No. No—I'm all right. It's not your fault. If I'd checked today's sheet when I came in, I could have... I would have been able to prepare myself..."

He was on the computer, feverishly clicking through the autopsy photos.

"What's this?" he asked, when he came to the close-up of the daisy-shaped abrasions on her right wrist.

"I don't know yet. It worries me. That, and the torn frenulum."

He opened that picture: the bright flash shot, Yarina's gloved fingers holding the corpse's lips open.

"No contusions on her face?"

"None."

"Petechiae?"

"A few in her sclera and conjunctiva, but nowhere else. And her neck was clean."

He kept clicking. When he reached the pictures of the fetus he said, "Did you take fetal DNA?"

"I dissected the fetus and kept it for testing."

"Good job."

Dr. Stone worked his way through the scene photos, one by one, never taking his eyes off the screen.

"Have you notified the family?"

"They requested a call, but it's the middle of the night in the Philippines now."

"I'll do it myself. Her mother ought to hear it from me."

"I want to talk to this boyfriend. Her roommate says she was pretty serious about him. Rebecca never mentioned a medical student she was dating?"

Stone was writing down the next of kin phone number, and took a moment to double-check it before he answered.

"Not to me."

"Were she and your daughter close?"

"Callie still speaks fondly of her, but she's growing up fast and we're not really in touch with Rebecca anymore. A tween doesn't want to hang out with her old nanny…"

Dr. Stone's expression brightened a bit; but then I saw his eyes glisten. "I don't know how I'm going to tell her."

We sat in silence. I was about to excuse myself when Stone said, "Neil."

Neil, he told me, was a guy Rebecca had been dating after she left his employ. "Rebecca had an interest in medical technology. My wife pulled some strings with a friend in the field, and helped her get a job at a biotech start-up. This Neil worked there, too."

I wondered if Neil was Bato the boyfriend. Maybe Rebecca had told her roommate that he was a medical student, or maybe Melodie got mixed up.

I said, "Do you know the name of the company?"

I put on my official-business voice and called Siloam Biologic. Someone with the title Director of Team Resources gave me three men named Neil in the company. I started with Neil Tanenbaum, a manufacturing science and technology cell culture engineer, because that sounded like something you could confuse for a medical student. But Neil Tanenbaum assured me he was definitely not dating Rebecca Corchero, because he was gay. He remembered her, though.

"She was tall, thin, Asian, right?"

That describes a lot of San Franciscans. I let him keep talking.

"She worked in the cell lines. I saw her at lunch sometimes. I heard there were some kind of—recriminations?—when she left."

"When was this?"

"Would've been…last year, in the fall." Neil Tanenbaum's tone changed, like he was cupping the phone. "Medical examiner means someone's dead, right? I hope it's not Rebecca…"

The phrase *not at liberty to say* popped into my head out of an old movie. I thanked him for his time and hung up.

Neil number two at Siloam Biologic was a biostatistician and told me the same thing. Stately, aloof Rebecca Corchero, cell lines division. Never talked about her personal life. Left the company under a cloud. The third and last was Neil Dupree, a software deployment specialist in the Engineering and Operations Leadership Team, whatever that meant. I got his voice mail and left a message.

I spent the rest of my afternoon clearing a single, tough old case. I didn't have any food at home apart from half a pound of graying hamburg and half a loaf of stale sourdough. I pictured the crush of people at the Ocean Beach Safeway. Making small talk with the cashier, the bagger.

No way. Not today. So I took myself out for an early dinner on the strange-bedfellows strip of leather bars, condo pods, and Cal-fusion bistros near my office. I pushed tofu curry salad around my plate and tried not to think about Los Angeles. I was trying not to see Mary Catherine Walsh on a stainless-steel autopsy table, or Rebecca Corchero on a white porcelain one. The splayed bodies, limp limbs, stringy hair. Corchero's conspiratorial smile when she offered me her parking space. Walsh's suicide note. The pill bottle and the cobalt blue car.

I was being haunted by two women I didn't even know. One was dead and buried—but the other waited for me in the morgue cooler at 850 Bryant Street. She waited for toxicology results, for phone calls and paperwork. She waited for a death certificate and the final disposition of her remains.

I wouldn't have peace until she did.

―――――――――――

Tuesday saw me running ragged—big morning, all hands on deck. I caught three cases, and Stone and Nguyen took seven more between them. Poor Yarina was hopping from table to table like we were running a combat field hospital. After I emerged from the morgue, good news and bad awaited me at my desk, in the form of a voice-mail message. The good news was that the police had arrested a suspect in the shooting of Eugene "Lumpy" Chen. The bad news: The assistant district attorney assigned to the case, the man leaving the message, was Anup Banerjee.

I called him back. He sounded harried.

"Where's the autopsy report on Eugene Chen?"

"I still have work to do on it."

"Prelim is next week."

"So you said in your message. I just got out of the morgue with three autopsies."

No tsks of sympathy from ADA Banerjee. "Can we go over the case now?"

"Right now?"

"Prelim is next week," he repeated.

"I'm starving."

"Me too. Let's get something to eat and review the case in my office. I know a great taco truck."

"Across Bryant, on the alley by the juror parking?"

"That's the one."

"Meet you there."

Banerjee loosened up a little while we stood in line for El Herrador, especially once we started discussing different iterations of the fish taco. You'd never know it from his sleek build, but Anup Banerjee was a foodie. He grew up in Cupertino with two doctors, both immigrants, as parents. He speaks Bengali like I speak Polish—fluent in curse words, proverbs, and food. He'd been an ADA in San Francisco for five years after three in Santa Clara County. I said that was a long time working as a prosecutor. He agreed, and left it at that.

Banerjee shared a tiny office with another ADA whose kid,

judging from the artwork, really, really likes red crayons and dinosaurs. On his wall Banerjee had diplomas from college and law school, no other decoration. When we settled down with our tacos, he popped the links out of his French cuffs with swift precision, rolled the sleeves off his dark brown forearms, and switched gears again—back to business.

"Video, witness statements, physical evidence. I need to match them up."

"The detectives told you about my assessment of the video?"

"The shooter had a limp, but it wasn't enough to stop him running Chen down. Here he is, by the way."

He handed me a mug shot. Josu Azarola, goes by Joe, born 1987. Pale complexion, dark hair and eyes and a mustache. His nose had been broken more than once. He had a faint, well-healed linear scar on his lower lip, extending to the tip of his chin. No visible tattoos or piercings. He cast his gaze beyond the police photographer's lens with studied boredom.

"There's more video," Banerjee said, clicking away on his city-issue computer, which looked easily as old and cranky as mine. "A camera outside a liquor store, looking west on Geary toward the café. The quality isn't good."

A pixelated Lumpy Chen sprinted into view, carrying the laptop in the crook of his right arm like a running back with a football. A man pursued at a lurching run. Something in his hand flashed while Chen went booking across the three lanes of Geary at a diagonal. Chen cut left to the curb, swung open the door to Kim Son 88 restaurant, and disappeared inside. The limping man followed him three seconds later, leveling his weapon as he stepped into the restaurant.

Banerjee froze the playback.

"The police recovered eleven casings altogether. I want to know how many hit Eugene Chen."

"Six or seven."

"You can't make up your mind?"

I opened my manila case folder and handed him the body diagram I'd done during the autopsy.

"See this one, on his right forearm? It's a shallow penetrating gunshot wound. I pulled a deformed slug out of the soft tissue in there, likely a reentry from one of the shots that went through his torso. One bullet, two wound tracks—in his back, out his belly, and then into his arm, where it stopped."

I held my own arm across my belly to demonstrate. Banerjee scrutinized the body outline and my blue pen notes.

"What's POL mean?"

"Point of lodgment."

He pointed to the three wounds I'd plotted in the center of mass.

"Are any of these ones fatal?"

"Not immediately. They went through his liver and lower lung, broke some ribs and did a number on his spleen. Could have been survivable with medical attention. He was definitely alive until the last shot, the head shot."

"How do you know?"

"Bleeding in the brain. His heart was still pumping when he got shot in the head. That one was instantly fatal."

Anup Banerjee was writing furiously on a legal pad, the top of his head hanging across the desk. I thought of the palm trees on Venice Beach all of a sudden, and realized his hair had a scent of coconuts. He kept talking while scribbling.

"Witnesses in the restaurant say Chen got shot in the open door and stumbled through, but was still on his feet. That's possible?"

"Yes. Sure."

"A customer at a table near the door saw the whole thing and gave us a positive ID of Azarola from a photo lineup. I need to make sure his account is reliable before we go into the prelim."

"What's he say happened?"

Banerjee clicked on the computer again, and read.

"'There was a noise on the street like fireworks, and this man opens the door. I heard loud bangs and the man went toward the kitchen. Another man came into the restaurant behind him with a gun, and shot him in the back of the head from real close, and the first man fell face-down.'"

He looked at me. "Can you support that?"

"Maybe."

Banerjee's big brown eyes clouded with irritation.

"Listen," I continued. "Your witness says it was a 'real close' shooting, right? I can tell you the gun was not pressed up against Chen's head—I would have found a burn mark matching the muzzle, and I didn't. What I *did* find is a blood-soaked hole in a dark-colored hoodie on the decedent's body. We've dried the hoodie so the police crime lab can do chemical tests. Once those come back, I can tell you how far away the gun's muzzle was from Chen's head."

Banerjee shook his head impatiently. "No time. His lawyer is refusing a time waiver."

"Prelim is next week, so I hear."

Whoops. Banerjee sat back, shoulders stooped inward, puckering his suit. *Brain first then mouth*, I chided myself, not for the first time.

"It's no joke, Doctor. The defense is Jackson Heffernan, a skilled lawyer with an excellent track record in getting guys like this off."

"Ugh." The sound came before I could choke it off.

"Oh good. You're familiar with Jack. He already called me this morning, looking for your report. I can guarantee he'll be breathing down your neck, too, and soon. So far all you've told me is that you can't tell me much, besides the fact that the shot to the head was—" he consulted his legal pad "'—instantly fatal.' Thanks for that." He leaned forward. "*But*. I really need to know, Doctor, if you can back up the statement of my eyewitness with the autopsy findings."

"The gunshot wound to the head is going back to front, consistent with what your witness said."

"Good. What about the range?"

"The distance from the door to where Chen's body landed is five or six feet. A handgun fired from five feet away certainly seems 'close' if you're in a closed room. I would say the scene and the physical evidence fit your witness's narrative of the event."

"Okay," Banerjee said, adding something to his legal pad. "I will be putting you on the stand at the preliminary hearing."

"Right."

I said nothing else and neither did he. He gave the back of his jacket a reflexive tug to straighten it, and then just looked at me and waited. I could not for the life of me tell what was going on in Anup Banerjee's head. The guy must be one hell of a prosecutor.

"What else?" I said eventually.

"What else? Anything else. Your report isn't ready, and I'm relying on it for the prelim. So tell me what's going to be in that report. Once you finish it, that is."

Once I finish it? *Sukinsyn!*

"Doctor?"

"Please call me Jessie, Counselor."

"Jessie, right. Call me Anup."

No smile passed between us.

"Right. Well, Anup. When I finish it, my report will also include the toxicology results. They show Chen had cocaine on board."

"How much?"

"Not a lot."

"Enough to make a difference in his death?"

"Not with a bullet in his head. Cause of death is multiple gunshot wounds. The cocaine is not a contributing factor."

Banerjee's eyes still hadn't left mine. "Let's see the rest of the video," he said.

He started it rolling again. After a few seconds, the door opened and the man with the gun and the limp left Kim Son 88 with the laptop. He slid it into his shoulder bag while walking with a brisk bob up Geary.

"Hold it!" I said. Banerjee stopped playback. "This guy just shot up a street corner and killed a man in order to retrieve a laptop. Now he's *walking* away? That's pretty cold-blooded."

"Is that your medical opinion?" A tight smile opened across Banerjee's face. "Watch this."

He hit Play again. The man with the limp continued up Geary—and stopped. He pulled something out of his back pocket and looked at it. Then he put the object up to his ear, and started talking.

"Whoa!"

Banerjee paused the video again. "What's that look like to you, Jessie?"

"Did he just get a phone call, check who it was from, and then answer it?"

"Yes."

"Who the hell could that call be from, that he pauses in fleeing a *murder scene* to talk to them?"

"There's only a little more."

Banerjee ran the surveillance video again, and we watched the man walking and talking. Then he put the phone away, turned left off Geary onto Larkin Street, and disappeared from view.

"How long was that talk?" I asked.

"Thirty-two seconds," Banerjee said.

"Phone records?"

"We got a subpoena, but haven't come up with anything in Azarola's name. Did you see him flip it open? Inspector Jones figures it's a burner."

"Can you get them to pull the cell tower activity?"

"Not without a phone number to start with. But it's not even worth it. We have witnesses, and we have this guy on video shooting Chen."

"You have the gun?"

"No. Probably down a sewer somewhere. Or in the bay."

"The computer?"

"Never recovered."

"Shouldn't that worry you?"

"We don't need it for a conviction."

I pointed to the screen. "What's so important on that laptop that Azarola would shoot up a whole block and murder Lumpy Chen over it?"

"Computers are valuable. Somebody steals one from you, you're going to want it back. We don't need any more motive than the robbery."

He closed the computer window and started gathering up his paperwork. "Besides, Jackson Heffernan's already giving hints that they're willing to plead out. I get more leverage if they're worried I can stick a murder one. Your testimony—the multiple wounds and the pursuit ending in a shot to the back of Chen's head—will help."

"Just a sec," I insisted, pressing my fingers on Azarola's mug shot and rap sheet. "Look at Azarola's priors. A bunch of trafficking offenses. Nothing violent. Why did he go psycho this time?"

The prosecutor's eyes lit up.

"You're right that he's only done short time, but that's because he got off or pled out. And you'll notice all those convictions are out of Tulare County. They run an adequate DA's office in Visalia, for a town of their size. But Mr. Josu Azarola is in San Francisco now, and I'm confident we'll be able to arrange some hard time for him."

Assistant District Attorney Anup Banerjee stood, took the rap sheet off his desk, and pushed the body diagram across to me.

"You'll let me know as soon as you finish your report?"

Again his expression didn't betray whether this was a courteous request or a challenge to my work ethic.

"I'll have it for you tomorrow morning."

I managed to type up the day's three cases in just over an hour, then ran down to the Ops Shop break room for a cup of their crappy but strong coffee before returning to Eugene Chen's case.

I started by proofreading the report, checking the trajectory each bullet took when it went through Chen's body. Entrance wound, pathway, organs and structures affected, and exit or point of lodgment. Every entrance wound has to lead either to a documented exit or to a description of the recovered bullet. The description I'd written of the penetrating wound to the right forearm tripped me up.

Path: The bullet penetrates the skin and soft tissue and lodges in the brachioradialis muscle without damage to large-caliber vasculature. The bullet is unjacketed, moderately deformed, and of medium caliber, and is embedded in the muscle along with pieces of uneven plastic or metal.

Pieces of uneven plastic or metal? How many pieces? No measurement of their size, no description of color or shape, no hint of what these foreign objects were, or how they had come to be found alongside a bullet inside the forearm of a dead man. Jackson Heffernan would shred me on the stand if my findings stayed that vague. I was going to have to track those things down and take a closer look.

I pressed the bare wires of the lab's broken doorbell together. A round man answered it with a scowl.

"What do you want?"

His outfit was like nothing I'd ever seen in a morgue: a tailored purple suit, gold lapel pin and onyx cuff links, and a yellow necktie done up with a knot of baroque complexity that must have taken half an hour.

Carlo San Pietro, our chief toxicologist.

"Well...?"

"I need to reexamine some evidence from one of my homicides. I deposited it in here about a month ago."

"I am locking up now."

"It's a rush. Going to prelim, and I need to finalize my report."

San Pietro's brow knit over lustrous tortoiseshell glasses that looked like they might have come from an actual tortoise. He sighed and pivoted, and held the lab door open for me.

"Case number?"

I told him, and he led us to a windowless room stacked floor-to-ceiling with cardboard banker's boxes. It looked like a broom closet. I was appalled.

"*This* is our evidence storage?"

Carlo San Pietro was on a stepladder, scanning handwritten labels. "No. This is evidence processing. Storage is downstairs. If you are lucky it is here, still."

He produced a box. Inside was a jumble of packaged evidence I'd recovered from Eugene Chen's clothing and body during the autopsy—heat-sealed pouches full of jewelry, bloodstained mail, the stolen wallet. Finally, he came up with the one I was looking for: a small manila envelope labeled *bullet from right arm*. San Pietro hopped to a computer terminal.

"Chain of custody," he said, and typed in a staccato flurry. "Seal, sign, and drop back in the slot when you finish."

He did not add, *Don't let the door hit you on the way out*. Not in words, at least.

I returned to my office, gloved up, and cut through the evidence tape sealing the envelope. The bullet still had visible rifling marks, but one side was deeply scored and its nose was flattened. It had hit something harder than flesh before it came to its point of lodgment—either bone or some other object in its path.

I gave the envelope a good shake and two pieces of uneven debris tinkled out. I measured the first as a quarter inch in diameter and the other as three-eights inch. They weren't bullet fragments. One had cornrows of tiny green and gold wires. The bigger piece was black plastic, and there seemed to be some writing on it. I pulled out my magnifying glass, shifted the light, and two clusters of tiny numbers and letters etched in white on the black plastic appeared. I transcribed the numbers and scribbled a note for myself. *Electronic circuits and plastic debris bearing serial numbers.*

This hadn't come from a medallion on a necklace, and it sure as shit wasn't credit card shrapnel from a pilfered piece of mail. The bullet I had pulled out of Lumpy Chen's forearm had first passed through his torso from back to front, and then through the stolen laptop computer he was clutching to his chest.

Computers are valuable, Anup Banerjee had said. How valuable was a computer with a bullet hole through it? Why would somebody kill to get it back?

I knew someone who could tell me.

CHAPTER EIGHT

Tommy sat across from me in the dim light of Jolie Brune Cajun Bistro and sucked on a crawfish with noisy relish.

"How is it?" I asked.

"Good."

Nothing more. But I was used to exchanges like this with my little brother.

"You speak to *Mamusia* lately?"

Tommy shook his head.

"I did. She asked about you."

He shrugged.

"You know what that means."

He laid on the Boston accent, thick: "Cawl ya muhtha."

"Cawl ya muhtha. Once in a while, *braciszku*. Don't leave it all to me. Right?"

Tomasz shrugged again, and savaged another Cajun critter.

"Wipe your hands," I ordered him. "Tell me what you think of this."

I had sealed the evidence envelope and its contents in a ziplock. The two little pieces of electronic circuit were lodged in the baggie's corner. Tommy held it up to the window.

"Piece of casing off a laptop, with the product ID and partial serial number. Where'd it come from?"

Before I could answer, he shook the paper envelope through the ziplock, and the bullet slug tumbled into view.

"*Oj, oj, boże mój,*" Tomasz rhymed, singsong, shaking his head just like our *mamusia* would when presented a grim piece of East Lynn gossip.

I told him the story of Lumpy Chen's shooting.

"So what," Tommy said. "He jacked the wrong guy."

"Azarola chased Lumpy down the street, blasting away the whole time. If he wanted the computer back so bad, why would he risk shooting at the thief?"

"He got the computer back."

"Yeah, but with a bullet through it! Dead thief and a dead computer…"

Amused condescension spread across my little brother's face.

"Well, Czesia. There's dead…and there's *dead*."

"Explain. And use ordinary words, or no dessert."

"A computer is a data engine. The data is stored in physical form as…as tiny magnetic switches. Those switches don't vanish just because you can't start the engine anymore. The information is still there. You can clone it onto another device. It's easy."

He asked if he could finish my shrimp and grits. I slid the plate across the table. "So Azarola didn't kill Lumpy to retrieve the computer, he killed him to retrieve the data?"

Tommy shrugged. "Maybe."

He held the ziplock in front of him and contemplated the mashed bullet while he chewed.

"Where'd this happen?"

I jerked my thumb. "Three blocks."

"You get the beignets," Tommy said, and handed the evidence bag back to me. "I'll take the bread pudding."

We hadn't gone five steps north on Polk Street before we ran into an ambulance crew outside a KFC franchise, loading someone on a stretcher. A man at a bus shelter stuck a needle in his arm. I smelled shit in a doorway. After a couple more blocks we reached the Café Oui-Fi. The big picture windows mirrored the pink and violet of the sunset's last moments—and I recalled them in flashing blue light, punched full of bullet holes.

Tommy went to the counter to order a coffee and get the Wi-Fi password. We took the table where Joe Azarola had sat, and Tommy pulled out his own computer.

"Wow. Eighty megabits."

"That's fast?"

"For a coffeehouse, for free? Wicked fast. How long was your bad guy here before the robbery?"

"Two hours."

"Wonder where he was surfing."

"That's what I said! But the detectives don't much care. They have him on video—and identified by an eyewitness—shooting Lumpy."

"But you're interested because…?"

"Because they *aren't*. It bugs me. Doesn't it bug you? Something on that laptop was worth killing for."

"You've got the whole product code and all but one or two digits of the serial number. With that, you can probably go to the manufacturer and find the MAC address."

"The what?"

"Media access control. Unique to the computer. The wireless modem uses it to interface with the router."

"So?"

"So if you know the MAC address, you could use it to isolate the IP address that the router assigned back to your target device's packet-switching network…"

"Tommy. English."

He rolled his eyes. He was typing away like mad on his own laptop.

"If you can get into the router's logs and cross-check IP addresses by MAC addresses, you could…well, you could isolate the data stream going to and from your bad guy's computer. Then you could scroll through the logs and reconstruct his browsing history while he was here." Strings of gibberish popped up from the bottom of his screen. Tommy seemed thrilled by them. "The ISP for this place is Sentorex. Terrible security. Give me half an hour and…"

"Thanks but no thanks," I said. "I'll find a way that won't lose me my job."

My little brother stopped typing and put on his puppy-dog eyes. I shook my head firmly. He gazed longingly at the strings of gibberish, but then hit a button and they disappeared. He called me a spoilsport. I asked him if the police could get the same information using subpoenas of records. Tommy conceded that they probably could, but that his way would be way quicker.

"And more fun," he added. I shook my head again.

We finished our coffees and headed outside, but then Tommy made a face and turned back into the Café Oui-Fi.

"Gotta see a man about a horse," he said.

"Don't forget to wash your hands."

The door closed and I was alone. It was a clear night. Panhandlers mixed with well-groomed young people in white earbuds hustling along Geary. Up Polk Street a shouting scuffle broke out. I looked toward Kim Son 88, the murder scene. It was midway down a long block, across a wide boulevard. No wonder witnesses reported so many shots fired—Azarola chased Lumpy Chen a good eighty or a hundred yards.

My phone chirped. It was a text. From: Arnie Spitz.

Can I see you again?

Well. Arnie Spitz was back from his trip. I found I was smiling. I started to formulate a witty riposte, but then made the tactical decision to let Arnie wait till morning for an answer.

Standing there on the curb with my phone in hand, I pictured fuzzy-video Joe Azarola stepping out of the café to the same spot, and placing a call on his own cell phone. He had been looking up—into the trees. I did, too.

Except that there were no trees up there. Following the direction of Azarola's gaze I saw only one thing.

Tommy came out the door behind me.

"Hey," he said. "What are you staring at?"

"The Hotel Somerville," I said.

"Whose case is that?" Homicide Inspector Keith Jones asked his partner, after I told them about Graciela Natividad, the drug mule who was gutted across the street from the Café Oui-Fi.

Inspector Daniel Ramirez shrugged. Jones turned to me. "Who did the autopsy?"

"Mike Stone."

The four of us were crammed into Anup Banerjee's office,

reviewing the Café Oui-Fi video again—this time at my instigation.

Jones said, "And you believe these cases are related—because Azarola might be looking up toward the hotel while he's on the phone...?"

"Not just that." I turned to Banerjee. "Freeze it right after Azarola appears."

He did, and I pointed out the second figure on the top of the screen, just a step behind Azarola: the young man with his hands full of white plastic bags.

"There's a KFC three blocks down Polk, and a bunch of KFC bags in the photos from the Hotel Somerville scene. Greasy fast food to try to help the girl pass the drug bindles, right? How much you want to bet those are the same bags."

"Okay. So what?"

"So what...? So then this guy with the takeout is one of the drug smugglers who's brought Graciela up to that hotel room so they can collect the bindles once she passes them! You said Azarola has drug priors in Fresno—"

"Visalia."

"Whatever. Maybe those bags are from KFC, and maybe the guy carrying them was with Azarola just before they got in range of the camera. If we can use that to connect Azarola to this guy, and this guy to the Hotel Somerville drug-smuggling case—"

"We don't need to connect Azarola to anything. We've got him on video shooting Eugene Chen."

"But *why?*"

Dead-eyed nonresponse from the cops, and impatient silence from the ADA. They were tired of telling me that theirs was not to question why, theirs was just to get the guy.

I pulled out the ziplock bag.

"Pieces of the laptop. I removed these from Eugene Chen's

forearm along with a deformed bullet. Azarola's computer had a big honking hole shot through it, and it's pinned underneath a man he just killed. Why take it?"

Ramirez barked a laugh. "It's got his fingerprints all over it, Doc. Literally. Or, if he left it behind we could've ID'd him through the data on it."

"Aha—I'm glad you mentioned that." I passed around the baggie and told them about the serial number.

"Again, so what?" Jones said. "We already know the laptop is his."

"You haven't recovered it, so you can't look at the data stored on it. And you say you can't get internet records from the café for that time interval. Too many users, too much data to sift through, right?"

I took the baggie back and held it up again. "With the information etched onto this piece of Azarola's computer, you can get its media access control address. From there you can track down the internet protocol address his computer was using while he was sitting in the Café Oui-Fi."

I turned to Anup Banerjee. "Then *you* can subpoena the records from the internet service provider. Zero in, find Azarola's traffic in the wireless router log, and look at what websites he visited."

"We can do that?" Jones said.

Daniel Ramirez nailed me with his cop eyes. "How'd *you* figure this out?"

"I know a guy."

Banerjee looked to Ramirez.

"What do you think?"

"Couldn't hurt—if the doc is right and it's that easy. We might come up with something to squeeze him with."

"And the mule," Jones added. "We can use that, too—depraved indifference."

"Felony murder rule," Banerjee said. "She died while they were trafficking."

"You're going to need two subpoenas," I said, trying like hell to mask my excitement. "One for the manufacturer, to get a list of network addresses that might match this serial number fragment. Then we need to compare those to the addresses of computers accessing the servers from that location at that date and time—"

"That's the second subpoena."

"Right."

Assistant District Attorney Anup Banerjee picked up the baggie with the computer shrapnel again.

"That's a good idea."

"Yeah," Inspector Ramirez agreed.

"You're welcome," I said, and held out my hand for the evidence.

Mike Stone wasn't in his office. Ted Nguyen told me he was in the autopsy suite, cutting. That was a surprise—we never cut in the afternoon.

"Tissue from one of Brian Sutcliffe's old cases," Nguyen said. "For the RICO trial."

"I thought Mike did that last week."

"That was a shooting. This one's a floater."

"Damn. Why don't they call Dr. Sutcliffe to testify?"

"From Maine? Interstate subpoenas are a pain in the neck. So Howe did the feds a favor and turfed it to Mike, since he's already doing that shooting for the same RICO case."

Dr. Stone was alone in the autopsy suite. He looked bent and bone-tired. In front of him on a cutting board was somebody's neck block—the trachea, thyroid, and esophagus from tongue to aorta. It had come out of a formaldehyde stock jar and was gray and green, ragged and wet.

"What?" Stone said without looking up.

"Strangulation?"

"Who the hell knows? A floater with neck trauma. Could be a ligature strangulation, or could be a corpse that got tangled in crab lines."

"Ugh," I said, and meant it. That's a shitty case. Postmortem injury caused by ropes wrapped around the neck of a man who died in an accidental drowning can look a lot like a hanging suicide or a garrote wound around the neck of a murder victim, if the body's been bobbing in the bay long enough.

"I remember that one," I said. "It's from the pile I found in my office."

"Yeah."

"Did Dr. Sutcliffe take histology samples?"

"No."

"At least he kept the neck block." I leaned in to take a closer look. "Is there a hyoid fracture...?"

Stone slapped his scalpel down and glared.

"I'm testifying on this tomorrow. You came in here for a reason?"

"Sorry—yes."

As I told him about the meeting with Anup Banerjee and the detectives, I watched a rosy flush rise from Mike Stone's collar, past his graying stubble and rheumy eyes, straight to his forehead.

"You went to the cops and a DA, and told them my body-packing case looks fishy...? You turned my accident into a homicide?"

"No! We were just talking about my case—"

"What the fuck does that have to do with Graciela Natividad? With my slam-dunk accidental drug overdose."

He cursed again and slammed a palm on the counter. His scalpel jumped and clattered.

"I… I tried to talk to you about it first."

"First! Before *undermining* me, you mean? Now those two assholes from Homicide are going to come in here and stir up all kinds of shit!"

He moved closer to me, still glaring.

"What do you think you're doing? If you're trying to show off, impress the DA, it's going to backfire."

That took me fully by surprise. I had no answer.

"Yeah," Stone scoffed. "Okay. Best of luck with your case. Stay away from mine."

I found my tongue.

"I am not trying to impress anybody."

He spat out a venomous laugh and turned his back.

"Mission accomplished."

Mission accomplished.

Stone was right. Why was I meddling in his case? Why was I even seeking to expand my own? I had a cause and manner of death for Eugene Chen, the police had a suspect in custody, and the district attorney had my autopsy report, ready for the preliminary hearing. Who cares about the damn suspect's browser history, or his phone calls, or his interest in a no-tell hotel in the Tenderloin? If I hadn't been so eager to show off to the detectives and the DA, my career wouldn't be in jeopardy once again.

And, once again, I was aching to call Barry Taylor. He was the only one I used to vent to, and I did the same for him. Though Barry only ever bitched about work—never the traffic, or politics, or the Dodgers. Or his wife, Cat. He hardly ever mentioned Cat.

I tried not to think about it. Barry and I knew what we had got ourselves into. I should have seen there was no clean way out. He was lying to Cat. I should have seen he was lying to me, too. He just needed a little more time, he said, and he'd work out a way to leave her for good. Barry was witty and smart and confident—dazzlingly confident, even for a cop. But he was no con man. He was lying to me because I let him.

I pulled out my phone. I opened the voice-mail app.

"Hey, it's Barry. I got the Catalina ferry tickets, and booked the tram tour to look at the bison. Bison...!"

I listened through to the end. Barry told me he loved me, called me "Doctor." He used to do that a lot. He used to profess how much he looked up to me, how much more I'd accomplished in my career than anyone else he knew, how many families I'd helped when they needed the answers that only I could give them.

"I know what that means to them, Doctor," he told me once. "I've rung those doorbells to tell a mother her kid was dead. It does her no good. I only opened a wound. It's you people who close it."

I played the voice-mail message again. One more time. When it ended, I put the phone flat on my desk. For a while I stared at the red-lettered word *Delete*.

Then I pressed my finger against it.

Delete this message? a dialogue box asked. *This action cannot be undone.*

"Psiakrew..." I said quietly.

"What is it?" Ted Nguyen asked from over the divider. He savored whatever agitation followed my Polish curses.

"Nothing," I said. "Just my stupid phone."

I touched the word *No* on the screen.

Message saved, the phone assured me.

"Enabler," I muttered at it.

I sat back in my office chair and stared at the paperwork piled all over the desk, trying to decide whether I should choose to feel panicky about pissing off my boss, or depressed over past harms I couldn't relitigate. I picked up the phone to stow it in my purse. When I did, a stray finger opened the text app. The top message caught my eye. It was from Arnie Spitz.

Can I see you again?

I hadn't yet replied. Our magical drive up the coast was... what? A month ago? Yes. The memory cheered me. Now Arnie Spitz is back from his business trip and, as promised, has reached out. The ball's in my court, and there Arnie stands, ready—waiting for me to bang it back.

So bang I did.

How bout 2nite. Someplc nice 4 a drink. Shitty day

I pulled out all the stops. There was a single red-carpet dress in my closet, left over from a Hollywood party thrown by a producer friend of a friend. I'd only ever worn it that one time. It was sleek and sleeveless, black as chipped coal with a hint of beading at the neckline, and expensive—like the BMW 235i, a gift to myself when Dr. Kashiman had offered me my first paying job at the Los Angeles County Department of Medical Examiner-Coroner. And, like my Beemer, the dress was a rare luxury. It had added to the mountain of debt I'd piled up through college and medical school... But—*o stary*—at the moment I'd laid eyes on it I didn't much care. It was one bloodthirsty killer dress.

I had to rifle through my drawers to find the special bra contraption that the Beverly Hills saleswoman had compelled me to buy, to save me from busting out of the scoop-necked bodice. I only owned one pair of high heels, and thankfully they matched the dress well enough. Slouching over an autopsy table has given me terrible posture, but the carefully engineered cleavage and the balancing act of heels forced me to stretch out my spine. I made a couple of circuits around the cable car's puny parlor to make sure I wouldn't totter, and was pleased to find that I was pretty darn tall and that the starlet dress played up all my curves.

It took me a lot of labor and leave-in conditioner to brush the stubborn ponytail crimp out of my hair. I usually kept it cut shorter—you don't want long hair in the morgue—but was glad now I'd been letting it grow. The contrast of honey-blond hair on the black dress made my gray-green eyes stand out like jewels—especially after I added a string of jade beads and earrings to match. Next I went rummaging for makeup. I winged my lashes with a deep kohl liner and chose matted-red lipstick for a full glam statement:

The Doctor Is In.

Arnie had texted me an address. I was alone there, shivering in the fog on a dismal street corner, outside a windowless building with a door that read *Hatchetation League*.

"Jessie!"

Arnie Spitz emerged from the back of a black car and trotted over, all apologies for tardiness. He looked me up and down, surprised and delighted by my choice of dress. He looked damn good to me, too, in a crisp pair of charcoal Levi's, a worn cotton shirt unbuttoned at the neck, and a trim taupe blazer.

"What the hell is this place?" I demanded.

That naughty glint came to his eye, and he took my hand. "Come."

The door had a knocker. Arnie used it to tap out an awkward signal, *rat-a-tat-tat, tat tat*. A peephole slat opened.

"And...?" said a man's voice.

Arnie was suddenly flustered, and asked the eyes in the door to wait a moment while he poked at his phone. Then he said, "Um... Shanghai Skipper."

The peephole slid shut and the door swung open.

"Oh, you're kidding!" I said as Arnie ushered me inside. "A *speakeasy?* With...what? An app for the password?"

He just grinned. That's exactly what it was. The door opened to reveal a zinc bar with copper trim, the bartender in a cornflower-blue seersucker shirt with suspenders and a handlebar mustache, his pomaded hair parted in the center. He served me the first of several strong, pretentious cocktails. Things with essence of tobacco. Hemp oil. Quince.

Arnie asked for my hand, and I gave it. He led me to an armchair, planted himself in it, and asked me if I would please sit on his lap.

"They have a strict no cell phones rule, you see—but I need to look for the second password. For the Sapphire Room."

"So you just need me for cover?"

"My intentions are pure."

My skin was starting to prickle. I put my drink down on the table, maneuvered a turn that allowed Arnie to admire every angle of my clingy dress, and then slid across his legs. I put an arm around his shoulder and undid a button on his shirt.

"Pure."

I kissed him. He shifted underneath me, and I could feel

very well why. I had a hand on his chest, he had one on my knee, and then under the hem of the dress. With the other he pulled out his cell phone.

"Splendid, Jessie. No one will suspect a thing."

He found the password with urgent speed, and we returned to our embrace, devouring each other. I slipped off a shoe and ran my bare toes along the back of Arnie's ankle. His socks were silk. I enjoyed the sensation. He did, too. I broke it off before too long, grabbing him by the head with my hands and pulling away, both of us panting.

The Sapphire Room could only be entered from behind the bar in the speakeasy. Arnie leaned close and said something to the bartender, who opened a hatch to a sunken staircase. I started giggling. Arnie shushed me, as if G-men with tommy guns were going to come busting through the place if I didn't maintain the illusion. The stairs led into a basement antechamber lined with knob-and-tube electrical wiring. On the far wall was a door. From behind it I heard voices.

"Permit me," Arnie said, and pushed it open.

The walls of the Sapphire Room glowed with a high-gloss sheen. I caught myself reflected back in the wainscoting—wavy and blue, like a funhouse mirror. We settled into a quiet corner. A hostess asked if she could refresh our pretentious drinks. Arnie ordered a bottle of Champagne instead. We drank it and talked mostly about work—mostly about mine.

"My world is sixty-eight degrees and fluorescent, one meeting after another," Arnie insisted when I pressed him. "You would not believe the tedium."

The man could not get enough shop talk from the morgue, though, so I unburdened my gripes about Nguyen's practiced crabbiness, Howe's arrogance, Stone's temper. It felt good to bitch and moan about the office.

"The place is falling apart. The pipes are exposed, my

morgue sink dribbles, the doorbell's busted. If Howe gave a shit about the facility—or us—he could find the funds to fix all that nickel-and-dime stuff."

I sipped the Champagne.

"Oh, enough, already!" I declared. "Think the rain'll ruin the rhubarb?"

"Pardon?"

"My dad used to say that when he wanted to change the subject."

"Well," said Arnie, "would you like to hear about my boat?"

I drained my glass. "You have a boat?"

"I do."

"Anyone ever die aboard it?"

"Not to my knowledge."

"Then," I said, shaking the empty flute at him, "yes. I'd love to hear about your boat."

Arnie smiled and refilled my bubbly and his own, and regaled me with tales of his sailboat. It was a sixty-foot sloop, "wing keeled and Bermuda rigged," worthy of a Magellanic voyage. He had sailed it to Hawaii, to Baja, to Vancouver.

"Vancouver was bloody hard going. Tacking against the wind the whole way."

"But you have Bermuda wings! And the sloopy keel dingus..."

"And she has an inboard diesel if I get desperate."

"What is *she* called?"

"The *Ann Marie*."

"Who's that?"

"No idea. I'm not the first to sail her. Never change the name on a sea vessel. It's dire bad luck."

"There's no such thing as luck."

"That may be."

He begged for another story from the morgue but I refused. "I'm sick of talking about what I do. Tell me about what you do."

"Will it get me on your good side?"

I sat up and planted my elbows on the small table between us. His eyes flicked to my cleavage. I vamped my voice down.

"That may be."

Arnie pulled his gaze away, found one of the waitresses, and said, cryptically, "Machine oil and the orange saucer, please, Marlene."

Then he leaned over the table himself. I enjoyed the scent of cologne off his close-shaved cheek. Arnie was growing tiny wrinkles on the skin by his ears. Just a hint of jowl softened the angle of his jaw.

"You know how GoFundMe and Kickstarter work."

"Yes."

"How about Facebook and LinkedIn."

"I don't live under a rock."

"Imagine taking the strengths of each, and discarding the weaknesses. Imagine a platform that combines crowdfunding with capital investment in a social media ecosystem. That's TechFolio."

"TechFolio."

"Do you like it?"

"No."

He was piqued. I wasn't going to lie, though.

"Well, *I* like it."

"That's what counts." I patted his hand. He started massaging my knuckles like he had during the long drive to Muir Woods.

"Our clients are high-capital global adventurers hampered by over-liquid investment challenges."

I raised my eyebrows silently at that line of pure BS, but he continued.

"You want to invest your capital in a fund that will bring you a good return—*and* will help create something worthy. But in every corner of the world, punitive taxes and other statist schemes prevent you from doing what you want—freely—with your own money. TechFolio is the digital asset platform that bridges that gap."

"Digital asset platform…?"

"Built on electronic currency. Bitcoin, for example."

"Sounds risky. Why do people invest with you?"

His eyes really lit up.

"Because we are at the very heart of the creative-capital nexus, surrounded by start-ups that need cash but aren't getting funded through traditional sources. The old brick-and-mortar VC firms have grown sclerotic. My company makes it possible for anyone—anyone, anywhere—to pay into a managed technology fund. Through the fund we incubate a range of start-ups and leverage the risk by spreading it out. Not in tranches but across the board."

"And, of course, you take a small fee for this service."

Arnie Spitz jerked back in surprise. Me and my big mouth again. But then he unfurled a cagey smile.

"You are a bold and direct person, Jessie. I do admire that trait."

"I didn't mean—"

"No offense taken—you're quite right. Great minds think alike."

The waitress arrived with a silver tray. "Your machine oil, Mr. Spitz. The orange saucer is on the house."

On the tray was a silver shaker and two martini glasses, and an orange plate with a brown lump of glazed goo garnished with sage leaves.

"What the hell is that?" I asked.

"Contraband," Arnie said wickedly. He scooped a bit of the

JUDY MELINEK & T.J. MITCHELL

goo in a tiny spoon like I've found among the personal effects of dead powder cocaine users, and held it out. I opened my mouth.

It was meat, or butter, or butter meat. It was salty and savory, lukewarm, and so rich I groaned. It was better than chocolate. It was a nearly sexual experience.

"*Foie gras d'oie.*"

"God, say that again."

He did. I took another spoonful.

"And now the pairing contraband."

Arnie tipped an amber fluid from the cocktail shaker into the glasses. I sipped. A Manhattan, with some kind of weird whiskey.

"Small-batch local rye," Arnie said. "They call it machine oil."

"Why?"

"It's illegal. So is the foie gras."

Arnie launched into an explanation—something about a tyrannical law banning goose liver, and about the rye being produced outside the cartel grip of the multinational distilleries—but I wasn't listening. I was watching his lips. They were beautiful lips, soft and peach, the upper one peaking on either side of a deep philtrum, the lower just loose enough to be lecherous. I couldn't stop imagining them on my neck, on my breasts. On the inside of my wrist. It had been too long since any man's lips had been.

I was enjoying our date more than I had enjoyed a night out since...well, maybe ever. Arnie's tastes and his personality and lifestyle were so different from mine, but we were having a blast together. I didn't want it to end. I wanted to find myself in a bed with Arnie Spitz, to wake up with him and not care whether or not I was late to the morning meeting or Howezit Goin' rounds. I was a little dizzy—and it wasn't from the rye.

"Arnie," I said. "I want to see your boat."

He stopped midsentence. His hand shot up and his head whipped toward the bar.

"Marlene, dear…! Check, please!"

We didn't even make it to the narrow bed in the *Ann Marie*'s cabin. We shredded the Beverly Hills bra. I heard metal shear when I tore at Arnie's trousers. His shoes stayed on, and my Hollywood dress bunched down and up simultaneously. We pressed against each other, across the cabin's tiny counter, over the sink, and, finally, onto a rug. We were grasping, frantic.

When we were done we laughed, panting, and rolled over. I ran my fingers through his hair. He ran his hands along both of mine, pinned me down, and kissed me again—but then stopped, and frowned at something.

"Naughty girl," he said.

"That's *Doctor* Naughty Girl to you."

"I mean it—you broke my boat!"

Sure enough, a slender brass handrail that I had gripped onto during our last spasm had popped right out of its fitting in the wall.

"Bulkhead," Arnie corrected while I was giggling about it. "Seagoing vessels do not have walls." He wrestled the handrail back in place, and repeated that I was a naughty doctor.

"Oh, Arnold," I said. "You ain't seen nothing yet."

My little black dress was still tangled around my belly. I stretched out with my arms on the floor—deck, whatever—and arched my back, performing bare-assed yoga.

Arnie stood. I crooked a finger to bring him closer, and started toying with him. He enjoyed it—and I was excited to find that I had chosen a lover who was going to give me exactly what I needed, after...what was it? Four months of abstinence—?

Jesus, yes it was. Almost four months since I'd last slept with a man.

Arnie, bless his heart and his yacht and his eager Aussie dick, did what I'd hoped he might do. He put Barry Taylor right out of my mind.

We made it to the *Ann Marie*'s bed that time, though not under the sheets until much later, when we were, both of us, fully and blissfully and repeatedly spent.

CHAPTER NINE

It was a little hard to tell the taxi where to meet me, since the *Ann Marie* was moored at the St. Francis Yacht Club and the only light in their parking lot came from the bruised glow of dawn under a high fog. The cabbie made not a single comment in judgment of my ravaged party dress, so I gave him a big, fat tip. I fed Bea and walked her around the block, took a quick bath and threw on an old pair of slacks, and was already outside with my car keys in hand before it dawned on me that I had left my Beemer parked across town at the Hatchetation League the night before. Then a text pinged my phone.

Good morning & wow. Sad to wake alone. Car find u?

Car...?

There was a black Prius waiting across the street. An earnest young man emerged from it.

"Dr. Teska?"

I stared at him, trying to fathom whether thought-of-everything Arnie was a sweetheart or a stalker. Since I was still feeling downright floppy from postcoital bliss, it wasn't hard to decide.

U true gentleman. Thx.

Call u later?

Yes

The driver got me to the morgue loading bay in the nick of time, but refused a tip. "My boss won't let me handle cash, ma'am," he insisted, when I tried to push five bucks on him. "TechFolio is a bitcoin-only account." I wanted to ask how the hell that worked, but I didn't have time—Stone's car and Nguyen's and Howe's were all in their parking spots, and I was late for morning meeting.

It had been a slow night on the streets of San Francisco. Stone—who somehow looked even more rumpled than me—took one case and Nguyen the other, leaving me with a much-needed paper day. I dived right into the Rebecca Corchero file.

While checking the photos I'd taken during autopsy against my written description of the external examination findings, I came across the "irregular band of contused abrasion and petal-shaped lacerations" on Rebecca's right wrist. They formed a matching pair, each with four indentations in the shape of a half-daisy, almost like two tiny handprints. Both wounds were surrounded by a small amount of dried blood, which meant they were fresh at the time of her death. Another picture showed a bruise on the inside of the same wrist. It wasn't a ligature binding, and handcuffs would have left a deeper, sharper margin. It didn't look like anything she'd get by a bang on a doorjamb, or by breaking a fall with her forearm, either.

I opened the scene photos on the computer. Rebecca's right arm hung limp at the side of the chair where she was slumped, dead; so she hadn't sustained that injury by passing out with her body weight pressing against her arm. In two pictures I could make out a fuzzy silver crescent at her wrist, obscured in shadow. The top sheet of the investigators' report had listed a bracelet in the personal property they'd removed from Rebecca's body—

The phone interrupted. I was surprised to hear Sophia Kalogeras on the other end. She wanted to talk about Rebecca.

Dr. Stone's wife told me her family was still getting over their shock. "Calliope is absolutely devastated. The poor girl's hardly slept. *I've* hardly slept. What happened to Rebecca? What *happened* to her?"

"Ms. Kalo... Mrs. Stone—"

"Sophia, dear."

"Sophia." I gathered my wits, and came up with a suitable nonanswer. "The case is pending while we investigate."

"She was alone, is that right?"

I said nothing.

"Rebecca is the sweetest, most generous girl you'll ever meet. And so young... I just don't understand this."

"I hope you believe me when I say I'm devoting myself fully to this investigation, Sophia. I can only imagine how hard it is for all of you, especially your daughter."

"Rebecca was like a big sister to Calliope. Calliope worships her. We took her with us on vacation every year—Thailand, Mexico, skiing in Banff... What am I going to tell my daughter? Calliope has to know that her loved ones aren't just going to drop dead. Doesn't she deserve to hear that?"

I slid a notepad under my free hand and readied a pen.

"It would help if you can tell me about Rebecca's health

history. Was she taking any medications? Seeing a doctor for any condition?"

"She was perfectly healthy. No medications that I know of."

"Did she use alcohol or drugs?"

"No! Did she die of—? What did she die of?"

"Do you know if she had a history of drug abuse?"

"Absolutely not. I did a background check when we hired her. She was spotless."

"I'd like to talk to a coworker of Rebecca's named Neil Dupree, but I'm having trouble reaching him. Does that name ring a bell? From Siloam Biologic?"

"Do you think…?"

"You helped Rebecca get the job at Siloam, right?"

"Yes—yes, when she left our employ. I was happy to recommend her to a friend, an old tech colleague. It was a great opportunity. Rebecca had very clear career goals. Michael and I were helping guide her—"

Sophia caught a wet breath. "Oh, God… Rebecca…"

I gave her a moment to compose herself, then continued, gently. "Sophia, can you put me in touch with Neil Dupree?"

Her tone turned cold as ice and twice as hard. "No. I don't know him."

Before I could respond, she wished me good day and hung up. Sophia Kalogeras had thrown me off balance again.

———

The day-shift 2578 investigator had gray hair and gray skin, and a nicotine baritone. "Is it a homicide?" he croaked.

"No—I mean, I don't know yet. It's personal effects from a probable OD pending tox, but there's some evidence of injury, too."

"Okay."

He ran a finger down a ledger sheet, pulled a ring of keys from a drawer, and came back with a sealed manila envelope. Inside it I found a gold cross on a chain and a silver bracelet. The bracelet startled me: It was a heavy bangle shaped into a gecko, life-size and lively in its expression, with polished green eyes in black sockets, the dark line of its mouth etched in a predaceous smile.

"That's some piece," the day-shift investigator said.

I agreed it was. Especially when I looked at its feet. They were identical, the toes flat and splayed and paddle-shaped, like a baby's outstretched hand.

Like the petals of a tiny silver daisy.

"Oh yeah, this case," the 2578 said. "We got a voice mail from the family—overseas, right? They want to hold an open-casket funeral. Is the body presentable for viewing?"

"Yes."

"Okay. They want us to mail them the crucifix so they get it in time for the service. I was gonna send the bracelet, too."

"Not yet. I'll call them myself to explain. And I need to sign this out, please."

I could make out something dark on the gecko's feet, something that didn't belong. It looked like rust. It wasn't.

I put the lizard bracelet under the desk lamp in my office. It wrapped around in a loop, so that the creature was biting its own tail when the wearer closed the clasp. An itty-bitty forked tongue hung out of its mouth as the release. It was ingenious, precise, and clearly crafted by an artist's hand. This was no bauble—it was the sort of piece that has meaning. The underside of the body was flat, designed to sit flush against the wearer's wrist with the feet spreading out to the sides. The words *Ajijic-Jal Mexico* were inscribed on the smooth metal of the belly, along with a silversmith's hallmark.

I pulled out my magnifying glass to examine the gecko's feet. There was dried blood on them. I clicked through the autopsy photos on the computer until I found close-up images of the daisy-petal indentations on Rebecca's right wrist, and the slender rivulet of blood that had run away from them, down onto her fingers. She would have used her right hand to shoot up in her left arm. So that meant the injury that drew blood on her right wrist had happened before that arm went limp at her side and the blood started running down. How had she received those two little wounds that were deep enough to draw blood?

I cut the fingers off an exam glove and slid it over my own wrist. Then I snapped the gecko bangle onto my arm and played around with it. If I mashed down on the top of the bracelet, all four feet buckled the latex evenly. The only way I could envision drawing blood with two of them was by wrenching the top of the bracelet forward at an angle—sideways, if you're the lizard—toward my wrist.

I tried it. The two left feet with the bloodstains dug in. They pinched the latex enough that I stopped for fear of breaking through. The bracelet's rigid underside made an opposing mark, a crescent on the glove over my inner wrist. I scanned through the thumbnail images and found a picture of the same spot on Rebecca's right arm. There was a faint pink line there.

I was going to have to go back into the morgue and pull out Rebecca Corchero's body again, this time with the gecko bangle, to compare against the injury pattern on her arm. If it matched, that injury wasn't accidental. It was a pressure indentation, made with considerable and sustained force. For those two gecko feet to cut bloody marks into Rebecca's skin on the dorsal surface of her arm and leave an imprint of the tail on the other side, something had to be squeezing her wrist, applying force in two directions at once. There were two planes of injury, outside and inside, on Rebecca's right arm. A single plane of injury might be a sign of an accident. Two planes of injury is a red flag for assault.

I clicked on the photo of Rebecca's death pose. The syringe, the tourniquet, the injection bruise. I still had to wait for the toxicology report, but this case certainly looked like a drug overdose. We classify drug overdoses as poisonings, because that's what they are. But not all poisonings are accidental.

Some are intentional. Intentional poisonings are homicides.

"Right now?" Yarina Marchenko was assisting Dr. Nguyen. It looked like it had been a messy job; bone dust and streaks of blood and flecks of flesh covered their PPEs from glove to cap.

"It's from three days ago. I need to reexamine the body for trauma and take new photos."

"I cannot help you."

The grocer's scale over their table rattled. "Right kidney one hundred seventy grams," Ted Nguyen said to a medical student, who jotted it down. Mike Stone glanced up. He was working alone at his table, collecting a black lung from a waifish woman with blue hair.

I asked Yarina if she could at least direct me to the body.

"Decomp?"

"No. Fresh."

She pointed a gory finger toward the far end of the morgue. "In cooler."

I hate the cold room. I pulled its meat locker handle, and the reek of a dozen corpses in various stages of bacterial putrefaction poured out. The dead feet peeked from under fresh white sheets. I flipped through toe tags, looked for Rebecca Corchero.

She wasn't there.

"She's not there," I hollered.

Yarina was using a zip tie to secure the biohazard bag of sliced organs. She cursed in Ukrainian, then said, "Moment, please, Dr. Nguyen." Ted just grunted. Yarina asked me the case number and padded across the room to the whiteboard. She scrutinized it.

"Not here," she announced. "Picked up already."

"Picked up...? Where'd it go?"

Yarina ignored the question and headed back to the autopsy table. She was all out of helpful.

"Look it up on your computer," Nguyen said. "The disposition field." He managed to sound simultaneously disdainful and amused. Stone kept working on the blue-haired chick and didn't say a word. I left for my office, barely swallowing a Slavic curse of my own.

Damn it, you should've put a hold on that body, I told myself as I stripped off the gloves and logged back into the computer. Under DISPOSITION OF BODY for case 955 it said McIntyre-Flynn/Cypress Grove. A mortuary way out on the Westside. I was going to have to drive over there to examine Rebecca's arm. I Googled their number—and just as my fingertips reached the phone, it rang.

Lo and behold, it was Siloam Biologic.

Neil Dupree apologized profusely that he hadn't returned my earlier calls. He claimed he had been stuck in work hell all week, sleeping under his desk for an hour at a time because the burndown on the latest sprint was still six hundred hours above plan, whatever the hell that meant. I informed him I was investigating the death of Rebecca Corchero. He was stunned.

"Dead…? How?"

"That's what I'm investigating. Were you in a relationship with her?"

"Yes. I mean, no… Not anymore. We dated for a while. Four months, last year."

I waited. I knew he would tell me how it ended. The boyfriends always do.

"She broke it off when she got fired. I think she wanted to wash her hands of Siloam, and I was part of that."

"Fired?"

"It was bullshit," Neil Dupree said hotly. "The angel investor's fault. Anson fired her, but the angel was behind it."

"Who's Anson?"

"Mark Anson, the CFO."

"Chief financial officer."

"Right."

"He was Rebecca's supervisor?"

"No. She was on the science team."

"Then what was the CFO's reason for firing her?"

Neil Dupree shifted his phone around and didn't answer right away.

"I don't know exactly. I think he accused her of skimming cash."

"Embezzling? But she was a lab worker, right? Not in accounting or—"

He scoffed. "You don't need to embezzle when there are grocery bags of cash lying around."

"Grocery bags?"

"Yeah, from Safeway. Filled with stacks of bills."

This time I said nothing—because I didn't believe my ears.

"Doctor…?"

"I'm here. Let me understand what you're telling me, Neil. This…outside investor…?"

"Venture capital, yeah—"

"...accused Rebecca of stealing from...grocery bags of cash."

"Becca never said so exactly, but I'm pretty sure that's what happened."

"You've seen these bags?"

"Sure. In an E & O-LT meeting."

"A what?"

"Engineering and Operations Leadership Team."

"Computers."

"Well, yeah. Anson wanted me and the CTO to talk to this guy, the angel, about turning some operating capital into bitcoin. The angel brought the bags in with him and put them in the middle of the conference table."

"Didn't that strike you as unusual?"

"Oh, no." He sounded genuinely blasé. "It's common in start-ups."

"Bags of cash."

"Sure. The only unusual thing is the bitcoin conversion. Turning one of those bags into bitcoin, I mean—using our servers. I told them it would waste a ton of IT resources that could be better used in other ways."

"What was this investor's name?"

"I don't remember. He wasn't part of our team. His company was called... TechnoFixer? TechPossible? Something like that."

I scribbled *TknoFixr/TkPossbl?* and gazed up at the towers of paperwork casting their fat shadows over my desk. I wanted to steer the conversation toward the decedent's recreational drug use, and here we were discussing the minutiae of biotech funding instead.

Time to shift to the direct approach.

"Are you a medical student, Neil?"

"No. Why?"

"And you've never been a med student?"

"BA in Engineering from Stanford."

"Did Rebecca use intravenous drugs?"

"What—! No way!"

So much for his blasé tone.

"She didn't even drink—had that gene that makes you turn red midway through a glass of wine. She was all into healthy living, went running every day. Was she… Doctor, how did Rebecca die?"

"I'm waiting for lab results. There were drugs at the scene."

"No way." He didn't pause, didn't hedge. "She was a nursing student! Rebecca had it all planned out, a career in medical informatics. RNs can earn good money in med tech. And no bedpans. That's what she would always say—an RN and no bedpans."

"When did you last see Rebecca?"

"A week after she got canned."

"Where was that?"

"At her place in the Sunset. I went over to talk to her."

"That was the last time you spoke?"

"Yes. She…she ended our relationship at that time."

I waited for him to continue.

"She said she'd be in touch. But she never was."

"So your breakup was amicable?"

"Yes."

"But not mutual."

"What's that got to do with anything?"

"Her roommate said she was dating someone," I said, flat and clinical. "I'm trying to find out who that is."

"I have no idea. I never spoke to Rebecca again after that day."

"Did you try?"

I have a novelty clock on my desk. The face is a pirate death's head, complete with eye patch. The crossbones tell hours and minutes, and a tiny slender cutlass serves as the second hand. I watched the cutlass slice away six full seconds before Neil Dupree answered.

"I told you. She didn't want to see me."

After we hung up I went into the activities section of the computer record to note the time and gist of our conversation. Mike Stone remembered right, that Rebecca Corchero's coworker boyfriend was named Neil, but that was old news. Neil Dupree was not Bato the magical medical student Rebecca was so crazy about.

I picked up the phone again and dialed the McIntyre-Flynn funeral home.

"Let me look," the receptionist said, and I heard the clack of computer keys. "Corchero? Scheduled for direct cremation."

Oh shit.

"Scheduled when?"

"I'll have to go ask. Hold, please."

When she returned, she told me that the cremation was already underway.

"Underway?"

"The body went into the retort at nine. So probably another hour and a half and it'll be done."

"But..."

"Hello?"

"I'm still here. Who...um, who signed this release from the medical examiner's office?"

Clack of keys again, and then the funeral director's receptionist said, "M. Stone, MD."

"For direct cremation?"

"Says so right here."

Great. Mike Stone had screwed up and checked the wrong

box on the release, and now I was going to have to break the bad news to the Corcheros. You can't have your beloved daughter's crucifix, and you can't have her body, either. We burned her for you. We'll mail the urn.

"Bułka z masłem," I muttered as I Googled the country code for the Philippines.

Camille Corchero told me her daughter had been proud of the good money she made in the States, and had been supporting her and a sister and several other family members. Rebecca always insisted she didn't need much, that it was easy to live frugally in a rich country.

"She said that people over there don't know how much they waste, they are born bathing in money. But she loved it there. We are a small town here. She loved the city, San Francisco."

I asked Camille what she could tell me about Rebecca's medical history, whether she took any medicines or drugs. She said Rebecca was never sick.

"Did she drink alcohol? Did she ever use drugs?"

"Oh no, no. *Never.* My daughter was going to be a nurse. She thought all that was stupid."

I asked Camille if Rebecca talked to her much about her boyfriend.

"She was dating someone at her job, but that boy was no good for her—he just work all the time, he don't appreciate my daughter. But she was never *serious* about that boy, and she stopped seeing him when the company went broke."

"The company went broke?"

"Yes. Rebecca didn't worry, though—she said that happens all the time there, with those companies. And then she got into the school for nurses and she met the new boy. That's different—he's a nice young doctor."

"Rebecca told you this?"

"Of course."

"Do you know this young man's name?"

"No, sorry. I think maybe my Rebecca was in love with him even, but when I try to talk to her about it, she don't want to. It's hard. It's hard to be so far apart from my daughter, so far away."

I asked Camille if she was familiar with the lizard bracelet. She wasn't. "But I want you to send us the cross she wore, the cross that belonged to my husband's mother. For the funeral. You will send it?"

I took a deep breath, bracing myself to give the poor woman more bad news.

"I'm sorry, Camille. We cannot send the cross back to you just yet. I promise we will send it as soon as we can, and I will keep it safe until then. But there's something else. Something difficult to tell you...about the funeral. Rebecca's body has been cremated."

"Yes. I know that."

Camille Corchero wasn't fazed in the least. I was.

"You...wanted to have Rebecca's body cremated?"

"Yes. Well—no. That is not our...not our tradition. But we agreed when Dr. Stone told us we cannot do an open funeral, open coffin. Because of the law."

"A law in the Philippines?"

"No, no. *Your* law. The...what did he say? The law about the spread of diseases."

"The letter of noncontagion?"

"Yes! Noncontagion. Dr. Stone explained about it when he called, to give us the...the news. Because of the way my Rebecca dies, he cannot send her body to us unless it is cremation."

There was a silence over the phone while I tried to figure out what to say to that. Camille broke it.

"You work with Dr. Stone?"

"Yes."

"You are lucky. Dr. Stone is a very kind man. He arranged everything for us. He said he wants to, because my Rebecca loves his daughter, Callie, they were like sisters. He says he will send us a beautiful urn, and then we can have the funeral right away, and not wait."

"That was…thoughtful of him," I said, only because I figured I'd better say something.

"Yes. The funeral is important to us. You understand? Are you a Catholic, dear…?"

I went for the simple answer to a complicated question.

"Yes."

"Then you understand. May God bless your Dr. Stone."

The letter of noncontagion is a formality, a single sheet of paper to certify that the decedent had no diagnosis of various dangerous diseases, like one of the spongiform encephalopathies or West Nile virus. SARS. Ebola. The scary shit. It made no sense. Did Mike Stone somehow think Rebecca had died with an active infection that I had missed on autopsy? I made myself a note to find out.

Rebecca had lied to her family about the way her job at Siloam Biologic ended. Why? What had happened there? Maybe nothing—maybe she worried she wasn't going to be able to send as much money home, and they would suffer for it. Maybe she was just worried *they* would worry. It's hard to live thousands of miles away, among strangers. Growing up, I heard about how hard it was most every day. I overheard my mother's cheery phone calls back to Poland. No one in Poland could see *Mamusia's* bruises through the phone line, and no one in the Philippines had any reason to doubt Rebecca when she told them the company she worked for had "gone broke."

I tried to get back to work, chipping away at my list of open cases, but it was no use. I kept daydreaming Camille Corchero trying to hold a wake over an urn—a beautiful urn, as promised. It was covered in filigreed silver lizards. They had green eyes and mocking smiles and rusty feet. Crowning the urn was a big gold crucifix, old-world style. Suffering Christ on the cross, crown of thorns, gaping stigmata. A thin red line ran from the lance wound in His side all the way to the urn's base.

I needed a break.

The wind, as always, carried a cloud of brake pads and diesel grit off the freeway viaduct and punched it down into our loading dock. I made my way down the block to Baby Mike Bail Bonds. Sparkle was on the phone while typing at her computer. I mimed coffee; she gave me the thumbs-up. She was finishing the call when I returned from Zeffiro's.

"Del Norte County," Sparkle said, as if that explained everything. "You look beat."

No doubt I did—and I may have blushed a little at the reminder of my intoxicating night aboard Arnie's boat. "I needed some air. A case is bugging me."

Sparkle's phone rang again. She punched a button and it stopped.

"Let's hear it."

I told her the basic outline of Rebecca's death and my conversation with Neil. "This girl told her family that the company she was working for went under. She also told them she had left her boyfriend for someone else, but when I talked to him about it, he either didn't know that, or didn't want to admit it to me."

"So what? She's lying to her family or he's lying to you. Or both. What'd the boyfriend say about the drugs?"

"Same as the family did—inconceivable, not her, not in a million years."

Sparkle rolled her eyes.

"Yeah," I conceded, "the family's always the last to know. But the roommate?"

"Oh—that's different. They tight?"

"Not especially. They kept different hours, and my dead girl was the private type."

"Still. If the boyfriend and the roommate both say no drugs—"

"Others, too."

"Who?"

"I can't tell you."

"Coworkers."

I couldn't hide my surprise, and that made Sparkle smile.

"Okay then. She got drugs in her system?"

"Toxicology results are still weeks away."

"So why not just wait?"

"Because this case started out as an accidental overdose of an injection drug, but now it's starting to look like a homicide."

"Well now." Sparkle leaned back and swirled her coffee.

"There's some trauma on her—not much, but enough to make it possible. The problem is, I have no reason why anybody would want this woman dead. The only thing in the story that doesn't make sense is her lies to the folks back home. That, and she's pregnant."

"There's your motive, then. The hinky ex-boyfriend killed her."

"They broke up too long ago for the math to work."

"Maybe they weren't so broke up."

"They were. That much I'm sure of. She had a new boyfriend, but I can't get anything on that guy."

"So background check her. You think your girl was lying? You're right. Everybody lies, and everybody's got dirt." Sparkle swiveled to her computer and poised her fingers over the keyboard like a pianist. "Just say her name, and I'll dig it all up right now."

"Thanks, Sparkle, but no."

"Inside twenty minutes I'll tell you what she had for breakfast."

"I have no doubt. But I can't accept your kind offer."

She looked a little deflated.

"You background check everybody?" I asked her.

Sparkle smiled ruefully. "I went out with this guy one time. Out for a drink, that's all. He was a smooth talker, handsome, a lieutenant in the fire department. We had a good time...but then he had to leave early, said he had an a.m. shift. When we left the bar, I took a picture of his license plate."

"You *what?*"

"Occupational reflex. And I'm glad I did. So I look him up—"

"You can do that?"

"I have my ways. Turns out he didn't have an a.m. shift. What he *did* have was an appointment at Department 17, across the street there."

"In the Hall."

She nodded. "Judge Meyers. You know Judge Meyers?"

I shook my head.

"Nice man. Funny taste in ties. Gets a lot of family law. He does quite a few restraining order violations, too."

"Don't tell me..."

"My handsome lieutenant had a pretrial hearing for stalking his ex-wife."

"*Sukinsyn!*"

"Whatever that is, you're right. I called him up the next day, confronted him about it."

I laughed. "Why?"

Sparkle looked genuinely offended. "What do you mean,

why? He lied to me. And you know what he says? He says, 'You don't understand! I love her! I just called her a couple of times and she took it the wrong way!' Jessie, he called the plaintiff thirty-three times in one day. From the firehouse! It was all in the police report."

"You told him all this?"

"Damn straight!" She swept her arm across the office. "I do this for a *living.* He knows I do. What the hell was he thinking?"

"Good point."

Sparkle grunted.

"I still see him around sometimes."

"What!"

"Oh, you'll find out, honey. This is a big city, but it's a small town. Hard to keep from bumping into people you've got history with."

"What do you do when you see him?"

"I yell, 'Hey, stalker!'"

"You do not!"

"Sure I do! He's a stalker!" Sparkle put on a hangdog face and dropped her voice an octave. "'Stop calling me that,' he says every time."

She crushed her coffee cup. "The big baby."

Back at my desk, I settled in to get some more cases cleared and plugged in my cell, which was going on twenty-something hours without a recharge. The screen lit up with the last string of texts between me and Arnie, from early that morning.

Good morning & wow. Sad to wake alone.

JUDY MELINEK & T.J. MITCHELL

Wow, indeed. Sparkle had worried me with her story about that date with the fireman. What did I really know about Arnold Spitz?

A Google search brought up pages upon pages of links. Half of them were tech websites written in a mix of gibberish and acronym and the other half were press-release puff pieces. Arnie Spitz was widely admired and envied among his peers. He unleashed innovation; he boosted visionaries. The word *bellwether* kept popping up. Arnie had a bare-bones LinkedIn profile and no Facebook account. His Wikipedia page consisted of a single vague paragraph and a list of links to the articles I'd already found. No Twitter handle, no blogs. No mention of a string of former wives or a notorious drug habit. No perp-walk photos.

You've completed your due diligence, I told myself. *Enough worrying. Get back to work.*

I was closing the open browser windows when a press-release headline caught my eye.

Siloam Bio: New Strategic Partner Announced

Siloam Biologic gained an ally today as it fights for position in San Francisco's crowded pack of medical-solution start-ups. The biomed firm will undertake a Series A preferred stock round with TechFolio Capital Solutions in exchange for an undisclosed amount of operating capital, and announced that their financing model has been structured to include a novel digital asset platform.

"We are thrilled to reach this pivot point in partnership with TechFolio Capital Solutions," Siloam Biologic CFO Mark Anson said, describing the deal as "the deepest involvement by a biotechnology innovator in crowdfund financing ever undertaken."

I pulled up the notes to my conversation with Neil Dupree. TechnoFixer or TechPossible—that's what he thought the angel investor was called. He meant TechFolio. Arnie Spitz's company.

Oh fuck.

Arnie Spitz was the guy with the grocery bags of cash who got Rebecca fired—? I knew that Arnie was an old pal of Sophia Kalogeras, and that Sophia had pulled some strings to get Rebecca that job at Siloam Biologic. Was Arnie on the other end of those strings? Did Rebecca Corchero and Arnie Spitz know each other?

Did I mention Rebecca's case to Arnie while he was plying me for morgue stories?

No, I hadn't. I was sure of that much.

Melodie the roommate claimed she'd never set eyes on El Bato—but maybe she'd met him without knowing he was Rebecca's boyfriend. I went back to Arnie's Wikipedia page and found a photo. He was at some kind of press junket, a folder in his hand, his head cocked just so. He made sure the camera caught him at three-quarters. He looked dashing. His eyes flashed, his teeth sparkled.

I printed it out in full color.

The Sunset District apartment where Rebecca Corchero died was in a scruffy and chipped row house. Rebecca's blue car from the scene photos wasn't in the driveway anymore. A grayish Nissan was. That gave me an opening for small talk; the Nissan belonged to Melodie Ortiz, who answered the door to 1461 30th Avenue in yoga pants and an oversize sweatshirt, toweling her freshly scrubbed young face. My Beemer was too long for the street space, so I was blocking her in. Melodie said that was fine, and we traded the customary complaints about parking in the city.

"I left Becca's room just like I found it. She's got like a cousin or something in Daly City who's gonna come by for her stuff, but they didn't say when."

"I'm sorry you have to go through this, Melodie," I said.

"I'm still pretty freaked out."

"I understand."

Melodie rocked back and forth. "So—you want to look around?"

"Sometimes coming to the scene in person I'll find things I might miss in the photographs," I said, and asked Melodie to re-create her coming home the morning that she found Rebecca's body. She wasn't eager, but agreed.

We started out on the brick stairway. The security gate was the typical local type, of dull galvanized steel, pitted white from the salt air. Melodie opened it with one key and swung it out, then used another key for the handle on the wooden door behind, which swung into the apartment. We stepped over the threshold and both looked at the ratty armchair in the entry hall. I recognized it from the scene photos, along with the off-white side table where the syringe had been.

"Right there," Melodie said. Her eyes were brimming. "Rebecca was *not* a junkie."

"I believe you, Melodie. She showed none of the signs I usually find of long-term drug abuse."

"So then…what?"

I examined the doorjamb. The wood was a little chipped and the cheap metal hardware dented, but didn't look like it had been forced.

"The lock wasn't broken."

"No."

"And you haven't replaced it."

She looked alarmed. "Should I?"

"No, no, it's okay—that's not what I meant. When you came in, like we just did, the gate was locked?"

"Yes."

"And the inside door?"

"Yes."

"It has a dead bolt. Was that locked, too?"

She paused, thought about it.

"No, it wasn't."

"Is it usually?"

"Not always. Sometimes Becca forgets."

"How about you?"

She smirked grimly. "I grew up in the Excelsior. I never forget to bolt the door."

I swung the door away from the wall. There was a doorknob dent in the lath and plaster, and a dusting of powder on the baseboard.

"When did this happen?"

Melodie scowled. "Oh. I dunno. We ding it by accident sometimes—you know, like, carrying groceries?"

"This looks fresh."

"I guess. I didn't notice it."

Her eyes fell on the badge clipped to my belt.

"Hey, Doctor…?"

"Teska."

"Yeah—I'll bet you can, like, help hurry the family for me, right?"

"The family?"

"In Daly City? The cousin or whatever? I need to get Rebecca's stuff out of here so I can look for a new roommate. Rent's due in two weeks."

I told her I'd see what I could do. Then she reached behind me to close the security gate. It clanged like a cage. Through

its bars I could see my Beemer downstairs at the curb. It reminded me of something.

"In the scene photos there's a bright blue Subaru parked in
the driveway."

"That's Rebecca's."

"Where is it now?"

"In the garage. The cousin is supposed to come get it."

I stepped aside while she closed—and dead-bolted—the
wooden door. I found myself right in front of the yellow hall
chair. Up close it was no more comfortable-looking than in
the photos. I sat in it.

Melodie gasped.

"What's wrong?"

"Sorry. It's just that…nobody's…"

"I understand."

It was a cramped spot. Dark. The chair's cushion sank on
one side, and the door had a draft. An odd place to choose
to shoot up when the cozy living room was all of fifteen feet
away.

"Did Rebecca's boyfriend have a key? Keys, I should say."

"I dunno."

It was clear Melodie didn't want to talk to me while I was
sitting in the haunted chair, so I got up and started down the
narrow hallway.

"You said you didn't think she was expecting anyone that
night."

"Right."

"Can I see her room?"

She took a deep breath. "Okay."

The hall dead-ended with one door in front of us and another to the left. Melodie turned the knob on the latter, but
then stood aside for me to enter.

"Like I said—I haven't been in here since... Rebecca passed."

"I'd appreciate if you'd come in with me," I said, falling back on my scene investigation training. "I'm going to examine the room, and I'd like you to witness that I'm leaving everything as I found it."

"Um, okay."

Rebecca Corchero's bedroom was small and perfectly neat. A desk held an open laptop with a dark screen, a smartphone plugged into a charger, and a single open textbook. More books, arranged by size, crammed her shelves. A couple were nursing texts, but most seemed to be investment self-help books—*Beat the Market!*, *Internet Investment While You Sleep*, *Blockchain Unchained*, *Beyond Borders: Be a Bitcoin Boss!*

I tried the cell phone first. It was locked with a passcode. I asked Melodie if she knew it. She didn't. I placed the phone back down, carefully, right where it had been, then sat behind the desk. I poked a finger on the computer's space bar, and, luckily for me, it whirred to life. The screen showed a browser window with a bunch of tabs.

"Um, wait," Melodie said. "Don't you need, like, a warrant?"

I told her I didn't. "This isn't a criminal investigation—it's a death investigation. I'm looking for documents that might help me understand Rebecca's medical history, and messages or social media posts that reflect her state of mind on the day she died."

I didn't mention evidence of an interest in experimenting with drugs. I also didn't mention that sometimes I'll find a suicide note in a computer's open documents.

The top browser window on Rebecca Corchero's laptop was from the University of California library, and had been logged out due to inactivity. Also open and logged out was an online music stream and a Netflix tab. A couple of social media sites were up there, too. On Instagram she'd posted a sepia photo of a chimpanzee wearing glasses, hunched over a huge book in a wood-paneled room. Rebecca had added a one-word caption: *Pharm!!*

I tried her email next, skimming for Arnie's name or Neil Dupree's, or anything that rang a bell. No dice. Half the emails were in Tagalog. I snapped pictures of those with my phone, in case I wanted to ask someone for translation later. There was a week-old email addressed to Michael Stone, asking if they could schedule a time to get together: She needed help with the nursing program paperwork. Not a single message to or from anyone at Siloam Biologic.

I opened a new browser window to check her history and found a bunch of links to bitcoin sites. One looked like a stock exchange portal that had been wrung through a random-letter generator. Another startled me with its black-helicopter rhetoric about coming global calamities, nuclear war survival zones, etcetera. A third wouldn't even open until I entered something called a First Level EGM Key.

Melodie was still hovering, antsy, in the doorway. I beckoned her over.

"Do you know anything about these sites? Internet investment?"

She squinted at the screen. "Oh, that. No, I don't, but Becca was, like, obsessed with it. Ever since she started work at that company, she's been buying books and talking nonstop about it. She said she was going to, like, make a million bucks and take care of her family in the Philippines."

I went into my bag and pulled out the picture of Arnie I'd printed. "Does this man look familiar?"

"No."

"You're certain?"

"Who is it?"

"His name is Arnold Spitz. Arnie for short."

"Never seen him."

"This isn't Rebecca's new boyfriend you mentioned, the one she called Bato?"

"No way. Bato's older, big nose, long face."

Wait a minute.

The penny dropped. And Melodie must have seen it in my eyes, because she turned hers away.

"You said you'd never met this new boyfriend."

Melodie started to make her way around her roommate's bed with its hospital-corner sheets and uniformly smooth coverlet.

"Well, yeah. I never met him. But I *saw* him. Couple of times anyway."

I waited. She reached the far side of the room.

"I had a job this one time down the Embarcadero, and it's, like, a pain in the ass to park down there, so I took the N-Judah line. I get off the train coming back, and a taxi pulls up to the corner by the stop. Rebecca gets out of the cab, and I can see there's this tall man in the back. Becca looks, like, surprised to see me? And embarrassed. The tall guy just sits there like a statue, staring straight ahead until the cab takes off. Rebecca went up the hill to our house without saying a word to me."

"Did you ask her who the man in the cab was?"

A flinty laugh. "Rebecca Corchero? No, I did not. Becca was chill—real responsible, no head games. A good roommate, and those are hard to find. But I knew what I could talk to her about and what I couldn't, and from the look she gave me right then? *En boca cerrada no entran moscas.* Keep your mouth shut and you can't, like, put your foot in it. You know?"

"Yes." I waited, but she didn't add anything. "What about the second time you saw this man?"

Melodie told me that a couple of weeks later she had booked a catering job over the bridge, at a winery in Sonoma. But then, only half an hour in, the prep kitchen caught fire. The whole place was evacuated, and the job got called off. She drove back to the city having wasted half a day burning gas, earning nothing.

"And then when I walk in the door I, like, really have to pee? It's a long drive. But when I get to the bathroom door, there's a flush, and then out comes this big tall man in Becca's bathrobe, barely to his knees..."

"Well, that's awkward."

"No shit! I say hello and he says hello, and then I call out for Becca. She yells from inside her room that everything's okay, don't worry about it."

"So what did El Bato do?"

Melodie Ortiz scowled at me in a mixture of disdain and amusement. "Not *El* Bato. Just Bato, okay?"

"What did he do?"

"How do I know? I had to pee, remember? When I came out of the bathroom, he wasn't in the hallway no more—that's all I cared about."

"It was the same man as you saw in the taxi?"

"For sure."

"But Rebecca never told you who he was?"

"No."

"You say he was older than the man in the picture I just showed you?"

"He looks it, yeah."

"But when we talked on the phone, you told me Rebecca's boyfriend was a student."

She shrugged. "That's what Becca told *me*. He didn't look like no student."

I waited for an explanation. Melodie sighed and sat down on the edge of the bed.

"I knew you'd be talking to her family. I guess—I don't know, I guess I, like, didn't want them to think…"

"That she was carrying on with an older man?"

Melodie swiveled to look at me. "Becca was in love with him, okay? Like, *really* in love. I mean, she didn't tell me that, but I could see it. Her family, though? They're Old World. Old school."

"They wouldn't have approved."

She shrugged.

"Can you describe this man for me?"

"Old enough to be, like, my dad? But not hella old. Real tall, round nose, long chin."

"Bald?"

"No. Well, I didn't get a good look. His hair was graying, I guess, but not all gray. The rest was kind of light brown."

"Eyes?"

"I don't know."

"Wedding ring?"

Melodie stood.

"Will this take much longer? I need to make dinner."

"Melodie. Did you see a wedding band on this man's hand?"

"I don't know."

I was running out of time and goodwill. I had told Melodie I didn't need a warrant, but had neglected to add that I was in her house as her guest. I could look around wherever she agreed to let me, but I was obliged to leave when she decided it was time for me to go.

"Just give me a couple more minutes, okay? Then I'll be out of your way."

She agreed.

I sifted through the trash can for draft suicide notes. None. I went through the drawers in the desk and bureau for a drug kit or paraphernalia. Nothing. Nothing in the tiny closet, either.

"That morning—nobody else was in here, you said?"

"Not that I saw."

Melodie was standing with her arms crossed in the doorway. I pointed my chin past it, to the bathroom.

"Medicine cabinet in there?"

"Yes."

"Did the investigators or cops check it?"

"I don't know."

"Can I? Quickly?"

She hedged.

"I won't mess with your stuff. I just need to look for medications that belonged to Rebecca." I held up my legal pad, all official-like. "I need to record them, and make sure they match what we find in the toxicology report."

Melodie stepped aside grudgingly.

It was easy to figure out which medicine cabinet shelf belonged to Rebecca: The items in it were ranged according to size, largest in back, all their labels facing front. No antidepressants or any other prescription medications. One pill bottle caught my attention, though.

"Everything in here is hers, right?" I asked Melodie.

"Everything on that shelf."

I opened the bottle of Goddess Essentials Women's Health Formula vitamins. The seal was broken but it was mostly full. I checked the expiration date. Months away.

"Do you know if Becca had been taking these for a long time?"

"No idea."

Women's Health Formula is a euphemism. One of the ingredients on the bottle was folic acid. They were prenatal vitamins. Rebecca knew she was pregnant when she died, and she was caring for that fetus.

The traffic crossing Golden Gate Park stopped dead, right when I had committed to Chain of Lakes Drive. I daydreamed of the Pacific Coast Highway down in Malibu, my BMW 235i gliding over miles of sand and palms, 320 horsepower growling under the shark nose hood just as God intended it to do. The long line of cars crept up. I feathered the clutch to inch closer to the bumper in front of me, going nowhere fast.

Rebecca Corchero was not an experienced drug user. If the toxicology report came back as I expected it to—showing drugs of abuse or their metabolites—I was going to have to determine a manner of death. I could remove suicide from the list—I had found nothing in her apartment that pointed to suicidal ideations. Natural, also—the autopsy revealed no disease at all. That left accident, homicide, or undetermined. If she was shooting up and overdosed, it was an accident. But the torn tissue inside her lower lip could mean that someone had assaulted her. Maybe someone killed her. And maybe not: the lacerated frenulum alone wasn't proof of homicide, and neither were the fresh abrasions on her wrist.

Too many what-ifs. That meant the possibility of an undetermined ruling also loomed over me—a decision that pleased exactly no one.

A gargantuan truck turned off Chain of Lakes Drive and chewed right into the park. It was hauling a multitiered sound stage decorated with nouveau-hippie, flower-power logos and a sign—*RHYTHM & DUNES*—in ironically groovy overstuffed lettering. I had overheard gripes about Rhythm

& Dunes at my neighborhood coffee shop; apparently it was some music festival that wrecks the Richmond District for most of August. The jam of cars on Chain of Lakes finally moved once the truck was out of the way.

When I got home I took Bea for an abbreviated walk, apologizing to her while trying to explain the concept of all-night lovemaking on a yacht. She didn't buy it.

Good morning & wow, my phone's last text string still said. *Sad to wake alone.*

Due diligence. I wanted Tommy's advice. Not about my love life; for that he was worse than useless. I wanted to talk to him about Arnie's company TechFolio, and the piles of cash.

"Yup," Tommy said, to my astonishment. "Seen that."

"Safeway bags full of money?"

"Yup."

I waited out the phone silence, but he added nothing.

"Tomasz."

"Uh-huh?"

"That doesn't strike you as unusual?"

"Nuh-uh."

"A weird way to do business?"

"Not in the start-up world. These enterprises move fast—if someone finds out about your idea before you can get rolling, your idea gets stolen. Cash is the quickest and best starting capital. No bankers, no disclosure statements. You bring me cash, I make cool thing. Period."

"So why is TechFolio making Siloam convert their operating cash into bitcoin?"

Silence. I had stumped Tommy. I relished it.

"Yeah, that's...puzzling," my brother conceded. "Arnie and his partners must have some e-currency angle. Otherwise their business model is backassward. You know how cyber-currency works?"

"That's why I'm talking to you, *braciszku*."

"You said they're 'converting' cash into bitcoin. That's not exactly right. You use computers to solve math problems, really hard math problems that require a lot of computation. You're rewarded with electronic currency."

"You're kidding."

"Dead serious. It's called mining. The bigger your computing power, the more currency you can earn. To do it right, you need a lot of money to buy a lot of computers, and to pay for huge amounts of electricity running them."

"So…what are they doing with the bitcoin?"

"You'll never find out."

I waited for him to explain. He didn't.

"Tomasz."

"That's one thing I can tell you for sure—you'll never figure out what the cryptocurrency angle is. Bitcoin is really hard to track if you do it right. Besides, these companies have nondisclosure agreements that will make your hair stand on end. Believe me—I've signed some."

An electric trolley bus on Fulton Street whined past my block and honked at something. Something honked back.

"But, hey," Tommy said. "*You* don't have an NDA with Arnie Spitz. If this bothers you so much, why don't you just ask him about it?"

"Well…" I hedged. "It so happens I do owe him a phone call."

"Oho! Of a romantic nature?"

"Maritime."

Stumped him twice. How I do love messing with my little brother. I hung up, stretched and yawned, and dialed again.

"You've been haunting me all day," Arnie said by way of hello. We purred at one another for a while. I was out of practice—Barry was never one for pillow talk. I found my opening when Arnie asked about my workday. I told him it was all paper-shuffling, nothing interesting, and asked about his.

"Exciting new avenues, though I can't go into detail. My team managed to appease a troublesome client, which always makes for a good day. Some of them require more hand-holding than others, you see."

I told him I did see, yes. Then I told him I had addressed a similar action item, by getting ahold of a recalcitrant witness, someone I needed to interview about an open case. Someone named Neil Dupree.

I asked him if the name rang a bell. It didn't.

I said, "At Siloam Biologic."

Arnie made a noise, a tiny plosive noise, on the other end of the cell signal. Then he said, "I know that company."

"Yes, your name came up."

"Really."

"I was asking Dupree about a woman named Rebecca Corchero. A case of mine."

I waited. He didn't respond.

"A coworker of his at Siloam Biologic. He told me she got fired after crossing swords with someone from TechFolio Capital Solutions—"

"Ah," he said. "*That* woman. Tall, dark, Asian?"

"Right."

"Yes, yes. Wait…she's a 'case' of yours?"

It had dawned on him that this is never a happy thing.

"She died last weekend. I'm investigating the circumstances."

"What circumstances?"

I told Arnie as much as I wanted to about the Corchero case, and then asked him to tell me about his dealings with her.

"I only ever saw her once. We are involved in financing that company, you see. One of our many ventures…"

"Okay."

"Jessie…"

"Yes?"

"Jessie, can we discuss this in person? It's not that it's especially complicated—but it was…contentious. I'm concerned that you may have received a biased report of the incident. Can we meet on Saturday for dinner? I have a spot you will *love*."

A dirty quip nearly popped onto my tongue before I bit it back. "Sure," I managed to say instead.

"I'll text you," Arnie said. Then he said something else that melted me, and something by way of goodbye that left me flushed around the base of my throat.

Bea had assumed that baleful, scolding look again.

"You'll understand when you're older," I told her.

CHAPTER TEN

"Here," Ted Nguyen said, and handed me one folder. Donna Griello the 2578 was silent and grim. The small flock of medical students looked spooked.

"Who died?"

No laughs. Mike Stone was absent. I asked about it.

"He's meeting with Dr. Howe," Donna said.

My single case file was an external examination. Nguyen only had two in front of him.

"Light day."

Still no chatter.

"Let's get to it, then," I said. Donna tore out of the conference room and I followed her—the Ops Shop would offer whatever gossip was available.

Both day-shift investigators were at their desks. Donna's night-shift partner, Cameron Blake, was behind his, too. I started to ask what was going on, but a look from Cam clammed me right up. Everyone's attention was focused on the chief's office. Dr. Howe was shouting. The door was closed, but his fury rattled the windows.

Cam motioned me over to his desk and sat me in front of the computer. It was open to a site called *KnowNowSF*. The headline read *ME Testifies in Fed Racketeer Trial*.

Crab trap or murder weapon? A San Francisco pathologist told the jury in a federal courtroom today that he couldn't tell the difference.

Prosecutors appeared exasperated by Deputy Chief Medical Examiner Michael Stone's testimony in their case against Hector Marroquin and two codefendants for murder and conspiracy in the death of Robert Falmouth two years ago.

"I would not conclude within reasonable medical certainty that these wounds are the result of strangulation," Stone said, when asked to present the findings of the medical examiner's office.

The story's text was interrupted by a close-up photo of a man with hair the color of ash and a mustache that matched. He had a face like a dead lawn. He stared at the camera with practiced menace. *Hector Marroquin*, read the caption. I scrolled down and the article continued.

Falmouth, who prosecutors say was garroted and dumped in San Francisco Bay on orders from Marroquin, was a longtime resident of San Francisco's Silver Terrace neighborhood. Stone told the court that "advanced decomposition" made it impossible to tell whether an injury to Falmouth's throat was evidence of murder, or of an already-dead body becoming tangled in fishing gear. "The postmortem investigation produced insufficient evidence to call this a homicide…"

The chief's office door swung open, and Dr. James Howe's voice roared through the silent Ops Shop.

"—different conclusion from the original pathologist? On a case you didn't even do yourself!"

Michael Stone came storming out. Howe's next words stopped him:

"Just because you think you know better!"

Stone swung back around to face the chief.

"You turfed me this case, Jim—and now you're going to undercut me? I did the best I could with the half-assed work Sutcliffe did on that neck block! No histo, and he didn't even dissect it all the way down!"

"It's a ligature strangulation homicide! Just look at the pictures!"

"You can't make that call on such a bad decomp—"

"Sutcliffe did, and he performed the damn autopsy! What makes you think you know more than the doctor who did the post?"

"Brian was wrong."

"Oh, don't you start on that nonsense again, Mike... I send you in there to represent our office, and you blow up a whole federal murder case? The prosecutor's gonna have to call *me* to the stand now, to clean up your mess!"

"Yeah? No surprise. Maybe you should have done it in the first place."

"I'm the chief, Mike. You aren't. Don't forget it—and if you ever want my job, you'd best recognize that working with the prosecution to make the case is part of it."

"I'm no sellout."

"What did you say?"

"You heard me. I'm not your lapdog."

Mike Stone pivoted again, marched straight through the Ops Shop, and was gone.

"Cameron—!" Howe thundered. *"Door!"*

Cam rose to close it. The other investigators exchanged mirthless grins. I thought I heard a sotto voce "about time" from somewhere in the room.

"What the hell was that about?"

"What...?" said Ted Nguyen. He was at his computer working on a death certificate, and I was standing by our divider, the door firmly closed.

"Down the Ops Shop. I just watched Mike Stone and Dr. Howe rip into each other over some testimony Mike did yesterday."

"Oh. That." Nguyen didn't pause in his work. "Sutcliffe's old floater. It's part of the whole federal racketeering mess. We're all getting called on related cases. Stone's already testifying in a shooting down there, so I guess Howe figured he could take this floater too. Plenty of bodies to go around. Pain in the neck."

I left Ted to his paperwork. The decomp floater Howe and Stone were shouting about was one of those files I had found locked away in my office cabinet, along with the semi-automatic pistol and a drug-cooking spoon and the evidence flotsam from a bunch of Dr. Brian Sutcliffe's other old cases.

I went to my computer and scanned the database for the autopsy report on Falmouth, Robert, then clicked through to the photos of his headless torso as it had appeared when it arrived at the morgue. The skin was mostly missing—the remaining bits in gray and green tatters—but the strap muscles of the neck were clearly apparent, and I didn't see any hemorrhage. All I saw was a bunch of vague lines across the tissue.

Sutcliffe had ruled this case a homicide. Howe concurred.

Now Stone had testified instead that the manner of death ought to be undetermined, since it looked to him like those ligature marks occurred after death, while the body was bobbing in the bay. And in spite of his rhetoric about critical thinking and open discussion, Dr. Howe didn't much like Michael Stone's dissenting opinion. Not if it complicated the prosecution's job in the courtroom.

I stared at the stack of brand-new toxicology reports perched atop my inbox. I could go home for the weekend with a load off my back if I buckled down and minded my own business instead of snooping into an argument between the chief and deputy chief.

Nie mój cyrk, nie moje małpy.

Not my circus. Not my monkeys.

First one down was SFME-0739, the John Doe with his face eaten by a coyote over Fourth of July weekend. He wasn't a Doe any longer—the name on his Veterans Administration ID card had been confirmed by fingerprints from the hand that wasn't gnawed up. His VA hospital chart documented post-traumatic stress disorder and alcohol abuse. Our lab's toxicology result showed low levels of diazepam and sertraline, and a high measure of blood alcohol. He died of liver disease due to acute and chronic alcoholism, natural manner. The body was still in the decomp freezer. Now that I had issued a death certificate, the old soldier could be interred with honors at the national cemetery up in Sacramento.

"Next," I said to the tox reports. "Step right up."

A thirty-year-old man dropped ecstasy in the alley behind a place called Club Bajaj and died half-naked in a puddle of vomit. Cause, MDMA intoxication. Manner, accident. A 295-pound man sprained an ankle at work in a big-box store and threw a clot to his lungs after planting himself across the living room couch for two days. Cause of death pulmonary embolism. Manner, accident. Four more cases—a jaywalker hit by a bus, a gunshot suicide, a skateboarder versus a hydrant, and a stabbing homicide—all came back tox-negative. I closed all of them and stood at the printer to do a little disco song-and-dance while it spat out my nice fresh pile of autopsy reports. Ted Nguyen peeked over the office divider.

"Ted! Coffee is for closers only."

"What?"

"Tox came in like Christmas morning! Finalized seven cases," I bragged. He scoffed, and registered a complaint about how slow the tox lab was, with San Pietro always away at conferences.

Sunshine Ted. I decided that was to be his nickname from now on.

I still had one monkey on my back: A case from July, an Alzheimer's patient who choked on a pork cutlet. The family was suing his convalescent home, and their lawyer had left me multiple strident voice mails. I figured I'd go ask the tox lab about it, and take the opportunity to log Rebecca Corchero's lizard bracelet back into evidence storage.

This time chief forensic toxicologist Carlo San Pietro wore an eggshell linen suit and spotted bow tie. He was bounding around the maze of cardboard boxes in his office. My question about the pork cutlet case's toxicology report had riled him.

"The case I'm looking for is almost six weeks old," I said, trying to stay out of his way. "I need the tox results to close it. Is something holding them up?"

"You are premature!" San Pietro ferreted through a pile of paperwork and came up with a file. "Here. I will show you something."

He pulled out a gas chromatograph report, the familiar range of peaks and valleys plotted across an X-Y graph.

"This is another one of yours. Case 955. Four days ago I

get it. It comes back positive, and the techs flag it for my review. It has some unusual peaks."

He grabbed another chromatogram, this one from the top of the pile.

"And look here: All the peaks match yours perfectly. This is 736, Dr. Stone's."

He mashed a manicured fingernail on the date.

"From? It was six weeks ago. But I had to wait for the *standards* to come in to identify the adulterants, the unusual peaks, in this batch of heroin. Without a standard I cannot confirm what it is, or give you an accurate level. Standards came yesterday. One indicates levamisole. You know levamisole?"

"It's an antiparasitic drug."

"Cheap, easy to buy, and it aids solubility of low-grade chlorhydrate powder drugs. It is the first time I have seen levamisole cutting heroin in San Francisco. A noteworthy finding."

He pointed to another spike on the paper. "Now, this one? This is a chemical peak I have never seen before, ever. You know what this is?"

I admitted that I didn't.

"Acetylfentanyl. A novel analogue of the synthetic opioid fentanyl. It appears in Eastern Europe heroin a few years ago. Not here, not yet until now. It makes a faster rush than heroin, it is orders of magnitude more potent, and it is cheaper. So now that I have identified those two peaks, I can write the report."

San Pietro lifted his round face, chin skyward. "I will have your report done in two weeks, and Dr. Stone has had to wait six weeks for the same result, exactly the same. Yet he does not complain."

Man, maybe Nguyen was right about this blowhard. I decided to soft-pedal.

"I appreciate the precision and importance of the work you do, Dr. San Pietro. I don't mean to rush you. I'm just looking for something to offer this family, the one that's been waiting almost two months for their tox report. Case 741. Can you give me an ETA for them?"

"No. You get it when you get it. We do not cut corners here, and we do not make estimates."

Cam Blake found me muttering to myself outside the door to the toxicology lab, and told me there was pizza for the taking in the Ops Shop break room if I wanted some. All four 2578s were together, using the shift change to throw a little birthday party for the daytime investigator with the gray hair and cigarette voice. The pizza was atrocious stuff: plasticine mozzarella atop dribbly sauce and crust like half an inch of drywall. But I was hungry and didn't want to hurt their feelings, so I hung around and chewed the plasticine while we all cracked wise about the birthday boy's advanced age. I left the Ops Shop grateful to the 2578s for putting San Pietro's arrogant asshattery out of my mind.

San Pietro had mentioned that Stone had an old case with the same drugs on board as Rebecca Corchero. I went into the computer and scanned down. Case SFME-0736—that was the one. Name: Graciela Natividad.

Psiakrew. The drug mule eviscerated in the Hotel Somerville the night Eugene "Lumpy" Chen got shot. The last time I'd mentioned her to Stone, he jumped right down my throat. Now toxicology showed that Natividad had died of the exact same mix of drugs that killed Rebecca Corchero...what, a month later? The Natividad case might inform my investigation of Corchero's death—which meant I'd have to talk to Mike Stone about Natividad again. And Stone was coming off that blowup with Dr. Howe about the RICO trial.

I girded myself and went down to his office.

"I'm busy, Jessie. What do you need?" Stone said right off. I asked him about Rebecca's cremation.

"I told you I would deal with the family. What's the problem?"

"I didn't see any evidence of contagious disease."

"There wasn't any."

"Then why did you sign off for direct cremation?"

"It was the best way to deal with the remains."

"That's my call. It's my case."

"The Corcheros are devout Catholics in a religious country, Jessie. They wanted to hold a funeral right away. Cremation was the best choice."

"They wanted the intact body for burial."

Mike Stone tipped his head to one side with a pained look, and massaged a crick in his neck. "Do you know how much it costs to embalm a body and transport it internationally?"

"Yes—"

"No. Not to the Philippines, you don't. And do you know where this family comes from? Their village, I mean. It's not Manila, let me tell you. On top of the air cargo cost, there's ground transportation of the casket. Even if the Corcheros could afford all that—and they can't—we're talking about shipping a body to the tropics. It won't be refrigerated. Try to imagine that. Cremation was the best choice."

"It isn't what the family wanted."

"Jessie. I understand your concern. But trust me when I tell you this—the best and only thing you can do for the Corchero family is to close the case." He swiveled to his computer. "You're waiting on tox, I'll bet. I'll push San Pietro to expedite it."

I said that wouldn't be necessary, because San Pietro was already finalizing the case.

"He tell you what she had on board?"

"Heroin. That's the other thing I need to talk to you about. Your body packer from the Hotel Somerville. The heroin on Rebecca Corchero's tox screen is identical."

"Based on...?"

I told him about the matching chromatogram peaks.

"Okay. Rebecca's dealer bought from the same batch as my mule was carrying. So what?"

"The dealer. I want to know if the detectives on your case have come up with any names."

Stone cocked his head and frowned at me sideways.

"Why?"

"You saw my autopsy diagram, Mike. Torn frenulum, orbital petechiae, and a wrist contusion consistent with restraint? I haven't ruled on manner."

"What do you mean? Corchero is an accident."

"Not yet it isn't."

His color was rising again.

"You aren't thinking this is a homicide!"

"It...it depends on..." I stammered.

Mike Stone balled his huge hands into fists and perched them on the desk. "How could you do that to them? Those poor people have suffered enough knowing that Callie—that Becca was a user!"

He leaned down on me, too close.

"Now I'm going to have to tell them...what? That maybe someone *hurt* her, too? What the hell is wrong with you!"

I rose—but Stone skirted around the desk and planted himself between me and the door. The room seemed to fill with his bad teeth, his lumpy nose, his jerking Adam's apple as he thundered on about the Corchero family and everything they'd already gone through, and how he would be damned before he let me put them through worse—

Then Stone's office door swung open and hit him. He was

so wound-up that he stumbled sideways into the wall, sending a diploma crashing.

"Jessie...? Are you—"

It was Cameron Blake, carrying four empty pizza boxes in one hand. They went toppling when Mike Stone shoved him back out the door.

Stone towered nearly a foot over Cam, but Cam was all muscle and ex-linebacker beer bulk. He shoved the deputy chief medical examiner back. Hard. Stone cursed and cocked a fist.

I stepped right into Stone's chest. I saw my career flash before my eyes, but did it anyway.

"Jail!" I yelled. "You wanna go to *jail*, Mike?"

That stopped him.

"*Again*, Mike?" Cam taunted from behind me.

Again...?

"Shut up, Cam," I said. I picked up a pizza box and handed it to him. "What the hell is going on? Can we all calm the fuck down, please."

Stone had lowered his fist and stepped back, but he certainly had not calmed the fuck down. His face was twisted into an ugly purple knot.

"Both of you," he said in a strangled whisper. "Leave."

We left.

The hallway was empty. Cam was bull-breathing through flared nostrils, pupils like hubcaps, bald pate mottled in red and yellow.

"Drink?" he said.

"I'm buying."

Cam took me to an alley across the street from the Hall of Justice where there was a sports bar that also offered bail bond service. It had gilded boxing gloves and a #16 Joe Montana jersey on the wall. The bartender wore a T-shirt that said IDENTITY THIEF. The ball game was on a TV by the door—bottom of the eighth, one man on—and the barfly Giants fans kept the place plenty loud enough for private shop talk. We went down the back, to the smallest and darkest leather banquette.

"That wasn't the first time I've had to get in Stone's face, and it won't be the last," Cam said, and had a long draw of his beer.

The charming and charismatic Dr. Michael Stone had a temper. You seldom saw it coming. You could screw the pooch on one of his cases and he'd laugh about it, or you could hand him a dead pen during morning meeting and he'd bite your head off.

"Too bad you had to find out this way," said Cam. "Talk around the Ops Shop is that all those scars on his arms aren't from his famous record of blood donation."

"Oh, come on…"

Cam shrugged and held his hands out. "I've heard that story from spouses of more ODs than I can count, that's all I'm saying."

I grew up with an alcoholic. I had to admit—silently—that the volatile display I'd just seen in Stone's office had sent me back to a lot of family dinners in the middle flat of an East Lynn three-decker.

I had watched my *mamusia* call around scrounging bail money more than once, too. "You were fucking with Mike about going to jail *again?*"

"I wasn't fucking with him."

"I don't so much as jaywalk. An ME with a sheet is no good on the stand."

"I didn't say he has a sheet."

"I don't want to play, Cam. Tell me or don't."

Someone shanked a breaking ball but managed to scramble for a base hit, to the general relief of the bar.

Cam slid closer to me.

"You were at that mansion of his, right? For the Fourth of July?"

"Yes."

"He has a feud with one of his neighbors. Started with parking, crabgrass, some such bullshit. Anyway, they get a notice from the city that their shared sidewalk is worn-out and they have to fix it. Stone wants to split the cost in half. The neighbor wants Stone to pay three-quarters 'cause that's closer to where the property line really is."

"Mike does not, I am guessing, agree to do this."

"They get into a shouting match over it. Then Stone goes and grabs a sledgehammer from his garage and starts smashing the fuck out of the neighbor's share of sidewalk. The neighbor calls nine-one-one, claims Stone threatened him with the sledge."

"They arrested him on that?"

"Oh shit, they didn't want to. The responding officers thought it'd be a he-said-he-said call—they went over there to settle everybody down. But then Stone gets in *their* faces."

"Uh-oh."

"Yes. He tells these two patrol officers what a bigwig he is at the OCME, and why don't they go back to ticketing old ladies for improper disposal of dog shit. They get fed up and arrest him on vandalism and assault."

"They took him to the *Hall?*"

"Briefly." Cam's gaze wandered over the dusty pool table and he assumed a wan expression. "Too, too briefly. His wife fixed it. You met his wife?"

"Yes."

"Well, she fixed it. There's this lawyer—"

I held up a hand. "Don't tell me. Jackson Heffernan."

"That's the one. She calls him, but before he arrives, the booking sergeant, who is no fool, alerts the district attorney's office, and the DA flips out."

I could see why. "An ME with an arrest record—especially for something violent? That's a real problem for the DA if they plan to put him on the stand in homicide cases."

"Right. So the DA and Heffernan *both* show up at the jail, *both* of them hollering for Stone's release! The arresting officers near shit themselves. They're both still doing night patrol on the Marine Unit boat, I hear."

"When was this?"

"Three years ago."

The TV crowd went wild as the Giants scored two on a beauty of a double out the right field line.

"The charges disappeared. Stone's wife wrote a fat check to the neighbor for the damage and then some. Mike never missed a day of work."

Cam hoisted his beer.

"To Mike Stone."

I arched an eyebrow. He clinked my glass.

"Don't forget this, Jessie: The DA was right. Stone is one hell of a good witness, and we rely on good witnesses to put away bad guys."

"Why do the homicide detectives hate his guts, then?"

"Because he's a dick. To them, at least. He has a highly developed sense of hierarchy, our Dr. Stone. If you're below him, he lets you know it—and he considers all cops below him. Even detectives."

"I've noticed."

"But at least..."

Cam hunched his shoulders and leaned his gleaming head closer. He smelled of hospital disinfectant and bad pizza.

"At least he keeps an open mind. I can't say as much for Dr. Howe."

I nursed my beer and waited.

"Jimmy Howe is the prosecution's best friend," Cameron Blake continued. "Someone is sitting at the defense table, Dr. Howe's pretty confident that's who done it. He likes to help the DA maintain a winning record."

The bar erupted in cheers. Some Giant had slugged a line drive to deep left field, bringing in another run on a double.

"Be careful alone with Stone," Cam said over the din. "I watched him tear a phone out of the wall once because he didn't like the answer he was getting from someone on the other end. When that man loses his temper, he really loses it."

He drained his suds and rose.

"Hell of an inning," Cam called to the bartender by way of goodbye.

———————

I couldn't sleep. The diesel din and shrill beeping alerts of construction equipment—the goddamn Rhythm & Dunes crew in Golden Gate Park—cut straight through the trees, crossed Fulton Street, and landed in my bedroom.

I tried to focus on something peaceful, and chose a long-weekend camping trip Barry and I once took to the Antelope Valley. It was early spring, cold after sundown in the high desert, and our attempts at lovemaking while cocooned in a single sleeping bag under a pup tent devolved into fits of hopeless giggling. A scent of sap, like pine pitch but richer, pervaded the tent as the starlit dark settled in. I asked Barry about it.

"Greasewood," he said. "It's strongest at night. You never smelled greasewood before?"

"I never been to the desert before."

Barry gathered mesquite branches and cooked bacon and eggs in the morning. I crawled out of the tent still wrapped in the sleeping bag.

"Every Angeleno needs to detox from the smog," Barry said. "It doesn't just get into your lungs—it gets into your clothes, your hair. It coats your skin like a stain."

He stood and stretched out his arms and filled his lungs. All around us the ground was glowing in the dawn light, a bloom of flowers so tiny that you couldn't see them individually. Then Barry crouched behind me and put his hands under the quilting. He kissed me behind the ear. "Close your eyes," he whispered. "Take a deep breath. This is the cure."

Lying alone in a defunct San Francisco cable car half a year later, I tried to bring myself back to that moment in the high desert. Eventually I did.

I tried to sleep in. Bea wouldn't let me, so we were running on Ocean Beach at seven. It belonged to me and Bea and the seagulls, and a couple of homeless making their beds in the yerba santa bushes. The free local newspaper littered the sidewalk on my block when we got back. The top story was a yawner about the fight to build a high-rise in a toxin-blighted industrial zone, but tucked in a corner of the front page was an article about Dr. Howe's testimony in the RICO trial. Though Howe wouldn't comment on the record, Jackson Heffernan certainly did—with predictable bombast about the chief ME and an overweening federal prosecutor engaging in a witch hunt, etcetera, etcetera, his client an upstanding community member, etcetera. I folded the newspaper in quarters and slid it into the bottom of the kitchen compost bin. It fit nicely.

I got a text. It was Arnie Spitz, sending me an address and asking if I wanted him to send a company car. I replied, *no thanks, I'll get myself there, look forward to seeing you for dinner.*

Etcetera.

One of Arnie's company cars. Prepaid in bitcoin. I thought of Rebecca Corchero's laptop, bitcoin websites still open on it. I thought, too, of Tommy's warning—that I'd never get past Spitz's ironclad nondisclosure agreements to find out about his electronic currency business angle.

My coffee was only half-drunk and my laptop sat fully charged on the tiny corner desk. A gust of wind shook Mahoney Brothers #45. It was blowing a gray curtain across my little garden. Bea lifted her head, considered the fog, and lay back down with a snuffle. I agreed with her. There were errands to run but I didn't want to run them. So I sat down to dig into Arnold Spitz again, deeper this time. I wanted to start with that online news site I'd read over Cam Blake's shoulder the morning before. What was it called?

KnowNowSF. That was it.

"We have tea," said the waitress when I asked for coffee.

"I want coffee."

"We have tea."

Sushi Sobakasu Omakase was squeezed between a Tibetan antiques shop and an organic meat market at the foot of the Transamerica Building. I wondered aloud where the menus were. Arnie informed me there weren't any. *Omakase* meant chef's choice. I tried to mask my dismay at being told I was expected to sit still and swallow whatever raw nuggets of sea critter this sushi place decided to foist on me. This is not how I like to eat. I like a menu. I like my fish cooked. I like coffee when I'm struggling to stifle a yawn, like I was at that moment in Sushi Sobakasu Omakase.

"Expand your horizons," Arnie advised, and reached across the polished bamboo table to take my hand. "Chef Tawara is a genius."

Arnie squeezed my knuckles and leaned closer, but was interrupted by the waitress, bearing our first course. It was a demitasse of strong, salty fish broth. It wasn't bad. Things were looking up.

"Jessie," Arnie said after the waitress left, "I know you want to talk to me about Siloam Biologic, and I want you to know that I am open to any of your questions and I have nothing to hide."

He sat back and sipped his soju cocktail. Time to fish or cut bait.

"Did you know Rebecca Corchero?"

"The dead woman you were asking about? Your 'case'?"

"She worked at Siloam."

"No, I didn't know her."

"Sophia Kalogeras helped her get that job by calling in a favor from a friend."

Arnie offered a jaundiced smirk. "I have never owed Sophia Kalogeras a favor. She is an old friend and a loyal one, but I would not want to find myself in her debt."

"Over the phone you mentioned Rebecca's involvement in an unpleasant incident when you visited Siloam Biologic."

"That woman knowingly violated protocol and compromised server security. I am enjoined from discussing the specifics, but I will tell you that her actions were reckless and a flagrant violation of her terms of employment. When confronted, she became abusive." Arnie downed the dregs of his cocktail, and signaled the waitress that he'd take another.

"Rebecca was a laboratory worker. Why was she hacking into the computers?"

"I don't know."

"This server intrusion—did it have something to do with bitcoin?"

Arnie threw a switch and put on a new expression: puzzlement. The condescension still lay behind it.

"Why do you ask?"

"I spoke to a man who was there at the Siloam meeting. The one where you brought in two grocery bags of cash. You ordered him to turn one of them into bitcoins."

"It's vastly more complicated than that."

"Here's what I see," I said. "Siloam Biologic is a promising start-up, but needs venture capital. You raise that capital from investors in your company TechFolio, and bring it to Siloam so they can get up and running quickly."

Arnie favored me with a tiny nod. "More or less accurate."

"But why do you dictate as part of the deal that Siloam has to take a bag of cash and convert it to bitcoins?"

"Ah. That's where I can't go into details."

"Nondisclosure agreements."

"I'm afraid so. Intellectual property is a bore."

"Fine. So blink once for yes, twice for no. A biotech company like Siloam requires a lot of computing power. You're using some of the space on their big fat servers to mint bitcoins."

"Mine," Arnie snapped. "One *mines* bitcoins."

"Machines invent math problems, and other machines solve them for money. Solve a problem, *mine* a bitcoin. And if you have enough computers solving enough problems, you can generate wealth out of thin air?"

"No. The act of buying, maintaining and operating large banks of servers involves significant costs—"

"Which is why you bring Siloam more cash than they're asking for. You stipulate they use the surplus to power their computers and mine bitcoins for you."

"It's called pay to play."

"Arnie, I understand brokering. What I *don't* understand is why your company would go to all that trouble in the first place. Why spend money turning perfectly green cash into electronic currency?"

"I'm sorry to be tiresome, Jessie, but I did tell you there are details about the mechanics of my business operations I'm not at liberty to discuss."

The next course arrived. Sushi topped with a runny, grayish-green blob. Arnie downed one and started on a fresh cocktail.

"Jessie," he said, "I believe in freedom and I believe in privacy. That's why I started TechFolio. I give ordinary people a place to invest their money with unassailable anonymity, earn a good return, and support innovation. Period."

"What does bitcoin have to do with the relationship between TechFolio and Siloam?"

"I'm certain I would be unable to explain it to you even if I were at liberty to try."

"Use small words."

He sighed and sat back, and went into a monologue about individuating corporate structure for the sequestration of gains and optimal risk management…and I decided it was time for the gloves to come off.

"Is this the kind of shell game that got you arrested for tax evasion back home in Australia?"

Arnie chuckled, and wagged an admonishing finger.

"You've been Googling."

"The internet is a vast and deep sea of everlasting data. Or some such horseshit."

"You must have read I was acquitted. Do you know why?"

"Because—"

"Because I was innocent of any wrongdoing."

"Then why leave Australia?"

"I didn't leave Australia. I came to California. I came to California for the same reason you did, for the same reason everyone does. It's the land of opportunity."

Arnie slid his hand across the table and grasped mine again.

"And I have never looked back," he said.

I've spent enough time in court to recognize a well-rehearsed witness. He has answers in his back pocket and takes them out when he needs them. Barry Taylor used to pull the same stunt. Arnie Spitz was better at it.

"What else did you find?" he asked. He was enjoying himself. My questions were sparring, a come-on. Foreplay.

The next course arrived, half-shell oysters with caviar. "Ah!" said Arnie, "I'm sorry the omakase hasn't been to your liking…but I *know* you're fond of these. Let's enjoy them and then go back to my boat."

"Your boat."

"I'm sure Chef Tawara will forgive—"

"Is it really your boat, Arnie?"

He released my hand and took up an oyster.

"I race her. I'm the skipper."

"But who owns the *Ann Marie?*"

"It's a company boat."

"TechFolio?"

"Siloam, actually. If you must know. They purchased her as a tax shelter. A friend of mine on Siloam's corporate board asked me to do them the honor of racing her—for my pleasure and their bragging rights."

He slurped the oyster and made a show of waving his empty cocktail glass for the waitress. If things didn't end up as planned, Arnie could claim tomorrow he had been drunk on the potent hooch of the exotic East.

"Who's the friend?"

"Oh, come *on!*" he snapped; and in a flash recovered. "Come on, now, Jessie. Why are you interrogating me? Is it this dead girl? Was she murdered? Am I a suspect…?"

"Are you?" I shot back. "Why'd you get Rebecca Corchero fired? Did she find something you didn't want her finding? Or was she just asking too many questions?"

Arnie looked left and right, then held out his wrists with a leer. "Do you have handcuffs?"

"Who's your friend with the boat?"

He ignored me. The waitress came with his fresh drink. He pulled out his phone and started fiddling with it.

"What are you doing?"

"Ordering a car. Let's get out of this place."

"No, Arnie. I'm going home."

Arnie's eyes came off the phone. He was shocked. Finally. "Jessie, be sensible—"

I shook my head. "I'm going home."

"Well…that's a shame."

I stood up from the bamboo table.

"Goodbye, Arnie."

He lifted his drink. He looked bored.

"Goodbye, Czesława."

CHAPTER ELEVEN

"I can have Baby Mike break his legs…"

"You're sweet. But, no."

Sparkle and I were at Caffè Zeffiro for lunch. I didn't have much of an appetite. I told her as much as I was free to tell about my Google search and Arnie's evasions when I'd confronted him with the things I'd found.

"He's hiding something," Sparkle agreed. "Why?"

A good question. Arnie had lied about the boat being his own. He denied getting Rebecca the job at Siloam Biologic, but he was lying about that, too. He clammed up when I pressed him over his cybercurrency business plan. Rebecca had been dabbling in bitcoin investment from her laptop at home and digging around inside Arnie's precious servers from work. What had she seen in there that Arnie didn't want her seeing? I was certain he had arranged to have Rebecca fired. Could it be he had also arranged to have her killed…?

"Who the hell knows?" I said, and discovered to my surprise I'd said it out loud.

Sparkle had a mouthful of sandwich and shrugged in response. I pushed pasta salad around, in no hurry to get back to the office. I had found an email in my inbox that morning with the eye-catching subject line *Probationary Hires Policy*, informing me that as a condition of my employment I was required to keep my open caseload down to twenty at any given time. "Please review the PHP carefully," Dr. Howe's pissy memo advised. "Failure to comply with the provisions therein may result in disciplinary action up to and including dismissal, criminal charges, and/or fines." I had come into work that morning with thirty-one open cases and picked up three new ones. I was on call for the whole coming week, and was certain to land some new homicides, which take ten times more work hours to clear. My open caseload was only going to get heavier.

The fizzling of my brief affair with rich and handsome liar Arnie Spitz had ruined the weekend, and a threat from the boss launched a shitty Monday. To top it all off, right after lunch I was due upstairs in Department 16 for the preliminary hearing in the case of *People v. Josu Azarola*—which meant a face-off between Anup Banerjee and Jackson Heffernan.

The opposing legal teams were just setting up, stacking papers and uncapping pens, when I walked into the courtroom. I greeted Banerjee and nodded at Heffernan.

"I hope you're settling in downstairs," Heffernan said.

"Nicely, thanks."

"You come from Los Angeles, is that right?"

"Boston, originally."

"Bahstin! Pahk the cah in Hahvid Yahd!"

I cringed. He winked.

"Ha ha. Yeah."

A back door opened and a sheriff's deputy escorted the defendant into the courtroom. Joe Azarola was dressed in a business suit, his hair cut conservatively—but underneath was a hard man. You could see it in his shoulders, the tension in his arms. I'd been right about the limp, too: He still had it.

ADA Banerjee started by asking about my qualifications and credentials. Medical school followed by pathology residency at UCLA and forensics fellowship at the Los Angeles County Coroner. Triple board certification. On paper I was impressive. At Banerjee's prompting I went over the specifics of the gunshot wound findings—the three shots in Eugene Chen's torso, back to front, the wounds in each arm, and the fatal bullet to the back of the head.

"What was the cause of death?"

"Multiple gunshot wounds."

"What did you determine was the manner of death?"

"Homicide."

That was pretty much all for the direct examination. ADA Banerjee handed me over to Jackson Heffernan for the cross.

Heffernan rose languidly, wished me a good afternoon, then asked if I'd collected any evidence off the body. I said yes. He asked what it was. I recited the long list from my autopsy report—the gold chains, the mail, the spark plug.

"You found a spark plug on the body?"

"Yes."

"Do you know what that's used for—? Besides running an engine, that is."

"It could be used to break car windows."

"This spark plug you recovered is a hard object that would fit in a fist, and it has a sharp metal point to it, right?"

"Yes."

"Would you agree, in your expert opinion, that it could do a lethal amount of damage to someone's head if wielded as a weapon?"

I thought about that for a moment.

"I've never seen anyone dead of a spark plug wound before."

"Is it possible?"

"It's possible."

Heffernan decided to accept that answer.

"Do you have redirect, Mr. Banerjee?" asked the judge. Banerjee said yes, and rose while Heffernan returned to sit.

"Based on the evidence on the body, you determined that Eugene was shot from behind, is that right?"

"Yes."

"Okay. Where on the body was this spark plug?"

"In the left pants pocket."

"When you visited the death scene, was there anything in Eugene's left hand?"

"No."

"Was there anything in his *right* hand at the death scene?"

"No."

"But you know that there was something in his right hand at the time he was shot, is that right?"

"Yes. A laptop computer."

"How do you know that?"

"According to the police reports, Eugene had stolen a laptop at the café. One of the bullets I recovered from the body ended its track lodged in his right inner forearm. That bullet was deformed, indicating that it had struck or passed through something hard. In that same wound I also found fragments of a laptop computer. This told me he was carrying the stolen laptop in his right hand, across his torso, when he was shot."

"You have testified that the gunshot wound to the back of the head would have been instantly lethal. Eugene was holding the computer in his right hand. So even if he had been gripping that spark plug in his left, he would not have been able to put it back in his pocket before he collapsed, would he?"

"No, he would not."

"No further questions."

Jackson Heffernan had one more shot at me, the recross.

"In your autopsy report you specifically documented finding computer circuitry with partial serial numbers on this debris you pulled out of a bloody wound. That's awfully specific, isn't it?"

I took my time thinking about the right response. Then I said, "If the computer were ever recovered, it could be possible to match it to the evidence found inside the decedent's body. So I considered it important to document that evidence thoroughly."

"Was the computer recovered in this case?"

"Not as far as I know."

"Could that serial number you mention in your report be important for anything else?"

"Objection," said Anup Banerjee. "Your Honor, Dr. Teska is not a computer expert."

"She wrote it down!" Heffernan reached over to the defense table, snatched the autopsy report, and held it up. "I want to know her reason."

"Overruled," the judge said. "Dr. Teska, answer the question if you can."

So I did.

"As I understand it, the serial number can be used to find the computer's unique media access control address. That information can help investigators reconstruct the computer's browsing history at the time and place of the shooting. That's why I noted the numbers I saw on the debris—in case it could help illuminate the circumstances surrounding Eugene Chen's death."

Jackson Heffernan was poleaxed. I stole a glance at Anup Banerjee. He was fighting to maintain his poker face.

Heffernan got a grip. "May I have a moment to confer with cocounsel and my client, your Honor," he said.

Sure, said the judge.

Heffernan slid into his chair behind the defense table and started whispering furiously to another lawyer, a young man with bad hair. Then he whispered to his client. Joe Azarola's expression, hard as nails and fishhooks, changed.

I sat there in the witness box, had a sip of my water, and waited.

After a couple or three minutes Heffernan made some low pronouncement, nodded at the other two men, and sprang up, relaxed and confident again. His hair was less perfect than it had been, though; and his tie just a wee bit askew.

"Dr. Teska. Is the utility of this information something you've discussed with the police and the DA?"

"Yes," I said.

Heffernan stood over the defense table and made a show of running a finger down his yellow legal pad.

"I have no further questions."

The judge thanked me for appearing, and told me I was free to go. I directed a professional smile to Anup Banerjee as I climbed off the witness stand, then turned to Jackson Heffernan and offered him the same overture. He gave me a sideways nod. He seemed to be dictating some internal memo.

Joe Azarola was staring straight ahead. He looked authentically frightened.

I took the elevator back down to the bowels of the Hall of Justice and went straight to my desk, where I fixed my eyes once more on Howe's memo, and then set about clearing old cases to save myself from getting fired. I'd been at it for hours when Anup Banerjee called to give me a debrief.

"You did great today," he said.

"Thanks. I was worried about the computer stuff getting out there."

"Oh, no, it's fine! Helps me, in fact. The idea of us trawling through his client's browser history gives us more to pressure Heffernan with. Did you see the look on his face?"

"He doesn't like surprises."

"Take it from me, no lawyer does!"

"Did Jones and Ramirez come back with anything from the web history yet?"

"No. The subpoenas were easy to get, but then the data went to the police computer lab, and God knows when they'll get around to looking at it. Heffernan doesn't need to know that, though…"

He let slip a diabolical chuckle.

"What was that nonsense with the spark plug?" I asked.

"Heffernan's only hope for mitigation is with a self-defense strategy, and for that he has to establish that his client was in plausible fear for his life."

"His client chased the guy half a block down Geary, putting a bunch of bullets in his back!"

"Heffernan was trying to make the case that Chen was menacing Azarola with that spark plug once he was cornered inside Kim Son 88, and that's why Azarola just simply *had* to kill him. But you put the whole thing to bed with your answer about the head wound. It was sweet!"

"Clearly you enjoy your job."

"Days like this I do—!"

My eyes wandered to the cubicle wall where I'd pinned Howe's threatening memo as incentive to keep putting cases to bed.

"I'm glad you were pleased with the outcome today," I said.

My cell rang at 2:17 a.m. It was the office. Body in a dumpster in a corner of Visitacion Valley called Little Hollywood—the opposite end of the city, exactly as far from my bed as a wee-hours death call could take me.

The cop at the cordon checked my badge and windshield pass. "Bad luck," he said, and pointed down the bleak road flanked by railroad tracks and the empty parking lots of light-industrial buildings. "Hundred yards that way's the county line—and it'd be San Mateo's problem."

I asked him what had brought us together here.

"Dead body in a dumpster. They called out Homicide."

"Why'd they call out Homicide?"

He shrugged. "That's what they do."

Donna and Cameron were waiting by the medical examiner van. I recognized the young man with the flame-red hair and newish suit who emerged from the police scrum as the homicide detective from my July Fourth animal-depredation case. I asked him if there was a coyote involved in this scene. He blushed right up to his naked pink ears and said no.

"What is it, then?"

"Homeless man saw the foot sticking out of the dumpster." He shined a penlight into the dark. It revealed a human foot, bare, probably male, grayish in color.

"Okay. Let's get it out."

"Don't you want to examine the scene?"

"I can't see a damn thing out here, Inspector. You got klieg lights?"

"No."

"Your guys took pictures?"

"Yeah."

behind.

"Then let's get the body out of the dumpster so I can look at it."

I didn't mean to give the rookie detective a hard time, but it was three in the morning in the parking lot of a company that made something called high-build floor epoxy, and I wanted to do my job and go home to a snoring beagle—because, no matter what was attached to that foot, I was going to have to be gowned up in the morgue in a very few hours to autopsy it.

Cam and Donna bitched and moaned as they climbed into the dumpster. I didn't blame them. Cam yelped as something wet went in his shoe. Donna asked the precinct cops to help receive the body when it came over the dumpster's edge. It was wrapped in blankets tied up with extension cords and a belt, the head swaddled in a blue towel. The thing looked like a garbage mummy. It smelled like one, too. We lowered it into a parking lot space marked *Reserved*. A smattering of maggots dropped out of the towel and did calisthenics on the pavement.

I managed to get the head unwrapped. It was a young man; Caucasian; definitely, extremely deceased. I lifted his eyelids to look for petechiae. None. No visible signs of trauma to the head or neck, either. The stench of garbage, paint products, and decomposing corpse was eye-watering.

"What is it?" the rookie homicide inspector asked eagerly.

"Drug dump."

"It's not a homicide?"

"Dollars to doughnuts a drug dump."

"How do you know?"

"Because that's what they always are."

By the time I got home from the Little Hollywood scene, it was nearly five and I had to be up by six thirty. So I fixed myself some coffee and tried to watch the sunrise. There wasn't one. The charcoal sky turned lighter shades of damp, and then it was day.

The autopsy of the dumpster corpse showed a lot of visceral congestion, lungs full of edema, and pink foam in the airway. He was in business-casual attire—minus the missing shoes. His hair was cut neatly, hands clean, no knuckle scars, fingernails in great shape. The rookie detective called me later that afternoon.

"This wasn't his first time with a needle," I told him. "Your decedent has track marks, but it's not like his arms are so scarred over that he was shooting up in the legs or feet, and his liver wasn't fatty or enlarged. Accidental overdose in a regular user of recreational injection drugs."

"Can you say what drugs?"

"The autopsy findings suggest heroin or another opiate, but until tox—"

The detective interrupted me with a groan.

"Soul Sister."

What the hell?

He continued. "I came up from Narcotics. We've been seeing this shit on the street called Soul Sister. It's heroin cut with a synthetic painkiller to give it more kick. It came in from China at first. Now there's a new batch that nobody knows much about, except that it's coming through Mexico, it's super strong, and it's killing junkies."

"The painkiller—is it acetylfentanyl?"

"Yeah! You're seeing it over there?"

"Couple of cases."

"ODs?"

I gave him a moment to rethink that question.

"Oh…right. You only see the dead ones."

"What makes you think our own dead one was using this stuff?"

"He's a regular user, you said. They're the ones overdosing on it. The kick is off the charts, so you only need a little bit to get the same high as you're used to—or better, even. So if you shoot up the same amount of Soul Sister as some of the brown sugar or black tar we usually see? Lights out. Even compared to high-grade white powder heroin, Soul Sister is dangerous."

"Well, Inspector, as we say around here—only tox will tell."

Carlo San Pietro had followed through on his boast: I found a report on case SFME-0955 in my mailbox when I went for a refill of the sludge coffee that keeps the Ops Shop humming day and night. The tox was in, and, with it, the last answers about Rebecca Corchero's death. She had 0.73 mg/liter of 6-MAM in her blood. Six-MAM is a metabolite of heroin, and 0.73 is a whole lot of it—enough to kill a seasoned addict.

Rebecca's roommate last saw her alive at around 8:30 on the night of August 8. Melodie was certain she had turned the dead bolt on the door when she left. When she returned the next morning and discovered the body, the security gate was locked but the dead bolt wasn't. The death scene was locked but not secure.

After Melodie left, Rebecca went to her room to surf the internet and study. At some point she ended up in the front hallway, slumped in a chair. She had a tourniquet and a sloppy injection wound on her left arm, and a used syringe on the table by her right. She was dead of enough heroin to kill a person twice her size, unless she had a high tolerance.

And I was sure Rebecca Corchero hadn't acquired such a tolerance. On autopsy I found no old track marks and no disease or damage to the liver or any other organs. Rebecca was a healthy and athletic nursing student in the first trimester of a pregnancy. She was taking prenatal vitamins. Why had she decided all of a sudden to start a heroin habit?

She hadn't.

Restraint injury. On her right wrist I had found two planes of injury, with abrasions and contusions that matched the lizard bracelet. There was dried blood on that bracelet, and more running down her hand. Someone had grabbed her. Someone held her arm down.

Lacerated frenulum. The tissue inside her lip was torn. That doesn't happen by itself. Someone had clamped a hand over her mouth.

Scleral and conjunctival petechiae. Damage to the capillaries in the whites of her eyes and the insides of her eyelids, from jugular vein compression. Someone had pressed something broad and soft, maybe a pillow or cushioned forearm, across her neck.

Someone had attacked Rebecca Corchero and killed her with a hot shot of Soul Sister.

I clicked open her autopsy report. In the template box for CAUSE OF DEATH, I typed *Acute mixed drug intoxication (heroin and acetylfentanyl)*. In the box below that, OTHER SIGNIFICANT CONDITIONS CONTRIBUTING TO DEATH, I typed *Blunt force trauma with restraint*.

And, finally, I pointed my cursor to the MANNER OF DEATH. In that box I typed *Homicide*.

Then I sat back and watched the cursor blink.

Our investigators had called the case in as a probable accident. The police Crime Scene Unit hadn't visited the scene. Now I was ruling the death a homicide, which meant homicide detectives had to investigate it.

"Hey, Ted," I said. He had a bunch of reports in his hand and was heading out of his cubicle. "I have a case that came in as an accident but now it's a homicide. What do I do with it?"

"Ask Stone," said Ted, and left.

Marvelous. I was already on Mike Stone's shit list, and

this new development would bump me higher. Same with Dr. Howe—the chief had made it perfectly clear, on paper and all official, that he expected me to be closing cases, not complicating them. But now that I was ruling Rebecca Corchero's death a homicide, I had to bring in the police. What was the protocol?

My eyes went to the corkboard behind the computer. A business card, for Keith Albert Jones, Inspector, SFPD Homicide.

"You've got a turd for us?" Jones said when I told him one of my accidents had turned into a homicide. "Glad I'm not on call this week."

"She has textbook restraint injuries, and toxicology just came in. Her levels are so high that it's gotta be a hot shot."

"She have priors for possession?"

"Clean all around. And everyone I've spoken to—family, friends, coworkers—they're all adamant she wasn't a user."

"Okay. So who would want her dead?"

"I can think of three men who might. Ex-boyfriend, ex-boss, and current boyfriend. The current boyfriend is top of my list."

"How come?"

"She was crazy about him and pregnant, and I'm pretty sure he's married."

"Who is he?"

"I don't know. The girl's roommate only knew him by a nickname. Bato."

"Bato."

"That's what the roomie said."

"The roomie could ID him?"

"Yes. And I've got the fetus, so we could do paternity if we need to."

"What about the other two?"

210

"The ex-boss had her fired, but I don't know why—it has to do with high-tech embezzlement or something. The ex-boyfriend worked at the same company and was stalking her after she dumped him."

"How old is this?"

"Nine days."

There was a sharp curse from the other end of the phone.

"You know the seventy-two-hour rule, Doc? There's a reason for it."

"Yeah. So what do I do now?"

"Talk to your chief."

"I was afraid you were going to say that."

"It's way better if it comes to our sergeant from your boss than from you. The sarge will send it down to the duty desk, and you'll hear from whoever catches it."

It was time for more coffee. Then it was time to dot my *i*'s and cross my *t*'s and sign the death certificate. Keith Jones was right: The best way to cover my ass was to deliver the completed case to Dr. Howe first thing in the morning.

I scrutinized the diagnosis section of the autopsy report, then the items submitted into evidence, to make sure that the lizard bracelet and syringe had been logged. Next, the inventory of biological specimens: blood, urine, liver tissue, vitreous fluid, bile, brain material, and the DNA card. Good and tight so far. But there was one thing on my handwritten autopsy sheet that didn't appear in the medical evidence database: the fetal tissue.

Dammit. To close the case I was going to have to go to Carlo San Pietro and endure another lecture to find out why there was a delay in logging the fetal tissue. Worse, it was four minutes past four. I called the lab and a tech confirmed my fear that San Pietro was gone for the day. The tech didn't know anything about logging fetal tissue. She advised me to try again tomorrow.

I wasn't about to let a clerical lag stop me from closing SFME-0955. There had to be a work-around. What if the fetal tissue had never left the morgue? I went down there to check the cold closet. My fresh-samples drawer was empty, so I scanned the shelves until I found the cardboard box for case SFME-0955. Vials of urine and bile and vitreous, and little boxes with bits of brain, liver, etcetera were all labeled in my handwriting—but there was no sign of the fetal tissue.

I was shivering by the time I came out of the cold closet and found Yarina in the autopsy suite, arranging tools for the next morning's work. I asked her if she remembered my case from two weeks ago, a pregnant Asian woman.

"I did this case with you?"

"Yes. I collected the fetus and I need to get it logged before I can close the case."

"I did all tissue collection for last two weeks," Yarina said. "There was no fetus."

"You're sure?"

"I would remember this fetus. It was not there."

"Then where'd it go?"

"The tissues from this case are in computer log?"

"Yes."

"But fetus is not in computer log?"

"Right."

"And you do not find it in the cold closet?"

"Right."

"Then no fetus."

"But…but I need it!"

Yarina stood stony and wordless until I recognized that she had no useful rejoinder to that sentiment.

"Please, Yarina… Couldn't it be somewhere else?"

She softened a little. "Let us look again."

We did. We went through my drawer and all the others. We pulled everything out of the cardboard box for that date range. We slid other boxes around to make sure there wasn't a stray fetus anywhere. There wasn't.

"Perhaps in stock jar?" Yarina offered.

"Perhaps, but I need it for DNA testing. Can't do that with preserved specimens."

"Why DNA?"

"Paternity."

"Oh," said Yarina. "I see. Well."

She looked off and nodded for another silent moment.

"Then, is problem."

Nothing puts a messy homicide investigation out of your mind like a newer and messier one. I was brushing my teeth before bed when the phone rang. It was Cameron Blake on call duty. A shooting in the Posada Village housing projects.

The road narrows when you cross into the projects. The concrete grows cracks and the windows sprout bars. You steer around an old washing machine and a stove dumped in the street. The buildings are long and low and boxy. Their bright paint has bleached into sickly pastels. I showed my badge to the cop blocking the top of Watchman Way, and followed the buckled sidewalk down to the crowd.

The crowd was segregated by race. Chinese and Samoans hung in the back. A single clutch of Hispanic men stood shoulder to shoulder on a stoop. Closest to the crime scene, right by the yellow tape, everyone was black. Three uniformed cops manned the tape line. They were white. The crowd wanted to know what was going on, and the cops wanted the crowd

JUDY MELINEK & T.J. MITCHELL

to back off. The crime scene photographer's flash bounced back off the faces at the cordon line. The children were curious. The adults were angry.

Watchman Way dead-ends at a weedy slope stretching down to the freeway, littered with every imaginable type of city jetsam. The noise and stink funnels up the hill and rebounds off the shoebox buildings. It is as bleak a spot as I have seen in San Francisco. A pair of homicide detectives elbowed through the uniforms to tell me they had a presumptive decedent ID based on witness statements. The crowd at the cordon line saw us conferring, and their overlapping demands got louder.

That's my cousin!

Is it Jamie G?

Let me in!

What are you doing?

Cutting through those voices, a woman keened, "I want to see my baby!"

I pulled on a pair of gloves and asked the photographer if she was almost finished.

The decedent was fifteen or sixteen, male, African American with a light complexion, a coltish kid who hadn't yet grown into his big hands and feet. He was sprawled face-down on the pavement in a pool of blood. He wore a Raiders jacket and baggy pants. His hair was cut short, and I could see a bullet entrance wound above the back of his right ear.

The photographer gave me the go-ahead to take over. I pushed up his jacket and pointed a flashlight. At least five more gunshot wounds on his upper back and shoulders. At first glance they all looked like entrances—round defects with raw edges and no laceration. The paramedics had left three EKG leads on the dead boy's back before I'd arrived, when they'd declared him dead and got their ambulance the hell out of there.

I asked Donna to help me roll the body. The bullet to the back of the head had come out under his left eye, leaving only raw meat and splintered bone where his nose should have been. Seepage ecchymosis—blood pulled by gravity—had settled in the soft tissues around the eye socket, distorting it into a grotesque purple balloon. If that really was the boy's mother calling out to us, there was no way we were going to ask her to make a visual ID.

When I pushed up the corpse's clothing to look for exit wounds on his torso, his arms pivoted and his hands flopped. I heard a voice yell that Jamie G was moving. He was still alive.

Why's there no ambulance?

I seen it leave an hour ago!

Where's the other medics?

Why won't you help him!

A gray-haired cop keyed his shoulder mic. "Ten twenty-five, Posada Village Watchman Way, all available units, all available…" I told the lead detective we'd do the fingerprinting and gunshot residue tests back at the morgue, and Cam hurried to slip brown paper bags over the dead boy's hands. Donna fastened the bags with zip ties around his wrists. Somebody near the cordon line yelled that we were flex-cuffing Jamie G even though he was still down and still covered in blood, and the crowd got a lot uglier. The uniformed police had batons across forearms, shoving the first line away from the yellow tape. One cop threatened to start swinging.

Cam unrolled a body bag. While he and Donna were shuffling the body into it, I spotted something in the puddle of blood where his head had been.

"Wait, don't zip it," I said.

I picked up the object with my gloved right hand. It was a stumpy piece of metal—maybe an expended slug. It could be evidence that the kid had already been down, prone, when he was shot in the head. I got the CSI photographer to take a couple of pictures, then pulled my right glove inside out and tied a knot, sealing the bullet. I tossed the glove into the body bag. Chain of evidence.

The police started clearing a path for the morgue van. People were crammed across the street and spilling onto walkways. I found some space to slip along the edge of the crowd. A young woman in a nightshirt and slippers saw the words MEDICAL EXAMINER on my windbreaker and stopped me.

"Is he dead?"

"Yes," I said.

"Why you won't let us see him?" demanded someone else, unseen, from the group behind her. I said nothing and kept making my way through the crowd. People—women and men, young and old—were moving in all directions, some hustling children toward the apartment buildings, many texting or talking on cell phones with expressions of worry and purpose. I came upon a group surrounding one woman who was crying silently. She came to meet me.

"That's my baby. That's my baby…! I want to see my baby!"

Her eyes were red, her hands shaking with grief. Even with the distorting damage to the dead boy's face, I could see a family resemblance.

"I'm… I'm sorry. He's not in a condition where you can see him right now. It'll be better once he's in the funeral home and…he's clean."

An elderly woman behind the dead boy's mother said, "What do you mean, *clean?*"

"He has blood on his face."

The mother's eyes went wide. "They shot Jamion *in the face?*"

She broke down and took her head in her hands, sobbing, wailing. I reached out and put my hand on her shoulder—

"Don't you touch her!"

I turned and found a man, burly, late-twenties, towering over me. He, too, looked a lot like the dead boy; a future that skinny kid would never have. He was spitting with hurt and rage.

"Get your hands off her! What's wrong with you?"

The boy's mother was still wailing. She hadn't looked up. I pulled away.

"I have to go," I said. "I have to go…"

I hustled through the crowd and the crowd let me, and I found myself alone on Watchman Way. The noise fell away. I made it to the cop with the cruiser at the top of the hill. He ignored me, head bent to the overlapping voices on his lapel radio. Another block, and I reached my Beemer.

I waited for the medical examiner van, running its yellow light bar, to come up the hill. I pulled behind to follow it—and jerked the steering wheel when something thumped against my door, loud. Out of the corner of my eye I saw figures on a slope above us, between two buildings. They were in motion. Pitching. A bottle hit the morgue van and shattered on its roof. I drove right through the glass as it rained down. Cam gunned the van. Sparks flew off its undercarriage when it hit a dip at the bottom of the hill and hauled ass up the other side. I pushed the Beemer to close the gap. Three police cars came at us and blurred past.

Cam braked hard and whipped right onto 20th Street, then slowed. I loosened my grip on the wheel and allowed a few feet between our bumpers.

I fought back tears for the boy's mother. I had screwed up. I made it worse for her. What good came of telling that poor woman that her child's corpse wasn't fit to view? It was a clumsy response to a cold, shitty situation: Your son is dead, and you can't be there for him, can't hold him, can't stroke his hair. All that's left of your boy is evidence. His young body, not yet cold, is evidence in a crime. How do you tell a mother that? How do you show up outside her home and spirit her baby away?

Brain first then mouth, Czesia. When will you learn? The fatal words MEDICAL EXAMINER are blazoned across your back. You're the angel of death. Do not reach out and touch people. Don't put your hands on anyone who isn't going back to the morgue with you.

At a stop sign I noticed amber fog lights in my rearview, well behind us. I followed Cam as he zigzagged the next couple of blocks. The amber lights did, too. When we turned left onto Mississippi Street, I slowed and kept my eyes in the Beemer's side mirror. The amber lights belonged to a Dodge Charger, a stepped-on muscle car with an oversize hood, fenders like shoulder pads, and a face mask grille. There were two people in it. A cigarette blinked in the passenger's mouth.

White lights and red lights snaked against each other on the Bay Bridge approach below us, with the skyscrapers beyond. On the next block, Mississippi Street pitched downhill, steep, plunging into the South of Market flatlands. Someone was following the Medical Examiner van, turn for turn, away from a crime scene and back to the morgue. I reached for my phone to alert Cam and Donna—but didn't dial. I figured first I'd go around the block and come up behind the Dodge. I could keep it in sight and get a plate number if we needed to involve the police. At 17th Street I banged a hard right.

So did the Dodge. They weren't following the morgue van. They were following me.

Seventeenth Street cranked around a dogleg and bounced over some potholes, then came out under the 280 freeway. I spotted an on-ramp and took it. The amber fog lights kept their distance, but followed. I accelerated and merged. The Dodge took another lane and held back ten car lengths. It was after eleven o'clock and traffic was light. I stayed at 65. He didn't pass. I slowed to 55, then 50. The Dodge did too. I watched the rearview and counted thirty seconds. Then I dropped a gear and put the hammer down.

The Beemer jumped to 70 and I whipped into the left lane. The yellow lights paced me. I went to 75 and swung across to the right lane, putting a couple of slower cars between us. The Dodge shouldered its way around them. I notched it up to 80. I was still pumped up on adrenaline from Watchman Way, and putting some real speed under my tires fed it.

We were coming up on the 280/101 split. At the last second I braked and swerved hard to the left, over the painted triangle of freeway exit no-man's-land. I heard horns from far back. Someone shot across my rearview, making the same move. We reached the 101's flat causeway stretch, about ten minutes from the airport—and its police substation. I floored the accelerator. We hit 85, and the fog lights started catching up. I went to 90. I went beyond.

My heart was racing. I concentrated on breathing steady. When we reached the end of the causeway and went into a curve, I cut from left to right in a slingshot. The Dodge did too. The traffic got a little heavier and I made use of it, bobbing and weaving, gripping the road and taking every inch I could. We came on a rising right curve. There were no cars ahead of me. I pushed the Beemer to 110 miles an hour.

I took my eyes off the rearview while I concentrated on the hill. The Beemer leaned into the curve and then evened out as the road straightened. I looked back.

No amber lights. I checked again. Nothing. The Dodge Charger had given up.

I loosened my grip on the wheel and eased back on the gas. My speed dropped down to 90 just as I reached the merge of an on-ramp. Just as the corner of my eye caught the cruiser in the bushes.

Then everything went bright blue and flashing.

CHAPTER TWELVE

The California Highway Patrol trooper kept me sitting by the side of the freeway while he took his sweet time writing me up, leaving Donna and Cam to wait in the morgue for more than an hour. By the time we ran fingerprints on the dead boy from Watchman Way and I got back home to bed, it was nearly three o'clock. Bea's baying got me up at six thirty. It was a good thing that Mike Stone made brief work of presenting the day's cases, or I might have fallen asleep at morning meeting.

I reached for the case file from the Watchman Way call, but Stone snatched it off the table.

"Ted," he said, "this is yours."

Nguyen scowled but kept his mouth shut and took it.

"That's my homicide from last night," I said.

"Come see me in my office after we cut," said Stone.

Every pair of eyes in the room was on me. I said okay.

I did two cases, both naturals, at the table next to Nguyen, who made a meal of bitching and moaning his way through the Watchman Way homicide. I finished quickly, cleaned up, and went to Stone's office. He sat at his desk in rolled-up shirtsleeves, his arms crossed in a way that let him massage the blood-donation scars in the crooks of both elbows with the fingertips of the opposite hands. He was scanning a hospital chart, and didn't bother looking up when I came through the door.

"Why did you turf my homicide to Ted?"

Mike peered over his reading glasses. "You have an order to appear before the traffic court, upstairs in this very building, on a charge of excessive speed and reckless operation of a motor vehicle?"

"*That's* why? A speeding ticket?"

"The trooper clocked you at ninety-two miles an hour. Then, apparently, you pulled your badge and tried to get out of it by telling him a tale about a phantom assailant who was chasing you away from a crime scene? He reported this to his captain, who thought it was serious enough to call me up and give me a piece of his mind about the way I train my staff."

Oh great. This CHP captain must be one more of the cops Mike Stone had pissed off in his long career of pissing off cops. I reflected privately that it was a good thing the trooper hadn't caught me while I was going a buck ten.

"Mike, my car has a dent in the rear panel where someone in Posada Village hit it with a rock. I saw a bottle break over the van's roof! The scene was dangerous enough, and then a car—"

"You realize I could put you on probation right now over this? It's a criminal charge."

"It's a speeding ticket!"

"It's an order to appear before a judge."

He wasn't kidding. So I took a breath, counted to three, and gave him the answer he was looking for.

"I regret my reckless overreaction to a perceived threat. I'll pay the ticket and it won't happen again."

I turned to leave.

"Jessie," Stone said, "we aren't done. Please sit down."

I did. He took off his reading glasses and laced his fingers. "You lost a fetus?"

The gentle way he said it brought me back to the confessional booth in St. Michael the Archangel—butterflies in my stomach and cramps in my knees, the sound of the wooden screen sliding.

"Yarina told me you spent nearly an hour yesterday tearing apart the morgue, looking for Rebecca Corchero's fetus."

Kurwa.

"Yes. We didn't find it."

"Well. That's no good."

"I know. I'm certain I collected the sample during the autopsy and put it in the cold drawer immediately after, but it never ended up in the specimen log. Yarina came to you because she's covering her ass."

"No, she is scrupulous about tissue specimens. And you, Jessie, are the doctor of record. Losing a specimen is bad practice—and it's especially unseemly when you lose a fetal specimen. Rebecca was only—what?—twelve weeks pregnant?"

"Yes."

"So this lost sample was really the entire fetus. All of five centimeters?"

"Something like that."

"Are you sure you didn't drop it in the stock jar?"

"I distinctly remember putting it in the cold drawer. I was

showing the students how we log samples. But, yes, I checked the stock jar, too. It's not there."

Stone nodded. He turned to his computer.

"Listen. I know Dr. Howe has been concerned about your caseload and backlog. That's why I took today's homicide away from you and gave it to Ted. I'm taking you off the call rotation until you catch up."

"What! Mike, you don't need to do that. I can pull my weight…"

"We'll see. Start with the Corchero case. Why haven't you closed it yet?"

"I'm ruling it a homicide. That's why I was looking for the fetal tissue, in case I need it for paternity testing."

Stone assumed a bewildered look.

"Corchero is an accidental overdose."

"No it isn't. I got the full tox report. She had too much heroin on board for an accidental OD. Somebody gave her a hot shot."

"What's the level?"

I told him about the 0.73 milligrams per liter of 6-MAM in the peripheral blood. About the open dead bolt at the scene. The restraint injury with fresh bleeding on Rebecca's wrist. The torn frenulum, the petechiae. Stone's head was shaking before I'd even finished. The bewilderment was gone from his face. In its place was a pitying worry.

"When did you put all this together, Jessie?"

"Yesterday."

"Why didn't you come to me with it?"

I said nothing. I didn't need to remind my boss how often he'd been blowing his top lately.

"There's nothing new in this litany apart from the blood morphine—and that's within range for an accident."

"Not at point seventy-three it isn't! That's a hot shot."

"Nonsense. Rebecca Corchero was a naive user—a first-timer, probably. She was experimenting with drugs, and she shot herself up with too much heroin. Period. It happens all the time."

"That doesn't mean it happened this time."

"There's some very dangerous stuff out there lately. Heroin with acetylfentanyl. Was this—"

"It's being called Soul Sister. And, yes, that's what came up in the tox. But it doesn't matter! Don't you see, Mike? The point seven-three morphine level alone is high enough to kill her—just the heroin, never mind the fentanyl!"

Mike Stone sneered. "How many ODs have you done? Total, I mean."

"I don't know."

"Couple dozen?"

"Sure."

"I'd have to check my log, but I'll wager I've done a couple *thousand*. I've seen levels higher than that in accidental overdoses. I've seen naive users make stupid and fatal errors in the cook-up. I've seen it all—and I'm telling you, this is no different. It's a simple case. Close it and move on to the next one in your backlog."

I pointed to a big red book on his desk.

"Baselt says—"

"Baselt says the range of blood tox data in fatal heroin overdose is *wide*. It depends on the user's tolerance, body mass, the purity of the product, a million things. Have you talked to the homicide division about this yet?"

"I was going to bring the case to Dr. Howe and ask for his help figuring out what to do with it."

Stone laughed coldly. "You're going to float this theory to the chief? Seriously? You're already in hot water with him over your backlog, and now you're going to try to convince him this slam-dunk accident is a new homicide—to *add* to that backlog? I'd reconsider that plan if I were you."

"The evidence is all there. It's a homicide."

Stone's chair squealed as he sat back.

"Evidence? Let me tell you about the hole you're digging for yourself here. If you rule Corchero as a homicide, you'll be impeached in court over the *lack* of evidence. The drug levels are not compelling. There's not nearly enough trauma. Where's the broken hyoid? The busted lip, bloody teeth? How about the scene—no breaking and entering, no stolen goods. There's no police report about neighbors hearing screams and a struggle. There's no police report at all! That's because this is an accidental OD, Jessie."

Stone looked down at his desk and shook his head. "Neither Dr. Howe nor I can back you up if you call this case a homicide."

He didn't couch it as a threat. Dr. Michael Stone seemed worried for me—for us, for the Office of Chief Medical Examiner. Very worried.

He pressed the fingers of one hand against his forehead. "And—wait—now you lost the dead woman's fetus? Okay, if the manner of death is accident, then all you've done is lose a biological specimen. That's an in-house disciplinary matter. But if this is a homicide? Then you've lost *evidence*. You'd be in deep shit. That's a career-breaking transgression."

He pivoted his computer screen around so I could see it. "Look. You have thirty-six open cases. Eight of them are homicides. *Real* homicides. Tackle those. Get your numbers down. You're off the call schedule and restricted to working in the morgue until you do."

"You're putting me on probation?"

"I'm giving you space to get your work done in a conscientious manner, and not screw anything else up."

"Mike—"

"No." He didn't raise his voice, but he was not fucking around. "No way. Get your caseload down. First, close Corchero—*today*. Then go back and hit your open files, starting with the oldest ones. Show me you can handle the ordinary workload in this office, and we'll talk about putting you back on homicides."

Mike Stone swiveled his computer screen back away from me. "Close the door behind you," he said.

Sparkle took one look at me and said, "I keep a bottle of emergency whiskey."

I declined and flopped into a chair. I told her about Stone's decision to take me off homicide duty. About my job—maybe my career—hanging by a thread.

"Shit. Well, then. I'm treating lunch."

"No, I'm gonna get a burrito and go right back to my desk."

"The hell you are. You're coming with me to Chinatown." Sparkle grabbed a frilled leather jacket, which matched her plum beret in color and her earrings in costume-jeweled trim. "I have some papers to serve up there. We're gonna eat at a place I know. The air will do you good."

Sparkle was right. It was a glorious day—sunshine, the barest breeze, fog falling off the hills. It felt like emerging on the steps of St. Michael's in Lynn after making those ten Hail Mary's and five Glory Be's as penance, the stale smell of pooling wax giving way to seagulls and salt air. We marched toward Market Street, passing a playground where nannies and young parents clung to the shade of a scrawny olive tree. A loose pack of boys chased pigeons while a toddler banged out the same two notes over and over on a carillon. Sparkle led the way up to Grant Avenue, dodging the lunch-hour suits pouring from skyscrapers into Union Square. I hustled to keep up.

"You're smiling," Sparkle observed.

"Memories of home. This could be downtown Boston on a summer day—when it isn't hazy, hot, and humid, that is."

We passed under the Dragon Gate and into Chinatown. Sparkle paused outside a souvenir shop and sat on a bench with bronze statues of three monkeys seeing, hearing, and speaking no evil. She patted a seat next to the see-no-evil monkey for me.

"Why'd you leave home?" she asked.

"Medical school. I went out to UCLA and fell in love with the place. Palm trees, and people live here—? They aren't on vacation—they actually *live* here? I stayed put for pathology residency and forensics fellowship. Eight years of training. At the end of it I was offered a position at the Los Angeles County Coroner. My dream job."

"You had a good boss in LA?"

"Dr. Emil Kashiman. The best."

"So why'd you leave *there?*"

I rubbed the speak-no-evil monkey's cool metal ear.

"Another time."

"A guy."

"No."

"Oh, come on. Had to be a guy. A guy at work?"

"I don't want to talk about it."

Sparkle relented, reluctantly. The two of us sat there between the monkeys and watched the crowd until I reminded her that I couldn't be AWOL all afternoon. She led me down the hill on Clay Street, under the white needle of the Transamerica Building. We passed at least three dodgy massage parlors on a single block before Sparkle announced that we'd reached the restaurant.

I looked at the sign. "Sparkle," I said, "this is a Vietnamese restaurant."

"So?"

"We're in *Chinatown*."

"Only tourists eat Chinese food in Chinatown. This place is the best."

And she was right. The food was great, and Sparkle didn't try to grill me about LA anymore. A steady stream of pedestrians flowed by, and we cracked each other up trying to guess their stories. I almost put the San Francisco Office of Chief Medical Examiner out of my mind.

Before heading back we made a stop for Sparkle's errand. A sign, *Bookkeeping and International Tax Services Enrolled Agent*, pointing to the second floor of a three-story brick building. On the ground floor was a jewelry store. I told Sparkle I'd window-shop and wait for her.

She wouldn't be but five minutes, she said. Maybe ten, tops.

I tried to distract myself from the memory of Mary Catherine Walsh in the Los Angeles morgue. She'd been in my head ever since I'd left Stone's office. His recriminations about Rebecca's missing fetus brought me circling back to Mary and hers, dead at twelve weeks just like Rebecca's. I had my eyes on a display window of gold chains, but all I could see was the suicide note in blue ink, the prescription bottle, the chalky white pills that killed Mary Walsh.

I trusted Sparkle. She'd been dead right about Arnie. She'd become an invaluable friend when I had too few—especially as the atmosphere in the OCME grew more poisonous. Our lunches together were salvation. I couldn't bring myself to tell Sparkle about Mary Walsh. I couldn't bring myself to risk losing her friendship; not now.

"Someday," I said aloud. But I didn't believe it.

A heavily jeweled Asian woman came out of the store to ask if she could help me. I said no thanks.

"A pretty lady like you should have something nice today. I will show you something."

She started talking pearls. I wasn't interested but nodded along to her pitch anyways. I looked over the jade and turquoise behind the pearls, and my eye went up to a painted sign over the window. It said *Gold, Sterling Silver, Gifts*, and under that a phrase, two words long, listed in at least a dozen foreign languages. The ones I couldn't read were Chinese, Japanese, Arabic, Russian. Right under Russian I was pleased to find Polish.

Kamienie Szlachetni the words said. It meant *precious stones*. I half wanted to point out the misspelling to the jeweler: It should be *Szlatchetne* with an *e*, not an *i*.

"Now, with your green eyes, maybe you want emerald, but I want you to try my amethyst instead..." She led me toward the door inside. I smiled off and said thanks but no thanks, and turned to go.

Then I stopped. In the window sign, well under *Kamienie Szlachetni*, another phrase caught my eye. It read *Mahalagang Bato*.

"Excuse me," I said. "This here, *Mahalagang Bato*. What language is that?"

The saleswoman's face clouded in irritation. She squinted at the sign. "Tagalog. Philippines language."

"What... Can you tell me what it means?"

"Jewels."

"Yes, but it's two words."

She scrutinized me, trying to decide if it was worth her time to humor the crazy lady. She poked her head inside and called to someone.

Another woman appeared. She was shorter, younger, with big, kind eyes.

"My friend. She speak Tagalog."

I asked her the same question.

"Mahalagang Bato?"

"Yes. What does it mean, exactly?"

"Precious stone," the woman said.

I darted to the window and pointed.

"This word, *Mahalagang*, what is it?"

"Precious."

"So *Bato* is—"

"Stone. *Bato* is stone."

Both women were now watching me with concern. I was reeling.

Bato is Stone.

I squeaked some rubber getting onto Harrison Street, weaved through Hayes Valley traffic and squeezed the yellow lights all the way out to the drab two-story house at 1461 30th Avenue. Rebecca Corchero's roommate Melodie Ortiz was not pleased to see me again. I told her I had one quick question, and then I'd be out of her hair and on my way.

"What is it?"

I pulled out my phone. On it was a screenshot from the article about Mike Stone's RICO testimony.

"Do you recognize this man?"

Melodie looked at the screen. Her eyelashes flashed wide.

"That's him!"

I held the phone out, told her to take it. "Are you absolutely certain? Is that the man you saw in the taxi with Rebecca?

The man you bumped into in your house while he was wearing her bathrobe?"

"Oh yeah. That's him all right. That's Rebecca's *bato*."

I took the phone back.

"Okay," I said.

"Wait—" said Melodie. "Who is it?"

I was already halfway down the brick staircase. "Thanks for your help," I said.

I parked the Beemer in Golden Gate Park and paced circles in an empty meadow.

"That's some funny fucking stunt, Becca. Your own little Bato, Michael Stone. Hilarious."

What now?

I pulled out my phone. Dial 911? And say what, exactly—? My boss is a murderer? The victim ID'd him a day late and a dollar short—and in code? In *Tagalog*?

"Motive, means, opportunity."

Motive was easy. Rebecca Corchero dumped Neil Dupree last year for another man. That man was Mike Stone. Rebecca figured her roomie Melodie would run into Stone now and again no matter how careful they were, so she assigned him the code name Bato and never—but never—talked about him. No one at Siloam Biologic knew anything about her love life. She shut down Neil Dupree's attempts to win her back by misdirecting him about her new medical student "boyfriend."

So, yeah, Rebecca Corchero was careful. Not careful enough, though, at least in one traditionally crucial regard. How did Mike Stone react when he found out she was pregnant? According to Melodie's account, Rebecca was in love with Mike. She came from a devout family. She was taking prenatal vitamins. She was going to bear that child. Tommy and I saw Rebecca in tears outside Stone's Sea Cliff palace during the Fourth of July festivities. Had Mike been making the usual promises to her, that he'd leave it all behind? Had she decided he was full of shit, and told him so? Or maybe she was trying to use the baby as leverage, and it wasn't working...?

"Conjecture," I warned myself. "And you don't even need it."

No, I didn't need to know what was going on in Rebecca Corchero's head in order to establish Michael Stone's motive for killing her. I'd heard the shouting match over the phone with Sophia—she knew her husband was screwing around. How was he going to keep denying it if Rebecca bore his child? In a divorce under those circumstances, Stone would lose big. He might even lose the thing he most values in this world—his daughter, Calliope. Hell, he'd lose Callie, divorce or no, the day she found out he'd been sneaking around with her beloved nanny. Her BFF, her surrogate big sister.

So Mike Stone had plenty of motive. Easy opportunity, too. He only had to make sure Melodie was out of the apartment for long enough, ring the doorbell, and unfold that toothy smile. Once inside, Stone cajoled or forced Rebecca into the lumpy hall chair, held her down, and stuck a hot shot of heroin in her arm.

"But what about that hot shot?" I sat on a cut tree stump and watched a pill bug flee under its ragged bark. "We've got motive and opportunity. So how about the means?"

Well, first of all Stone had successfully made it look like an accidental overdose. He left the syringe on the table next to Rebecca's dominant hand, the tourniquet still around her arm. He was careful to disturb nothing else, and slam-locked the door on his way out. He left the body right where it lay, even if it seemed like a weird place to shoot up. Killers tip us off to their faked accidents by trying too hard to dress the scene, dragging the corpse around. Stone knew that from his own crime scene experience. He knew he had to keep it simple.

So the police treated the apartment as a death scene but not a crime scene. No police investigation meant no canvass of the neighbors, no witness interviews by a detective. Stone knew that he could steer whoever caught the autopsy, me or Nguyen, to manner it an accident. He'd been pushing me in that direction every chance he got, and now was openly ordering me to sign off case number SFME-0955 and make it go away.

"Oscar material when you pretended to learn she was dead, Mike." That afternoon in his office, after he turned white and teared up and started stammering about how devastated Callie was going to be, he sent me on a goose chase after Neil Dupree. And he...

Boże mój.

He told me *he* would call Rebecca's family in the Philippines. Better they should learn it from me, Mike said. Then he gave the Corcheros his bullshit line about the letter of noncontagion, and convinced them to let him cremate the body. I couldn't reexamine the body's wounds after he destroyed the evidence.

"But the body never lies."

Rebecca had fought him, and Stone couldn't avoid inflicting those restraint injuries that I found on autopsy. She had abrasions to her wrist. She had petechiae and a torn frenulum. Sure, he had doubtless worn gloves so he wouldn't leave fingerprints behind. But he left assaultive damage in Rebecca's flesh.

Wait. He left something else, too. His DNA—in the fetus. That's why it disappeared. Dr. Michael Stone has access to the morgue cold closet anytime he wants.

"I'll bet he fucking flushed it."

I headed for my Beemer. Only one thing was still missing: The murder weapon. I had a good idea where I could find it.

I turned the key and the loading dock's electric lock clicked. The doors slid open and I hustled through the sally port, past a body on a gurney awaiting funeral home pickup. As soon as I cleared the air lock's swinging doors, I could hear Mike Stone's voice, at its usual booming volume, coming from his office down the corridor. He was on the phone with someone at a hospital, trying to get radiology on a case.

I slipped into my own office and fired up the computer. In the OCME's database I found Stone's notes from the autopsy he performed on July 6: Graciela Natividad, SFME-0736.

Upon resection of the bowel there are 17 bindles of gray-specked white crystalline material wrapped in layers of latex condoms, each measuring approximately 3 to 4 cm in diameter. One of the bindles has ruptured and apparently spilled its contents in the bowel, but is still partially full.

Okay. Seventeen bindles.

I went to the Natividad autopsy photos and scrolled through gory thumbnail images. There were in situ pictures of the bindles as Stone ran his scissors down the intestine to remove them. He also had a close-up of the burst condom, chalky white powder visible through a tear in the latex. One of the last autopsy photos showed the bindles immediately after Stone removed them, white blobs against the blue of his cutting board. I counted them. Seventeen, including the fatal ruptured one. I toggled back into the database and found the evidence list for SFME-0736. A technician in the toxicology lab had logged them into evidence at 14:04 that same day.

The toxicology tech had logged sixteen bindles.

The corridor was silent but for the buzz of the lights. Stone's office door was open. I slipped past it and down to the tox lab, and touched the bare wires of the doorbell together. A chipper young technician answered and led me to the evidence room, where she sorted through boxes and found the right evidence envelope.

Michael Stone had signed the red tape sealing the flap. I cut open the envelope, dumped its contents, and counted. Sixteen bindles, the broken one preserved in a thermoplastic bag and labeled with a biohazard warning. I counted again to be sure.

Sixteen.

I thanked the technician, returned the bindles to the envelope, and signed the red evidence tape myself to preserve chain of custody. The tech put the envelope back in the box and made a joke about how, if that was my idea of examining evidence, I was now her favorite doctor. I joked back that my trip to the lab was really just a ruse to get out of the morgue and talk to living people for a change. She thought that was a riot. I faked a good-natured grin.

I knew the toxicology technician only in passing. She seemed like a sweetheart. Part of me was glad I hadn't caught her in a serious error, miscounting drug bindles.

There had been no error. Michael Stone took seventeen condoms stuffed with heroin out of Graciela Natividad's cecum, and submitted sixteen into evidence. Between the morgue and the tox lab, one bindle of Soul Sister had gone missing. A hot shot of identical heroin later killed Rebecca Corchero.

I was ready to go to Howe.

The chief's door was open. He waved me in. He was enjoying a set of blueprints that paved over the detritus on his massive desk.

"The future is now, Dr. Teska!" Dr. Howe said, and swept a hand across the expanse of ink lines. "Funded, approved, and ready to start construction."

He flopped happily into his swivel chair and asked me to take a seat. The only space that wasn't covered in case files and legal briefs was one corner of the sofa, and the shotgun with a toe tag tied to its trigger guard was still leaning there, gathering dust.

Howe noticed me eyeing it. "Evidence from an old suicide. I keep it there for PD recruits when they come through on training. They have a hard time understanding the mechanics of suicide with a long-barreled weapon if they don't see that method demonstrated."

I took a seat on the couch, under the gun, with the Corchero file in my lap. I had to be clinical. I had to treat this case like any other, like a presentation at Howezit Goin' rounds. So I told Dr. Howe the case history. In the course of a death investigation, I had discovered that his deputy chief, Dr. Michael Stone, had been in a sexual relationship with my decedent, a twenty-four-year-old woman named Rebecca Corchero. Corchero was found dead with drug paraphernalia in her unsecured apartment. There was evidence of restraint injury. Tox came back positive for heroin in the peripheral blood, at a level that was certain to have been fatal to a naive user. On autopsy I had found a fetus near the end of the first trimester of gestation. Scene evidence suggested the decedent had intended to bring the pregnancy to term.

I had discovered that Michael Stone deceived the Corchero

family into cremating the body. Then I had found that the fetus went missing somewhere between the morgue's cold closet and the tox lab. Also missing was a bindle of heroin from one of Dr. Stone's earlier cases, a body-packing drug mule. The heroin in that case had precisely the same chemical signature as the drugs that killed Rebecca Corchero.

Dr. Howe's lips formed a thin line. Somewhere behind them he was processing furiously; but he didn't say one word. I lost my grip on clinical neutrality and got to my feet.

"Mike destroyed the fetus and saw to it that Rebecca's body was destroyed, too. Now he's ordered me to sign out her death as an accident. I won't. This is a homicide. Mike Stone injected Rebecca Corchero with that heroin from the Hotel Somerville mule. He killed her and he's trying to cover it up."

"Jessie…"

"Yes."

"Won't you please sit back down."

I returned to the sofa.

Dr. Howe pressed his palms together, silent. Then he said, "Have you contacted the police?"

"No. I…wouldn't know who to call. I didn't want some detective showing up here and arresting Mike without you knowing it was going to happen."

"Good. You did right. Is that the case folder?"

"Yes."

"Let me have it."

I did.

"Thank you for coming to me," Dr. Howe said, leafing through the file. "Be aware that I will be obliged to initiate an internal investigation." He closed the folder and placed it carefully on the desk. Then he locked his eyes on mine.

"Does anyone else know?"

"No."

"You are not to discuss this matter with anyone other than me."

"I won't."

"*No one*. Do you understand that, Jessie?" His gaze hadn't wavered and he hadn't blinked.

"Yes, Dr. Howe."

He rose. I did too.

"Don't worry," the chief medical examiner said. "I'm going to make sure this is handled properly. Everything will work out."

Dr. James Howe proffered the smile we usually reserve for a decedent's next of kin, and steered me out his office door.

CHAPTER THIRTEEN

I was surprised to find Mike Stone running Thursday's morning meeting. What the hell was he doing at work? The best I could figure was that Dr. Howe didn't want to confront him until he could get Mike alone—after we had cut our cases and separated into our own offices for paperwork. It was a light day; one each: suicide, accident, natural. Mike took the suicide, gave Ted Nguyen the natural, and assigned me the accident—an elderly man who tripped down the brick stairs of his apartment in Russian Hill on his way to the farmers market, his Wednesday routine.

"He had his canvas shopping bags in hand," Cameron Blake reported, "wallet still in his pocket when a neighbor found him. No signs of foul play. Medics took him to the General where he coded during surgery for a subdural." He slid the folder across the table.

"Don't say I never throw you a bone, Jessie," Mike Stone said, and twirled a pen playfully.

I stifled a shudder and smiled a glare. Let's see how cocksure you feel in an orange jumpsuit, Mike. I hope the boys in

Homicide take a rubber hose to you before they perp-walk your sorry ass the long way to the jail upstairs. I devoutly hope they do.

When the meeting broke up, I buttonholed Cameron. "What's he doing here?" I whispered.

"Who?"

"Mike."

"What do you mean?"

"Didn't Dr. Howe… Did he say anything about Mike?"

"Dr. Howe's not in yet. I don't know what you're talking about. Something up with Mike?"

"I… I can't discuss it."

Cam was coming off the night shift, tired already. Now he was tired and peeved. "You asked me the question, Doctor," he said, and left me alone in the conference room.

I chose the autopsy table farthest from Stone's and made quick work of the dead man from Russian Hill, then retreated to my office, ignored the flashing message light on my phone, and managed to clear three of my old cases. If I walked over to grab a quick lunch from El Herrador, I could close several more before the day was done.

Outside the Hall of Justice, I got stalled behind a knot of people at the crosswalk light. An aging frat-boy type with slicked hair flashed me a smile too cocky by half. I returned it with courtesy but no encouragement. As the light turned and the crowd untangled, I saw another man checking me out, this one in his midtwenties, pasty, with a bramble of black hair and a double chin boldfaced in stubble. When our eyes met, he broke right off and joined the crowd peeling away toward the Bear Flag Deli.

I went the other way, toward Sparkle's office. It was closed and dark, but through the window I saw someone moving in the back room, so I went down the alley and knocked on the back door. No answer—and my stomach was growling impatiently for tacos.

When I turned back toward the alley, I found myself face-to-face with the pasty young man from the crosswalk.

"Dr. Teska!"

His eyes were bloodshot, but the pupils weren't dilated. No track marks on his bare arms. He was a stranger to me.

"You didn't return my calls… I need to talk to you!"

"Who are you?"

"Why did you send the cops?" the man demanded, and took a step.

Something on his polo shirt caught my eye. A little red logo said SILOAM BIOLOGIC.

"Siloam," I said. And then, "Are you Neil Dupree?"

"I called you—a bunch of times! Why did you send the cops after me?"

"I don't know what you're talking about."

"The *cops!* Two cops in my office this morning! They said you sent them. They wanted to talk to me about Rebecca…"

"Neil—"

"Cops? At Siloam? *Inside* Siloam? You can't do that!"

"Neil, it's okay." I backed up against a line of garbage bins. "The police are trying to figure out what happened to Rebecca, that's all. You knew her, they need to talk to you. It's routine."

"I don't know what happened to Becca! You tell them to stay away from me!"

Neil Dupree's face crumpled. He dropped his chin to his chest and ran a hand across his bald spot. I assured him again that there was nothing to worry about. His head snapped back up, red-rimmed eyes narrow with anger. He jabbed a finger toward my throat.

"What do *you* know? I can't talk about Siloam. *At all.* But bright and early this morning, right there at my desk with everyone watching, I'm getting interrogated by two detectives?"

I held up an open palm. "What are you even doing here, Neil? If you needed to talk to me so badly—"

"I told you! I *called!*"

"And you didn't hear back fast enough, so you decided… what? To stake out my workplace until I left for lunch, and jump me in an alley?"

He thrust closer—too close. There was white crud forming at the angles of his mouth. He was undershowered, and his breath stank like a dead man's teeth.

"*You* sent those detectives to Siloam. *You* get them to leave me alone!"

"Hey," said a voice, calmly, over my shoulder.

Dupree's red-rimmed eyes went to the sound. They widened. A form filled the entire back doorway of Sparkle's office.

"I'm going to ask you folks to take your dispute somewhere else."

A man—young, bald, and black, carrying 280-plus pounds of brawn on a six-foot-four frame—emerged. I recognized him.

"Baby Mike?"

Baby Mike's mouth scrunched, puzzled—but his eyes didn't leave Neil Dupree.

"I know you?"

I told him I was a friend of his cousin Sparkle's. He nodded, but otherwise didn't move. He didn't have to. Dupree was already backing away. It wasn't until he had made it into the middle of the alley that he found his voice again.

"Call them off, Dr. Teska. *You call them off!*"

He shouted it, stabbing that index finger of his into the air between us. He marched back up the alley toward Bryant Street.

Baby Mike watched Neil Dupree until he went around the corner. Then he peered down at me.

"I bet you're that autopsy doctor."

I told him I was. He extended a frying pan hand.

"I'm Michael."

"Jessie."

"You looking for Sparkle?"

"Yes."

"Well...come on in, Jessie."

Baby Mike reached down and grabbed something as he went over the threshold. It was a sawed-off baseball bat, propped against the wall. I followed his double-wide chassis into the front office.

"Who was that?" he asked.

"Witness in an investigation."

"He gonna be back?"

"I doubt it."

Baby Mike slid the cudgel into a bracket on the underside of Sparkle's desk and told me he'd been changing a leaky faucet in the bathroom. "Sparkle's on her way in," he said as he headed back to it. "Pleasure to meet you."

"Same, Michael," I said. "Under the circumstances."

Cops at Siloam Biologic that morning. They sure freaked out Neil Dupree. The homicide squad can have that effect on people. If they'd visited Siloam, then they were doing background on the decedent and closing out witnesses before they went after Michael Stone. They were probably talking to Melodie, too, checking the Bato story. Maybe they were ready to detain Stone. Maybe he'd be gone from our office before I got back from lunch. That would be a relief.

When Sparkle arrived and I told her about my visit from Neil Dupree, she zeroed right in.

"This is your dead girl's hinky ex, the one from the bio-tech company? How do you know it doesn't have something to do with that?"

I rolled my head around on my neck. Then I said I was already late to grab some lunch and get back to the office.

"Jessie. Tell me."

"Do you people have client privilege in bail bonds?"

"Not like an attorney, no. But when somebody sits in that chair, nothing is more important to me than confidentiality."

I pulled out a dollar bill, put it on her desk. She looked at me sideways, assessed that I wasn't joking, and said, "Consider yourself covered."

So I settled into the chair Sparkle reserves for her hard-luck clients and their long-suffering parents and girlfriends, and I told her the whole story of Becca and Bato. When I finished, Sparkle looked like she'd eaten a bad clam. She had only one question.

"Do you think the cops are gonna follow through?"

"Why wouldn't they?"

"Your dead girl is a drug-overdosed foreigner with no family in San Francisco. The suspect you've dropped in the DA's lap is a prominent member of the law-enforcement community—"

"The cops hate Stone! And we are not law enforcement—"

"Okay, yeah, but you are, though. Or the DAs certainly see you that way."

"They're wrong."

"It's the DA who makes the charge, and the cops will listen to the DA. So I repeat: Do you think the cops are going to follow through?"

The answer to that question unsettled me enough that I said nothing. Sparkle swiveled to her computer.

"Well, Jessie, I don't know, either. Maybe they will and maybe they won't." She typed in a password. Then she confirmed with me the right spelling for Neil's last name, and asked if I knew his middle.

"Write down your email address—*personal*, not city. I'll let you know what I find," Sparkle said. "In the meantime, I'd stay far away from Michael Stone if I was you."

I heeded Sparkle's advice and came in the back way, through the electric sliding doors at the loading dock. Stone's door was closed, and I heard nothing coming from behind it. Nguyen was at his desk in our office, flipping through a medical chart. I unwrapped my tacos and dialed into the phone messages.

"Zasrane to życie!"

"What…?"

"Sorry. Whole bunch of messages."

Neil Dupree had called me five times while I was in the morgue that morning, starting with frantic babbling about the cops coming to his office, and culminating in a string of demands and a promise—or threat—that he was going to come find me. The other messages were routine: a risk manager at a nursing home, a mortician, human resources needing me to complete a missing piece of insurance paperwork. I snarfed some taco. The next voice stopped me chewing.

"Jessie, this is Sophia Kalogeras. I need to speak to you in private. This evening." She left her cell number and asked me to text a confirmation. What did Mike Stone's wife have to discuss with me in private? Before I could worry much about it, the last message started. It was Anup Banerjee, characteristically terse, telling me to call him.

I did.

"We've got the warrant results in *People v. Azarola*," he said.

"Lumpy Chen. So it worked, using that partial serial number to—"

"Yeah, the server logs showed us everything Azarola was doing online from the time he sat down until Chen jacked the laptop."

"You're welcome. What do you want from me now?"

"You floated the theory that the Chen case is related to that drug mule death. I found websites in Azarola's browser history that have something to do with pharmaceutical supplies, mostly overseas. Take a look and see if they mean anything to you. I'm emailing you the list right now."

"I'm a busy lady."

"Yet here we are."

"And you're pushing your luck..."

His email appeared on my screen. It was pages long, links and screenshots. Joe Azarola had whiled away some of his time at the Café Oui-Fi on Facebook. Instagram, too. Plus forays to websites with lots of variations of XXX.

"Just concentrate on the pharma stuff," Banerjee said when I pointed out that trawling through porn was normally outside my job description.

"I'll see what I can do."

I put the email list on the back burner and returned to the pile of cases hanging over my head. They kept me plenty busy till Ted Nguyen got up to leave, at 4:30 on the nose. I followed him. Sunshine Ted made a crack about how he kept hearing how much backlog I had, but here I was quitting at quitting time. I responded I had a date, which shut him up and made him blush. It was half true—I did have to meet Sophia Kalogeras. But I didn't much want to hang around our office alone, either.

O wilku mowa. Dr. Michael Stone was in the corridor. He had just turned the key and pushed open his office door. He was pale and stooped, his tie loose, and was having trouble mustering the dexterity to pull the key out. Ted noticed none of this. He wished the deputy chief good-night and headed in the other direction, toward the loading dock parking lot.

I caught a glimpse inside Stone's office. There was a cot there now, with a pillow and rumpled sheets. Mike's eyes found mine. They were filled with white-hot silent rage. I hustled to catch up with Nguyen.

Stone's wife wanted to talk to me. If he was sleeping in his office, that meant she had kicked him out. On top of that, the police had probably been grilling him all afternoon. No orange jumpsuit, not yet. It had been, what, ten days since Rebecca Corchero died—? Not quite a cold case but not an easy one, either. The cops would take their time with such a high-profile person of interest, and I would have to continue working with Michael Stone, pretending not to know he was a murderer. That rattled me. I was going to have to figure out ways to avoid him.

Sophia Kalogeras arranged to meet me at a café way out on Balboa Street. The fog had come back in like a bastard, heavy and gray as gutter slush. At least it gave us a conversation starter. Griping about the August fog is a social custom that crosses San Francisco's class lines.

Sophia wore pearls. Her hair cascaded onto her shoulders, impossibly luminous, an even chestnut hue all the way to the roots. I've cut into the scalps of enough mature women to know a pricey dye job when I see it. The same with her makeup—inconspicuous and flattering, even this late in the day. There was no concealing the hollow look behind the mascara, though.

"I have to talk to you privately about Rebecca's autopsy," she said without small talk. "The police came by my office yesterday asking questions. They told me she was pregnant."

Sophia was peering into me, digging deep, and she didn't miss my true reaction, which was *Oh shit—why would they divulge that?*

"Is it true? Was she…?"

"I'm sorry. I can't talk about an ongoing investigation."

"From the tone of their questions, it seems they are treating Rebecca's death as a homicide—and my husband as a suspect…" Sophia waited for my reaction, and I tried like hell not to give one. She pressed on. "Do you know how absurd that notion is? Michael loved Rebecca like a daughter. He was instrumental in getting her into nursing school, in helping her achieve her *dream*. We all supported that girl, in so many ways."

"Did they… Did the detectives tell you they were going to arrest Dr. Stone?"

"Of course not. You know how it is with those people— the questions all go in one direction. It was insulting. It was *fantastical*. They all but accused my husband of having impregnated Rebecca! I was so angry I could spit…"

Some of that anger slipped her grip—in a brief glower that could strip paint. She sipped her tea, waited for me to speak. When I didn't, she said, "Rebecca was dating someone at work, at that biotech company. I told the detectives, of course, but they just kept harassing me with…with *alibi* questions! What was Michael doing that night, when, where…"

"The job at Siloam Biologic—you helped Rebecca get it, is that right?"

"Yes. Through an old friend."

"Arnie Spitz."

Sophia cocked her head. I had caught her off guard, for once. "Yes. Arnold and I worked together years ago, before I went into academia."

"Spitz is only an investor in Siloam. How did he get Rebecca a job there?"

She unleashed a dry smile. "He's persuasive."

No shit, sister. "But Spitz got her fired, too. How come?"

"Arnold once mentioned that Rebecca had involved herself in some financial improprieties. I didn't want to pry. I was…a little embarrassed, you see—having recommended her. Rebecca worked for us for more than three years. We trusted her with our child! I suspect her dismissal from Siloam came out of a misunderstanding."

A pair of studious high school girls took the booth next to ours and flipped open laptops and textbooks. Sophia Kalogeras leaned closer.

"Jessie, I need to know if Rebecca…if she really was pregnant."

"I can't discuss the autopsy."

She squared her shoulders. "You're new to this city, Doctor. You don't know how corrupt our police force is. Michael has stood up to them so many times. They will do anything, tell any lie, to bring him down. Michael told me Rebecca died of a heroin overdose. It was an accident. It happens. It happens to all sorts of people you'd never think of using drugs. Jessie…surely you agree?"

"I have some concerns."

"Did you rule Rebecca's death a homicide?"

"I can't discuss the manner of death on a case pending investigation."

"Have you done paternity testing on the baby?"

"I can't talk to you about that."

Sophia sat back in the booth and we went into a silent stare-down over the chipped mugs of tea. She broke it.

"The night Rebecca died, Michael was teaching. He lectures at Hastings Law School once a week. He came home after. He was with me the rest of the night."

It was a lousy alibi. The detectives were going to have a field day with Dr. Michael Stone. Sophia's eyes went hard enough to bring back the crow's-feet banished by Botox.

"The police do not appreciate everything Michael has done for them. He's caught some of them misrepresenting facts. My husband has little patience for incompetence, and they resent having to rely on him for his expertise. Michael is a widely sought-after expert, you know. Nationally renowned. He only keeps working at your office because he has such a passion for teaching. And mentoring. He speaks very highly of you, Dr. Teska. He's told me that you also love to teach…?"

"I do."

Sophia smiled with her mouth, but those hard eyes weren't up to it.

"Well. Your students are lucky to have you, and you certainly landed at the right office." She held out her hand and I shook it. "I want to thank you for taking the time to talk to me. I'm confident this will all blow over."

That was a lie. So was my response.

"It was my pleasure, Sophia."

───────────────

Mike Stone was back in place at the head of the conference table for Friday's morning meeting. He had bags under his eyes, and his shirt collar was grimy. He hadn't shaved. He looked like he had aged a good few years. I caught two naturals and an accident. When he handed me my case files, our eyes met. There was none of the wrath in them I'd seen the day before. There was nothing in them at all.

"So what'd you find?" Anup Banerjee asked. I was standing in the assistant district attorney's doorway, a pile of paper in my arms—the fruits of my search through the Café Oui-Fi data dump. I spread them across his desk.

"Joe Azarola was browsing at least four Canadian pharmacy sites, two Chinese chemical processors, a Russian black market clearinghouse, and a farm supply company in India."

Banerjee grabbed a yellow legal pad and uncapped a pen. "What's up with that last one?"

"He was online-shopping for a synthetic opioid used in veterinary drugs. An elephant tranquilizer."

"No shit—?"

"We've been seeing a whole range of fentanyl analogues mixed into heroin. Remember the body packer who died the same night as Lumpy Chen?"

"Somebody mutilated her in that hotel right across the street from the Café Oui-Fi."

"Right. Her name was Graciela Natividad. The heroin bindle that burst in her gut and killed her was augmented with one of these opioid drugs. Acetylfentanyl."

Banerjee scribbled. "Smaller packages and bigger profit margins."

"Right. Or maybe they're looking to diversify the supply chain. If you can order your fentanyl analogues shipped internationally, there's no need to pack the drugs into condoms and feed them to some desperate peasant girl. Especially if you might kill her doing it."

"They don't give two shits about that girl, believe me." Anup Banerjee's gaze pulled back and took on the cold, sharp focus I had seen in the courtroom. He shuffled through the website printouts for the Chinese chemical labs and the Russian mail-order pharmacies. "This is good. What else you got?"

I leaned across the desk and flipped the sheet on his legal pad.

"You're going to want a fresh page."

A corner of the ADA's tight lips inched up. I surveyed the paperwork and found the printout I was looking for. "Do you know what bitcoin is?"

"Sure. Electronic currency."

"Your man Joe Azarola spent a whole lot of time moving bitcoin around."

"Dark net drug buys?"

"No."

I handed him the paper. He took his time, read it over. Then he said, "TechFolio. What's that?"

"Let me tell you about a man named Arnold Spitz."

I explained the convolutions of Arnie's business model. Anup Banerjee's expression grew cloudier as I did. When I finished, he dropped the pen on the desk, planted his elbows, and spread his palms upward.

"So what?"

"So what...? So, over here we have a shady company that plays corporate shell games with other people's money. They also disburse bags of cash. Over there we have Joe Azarola shooting Lumpy Chen dead so that he can retrieve his laptop. That computer was worth killing over, even with a bullet hole through it. And here's why."

I pointed to a line of repeated text on the page I'd handed him. "Know what those are?"

Banerjee examined them. "Log-ins."

"And log-outs. Followed by more log-ins. Each with a different username."

"So what?" Banerjee repeated. How thick is this guy, I asked myself.

"Azarola has a different username each time. He's sending funds to TechFolio under aliases. Small amounts. Hard to trace. Money laundering, Anup! Right there, sitting in a café, on a laptop. It's not the computer's hard drive that Azarola was so worried about—it's the browser history!"

Banerjee looked over the sheet again. Then he shook his head.

"I don't see it."

"What?"

"That's a theory. I can't use theories."

"What!"

"You heard me. You're so sure he's setting up multiple accounts—so where's the transfer? What's the amount?"

"The log-ins came off the server records, but after that he went into the TechFolio website—behind a firewall."

"So you don't have any proof of money laundering?"

"Azarola is a drug dealer..."

"So?"

"So he has money that needs laundering!"

Anup Banerjee rolled his chair back. "Jessie, I have Josu Azarola dead to rights on a homicide. I am looking for evidence—not theories, evidence—to bolster *that* case. Now, if you give me indictable proof of money laundering, maybe I could bump it up to the feds, especially if I can connect Azarola to the guys they're already going after."

"In the RICO case?"

"Yeah."

"Hector Marroquin."

"If you say so."

"Anup, Marroquin has the same lawyer as Azarola!"

"Jackson Heffernan?"

"The one and only."

Banerjee mulled. Then he shrugged.

"That does nothing for you?"

"Not much. Heffernan is a prominent defense attorney."

"He defends drug dealers!"

"He defends a lot of people, as long as they can pay."

"But…look at what's in front of you here! These guys are all on the same page! They're working together…"

Banerjee pulled that stunt skilled courtroom attorneys have, where they let you run out of steam and trail off. Then he assumed a softer expression and picked up a sheaf of papers.

"Thanks for this. I mean it. The online fentanyl shopping you've uncovered is immensely helpful. It supports my effort to make a stronger connection between the Chen case and the mule death—before you gave me this, all we had was the video of Azarola walking past some guy carrying takeout bags, and Azarola looking up at the hotel. If we could find the two people in the hotel room who were trying to get the girl to pass the heroin, and link them to Azarola, then we might have something."

"How do you know there were two?"

"Shoe prints at the scene." He reached across to the far corner of his desk and fanned out another stack of photos, these from the gruesome Hotel Somerville crime scene where Graciela Natividad died and was mutilated. The bed black with blood, the girl splayed on the floor, intestines spilling out—and, all around the room, two distinct sets of footwear impression evidence. One pair of shoes had formed a zigzag pattern and the other had left crosses and circles. Bloody footprints.

"Footprints…" I said.

"What about them?"

"Azarola left us digital footprints. On Facebook. There are screenshots. Pictures…"

My fingers flipped through the Café Oui-Fi data dump until I found them. Mostly they were photos of Azarola posing with other men—showing off guns, waving around fans of cash, sometimes with half-naked women. Sometimes with bags of white powder.

"This guy." It was a buddy selfie. A man had an arm gripped around Joe Azarola's neck. The man was in his early twenties, light brown skin, a lupine face with a long, slender nose and narrow chin. He had remarkably beautiful eyes—pale green, almost yellow. His hair was gelled up in spikes and bleached except for the dark sideburns, which he kept crisp and shaved close. Big diamond studs in his earlobes. He was all smiles. He had great teeth.

"I keep seeing him," I said, pulling out a full body shot of the same man posing with a black pistol in one hand and a silver revolver in the other. Here he was with his feet on a table covered with beer bottles. You could make out the bottom of one boot: crosses and circles. I pointed it out to Banerjee.

"Again," said Banerjee, "same guy." He pointed to a close-up. It was Yellow Eyes on his own, head thrown back, downing a shot of liquor.

"Tattoo," I said. On the right forearm's proximal volar surface was a bold black image: a rose and a pair of dice. Below that, *RIP Paquito 12.20.13.*

Banerjee scribbled more notes and said he'd send the screenshots to the detectives working the Graciela Natividad investigation. "Maybe they can ID this guy. The tattoo helps. The shoe pattern, too. If he's one of the two people who left those footprints in the Hotel Somerville, we can use him to connect Joe Azarola to their case. And I'm sure they'll be eager to hear what you've uncovered about Azarola's foreign fentanyl sources. I'd love to see solid evidence that connects the shooting of Eugene Chen to the death of Graciela Natividad—it gives me leverage if Azarola knows I could get him on conspiracy and accessory in the felony trafficking that killed her. But there's another problem with that approach."

"What problem?"

"Michael Stone."

I made myself busy gathering the papers off the table and avoided Anup Banerjee's eyes.

"Were you in the morgue when he did the autopsy on Graciela Natividad?"

"Yes."

"I might need you to testify to the cause of death for Natividad if it gets to trial. I can't call Stone."

I tapped the papers into neater and neater piles and said nothing.

"What do you know about homicide detectives investigating Dr. Stone?"

I faked a laugh. "You forgot to swear me in."

Banerjee repeated the question, serious as cancer.

"I can't answer that."

"Can't, or won't?"

I didn't.

He cocked his head. "Jessie—Michael Stone is a crucial expert witness in three of my current charged cases, not to mention the Natividad investigation. I'm being told I can't put him on the stand. I need to know why."

"I can't talk about it."

"There are rumors Stone had a mistress, and she got pregnant and he killed her."

"I can't talk about Dr. Stone. I could lose my job."

Banerjee's black eyebrows screwed down. "There are serious stakes here. Stone is the expert in a lot of homicides, and not just my cases. If you have knowledge that he is tainted as a witness, tell me now."

I said nothing.

"Has Dr. Howe ordered you not to talk about this? Because if he has, I can subpoena you. You'll be compelled to answer before a judge."

I went to the door.

"You do whatever you have to do," I said, and walked out.

Dr. Howe was behind his desk, fiddling with one of the doodads cluttering it—a spent .40-caliber bullet slug, splayed open like a lead lily and encased in a Lucite prism.

"Dr. Stone took you off homicides?"

"He… Yes."

Howe scowled. "I'm putting you back on. This police investigation you instigated has the DA's office worried. Very worried. They don't want Mike's name on any new cases other than straightforward accidents and naturals. I can't very well leave Ted doing all the homicides. He more than pulls his weight around here. So I'm countermanding Mike's decision to take you off homicides—starting tonight, with weekend call."

He spun the pyramid end of the prism like a top. I thanked him.

"Don't thank me—show me," he shot back. "Show me

you can work hard in the morgue and still get your old cases closed."

"I will."

The chief planted his paperweight on its flat end with a bang like a gavel. Then he dismissed me.

I buckled down as ordered, well into overtime. By seven I had put three cases to bed and was working on one more. Hunger drove me in search of cold pizza, leftover sandwiches—anything—from the guys on call in the Ops Shop. I stretched, did a couple of knee bends, and was reaching for my office door handle when I froze. I heard steps coming down the hallway. From the left. Long strides.

Michael Stone.

The steps stopped. I looked down. Shadows leaked under the sill.

I gripped the handle. It rattled and twitched. I tightened my hold. It twitched again. Then the shadows under the sill shifted and vanished, and long strides beat down the corridor toward the loading dock. The sally port's swinging doors squealed.

I waited before I came out. The hallway was empty. My heart was drumming in my ears. I headed for the Ops Shop—after locking my office door behind me.

I caught Cam and Donna just as they were heading out on their first trip of the night shift, to collect a drunk who'd wandered onto 19th Avenue and got smeared by three cars heading in two directions. They had nothing to offer me but stale doughnuts and sludge coffee. I was hungry and spooked enough to take both with thanks.

"Hope we won't see you later," Cam said, and pointed to the blackboard. Under *Doctor on call*, one of them had drawn a chalk line through Stone's name and written mine next to it. I pointed out they could have just used the eraser.

Donna shook her frosted bangs. "No fun in that." She asked

if I'd noticed any signs of life when I passed Stone's office. I told them he'd just left through the loading dock.

Cam used a pen to ring his coffee mug like a bell and sang, "Diiinn-ner tiiime…"

Donna chuckled and urged the last doughnut on me. "You better take this before Mike comes scrounging. He's eating in that office and sleeping there, too."

"Showering and shaving in the locker room," Cam added, and hoisted the mug. "Here's hoping he finds someplace else to go. He don't look so good."

Donna raised her own. "I mean, imagine the paperwork if he wakes up dead in there."

"Rumor has it the wife won't let Mike darken her door," said Cam. "Serves him right—if the rumors are true."

I thought of my *mamusia* and what she'd say about that. *Plotki nie kłamią.*

The rumors are always true.

I returned to my own lonely office to proofread a histology report. I figured I could leave Bea alone without her walk till about nine. The Corchero call wouldn't take long, but with the twelve-hour time difference I didn't want to ring the poor people out of bed. I waited till eight.

Camille Corchero, Rebecca's mother, wished me good morning from halfway across the globe. She thanked me for having sent her daughter's ashes so quickly. I asked if they'd held a service, and she told me all about it—the funeral Mass, her family coming together in grief, the community rallying behind them.

"No one…said about how she died, except it was too soon. Our priest spoke well of my daughter. We buried her. She is at rest now."

A lump of bile rose in my throat. No, Camille. No, she isn't.

"Doctor—you will send us the cross necklace? We have

a…a place for Rebecca. In the house, with her picture. The cross will go there. It is important to us."

I pictured the sepia photograph of my own grandmother, framed in fading gold paint, that my mother laid out every March 20, *Babcia's* saint's day. I don't remember ever missing a year praying over it. Votive candles. A Mass card from the funeral. And a letter, on flimsy, pale blue airmail paper—the last letter *Babcia* wrote *Mamusia*, in her slanted and precise old-world hand.

"Doctor…?"

"I…yes, Camille, I'm here. The crucifix. I apologize for the delay. Sometimes these…types of death…require a little more time than others."

"I see," Camille replied. "I understand. I trust you, Doctor. I know you will hurry how you can."

"I promise you I will do that, Camille. I promise I will… close your daughter's case as soon as circumstances allow."

After I hung up the phone, I sat looking at it for a long time. I wanted, very badly, to take the letter opener off my desk, go find Michael Stone, and stab him in the fucking neck. Maybe then Rebecca would rest in peace.

No. She wouldn't. It had to be the right way. Stone would pay. I only hoped the PD and the DA would make a public show of it, that I would be rewarded with the spectacle of that bastard marched out of our office in handcuffs. And I offered a silent prayer that I, as the doctor who performed Rebecca Corchero's autopsy, would be called to testify to the forensic findings at Michael Stone's trial for her murder.

The dog. The time. I looked: 8:17. I gathered my things and hustled down the dark hallway, through the swinging doors and into the sally port with its empty gurneys staged neatly along one wall. I pressed the button to operate the sliding electric doors and emerged outside, into the August twilight.

I had crossed half a dozen steps toward my car when something caught my eye on Harriet Street, just past the loading dock's low wall.

A Dodge Charger.

I stopped in the middle of the loading dock. I focused on the windshield. In the driver's seat I made out a shadow. It moved.

I opened my purse and pretended to root around. Then I swiveled, walked briskly back to the morgue, and pulled out my keys. On the street a car door closed. I glanced back. A male figure in dark clothes with a hood over his head was hurrying toward the loading dock parking lot.

There's a lag between the electric lock clicking open and the ancient steel doors sliding away from each other. I held my breath. As soon as there was room for my body, I slipped through. I looked back. The hooded man broke into a dash. The door's panels started to slide back together.

They weren't closing fast enough.

My hands clasped the closest heavy object in the sally port—a gurney. I whipped it around and jammed it against the door frame. The man ran into it, and the gurney bumped back. I rammed it into place again.

The gap was shrinking. The man spat the word *bitch* from under his hood and tried to scramble over the gurney. I yanked it out from under him. He stumbled and fell backward. The doors were a foot away from sealing. The man leaped up again, and his hood fell away. Our eyes met. His were pinpricks of violence.

They were pale green—almost yellow.

His right hand, in a black glove, came at me. I ducked. The steel panels closed on his forearm. Then the gloved fingers of his left hand reached through the gap and gripped the edge. He heaved it. The motor in the wall whined and the panels budged a little, enough for him to get his right hand free, and into the effort.

The whine turned to a rattle as Yellow Eyes started to pry open the electric doors.

I burst into the autopsy suite and stumbled in the dark, grabbing for the phone, but knocked it to the floor with a plastic clatter. I dropped to my knees and swept my hands back and forth. I heard the crash of a gurney against the sally port wall. My fingers found the phone cord, then the receiver. The doors flapped open behind me.

No time for 911 and nowhere to hide.

Yellow Eyes turned the wrong way. I jumped up and brought the receiver down on the back of his head with all my might, then dashed for the exit at the other end of the autopsy suite. He sprang and caught me in the back with a tripping shove, and I went down. When I scrambled up he hit me, twice and hard, on the side of the head. I saw stars and heard ringing, but kept my footing. I swung at him but he blocked the blow and punched me on the right brow. That sent me spinning. He got behind me and grabbed me in a headlock. I flailed and kicked and screamed. Yellow Eyes locked his right arm with his left and tightened the choke hold. He bulldozed me up against the lab counter next to my own autopsy station and bent me over at the waist.

I clawed at his arm and felt the sleeve tear, but he didn't let up. He knew what he was doing: squeezing my carotid arteries and trachea while crushing my rib cage under his body weight. I knew what that meant: I had only seconds before I blacked out. I couldn't break his grip and I couldn't get enough leverage in my legs to mule-kick him. I tried to wrench my torso sideways, open up some breathing space, but he just leaned harder. In my right ear, where he'd punched me, I couldn't hear anything but ringing. In my left, I heard his voice. It was strained with the effort of strangling me, but soft. It was telling me to relax, don't fight. He didn't want to hurt me. Just relax and he'd let me go. That's what he said.

"Okay…" I croaked, to see if he'd loosen his grip.

"Yeah, it's okay," the man said in a gentle way, and squeezed harder.

He said something soothing again, but I couldn't make it out. The blood was pounding in my eardrums. My field of vision was going green. I felt my jaw jerk in spasm, my nostrils flare. My lungs were burning. I fought the panic of air hunger. I willed my hands to slacken their grip on his arms and fall to the countertop. I relaxed my body. And carefully—very, very carefully—I walked the fingers of my right hand across the table. They dipped over the edge. They found the drawer pull. They went into the drawer. They came back out with my pink #22 autopsy scalpel.

I stabbed straight down. The knife went into his leg, deep. The man screeched into my one good ear. I pulled the scalpel out and slashed at his arms—but it wasn't cutting. I dropped the scalpel, raised my right fist, and slammed it down on the spot where I'd stabbed him. He howled again, and the leg crumpled. He lost his grip and I caught one great, glorious, life-giving breath. Then I elbowed him in the gut with my right arm and reached with my left for his face, jabbing at his eye with my thumb. I screamed bloody murder.

The man twisted away. I slipped out from under him, wheeled, and kneed him square in the nuts. He doubled over. I knit my hands together and swung them up to slam the bridge of his nose. I felt bone snap.

Yellow Eyes stumbled back. I was coughing and gasping. He was bleeding freely from the nose. His left hand clutched his groin. His right leg was bent. He looked pretty wobbly.

"Fuck this," Yellow Eyes said. His right hand went into his pocket and came out with a gun.

To my left was a shelf lined with tissue samples. I grabbed the biggest one: a brain bucket. I heaved it. The bucket burst open in a wild splash of formalin solution when it hit him in the chest. The brain whacked him in the mouth, and its spinal cord wrapped around his neck like a noose. He shrieked and clutched at his eyes. He lurched and his feet went right out under him. Formaldehyde is slippery. Caustic, too—it could blind him. I hoped it would, at least long enough. I ran for the glowing exit sign over the morgue's far door.

The hallway. I sprinted past the locker rooms, past my office and Stone's. I reached the end of the corridor, the door to the public entrance. Shit! After hours—it was locked! My keys? Had I...yes—they were in my pocket...

Before I could find the right one for the doorknob, the morgue door slammed, an explosion filled the hallway, and a bullet slapped into the wood paneling over my head. I dropped to the floor, and Yellow Eyes took another potshot, closer.

I wasn't going to make it outside. I reached for the only unlocked door and pushed through into the Ops Shop. It was empty—Cam and Donna were still out at the traffic fatality. I killed the lights, scrambled to the farthest desk in the labyrinth of workstations, and hid.

Hid, and waited. Yellow Eyes was probably still half-blind, hacking and heaving from the fumes off his formalin-soaked clothes. His knee would be hurting like hell. He had just squeezed off two gunshots inside a police building. I had thrown a human brain at him. I hoped and prayed that he knew it was time to call it quits.

He didn't. He came through the door. He didn't curse me or try to sweet-talk me again. He didn't say a thing. Gun drawn and stifling a gagging cough, Yellow Eyes made his way methodically desk to desk, looking to kill me.

Unless I could make my way back out that same door, I had nowhere left to run. I needed a weapon. I was crouched behind Cameron Blake's desk. A plastic jar of M&M's, a mug full of pens, a bobblehead in a Giants uniform. I made a mental note to buy Cam a shotgun for Christmas.

A shotgun!

Yellow Eyes had finished with the first row of desks and was making his way to the second. I waited until he'd disappeared behind the chimney column, then I crawled toward Dr. Howe's office. I stayed low and reached up—slowly—to the door handle. It turned. It clicked. I peered back into the gloom of the Ops Shop. Another stifled hack from behind the dispatch column. I eased the door open.

It creaked.

The gun whipped around from behind the column, followed by an arm, followed by Yellow Eyes. I stumbled through Howe's door and lurched for the dusty double-barreled shotgun leaning against the sofa. I threw myself behind Howe's oak desk and opened the shotgun's breech.

Yeah—empty.

My assailant came through the door. I waited until his damaged eyes had scanned the room—then slammed the shotgun breech shut. He swung his gun arm toward the source of the sound. I pointed the two fat gun barrels over the desk.

Yellow Eyes gasped, jumped back, and twirled out the door.

"Get out!" I screamed—and again, over and over. My heart was pounding in my temples. My breath was coming in gulps. I slowed it down and shook the terror out of my battered head.

"Okay, numbnuts," I yelled. "I'm going to call nine-one-one now! If you come in here, I'll shoot you. This is a twelve-gauge loaded with Remington number four buckshot. I know that because I did the autopsy on the guy who offed himself with it. Left a big fucking hole in his belly. Ribs all over his rec room."

I paused. No answer but another stifled cough.

"He fired off one shell. Come through that door, and I will shoot you in your center of mass with the other one."

"Fuck you," Yellow Eyes said, and coughed again.

"Nope! His diaphragm was torn into three pieces. That's how you breathe, your diaphragm. His aorta was ruptured. That's the biggest artery in your body. It's, like, a garden hose for blood. I shoot you with this, same thing's gonna happen to you. You'll lie on the floor spurting blood all over the place for as long as maybe two minutes. You will feel everything. You will have the chance to wonder why you came through that door…"

My hands were shaking and I fought back the need to retch. I readied my legs in a crouch. He'd have to come awful close to get a good shot at me over the desk with that pistol. Maybe I could swing the gunstock at him before he pulled the trigger. Maybe his first shot would miss, and I'd get a chance at a second swing.

I reached for the phone. Before my fingers made it there, the lights came on in the Ops Shop. Through the open door of Howe's office I could see the gloved hand with the semi-automatic pistol swing across the Investigations Department. It settled on a man who had just come in through the locked lobby entrance.

Michael Stone.

When the man with the gun pointed the muzzle at him, Stone threw his hands in the air. His keys jangled in his right. A takeout bag rustled in his left. "I—heard voices," Stone said.

"Shut the fuck up," Yellow Eyes replied. He limped toward Stone, gun arm locked.

"Look…whatever you want…" Stone said.

"Shut the fuck up," Yellow Eyes repeated. He didn't sound angry or even agitated. He stopped two or three yards away from Stone. Yellow Eyes stared at him. He cocked his head.

"Well, damn."

And he lowered the pistol.

"Damn…" Yellow Eyes coughed and wheezed, and coughed again. Then he said, "Go get in there with that bitch."

"Wha…what?" Mike Stone stammered.

"You heard me, man! Go get in that room over there." Yellow Eyes pointed to Howe's office—with his left hand. His right held the gun, but now it was pointed at the floor.

Stone came in, still clutching the keys and doggie bag. "Shut the door," Yellow Eyes instructed him from across the room. He did. I heard the door to the hallway open and close.

I was still crouched behind the desk, trying to figure out what the hell had just happened. Mike Stone stood in the middle of our chief's office, trying to do the same. We stayed that way for half a frozen minute. Then, as it dawned on both of us that the man with the gun really had gone away, Stone dropped his keys and bag on the floor, and moved toward the desk.

I jumped up and swiveled the shotgun and started screaming at him to stay away from me. I still couldn't hear out of one ear. My right eye was swelling shut. My chest ached and my throat hurt like the dickens. Maybe I was on adrenaline autopilot or maybe I was hysterical—but, either way, I aimed that shotgun at my boss.

Mike Stone's expression softened from shock to pity. "I'm going for the phone, Jessie. Our cells don't work in here, you know that. We have to call nine-one-one."

He took the last step to the desk, staring down the barrel of the gun, and picked up the receiver.

"Besides. That thing isn't loaded."

CHAPTER FOURTEEN

"Careful not to slip in the formaldehyde in there," I warned the cops who arrived first. "And watch out for the brain on the floor." I advised them where to look for the two bullets, for my pink scalpel, and—hopefully—the assailant's blood spatter. I declined an ambulance but requested an ice pack for my eye.

The detectives on call turned out to be Keith Jones and Daniel Ramirez. I was relieved to see their faces. Mike Stone was not. He started yelling that he wanted his lawyer. Inspector Jones told him to calm down; first they needed to get us out of there so that CSI could secure the crime scene.

"Calm down?" Stone raged back. "That's the goddamned police department parking garage next to our loading dock! You'd think you clowns could keep our employees safe from *assault* in your very own *driveway!*"

Jones glared back at him. "Heffernan, right? Jackson? I think they got that guy on speed dial at the jail phone, if you want to go straight there."

"Am I under arrest?"

"I didn't say that."

"Am I under arrest?"

"No."

"Am I free to go?"

"No. You're a witness. We need a statement. Upstairs." Jones nodded his brown fedora at one of the patrol cops, who squared up on Mike Stone.

Mike waved his hands in disgust and stalked off toward the public entrance, Inspector Jones and the uniform flanking him. Inspector Ramirez waited till they were gone.

"You're with me, Doc. Your head all right?"

I assured him it was, and tried to hide how shaky I actually felt as I followed the detective outside and around the cloisters to the Hall's elevators. On the fifth floor a gray corridor with dull olive floors led us to the Homicide Division. Ramirez pressed his ID against a sensor and led me into an interview room. It was small and overlit, with a crummy whitewash paint job. Ramirez sat me in a straight-backed chair behind the metal table. He asked if I was hungry.

"I can ID him."

The detective's loose limbs locked tight. He pulled out a pad and pen.

"You can?"

"He's a buddy of Josu Azarola."

"What?"

"The Facebook pictures you guys got off Azarola's browsing history? The man who tried to kill me tonight is in those. In a bunch of them."

"You know his name?"

"No."

"Okay," Ramirez said. "Sit tight." He went out the door in a hurry.

I wanted to call my brother; it was getting late and he's an early-to-bed type. I was just about to go ask about a landline when the interrogation room door opened again—and a haggard Dr. James Howe stuck his head in. I was thrown off by his street clothes. I'd never seen Dr. Howe without a suit and tie. He had some stubble. I'd never seen that, either. His expression betrayed genuine shock.

"Oh, God," he said. "Jessie. Are you all right?" I told him I was fine. He said he heard I had taken some blows to the head and wanted to know why I didn't go to the ER for an evaluation. I said that my injuries looked a lot worse than they felt.

"You're sure you're okay?"

"Certain."

"Maybe I should take you off call? I can check with Ted…"

"No—! No, please don't. I mean it. I'd be lucky to get called out—it'll distract me."

Dr. Howe gazed down at me like a proud uncle. "Remarkable dedication and grit! Have the 2578s contact me if you change your mind. Otherwise, I'll see you on Monday."

"Yes, you will, Dr. Howe."

Behind him a policewoman came in with a fast-food turkey sub. It was soggy and acrid and altogether nasty. I choked it down anyway, and sucked up the tepid Coke that came with it. Someone from CSI arrived to escort me to a room called Photographic Services. Along the way we kept passing signs warning *Restricted Access: Law Enforcement must prominently display badge/ID*. I patted myself down looking for my badge and realized I didn't need it. I wasn't there as a peace officer. I was a crime victim.

The photographer and I recognized each other, though neither of us could recall from where. We tossed cases back and forth before we settled on it—the coyote depredation, up in the woods by the Lincoln Park golf course. That memory put a damper on our chitchat. She asked me to strip to my bra so she could shoot my neck injuries. Close-ups of my ear and eye. She asked if I needed to take my pants off so she could document any areas underneath them.

"I...no... But if you need to check, I can—"

"Oh, no—no, it's up to you."

"Then, no. He didn't... I don't have any..."

"Right. Let me get your hands?"

The photographer walked me back up to the interrogation room, where Jones and Ramirez sat waiting in folding chairs. I was surprised to find another man waiting—pacing, actually—behind them. Anup Banerjee. His eyes widened when he fixed them on my battered face.

Jones opened his notepad and his mouth, but I wasn't about to let him get the first question in. "From your reaction downstairs, I figure you two are investigating Michael Stone for the murder of Rebecca Corchero. I want to know why you haven't arrested him already."

Jones glanced at his partner with about as much surprise as a homicide detective can muster.

"Dr. Teska, we're here to investigate what happened to you tonight. So let's stick to that, okay?"

"No. Not okay." I pointed to the ceiling—the county jail, one floor up. "I want to know when you're going to put Stone in a jumpsuit."

"We are not going to talk about that."

Before I could protest again, Anup Banerjee spoke, gently and without guile. "Please, Jessie. The man who assaulted you is still out there. Right now we need to find out whatever we can about him."

So I went through the whole awful story, from the moment I spotted the shadow figure in the Dodge Charger to the moment Mike Stone called 911.

"This man. You don't know his name?" Jones asked.

"No."

"And at what point did you recognize him?"

"In the doorway, when his hood fell back. He's the man in the Facebook posts with Joe Azarola."

Inspector Jones went through his notes. "He hit you...how many times total?"

"Twice to the side of the head and once to the eye."

"Then he grappled you from behind and tried to strangle you."

"He didn't *try*. Look!" I pointed to my neck.

Inspector Ramirez piped up: "You need a new ice pack?"

"No!"

"And remind me when you left your office...?"

"Eight twenty."

"Why so late?"

"She had to call the Philippines," Ramirez said.

"Oh, right. Eight twenty—do you frequently work at that hour?"

"No."

"Why did you go out to the loading dock alone?"

"What?"

Jones repeated the question. Then Ramirez expanded on it. "Why didn't you ask for an escort from one of the other staff?"

I let the question sit there before I answered. "I'm a big girl, Inspector Ramirez."

He laughed nervously. "No, no—that's not what I mean. It's this policy Dr. Howe mentioned..."

"The memo," his partner added, as partners will.

"The memo."

"Yes."

"You'll have to be more specific. I get a lot of memos."

"Dr. Howe told us about this...uh..." Ramirez flipped his own notes back a couple pages. "Here—this 'New Worker Safety Directive.' That all OCME employees are required to seek an escort when leaving the workplace through the loading dock after hours."

"He said you signed it," Jones added.

"The investigators were out on a call."

"Dr. Stone mentioned there are a number of transients who sleep under the freeway there," Ramirez said. "By Harriet Street. He said some of them have accosted OCME staff before."

"Dr. Stone mentioned that, did he."

"Yes. Well—Dr. Howe, too."

"So what?"

"We want to make sure we're looking in the right direction," Jones said. "It's not unusual for the victim of a sexual assault to—"

"Sexual assault!"

Ramirez produced a pocket pack of Kleenex and put it in front of me. "Would you feel more comfortable if we asked a female officer to be present?"

"Sexual assault? You think this was a *rape* attempt? You're not listening—that man came here to *kill* me."

Ramirez leaned in, all earnest-like. "Dr. Teska, we appreciate this has been traumatic for you. We're trying to get a direction for our investigation, while the events are fresh. Has anyone ever accosted you on the loading dock before?"

"I've only been working here for two months!"

"So you've never seen this man back there?"

"No! I told you I saw his car before, though."

"The night a car with yellow lights chased you."

"Amber fog lights. Right."

"You saw his face then?"

"No."

"Oh..."

"Was that the night you got the summons for reckless speed?" Jones said.

"Dr. Stone mentioned that, too, did he?"

"Was it that night?"

"I was being *chased!* By the same car I saw this guy get out of tonight!"

Jones sighed impatiently, and Ramirez nodded the way you do to a child ranting in all earnestness about the monsters under the bed. Then, to my surprise and theirs, Anup Banerjee spoke up.

"What's the angle for Azarola?"

"How do you mean?" I said.

"If your assailant is a buddy of his, how's it help Azarola if you get killed? If you're right and this man came here to kill you, it can't be for Joe Azarola's sake. Azarola wants a plea deal. Killing you does nothing for that. In fact, it puts him in significant jeopardy."

He was right, damn him. "I don't know, Anup. But I'm telling you, the man who attacked me is in those pictures off Azarola's Facebook feed. Let's get them printed." I swung to the cops. "Then you two can go get him. That's what you do, isn't it?"

"We already have the precincts canvassing ERs for a man with a deep cut to his right knee," Ramirez offered.

"Yeah? Tell them I broke his nose, too." I found myself massaging my knuckles.

Keith Jones rolled his shoulders and pivoted his neck in fatigue or the affectation of it. He and Anup Banerjee went out to a computer terminal and returned with a glossy eight-by-ten of the Facebook image from the case database. There he was—the wolf's grin, the pinched features, the asshole haircut. The yellow-green eyes. Jones handed me a Sharpie and asked me to sign the bottom of the picture, and then it was official: The San Francisco Police Department had a person of interest in the assault of Czesława Gladys Teska.

Inspector Jones tagged open the door with his ID and said I could go. I made a beeline for the elevators, the clack of my shoes filling the mausoleum of marble that led to it. Anup Banerjee caught up.

"Jessie—wait."

I did.

"Don't you live alone?"

He had a point. "I'll stay with my brother on the Peninsula."

"That's good. I'll walk you to your car—"

"But I have to go home first."

He tightened up. "What for?"

"My dog."

"Oh. Right." Banerjee ran a hand through his black bangs, trying to figure out how to say something. Then he said it.

"Let me come with you."

A joke about at least taking a girl out to dinner first fought to surface, but my fatigue and bad cheer squelched it. I didn't want to be alone. Anup Banerjee was standing there before me, his suit rumpled and his tie missing. He probably hadn't been home since he got off work. He didn't have to be in the interview room with Jones and Ramirez. He was there because he was concerned about me. Now he was offering to help in the only way he could think of.

"Thank you, Anup. I'd appreciate it."

He slouched in relief, and we continued together down the corridor. We were alone in an elevator and the doors were closing when a man's voice rang out to hold it.

In came Jackson Heffernan and, a few paces behind him, Michael Stone.

Stone said nothing. Heffernan looked me up and down and shook his head in sorrow.

"What a terrible thing. Shocking! I hope nothing's broken...?"

"Nothing's broken."

"Thank goodness."

The antique elevator seemed to be taking its sweet time dropping five floors.

"I understand this man shot at you?"

I didn't answer.

"It was lucky for you that Mickey came in when he did, wasn't it?"

I answered Heffernan but addressed myself to Michael Stone.

"It was lucky for Mickey that the shotgun wasn't loaded."

The elevator jerked to a stop.

"Kidding!" Anup Banerjee yelped from over my shoulder. "She's kidding... It's been a long night—"

"I'm kidding," I said, deadly.

The elevator opened and the four of us crossed the empty lobby of the Hall of Justice together. We split at the staircase onto Bryant Street. No one offered a backward glance. Once we were out of earshot, Anup started to admonish me for the stunt—but a swift side-eye clammed him up. We turned the corner by the McDonald's toward my Beemer, still parked in the loading dock lot. Anup started giggling. I shot him another side-eye. He tried to stop, and out popped a wet snort that started me going, too. It got worse. Pretty soon the pair of us had dissolved into stifled, clucking hysterics.

"Oh God," I managed to say, and pointed at one of the video cameras staring down at the morgue loading dock, and us. "Good thing those don't work...!"

That slayed Anup. I reached to hold him up as he gasped for breath. He put his hands on my shoulders, and I laced mine over his, and we leaned against each other by the crowns of our heads, laughing till we were both in tears.

It felt good.

It was well after midnight by the time we reached the Richmond District. The Rhythm & Dunes concert was over but a crowd lingered, warbling their favorite tunes and pausing to piss on the rosemary bushes.

I opened the wooden gate to 892 41st Avenue. The concert's colored searchlights cast the fog in a kaleidoscope glow, but my tiny overgrown yard was pitch-dark, and sinister. It had never felt that way before. Anup made small talk about the bright yellow cable car cottage to mask his own nervousness. I turned my door key and flipped the light—and we gasped in unison.

Mahoney Brothers #45 was ransacked. Rubbish—bits of fabric, foam rubber, shredded paper—covered the floor and the bench seats along the wall. Chairs were upended. The kitchen was a junk pile of canned food, plastic forks, and take-out chopsticks. The whole place had a terrible sewage reek.

"Oh my God!" Anup yelped. He grabbed me by the hand and dragged me back out the door.

"Anup...hold on..." He was pulling me across the yard.

"Whoever did that could still—"

"Relax!" I planted my feet to stop us, and put my other hand over his. "You're half right..."

I went back to the cabin and opened the door again. I called for Bea. I had to do it three times—but then she appeared, whimpering, tail between her legs, head down.

"The culprit," I announced.

It took Anup a minute to put it together. "Your *dog* did that?"

I pointed a finger at Bea. "Bad dog! Bad dog, scaring the crap out of the nice lawyer man!" She whimpered some more. I figured that was guilt trip enough. It was my fault, after all. Well, technically it was Yellow Eyes' fault, the fucker. I knelt to scratch Bea's ears and give her a couple of little kisses, and she perked right up, tail wagging, tongue flapping gratefully.

"Oh my God..." Anup said again, and slumped.

"You two have met, I believe."

Bea loped over to sniff at Anup. He held out his knuckles for her.

"What's the little terror's name?"

"Bea."

"Short for Beatrice?"

"Short for Beagle."

Bea snuffled a circle around Anup's loafers. Anup stared at me.

"She's a beagle," I said.

Bea went inside. She came back with the leash in her mouth and jumped up on me.

"Will you come with us?" I asked Anup.

We headed down Fulton Street along the park. I made two calls to Tommy that bumped straight to voice mail. I cursed in Polish.

"You can't stay alone tonight," Anup said.

"I'm going to Tommy's. I'll be fine."

"He's not answering his phone."

"It's off—but he's there."

"Where's he live?"

"Menlo Park."

Anup looked at me in astonishment. "Jessie," he said, "Menlo Park is forty-five minutes away, minimum. You're injured and exhausted. You can't drive down there not know-ing if you can get in."

I dialed Tomasz again. Got the same result.

"Wait!" Anup said brightly, pulling out his own phone. "Victim Services! Why didn't I think of that before? They'll put you up in a hotel."

"What hotel?"

"The Holiday Inn."

"The one on Van Ness?"

"Yeah, exactly."

"No way! You know how many bodies I've trucked out of that place?"

"Oh, come *on*—"

"I did an OD there last week! Thanks but no thanks. I just wish Tommy would answer his goddamn phone..."

A drunk concertgoer crashed through the cypress trees, cursing as he ran into a branch. A pair of tottering girls fol-lowed, screeching with laughter. Bea barked in alarm.

"Okay, look," Anup said, "I have a futon. A really fancy futon—"

"No."

"Hear me out. I've sheltered clients before, in emergencies like this. Well, not like *this*...nothing's like this. The futon is downstairs behind the garage—"

"You want to lock me in your basement."

"It's not a basement and that's not funny."

"Anup. Fancy futon or no, I am not going to impose on you like that."

"It's no imposition! I've got nothing going on tomor-row. You can sleep in and I'll leave you alone. You must be starving—I know I am... I've got a leftover casserole we can nuke—"

He jumped as the crash of something being loaded onto a

flatbed shattered my one good ear, and Bea went bananas as a truck hauling chemical toilets roared past us on Fulton. I had to holler over the diesel din.

"The dog comes too!"

Anup Banerjee rented a house in the Outer Sunset District, the only neighborhood even foggier than mine. He had beers in the fridge. Good beers. I drank a couple with the casserole. "Casserole" didn't do it justice: The dish was some thick chickpea-and-lamb stew, fragrant and wonderful over fluffy rice. Anup said we had his mom to thank for it.

"She drives up here from Cupertino every Sunday to check that I'm eating, and brings food just in case I'm not."

"You said she's a doctor?"

"My dad, too."

"Well, there you go, then. Nutrition is very important, young man. What flavor of doctors are they?"

"Mom's an ob-gyn, Dad's a cardiologist. They wanted me to be a physician. I'm a huge disappointment."

"You're a lawyer! That's not good enough?"

He shook his head ruefully. "A corporate lawyer, maybe. Or a professor of law. But a prosecutor? Law enforcement...? They expected more of me."

I stuffed my mouth with chickpeas and lamb before I could put my foot in it. My mother never expected much of me. My father did. But he was—and, as far as I know, still is—a bitter, abusive bastard, and I never put much stock in his opinion. My mother got her green card after she married him, but that's not why she did it. To hear Danuta Repczyńska tell the tale, she married Arthur Teska because Arthur Teska was her very own American Dream. He was tall and wavy-haired and handsome, charming and open as a book, gregarious and funny. He wasn't kind, though; and he drank.

Dad didn't start beating *Mamusia* until after I was born, and the only thing that stopped him was getting thrown out of our house on Pinkham Street in East Lynn fifteen years later. Tommy did the throwing part, and I arranged for a locksmith to rekey the door. I chose the wording on the restraining order, too. *Mamusia* signed on the line.

Tomasz was only fourteen then, and he wasn't a big boy, either; but he was tough—tough enough to stand up to the old man that one time. That's all it took. *Mamusia* blamed Tommy—still blames Tommy—when her beloved Arthur didn't come crawling back. She claimed he'd run off in fear of child protective services, but that wasn't the reason, and she knew it. Dad was looking for any excuse to cut loose from us. We shouldn't have bothered with the restraining order. He made himself good and scarce.

The last time I saw my father was a dozen years ago, at Central Square Lynn, when he followed me onto the commuter rail and spent the whole ride over the marshes and through the switchyards to Boston North Station telling me how everything was my mother's fault, that she drove him to drink, that he missed me, that he loved me. I was nineteen. I hustled down the platform and Arthur Teska ghosted into the crowd. Behind me I heard him say, "I'll see you, Jess, okay? Be good..."

Anup Banerjee's family situation sounded pretty damn cozy to me. I didn't hold it against him. People from happy families can't comprehend what it's like to live in a hostage situation with people who tell you they love you.

I had a nice, hot shower upstairs while Anup made up the futon in his spare room behind the garage. A high window looked out to the backyard, where he kept a fire pit and some lounge chairs. Bea was romping around out there under a dim light. I commented that she seemed to enjoy snuffling through his little vegetable garden.

"She's probably after the gophers," he said. "I'd be a better farmer if it wasn't for them—them and the fog."

The futon room seemed to be his home office. He had plastered one wall with awards and certificates. I ran a finger along the top of a boxy prize for legal scholarship. No dust. The smallest frame had pride of place, set apart in the center. It contained a handwritten letter.

Dear Anup, it read, *You helped give me my life back. I don't know how to thank you. With love and gratitude—Daryl and Elaine.*

Alongside the letter was a stamped and sealed ruling from the Superior Court of California and a newspaper clipping headlined *DNA Frees Man after 15 Years for Murder.*

I asked Anup about it. "It's a long story," he said, "and it's been a long day." He gave the pillow a final jab and started for the door.

"Give me the short version."

Anup stopped on the threshold. "It's a case I worked on when I was a law student at Santa Clara University. An exoneration."

"Really?"

"A stabbing down in San Jose. Daryl Harrick was nineteen when he was arrested for it. The knife had partial prints, inconclusive for a match, and they never did DNA. Daryl got convicted on circumstantial evidence and sentenced to life. He spent twelve years in prison before the Innocence Law Center took up his case. I was an intern there, and it was my job to reexamine the evidence. I started with the knife—"

"You sent out for a low copy number DNA analysis, which didn't exist at the time of the original trial."

Anup lit up. "Exactly! But that's not all. In the evidence box

I found swabs from blood spots collected at the scene. Those hadn't been tested, either—"

"What the hell?"

"Right. The technology *was* there to test that blood—but the DA never did."

"So you tested it, and…?"

"Both the knife and the droplets contained the victim's DNA and another person's—a man who was already in prison for a different murder. Another stabbing, two years after this one."

"Wow."

"Yeah. We got an appeal. It took us three years and a lot of work, but Daryl's a free man now."

"Who is Elaine?"

"His mom. She still sends me Christmas cards. Daryl's doing all right. Not great. No one can give him those years back."

"And the second victim would still be alive today if the district attorney hadn't prosecuted an innocent man."

"Imagine being that second victim's family."

I could. I've talked to those families.

"And now," Anup said wryly, "you're wondering why, after that experience, I got out of law school and went straight to work as a prosecutor."

"It did cross my mind."

"I was idealistic. I believed that by working each and every case with integrity and discipline, I would be able to prevent the miscarriage of justice." He sighed, and his head tipped sideways, pulling his whole frame into a stoop. "*But.* Then I started working at a real-life district attorney's office. The understaffing, the overwhelming volume of cases, the culture of winning that pushes ADAs everywhere to cut corners in pursuit of convictions. It's hard to work up every lead. I don't have the time, I don't have the resources."

Anup contemplated the handwritten letter. "I keep this as a reminder. It's here and not at my office because it's not something to show off. It never should have been written."

"Anup—! It says right there, in the man's own handwriting, that you gave him his life back!"

"That's Elaine's handwriting. She was just so happy to have her son out. But Daryl never should have gone into that prison."

Anup Banerjee smiled in a tired way, an ivory sliver in a dark face, in a dark room. "You get settled. I'll bring the dog in."

I slept through the night on the fancy futon, but had bad dreams, and woke, bleary, sometime after ten. Bea wasn't there. I dragged myself upstairs, calling the dog, surprised she hadn't woken me sooner for her walk. I called again, but she didn't answer and didn't come running.

"Anup…?"

His house was silent.

My stomach tightened. I stood in the elbow of the L-shaped kitchen and listened. Something in the next room creaked.

I swept my head around until I located the handle of a chef's knife in the drying rack. I moved toward it.

The coffeepot stopped me. It was a fancy vacuum thingy sitting on a twee table—laid out with a mug, a sugar bowl, and a pastry on a plate. A spoon on a folded cloth napkin. A note.

I couldn't bear to wake you & Beagle was antsy so I took her out running with me. Enjoy the Danish. Milk & half-n-half in fridge. Mi casa es su casa!

"Jesus, Mary and Joseph," I said aloud.

I was finishing the coffee when I heard Bea loping up the front stairs with Anup. He wore a faded red Stanford Athletics T-shirt and skintight black spandex shorts that immediately brightened my outlook on the day.

"Good morning," he said.

"Hello there."

Bea barked happily and hopped her paws on my lap.

"Down, girl," I warned.

Anup insisted that he wanted to come back to my place to help me fix it up. I said yes, I would be grateful; both for the labor and the company. He flashed another smile—genuine, this one, and wide—and I watched him go bounding up the stairs to take a shower. I reminded myself we were colleagues—and never again was I going to get mixed up with a colleague.

The last time Bea trashed my house it was the place on Midvale Avenue in Los Angeles. Barry and his wife had separated by then, and though Barry had rented his own place, he was spending most of his free time at mine. He came home from a shift one day with a puppy. I knew why he brought me the dog: It was a diversionary tactic, a way of muting the ticktock of my biological clock. I had given him a key but he rang the doorbell. I was in an apron when I answered it.

Barry Taylor was a native Angeleno and looked the part—a suntanned, boyish dirty blond with clear emerald eyes, a square chin, and sharp jawline. If he hadn't been a cop, he could've worked as a surfwear model. The beagle was licking his chin and he was grinning like a little kid. I think I was never more in love with Barry than at that moment.

We woke the next morning to find that the puppy had escaped her pen and chewed up every shoe she could hunt down. She'd left turds and puddles all over the apartment. Barry was still naked but for a T-shirt while he scrubbed the wall-to-wall carpet, grousing. It was a ridiculous, hilarious sight. He proposed that we should name the puppy Brody, the hero cop in *Jaws*. I told him I liked that name too much to give it to a dog. What I didn't tell him was that I didn't want to play around with naming any creature we were raising until it was our baby.

Barry and Cat had been high school sweethearts, still practically kids when they married. He worked; she stayed at home and had an Etsy business or something. They always wanted a family, but the time was never right. Barry was working Narcotics. He wanted to make sergeant, and spent a lot of time undercover, gone sometimes for weeks on end. Cat bugged him to transfer to Robbery, and eventually he did—but then it turned out he was working just as hard, trying to make detective. They were fighting constantly. Then came the trial separation.

I mostly steered clear of boys growing up. Slogging through state college on a shoestring of loans and side jobs didn't much change things. I still lived with my mother and commuted by train from Lynn to Boston every day, a townie in a college town, a bitter sort of internal exile. If you really wanted to get laid, you could always show up at a frat party—BU or BC or Northeastern, take your pick—but I was never much interested in hooking up with some drunken arrested-adolescent who laughed at me for dropping my *r*'s.

California was different. No one cared where I came from. In Los Angeles I shed the chip on my shoulder and started enjoying the occasional man in my life. I enjoyed Barry Taylor especially. Barry was still working Narcotics back then. He kept showing up at my office in the company of a corpse, usually one of his confidential informants, terminally over-dosed. We hit it off right away. Barry has a dry sense of humor and an eye for the absurd. He keeps an even keel. He's sharp as a tack, well-read, engaged in the world. He seemed a no-bullshit kind of guy, and I value that. Detective Barry Taylor never asked me out, nothing like that. I enjoyed flirting with him because he was safe—safe, because he wore a wedding band and safe because medical examiners dating cops is taboo at best, cause for dismissal at worst. Our flirty pas de deux changed one late-winter afternoon when he came to my office and I noticed the ring was gone.

"I thought you were married," I said.

"Divorced," he replied; and then hedged. "Well, it's not finalized…"

I accepted Barry's invitation to a casual dinner that Friday. After, we went to his bachelor pad apartment. The key was still so fresh-cut that he had trouble opening the door. The place had the smell of cheap new carpet and barely dry paint. I stayed for a drink but that was all. It wasn't long before I was staying the night. It wasn't long before I was in love. Barry wasn't a homicide detective, so we both figured that neither the LAPD nor the county coroner had any business telling us who we could fraternize with outside the workplace. Not as long as we could still do our respective jobs without letting our relationship get in the way, that is. As long as we both maintained our integrity.

We were together for three months. The divorce was proceeding slowly. There were financial complications, community property issues.

"Cat is my past," Barry kept telling me. "You're my future, Jessie." The one time I pointed out that my own future, my opportunity to bear children without medical complication, was narrowing as I passed my thirtieth birthday, he embraced me and told me how proud he was of everything I'd accomplished—putting myself through school, earning my MD, the hard work I did that he couldn't imagine doing—and he acknowledged that I'd only been able to get where I was because I had done the opposite of what he had. I hadn't married young; I didn't make that mistake. I had kept my goals in sight and gone after them.

"That discipline," he said. "I wish I had that discipline of yours."

He said he, too, wanted to have children. He wanted to have my children. He assured me I was going to make the world's greatest mother. Soon. Both my Midvale apartment and his bachelor pad were too small for us to move into together, but we'd find a place once his lease expired at the end of May. Then, after the divorce was finalized, when nothing was in our way, we could get married. It wouldn't be a June wedding—but maybe by the Fourth of July. For sure before the summer was over. Barry promised.

I believed him.

I never did give the dog a name. I just kept calling her Beagle.

The single pile of dog shit in Mahoney Brothers #45 lay in the far corner of the kitchen. On linoleum: Thank heaven for small mercies. Bea had wet the rug in my bedroom, too. Anup donned biohazard autopsy gloves out of my call bag and decontaminated the linoleum while I threw open all the windows, hauled the rug to the yard, and gave it a good hosing-down on the clothesline. Then we stuffed garbage bags with the mauled remains of my sofa cushions, throw pillows, cardboard boxes, and kitchen jetsam.

"Zasrane to życie."

"I'm going to guess I agree."

"It's a shitty life."

"Well, literally."

I had to sit down and hang my head. My right ear was throbbing and tender, the hearing wooly. My right eye had blossomed overnight into a purple shiner. The whites were bright red. I imagined my own gloved fingers jotting *right orbital diffuse scleral hemorrhages* on an autopsy sheet. The dull blush of choke-hold marks on my neck was something I'd only ever seen in victims of strangulation. Dead bodies under the knife—my body in the bathroom mirror.

Anup righted a chair and sat beside me. He put a glass of water in my hand.

"Last night, you told Jones and Ramirez that Michael Stone belongs in jail. I want you to explain to me why you said that, Jessie—and this time it's not because I'm worried about what it might do to my cases. I'm worried about *you*."

His big brown eyes, which had been so probing the last time he interrogated me about Stone, were full of compassion and, yes, worry. No artifice, no misdirection.

I believed him.

"You were right. Dr. Howe told me to talk to no one but him about Stone."

Anup didn't press it. I examined my hands. The knuckles on my right fingers were bruised like a fighter's. My left had a jagged nail from clawing at Yellow Eyes. I remembered Rebecca's right hand on my autopsy table: her manicured false fingernails, except for the index, that nail broken in an irregular line.

"I believe Michael Stone murdered a woman named Rebecca Corchero. She came into our morgue and I caught the case. He made her death look like an accidental overdose of heroin jacked up with acetylfentanyl. We've been seeing a lot of those."

"Why would Stone kill this woman?"

"She was pregnant with his child."

Anup sat back. He told me to go on, to tell him everything. This time I was willing to. I wanted to. So I did.

I finished by saying that I thought it was possible Stone was connected to Azarola. "The drugs that killed Rebecca were chemically identical to the drugs that killed Graciela Natividad in the Hotel Somerville, and one of the packets of heroin from that autopsy is missing. Unaccounted for."

I watched his eyes travel back and forth across the bent-wood ceiling.

"You think Stone stole the heroin and used it to inject Rebecca."

"Yes."

"That's hard to prove."

"Not my job."

"Jessie… Jackson Heffernan had a point last night, in the elevator. Michael Stone may have saved your life."

"Don't think that hasn't occurred to me. If Jones and Ramirez had done their damn job and arrested him, he wouldn't have been there and I might…"

Anup shook his head.

"I might still be in the morgue right now."

Anup took the empty water glass out of my hand and re-filled it.

"It was a mistake to go to Howe instead of the police, but I can fix that. I'm the doctor of record. It's my death certificate and my report. I'm going to file it—and then Jones and Ramirez will have an open homicide on their hands, and they'll *have* to do something about it."

"But that's why they're dragging their feet—they can't arrest someone as prominent as Stone without probable cause. You uncovered his infidelity, but you can't prove that the baby was his without the fetus—"

"That he destroyed!"

"His lawyer will say *you* lost it in the morgue, and it'll be hard for a prosecutor to prove you didn't. You're accusing Stone of evidence tampering and murder. The circumstantial evidence isn't enough to support those charges. Maybe you can prove he was an adulterer, but adultery isn't criminal."

"It wrecks lives, Anup! It…"

Anup Banerjee was gathering bits of debris, dropping them in a garbage bag. He turned to face me, a handsome young man in old jeans, cleaning dog shit out of my house because he's decent and kind, and maybe wants to connect with me. I wanted to connect with him. Oh, God, did I.

But I wouldn't. I couldn't, not unless I wanted to notch one more wreck on my belt.

"I don't want to talk about it anymore." My throat was raw and my voice, which had been hoarse since Yellow Eyes had tried to strangle me, was giving out. "I just want to finish up here so I can get down to my brother's place. I'm sorry, Anup."

"It's okay. I mean it. Just… I hope you'll trust me when you need to."

"I…"

The bitty room only took me three steps to cross. I placed my right palm on Anup Banerjee's warm breast, over his beating heart.

"I trust you," I said.

I spent the whole drive to Menlo Park with one eye glued to the rearview mirror, watching for Dodge Chargers. The farther south I went, the faster the traffic and the pricier the cars. I set cruise control at the speed limit and watched Teslas and Bentleys flow around me.

When he saw my swollen face, my little brother went pale with fury. I tried to talk him down by joking about all the times he'd gone out looking worse, but he wasn't buying. Tomasz and I had always watched out for one another. The beatings he took were ones I couldn't protect him from. Now I'd taken one of those.

He poured himself a Coke and brought me one of the beers he kept for guests, and I recounted the whole thing. A proud twinkle replaced the flame in my brother's eyes. "A scalpel to the knee? That'll leave a mark."

"Pretty sure I hit bone."

He hoisted his glass. *"Na zdrowie!"*

I clinked it with my bottleneck. *"Sto lat!"*

We drank—to "a hundred years" of birthdays.

"And that's what gets me," I said. "This guy's nose is busted, he's got a stab wound, formaldehyde is burning his eyes and his airway, and I'd bashed him in the nads. What's he do when I get away...? He follows me down the hall, deeper into this building that's crawling with cops—and he's shooting!"

"He was motivated."

"The detectives want this to be a rapist. I think they're wrong. I think he's a hit man."

Tommy paced a rectangle in his living room, wheels turning under his mat of curly hair.

"Why didn't he shoot Stone?"

"He... I don't know."

I replayed it: Stone with his hands in the air, frozen in fear. Then that tilt of the head. Yellow Eyes lowers his weapon. His body relaxes. Damn, he says.

Damn.

"He recognized Stone."

Tommy nodded.

"So does he *know* Stone?"

"Ask Stone."

"Psiakrew."

"Jessie," Tommy said quietly, "why didn't he shoot you anyways, after Stone showed up?"

"Maybe he was instructed to make sure it happened without witnesses. First plan—a carjacking. That went south when I recognized his Charger outside. Backup plan—a rape attempt. He was probably still trying to make that work when he chased me into Howe's office. And he didn't have a backup plan to his backup plan."

"To dobra rzecz."

"Most of the time these guys are not terribly bright, Tomasz."

"To dobra rzecz," my little brother said again. He was right: It's a good thing.

I pressed the cool bottle to my black eye. It was starting to open, sticky and blurry and still drumming my pulse back. Who wanted to ambush and kill me after a late night at the office, and who would keep after me so recklessly—right up until he recognized Michael Stone's face?

No one I could imagine. That scared me more than anything else.

Tommy's phone chirped. He snatched it off the coffee table, and I ragged on him for ignoring me all night at my time of extreme need, but jumping on some stupid text now.

"This stupid text is important," he said, thumbs aflutter. "You'll find it interesting." He'd been offered an opportunity to go for a technical interview as part of a job recruitment pitch.

"I thought you were happy at your job."

"I am. I'm just curious about this place. It's a raw start-up called Redoxx PicoApp. I did some homework—Redoxx is receiving venture capital that's being kept very hush-hush for now. Guess what company is supplying it?"

"How the hell would I know?"

Tommy smirked and said nothing.

"What?" I demanded.

And then it came to me—

"No!"

Tommy nodded.

"TechFolio?"

He held up his phone with the text thread. "The funding for this company comes from Arnie Spitz."

"Son of a bitch!"

"I know, right? I'll get in there to do some tree structures, and then I can get a peek at their—"

"You can't!"

Tommy cocked his head. "What?"

"You don't understand! Arnie Spitz is...oh God, where do I start...?"

I told Tommy about the links between Arnie and Joe Azarola: The multiple, anonymous TechFolio accounts Azarola had accessed on his laptop the same evening he was shopping online for elephant tranquilizers and waiting for his accomplices to cut open a dead woman and collect a pile of heroin-filled condoms. The same evening he'd shot dead Eugene "Lumpy" Chen after Lumpy tried to steal that laptop.

"That's all connected? Through *Arnie Spitz?*"

"I tried to make a district attorney see it that way, but he says there's not enough for probable cause. It's only a *theory*, he says."

"Well." Tomasz shoved his right thumb under his chin and

his index finger across his top lip. I knew not to break the trance. "Well," he said again. "Then I *have* to go in there."

"What? No!"

"Yes. The evidence proving your theory is behind Tech-Folio's firewall. I can go get it."

"But Spitz knows you're my brother and he knows I'm onto him—he won't let you through the door!"

"He won't even know I was there."

"What makes you think that?"

"Companies like this are super compartmentalized. I'll get behind the firewall, hack around and see what he's got."

"You'll be breaking the law..."

He flicked his wrist at the quibble. "Civil, not criminal."

"Still!"

"Czesia. You want answers about Arnie's bitcoin shenanigans?"

I conceded I did.

A familiar felonious glimmer brightened my brother's features.

"I'll deliver."

My cell phone said 4:02 a.m.

"Dr. Teska?"

It was a woman. She sounded familiar.

"Where am I?"

"Dr. Teska? It's the office calling."

"Wait."

I sat up, blinked around. I was in a strange room. No: I knew the place. It was my brother's spare room, at his apartment in Menlo Park. It was Sunday night. I was at Tommy's, it was Sunday night, I was on call. The woman on the phone was Donna Griello. I rubbed my face, felt sweat. I had been dreaming. Another nightmare. It was slipping away. I let it.

"Okay," I said. "What's up?"

"A floater."

Donna gave me the details—Pier 39, look for the police Marine Unit boat moored on the north side.

It was a few minutes before five when I got there; still pitch-dark. The lighthouse on Alcatraz Island cut a white pinwheel under the fog. A patrol cop pointed to a floating dock and told me to watch myself on the gangway. It made me seasick, bucking and skating in the windblown eddies of San Francisco Bay. Sudden flashes from the CSI photographer didn't help my balance any—and then there was the fishy fecal reek from sea lions barking and braying one on top of another.

The police boat had its searchlight pointed at a blue tarp. "What do we got?" I said.

"Holy shit, Jessie!" The voice belonged to Cameron Blake. Damn. My face.

"You should see the other guy," I said, and sidled past Cam and Donna and the boat cops and the CSI tech to the soggy corpse on the tarp. It was face-down. Well, it would have been, if it had a face: The head was missing. I pulled gloves out of my kit bag and took a closer look.

The body belonged to a man wearing a ripped T-shirt and blue jeans. His feet were bare, hands bound behind his back with what looked like fishing line. The fingertips had all been cut off. The wound margin on the stump of his neck had a ratty look, and the vertebral bones had been hacked apart. Deep furrows ringed the base of the neck: ligature strangulation. Cam and Donna joined me and we patted down the wet clothing. No wallet, no phone, nothing.

I snapped off my gloves and the homicide detectives stepped up: a hard, ball-shaped woman and a lumpy man with a stiff crew cut, brown but for a single white patch, like a baby's first tooth. I asked where the body was found. It had got snagged in the pilings at the end of Pier 39, Inspector Baby Tooth said. A security guard thought it was a sea lion till he noticed it wasn't moving. Baby Tooth's partner asked me what I could tell them about the remains.

"Definitely an intentional beheading, probably postmortem, along with the fingertips, to prevent ID." I pointed to the ligature furrows, uniform depth going all the way around the neck except for a shallower spot over the nape. "Garroting. Maybe the same fishing line that's binding his hands—it looks like the same gauge." I got down on my knees and shined my penlight on the dead man's forearms and hands, clean but for his mangled fingers. "I don't see any defensive injuries, so he was probably bound first then strangled."

"Can you estimate age?" Baby Tooth asked.

"Maybe on autopsy, for sure by forensic anthropology."

"Race?"

"His pigmentation looks light, but there's enough decomposition that I won't guess until we get him back to the morgue."

"The sooner the better, Doc," the detective said, and ordered the police boat to kill its flashing blue lights. The sky was lightening. Our floating dock was attached to the backside of Pier 39, the go-to tourist trap in a tourist town. Neon signs were blinking on, lookie-loos had started to gather, and two big ferries were firing up their engines. I agreed; high time to get our mangled cadaver out of there.

Donna and Cam counted to three and flipped the sodden carcass onto its back, into the body bag.

"Hold up," I said, and pointed my light. I pushed up the shredded T-shirt. Green belly. I asked the boat cop the water temperature.

"Fifty-nine degrees."

I turned to the woman detective. "He's been dead about two days."

A perfect V of pelicans soared silently overhead. Alcatraz Island was unveiling itself in the pewter dawn. It was turning into an altogether lovely morning. The 2578s hoisted the body bag by its corner handles. One of the cops offered to help them carry it up the gangway. Donna declined.

"Piece of cake," she said. "Ten pounds lighter without the head."

———————

Cam backed the van right up to the electric sliding doors on the morgue's loading dock. I parked the Beemer next to them and stayed put in the driver's seat till my heart rate and the hairs on my neck both came down. The 2578s off-loaded the gurney and maneuvered it onto the floor scale in the sally port. Cam made a lame joke about fingerprinting while he did the math to come up with the weight of the remains.

Donna asked, "You want us to put him in the cooler, or leave him by your table?"

It was 6:20, only an hour and change till morning meeting. No point going home.

"Bring him to X-ray. I might as well clock in."

They rolled the gurney to the cramped radiology room. I followed. My station's lab counter was in its usual rickety and scarred state, no worse for the violence that had happened there. I gasped from a sharp stitch in my chest and realized it had been there since the attack, that it hurt to breathe and I'd been ignoring the pain. *That was a stupid fucking thing to do, Jessie. What if it's a closed rib fracture that decides to avulse? Bend over the wrong way and you'll end up with a pneumothorax, and—*

"Doc...?" said Cameron. He and Donna looked anxious.

"What."

"Do you want some help doing the X-rays?" I realized that he'd asked me this already and I hadn't answered.

"What I could really use is coffee," I said.

Cameron smiled, relieved. "We're going on a Mickey D's run. I'll bring you a muffin puck, too."

Without the head, X-ray was a little quicker than usual—but it was hard work, shifting the sodden body around. I inspected the images on the monitor as they appeared. The body was still clothed, so the studs and zipper on the floater's jeans showed up. I noticed one other piece of metal, in the right leg, embedded in the stout bone of the femur's distal end. Bullet shaped—a straight line on one end and oblique curves everywhere else. I checked the jeans for a bullet hole and didn't see one. Maybe it was a souvenir from an old injury. I'd find out when I cut in.

But that was for later. It was time for morning meeting. I was grateful for the lukewarm coffee and canary-cheese Egg McMuffin Cam handed me.

Dr. Stone was absent again. This time there was no explanation at all, and Howe was forcing Ted Nguyen to act as deputy chief. I already had my floater homicide. He handed me two more cases, a natural and an accident, and kept a stack of folders in front of himself.

"How many you taking, Ted?" I asked.

"Five."

"Five...?"

"Two are externals."

Cameron caught my eye. He shook his bald head tightly. I jerked a thumb toward the students huddled against one wall. "Our future doctors ought to hear what they are, don't you think?"

Nguyen assented with a grunt. "One, sixty-two-year-old male, anesthesia complications during a prostatectomy at St. Francis. Two, forty-five-year-old male with history of heart disease and diabetes found decomposing in his bedroom. Three, a ten-week-old infant found dead amid abundant bedding in her crib. Four, elderly woman slipped and fell at the Stonestown Mall, skull fracture. Five, pedestrian versus truck. Dead at the scene with devastating injuries to the torso and extremities."

I didn't have to fake my confusion. "Which ones are the externals?"

"The last two."

"A fall in a public place and an MVA?"

"Yeah."

"Don't you think they should have autopsies?"

"No."

Donna Griello snickered. Nguyen glared. "Whatever," Donna said. "My shift's ending."

I said, "What if that truck driver turns out to be drunk? The DA might want—"

"What do you want me to do? Either we can do external examinations or we can stack the leftovers in the cooler till tomorrow and hope that Mike deigns to join us then!"

Yarina piped up. "Dr. Howe says this is okay?"

"You go ask him," Ted snapped back. He scooped up his pile of case folders. "Let's get this over with."

Under his clothes, John Doe #76, my floater homicide, was young and fit, what was left of him. Early decomposition— that green belly I had seen on the wharf and some marbling, but no skin slippage. He had a round purple contusion two inches in diameter on his right thigh. On the inner left wrist

I found a distinctive pattern of injury pressed into the skin: an oval bruise with wave-like striations running through it, and two healing scars, each radiating from a central divot. I had to stop my autopsy to write out a detailed description and take a bunch of pictures. I found a defect to the right forearm, too. I called all the medical students to gather around. The affected area was olive drab, black in spots, ochre along its ratty edges.

"Chemical burn," I said, "postmortem. How do I know that?" There were some wrong guesses; but then one student, a black woman with a gold dumbbell piercing one eyebrow, offered that she didn't see any inflammation.

"Exactly! Look at those margins, too. There's no redness or swelling surrounding the burned area. No immune response and no vital reaction—because he was already deceased when this happened."

"*How* did it happen?" another student asked.

"I believe it's intentional. It's too specific and localized to be a spill. So, then…you guys already know the next question."

Several voices answered together: "Why."

"Any ideas?"

Nobody had the right one.

"Consider this. He's missing his head and his fingertips. That's probably part of an attempt to prevent us from ID'ing him with prints or dental records. The burn is another part of that effort."

"A tattoo!" the student with the eyebrow said.

"Right again. I'll bet he had a distinctive tattoo here, and now we can't search missing-persons reports and other databases for that identifying mark."

Some of them stayed around while I opened up the decapitated body and examined the organs. Didn't find much. He had a moderately fatty liver consistent with drug or alcohol use, and pretty gnarly smoker's lungs with a lot of anthracotic pigmentation, but no signs of pulmonary disease. Booze and cigarettes didn't kill John Doe #76. A garrote did.

"Look at that," I said to the students who remained for the neck dissection. "Horizontal hemorrhage in the strap muscles. The force here was administered from directly behind, not from above, like in a hanging. Textbook ligature strangulation homicide."

I thought of Dr. Sutcliffe's floater case, the one that had caused such trouble. Sutcliffe ruled the manner of death as homicide, but Stone argued that it could be a suicide or accident with postmortem injury—and right there the jury in Hector Marroquin's RICO trial got a dose of reasonable doubt. What a headache. If my John Doe had marinated in the bay for a few more days like Sutcliffe's floater had, it might have ended up as ambiguously. At least my determination of cause and manner would be ironclad.

My last task was to retrieve that souvenir bullet in the right leg. It had to be an artifact from an old shooting; I didn't see a fresh gunshot wound anywhere. I studied the radiology images to pinpoint where it was, then started cutting. Just under the skin I discovered a wound track filled with clotted blood. It led into the center of the bruise on the lower thigh.

"Hand me that magnifying glass," I said to the student with the pierced eyebrow. I spotted a defect I hadn't seen with my naked eye and cut down, following the bloody track of the wound until I reached the egg-white bone of the patella. I dissected around it.

"Bingo."

A slender, sharp piece of metal glinted at us. I took a forceps and grabbed it—and one of the students objected.

"No metal implements! That's what Dr. Howe—"

"That's only for bullets. This is something else."

I pulled. It wouldn't budge out of the bone.

"Somebody go in my tool kit and get me a surgical clamp."

I squeezed the clamp until its ratchet locked, pinching the edge of the shrapnel lodged in John Doe's knee, and I yanked—hard. On the third try the leg jerked and the foreign object came out.

I held it right up to my plastic face shield, but didn't believe my eyes.

A student's voice over my shoulder said, "Well, look at that! It's a scalpel blade…!"

San Francisco's homicide detectives share an open office on the Hall's fifth floor, a cavernous chamber that must once have been a courtroom, with grand grimy windows climbing to the thirty-foot ceiling. It looks like a newsroom and smells like a gym. The place was largely empty for lunch— but detectives Keith Jones and Daniel Ramirez were at their workstation, chewing on sandwiches.

"Hi, Doc," mumbled Ramirez through a mouthful. "How's the eye?"

They offered some fries and I snarfed them gratefully; I'd been up since four and had only eaten the breakfast puck. They were hovering over a desk covered with photo printouts of the man who'd tried to kill me.

"Look at this," Jones said. On their computer screen was a press release with the headline *Wanted: SFPD Seek Public's Assistance in Assault Case.* Under that, a mug shot. Yellow Eyes' hair was dark, not bleached like in the Facebook posts, and he wore a thin mustache.

"That's an old picture," Ramirez said. "The public information office wants us to add a fresh one."

I scanned the Wanted poster: physical description, age 29,

comes from Visalia. They listed the plate number of his late-model orange Dodge Charger, phone numbers for the homicide detail and the anonymous tip line. And there was a name.

"Emilio Viscaya."

Giving Yellow Eyes a name brought that stitch back to my ribs. I massaged it and asked the detectives how they had ID'd him.

"Facebook," Ramirez said.

Jones lifted his soda and showed me a sheet underneath. "Viscaya did time twice, first for schedule one possession and then violating parole with felony trafficking and a side of reckless evading. Last year he beat a charge for assault with a deadly weapon. And—" the detective planted an index finger on the paper "—three years ago he was a person of interest in a forceable rape."

"I'll bet you haven't found him."

"We're close," said Ramirez.

"Closer than you think, Inspector."

I showed them the clear plastic sharps container I'd brought from the morgue. "This is a broken scalpel blade. I just pulled it out of a dead man's knee. We need to take it down to evidence and see if we can fracture-match it to the handle CSI recovered from my office Friday night."

"Whoa, whoa!" Ramirez said, choking down his mouthful of lunch. "What dead man?"

"The John Doe I picked up last night."

"The floater from Fisherman's Wharf, missing the head and hands?"

"Fingers."

Jones was already punching at the computer keyboard.

"That's Lynch and Wong's case," Ramirez mused. "If it's the same guy—"

"We ID their homicide and close our assault," his partner said.

Ramirez beamed at me. "A twofer!"

A printer whined. Jones grabbed the sheet it spat out, and with a Sharpie pen he circled *0012 DESC= SCALPEL*.

"Let's go."

We took the elevator down to B Level, the bowels of the Hall of Justice. Ramirez handed the printed sheet to a clerk behind the evidence room window. The clerk returned after a few minutes with a slender box.

"Signing it out?"

"No, we'll look at it here."

"Okay." He buzzed us through to a brightly lit room with a centimeter-grid counter, and offered us latex gloves from a box labeled *XL*. The detectives took theirs.

"I need size small," I said.

The clerk sighed, left, and came back with a box of medium gloves. "Smallest we got."

I gloved up and sliced through the evidence tape on the box, doing my best to handle a utility knife in floppy rubber fingers. Inside lay the pink scalpel handle Yarina had given me on my first day at work. It still had a shard of steel attached. The shard was smeared with blood. I put the scalpel on the grid table and fumbled with the sharps box from the autopsy until I got the broken blade out of it. I lined them up without letting them touch.

Perfect.

"Do you have a date of birth and next of kin contacts for Mr. Viscaya?" I asked.

"Back upstairs we do."

"Well, then, boys," I declared, "I've got your person of interest in our cooler, and you've got an ID for my John Doe."

I pulled my shoulders back and pushed my chin out. "It's not every day you get to solve your own attempted murder!"

I held up a gloved fist. Both detectives grinned and bumped it.

While Ramirez fiddled with the computer, searching for Emilio Viscaya's next of kin information, I leafed through Joe Azarola's Facebook photo printouts. Many were new to me: the dead man with a big, scary dog, the dead man with a busty woman. The dead man a blur in a crowded club, clowning around. I wanted a good look at that tattoo on his right arm. The picture I'd already seen, of Viscaya downing a shot, seemed to show it best. Underneath that print was a close-up of his face in profile as he reached for something with his other hand. It gave me a view of the scar I had just seen on his decomposing body. Before it had healed, the injury on his left wrist was an oblong abrasion with four thin, scalloped lacerations.

A chill went through me, through flesh and bone. I had seen those lacerations before. They were shaped like a startled baby's outstretched hand.

Or the petals of a daisy.

"Inspector Ramirez," I said, "tell me the date this picture was posted."

He took the print and flipped it over, read the number on the back, punched at his keyboard, and said August 9.

"Give me a calendar."

He pointed to one on the wall.

August 9 was a Sunday.

Rebecca Corchero had been killed the night before.

I sat on the edge of the desk.

"What's up?" Jones said, crumpling his sandwich wrapper and eyeing me.

"Got any soda left?"

"Sure."

"Let me have it."

He did. It was watery and flat, but at least it was cold. Ramirez made a joke of asking Jones about his herpes, but I hardly heard it. I stood and faced the two homicide detectives.

"Michael Stone didn't kill Rebecca Corchero. This guy did. Emilio Viscaya did."

They both stared for a while, to see if I had anything more to add. When I didn't, Jones swore and flung the sandwich wrapper into the trash.

"You mean that's a homicide again? Why don't you people make up your goddamned minds?"

"What do you mean, 'again'…?" I looked from him to his partner. Ramirez was staring at the ceiling and shaking his head.

"What do you mean, *again!*"

Ramirez brought his eyes back to mine. "The case against Stone is closed. We closed it Friday. We weren't getting anything good, and with his girlfriend's manner of death an accident, there was no point flogging that horse anymore."

"Wait. Wait, wait. *What?*"

They just glared at me.

"Who… Where's the death certificate? Show me the DC…"

"The sergeant called us to his office for a meeting. He was in there with Chief Medical Examiner Howe. Dr. Howe told us the Corchero manner of death was final—as an accident, not a homicide. The sarge told us to close the Michael Stone investigation. So we closed it."

"Waste of time," added Jones.

Ramirez had assumed his puzzled look. "Why are you asking us for the death certificate? Corchero is your case. Didn't you sign it out?"

I didn't answer him.

Other detectives were returning from lunch. They all seemed to pick up their phones at once. Their voices filled the vaulting space above.

Jones laughed in a sour way.

"So now you're telling us Michael Stone didn't kill Rebecca Corchero, huh? No shit. No one killed Rebecca Corchero."

He held his hand out across the sea of desks. "If you'll excuse us, Doc, we have homicides to solve over here. Accidents are with the Hit and Run squad. Out the door, make two rights, end of the hallway."

CHAPTER FIFTEEN

I hustled into the autopsy suite, found Yarina, and ordered her to wheel the morning's John Doe out of the cooler.

"Now?"

"*Right* now."

I went to the toxicology lab. Carlo San Pietro himself answered.

I said, "I need to sign out a piece of evidence."

San Pietro shook his head. "You people. You do not understand that the evidence, it belongs in the evidence room! If you need it, keep it until you are done—"

"New information changes the course of an investigation."

"Excuses! Dr. Stone's excuse today is the court for an exhibit. Your excuse is 'new information.' I cannot keep—"

"Dr. Stone—? Today?"

"Yes. I just finish with him, and you ring my bell. I have responsibilities..."

I let San Pietro prattle on about how important he was while he unlocked the door to the evidence closet and climbed up to retrieve the box from case SFME-0955. He asked me what I was looking for.

"An envelope marked *white metal bracelet lizard design*."

———————

Yarina had parked the macabre remains of Emilio Viscaya under the light by my autopsy table. I removed the gecko bracelet from the evidence envelope. Along its back marched rows of deeply etched scales. They matched the brown waves rippling across the yellow bruise on the corpse. I held the bracelet directly over it and pivoted the gecko out. When I did, the splayed toes of its feet aligned with the tiny wounds on the dead man's skin.

Emilio Viscaya and Rebecca Corchero had mirrored injuries, hers from one pair of the lizard's legs, his from the other. Viscaya was holding her arm down while he fought to inject her with a hot shot of Soul Sister. Two weeks after killing Rebecca and disguising it as an accidental drug overdose, he had tried to kill me and disguise it as a carjacking or a rape. He failed—and immediately someone killed *him* and tried to hide his identity. If it weren't for the scalpel blade, it might have worked.

I aligned the gecko with the injury on the corpse and Yarina took pictures. Dr. Howe couldn't ignore matching injury pattern evidence. The cops could drag their feet and stonewall Rebecca's murder case all they want. The body never lies.

———————

"I hope it's good news. I could use some." The chief recited a litany of snafus at the construction site—union headaches, fire marshal issues, something about rebar. He was leaning back in his swivel chair, playing with another of his desk doo-dads. He looked old and tired.

"Oh, it's good news. The case I did today, the John Doe? I got him ID'd."

"You mean the one with the souvenir bullet?"

"It wasn't a bullet. It was a broken number twenty-two scalpel blade."

"A twenty-two scalpel? But…"

It took a moment for him to put it together—and then dawn broke on Marblehead. I had managed to shock Dr. James Howe.

"You're joking."

"I'm not."

"Your John Doe this morning was the man who attacked you on Friday night?"

"His name is Emilio Viscaya. I photo-identified him to Ramirez and Jones."

"That's…amazing! God, Jessie, what a relief." He slapped a hand on his desk, and the smaller pieces of flotsam jumped. "You have cheered me right up, Jessie! Right up! I'm sure you've been concerned about your personal safety here in the Hall since Friday. We have all been. Did he have a record?"

"Yes."

"Did it include sexual assault?"

"Arrested but not indicted."

"My goodness—what a relief. I'm certainly glad that case is closed."

"It isn't."

"What do you mean?"

I laid out the pictures, the bracelet, the physical evidence. "This man Emilio Viscaya killed Rebecca Corchero."

"What?"

"The homicide detectives seem to think the Corchero case

is off their list," I said. "They told me the death certificate is finalized, with *accident* as the manner of death."

Dr. Howe crossed his arms.

"That's correct."

"There is no death certificate. I still have that case open, pending investigation."

"I signed it out."

"You…what?"

"I signed it. When you handed it off to me—"

"Handed it *off?*"

"—when you handed it off to me, the Corchero case became my responsibility—"

"You took it away from me!"

"You came to me looking for help because you had dug yourself a hole. You accused Michael Stone, your supervisor and my deputy—my friend and valued colleague—of *murder!* And when you did that—"

"You're making it sound like I couldn't—"

"Dr. Teska, I see that this is upsetting you, and I can't allow you to exacerbate your condition while you are still recuperating from a traumatic event. It might be best if we continued this discussion another time."

I clamped my lips together. I balled my fists. I said I was sorry.

"Have a seat."

I sat.

"I'm not alone in coming to this determination," Howe said. "Inspectors Ramirez and Jones were very thorough. I reviewed all of their findings. Miss Corchero's death is not a homicide."

"But she wasn't a user! She got a hot shot of the same heroin Joe Azarola was smuggling. This guy Viscaya has a felony drug record and was a known associate of Azarola's. Hell, the pictures I got off Azarola's computer show him and Viscaya posing with piles of drugs and stacks of cash!"

"Intentional poisonings are vanishingly rare—and your findings don't prove that Miss Corchero was forcibly injected at the hand of another."

"The physical evidence for assault is all there!"

A cutthroat glint came to Howe's eye. "She had the visceral congestion that comes from an overdose, and with her head slumped down—as we see in the scene photos—she ends up with petechiae. Her torn frenulum? Drug users fall. She tripped and hit something. I've seen that many times. I'll bet you have, too."

"I've never seen a blood morphine level that high."

"Point seven three milligrams per liter? I've seen naive users with *higher* numbers. She was a nursing student with easy access to needles, and you know from your own training that clinical care professionals frequently build a rapport with drug-addicted patients. Some of those patients are also dealers. This girl was a risk-taker, impulsive, we know that. Risk-takers use drugs, and drug users die disproportionately of accidents."

I accused him of circular logic. His pupils tightened. I didn't care. Maybe he'd lose his cool and say something that wasn't unalloyed horseshit.

"Rebecca died of the same heroin mix that Azarola was smuggling with a body packer," I said.

"Soul Sister. The detectives tell me it's all over the streets now. No way to trace it—Miss Corchero could have bought it anywhere. Oh, and that drug bindle you accused Mike of stealing out of evidence, after he did the autopsy on the body packer? It was in the police lab all along."

"What!"

"Mike took it straight there for testing. Yes, he should have logged it in with us first, but he didn't. This is why it's important to follow proper protocol. That missing bindle of heroin never was missing. All of the drugs that came through this office have been accounted for."

Howe stood, energized, and strode to the door. He closed it.

"That reminds me—protocol. You lost a specimen from the autopsy. A fetus. That's bad enough—but now you're trying to cover your ass by blaming Mike...?"

He swept an arm across his garbage patch of an office. "Specimens get lost. It happens. We're crowded and underfunded. That's why I was down at the building site today, trying to get our new facility finished. We need it. Desperately—before a mistake like yours becomes a scandal that will damage this whole department."

"Dr. Howe. Just because Mike didn't kill Rebecca doesn't mean he wasn't interested in hiding her pregnancy from—"

"Oh yes, let's talk about *that*, Jessie!" His voice had risen. The tap of someone's keyboard fingers in the Ops Shop on the other side of the door ceased. "Do you realize just how much damage you have done to the Stone family? The police investigation you instigated has caused Mike and his wife—and their daughter Calliope—a great deal of suffering..."

Calliope Stone, pointing to the Presidio hills smothered in fog on the Fourth of July. Sophia Kalogeras, her gems and expertly dyed hair. The pale outline of a watch band on Rebecca Corchero's tanned arm. The chalky pills in Mary Walsh's stomach. My own stomach lurched. Howe got to me. He didn't even know how bad.

"Rebecca Corchero was a consenting adult," he continued, softer. "Mike made a mistake, as many men do at his stage of life. It may be that this unfortunate, untimely death—in an accident of recreational drug use—is a blessing in disguise."

"Good riddance to the homewrecker."

"Don't be crude."

"You're blaming the victim!"

Dr. Howe shook his head and affected an air of disappointment.

"We are done here. I hope you've learned a lesson. You need watertight *evidence*, not innuendo, before you accuse a person of Michael Stone's caliber of wrongdoing."

"Evidence?" I was on my feet, but I sure as shit wasn't heading for the door. "Evidence… You're right that Stone didn't kill Rebecca Corchero. Emilio Viscaya killed Rebecca Corchero. You can dismiss my findings that the petechiae and the torn frenulum are indicative of a struggle. You can contest my opinion that the tox level points to an intentional poisoning. But you cannot ignore *this!*"

I planted a finger on the photographs of Rebecca's wrist and Viscaya's, the evidence right under his nose. "What are the odds that two people have mirroring lacerations with this kind of patterned injury?"

"What are the odds?" Howe sneered. "I don't know—what are they? Do you have peer-reviewed literature on matching patterned laceration injury between two individuals separated in time by two weeks and a whole lot of decomp? How would you defend your opinion under cross-examination?" He waggled a hand over the photographs. "This is, at best, a tangentially interesting artifactual finding. It isn't enough to make the manner of death homicide."

I grabbed the silver gecko in its plastic evidence pouch. "There is *blood* on this bracelet! We can type and test it, and some of it will come back belonging to Emilio Viscaya! *Look!*" It was all I could do to keep myself from shaking the thing under his nose.

Howe met my eyes. He held out his hand. I put the bracelet in it. He examined the lizard through the baggie, massaged its surfaces between his fingers and thumb. Then he leaned over the photos.

"These things you're calling grab marks on Rebecca Corchero could be from prior injury. As you've pointed out, this bracelet has sharp edges. And this healing injury on the decomp's arm—you have no way of telling what caused that."

I made no rejoinder. Not because Howe was right—but because I knew there was none to make. Howe had found a politically expedient reason to rule Rebecca Corchero's death an accidental drug overdose. Keeping his deputy chief away from a screaming-headline scandal involving a mistress, a drug ring, and a murder? Expedient enough.

Howe hollered through the door for the 2578s, and Donna Griello came in. She glanced at me, worried. Howe handed her the silver gecko in its evidence bag.

"This has been misfiled as evidence. It's property of the next of kin in a closed case. Release it to Yarina and make sure she doesn't leave today till she gives it a proper biohazard cleaning. Then expedite it to the Corchero family. *Immediately*, Griello. God knows they've waited long enough, the poor people."

"Yes, Dr. Howe," said Donna, and left.

I followed.

Howe said softly, "Wait. Please."

I stopped in the doorway.

"Jessie… I realize I haven't been forthcoming with you about the dire condition we're in here. We are at risk of losing our professional accreditation. We're already on probationary status because we just aren't clearing cases fast enough…"

Dr. Howe sighed and ran a hand through his thin hair. He looked up at the wall next to his desk, where he'd hung the blueprint plan for his cherished new morgue. He had bags under his eyes. His mouth drooped.

"If we lose accreditation we lose the confidence of the

mayor. She's told me as much. She'll pull the plug on the new building. It would end my career."

He rose and lifted the sports coat off the back of his chair.

"Rebecca Corchero died of an accidental overdose of recreational drugs. The final ruling is mine. I have issued the death certificate and closed the case. There's nothing you can do about it, and nothing you should want to."

He joined me by the open door.

"Let Rebecca rest in peace. Let her family say goodbye to her, finally. Other families need your help and are waiting for it."

Dr. Howe shut off the lights. In the sudden flat shadows he said, "Don't let them down."

I went back to my empty office and sat in the dark. I was desperate to talk to Anup Banerjee. I wanted to…what? Unburden? I wanted to hear his voice. I stared at the phone for a while, but didn't lift the receiver. Anup would ask me why I didn't fight. Because, Anup, if Dr. James Howe signs a death certificate, then it is carved in granite. Rebecca Corchero's death was an accident. Officially and finally.

The message light was flashing. I checked it. Neil Dupree again, insisting—in a civil tone, this time—that he still needed to talk to me. He swore up and down he had nothing to do with Rebecca's death, but ever since the police visit at Siloam Biologic, his boss had continued to give him heat about it.

"If you could just please find time in your schedule to come by our office and tell our CTO that I had nothing to do with—"

I erased the message. I was hungry. I chewed the edge of a ragged fingernail that got mauled in the fight with Viscaya and thought again of Rebecca's right index finger with its torn fake nail.

My phone chirped a text: Tommy.

Got news

I texted back.

Meet me Baby Mike Bail Bonds ASAP

BRT

U ate?

No

I'll bring tacos

Tripas?

Will see

K

Sparkle hadn't seen me with my black eye. She was pleased to hear that the man who gave it to me was dead—but worried when I told her how.

"Who strangled and dumped him?"

"I don't know. But it's the same—"

The Baby Mike Bail Bonds door chime rang for my brother, Tomasz. He greeted Sparkle. I pounced on him.

"What'd you find out?"

"They had tripas?"

I stuck the tripe burrito under his nose and he took a deep whiff of the foil wrapper. Then I yanked it back. "Show me what you've got. Now."

My brother's eyes followed the burrito with manifest longing while he put his foot on the edge of Sparkle's desk and produced a tiny black thumb drive from his sock.

"They didn't let me bring in any of my own devices, of course—but they didn't strip-search me, either."

He asked Sparkle if he could use her computer.

"I don't want any viruses."

"Trust me."

Sparkle looked to me, skeptical. I said, "Trust him."

Sparkle groused, but typed the password and gave up her chair. Tommy plugged in the data drive.

"They walked me around and showed off their hardware and introduced me to the chef who makes the free meals. It was pretty slick."

"Did you manage to get into the TechFolio computers?"

"At first I had no privacy. But then they handed me off to one of the senior programmers, who left me alone to do a hash table just to see if I had, you know, a functioning brain stem. From there I had access to force the ports. Their defenses are top-shelf, but I found an opening. See, first I had to sudo in using the default admin…"

Goddamn it.

"Tomasz. *Braciszku*. Did you get into TechFolio?"

"Yes."

"And…?"

"You were right. About Azarola. I found the other side of the trades he was making from his laptop."

"How?"

"TechFolio is funding Redoxx. They're connected on a foundational level. Once they sat me down at a machine on Redoxx's network, I was able to explore ways to hack into TechFolio. It wasn't easy, but I found one—a good and stable one, too. From there, it was a breeze to find Azarola's trades."

"So where did Azarola's money go once it was in the Tech-Folio system?"

"Bitcoin…" Tommy looked like he'd bitten into rotten fruit. "That's Arnie Spitz's brilliant new venture—a money laundering pyramid scheme. Just like Arnie told you, they really are turning dollars into bitcoins, then investing the bitcoin in other start-ups and paying dividends back to an investment earnings account at TechFolio. What he *didn't* tell you is that Azarola's account is earning a lot less than he's putting in."

"He's taking a loss? Why would he do that?"

Sparkle cut in. "Drug dealers don't mind paying for clean currency. As long as they get *most* of their money back, they're happy not to have to figure out a new place to pile up their stacks of greenbacks."

"Oh, it's clean," Tommy added. "I looked at some of the other accounts in there, on the TechFolio end. A lot of them are small investors, like you'd see in any mutual fund. I saw some tech fund heavy hitters in there, too."

I started to pace. "So Joe Azarola is a middle manager, collecting cash from street dealers. He bundles it and then sits at his laptop moving the money around, through multiple fake investor accounts at TechFolio. Dirty cash comes out laundered bitcoin."

"Laundered and anonymous," Tommy added.

"That creep Neil Dupree told me that Arnie Spitz would come into Siloam with bags full of cash. Most of that was investment capital for the company's operations—but as part of the deal, Siloam had to use the rest of the cash to put their own computers to work mining bitcoins for TechFolio."

"Spitz is subsidizing legitimate businesses with laundered drug money," said Sparkle. "There it is. You've got your closed loop."

"Hearsay. *Stolen* hearsay."

"Point the feds in the right direction, and they'll find it too. They've got subpoena power."

"Czesia," Tommy said from behind Sparkle's computer. "There's something else."

I joined him. "The investor list," Tommy said. It was mostly line after line of alphanumeric gibberish, but there were some actual names in there, too. Tommy scrolled through the *A*s and *B*s into the *C*s, and stopped.

"Corchero."

"That's your dead girl's name, right?"

"Yes. But that's not her."

Sparkle joined in. "Who is it?"

The cursor was pointing at *Corchero, Camille.*

"Rebecca's mother," I said.

"Huh," said my brother.

"Well, that's…" said Sparkle, and left the thought to float off.

I looked out Sparkle's picture window. A shirtless man pushed a shopping cart down the sidewalk. He had a scaly red scab on his left flank. A vermiculated ventral hernia pushed against the skin of his abdomen like a ball python fighting its way out of his belly. He was having a heated argument with himself as he shuffled along. I wondered when I would be seeing him on my table.

I turned back to Tommy. "You said it's wicked hard to open a channel between Redoxx and TechFolio by computer, right?"

"Yeah."

"Siloam and TechFolio are connected the same way Redoxx and TechFolio are. Would it be easier for an employee at Siloam to hack into TechFolio than it was for you to do it from Redoxx?"

"If they worked in IT, maybe."

"An in-house software engineer could do what you did?"

"It'd be easier. Still not *easy*. And you'd shit sure get fired if anyone found out."

I opened a browser window and Google-mapped Siloam Biologic. Four blocks away, straight down Brannan Street.

"Did the people at Redoxx figure out what you were up to?"

Tommy smirked. "Doubt it. Their own security is so tight that once you break out, they can't watch you." He pointed to the thumb drive sticking out of Sparkle's computer. "And I used some old toolkit tricks that make it even harder."

"Braciszku," I said, "Joe Azarola killed Lumpy Chen to protect the information stored on his laptop."

Sparkle was staring at the thumb drive like it was a scorpion in flex. My brother was staring at his tripe burrito.

"Can I dig into that now, before it gets cold?"

Siloam was in a spruced-up warehouse building. The lobby featured Scandinavian chairs, tinted glass tables, a pert receptionist, and an instant espresso machine. I strolled its perimeter while waiting for Neil Dupree to come meet me. There was a mirror; I checked the makeup job I'd done to cover my black eye and bruises. The walls held up the usual pieces of corporate art: carefully edgy, innocuous. The most interesting thing in the sleek and sterile room was a long glass case holding a scale model sailboat. A sign above the case read: *A gift of friendship from TechFolio Ventures to our partners at Siloam Biologic—may Fortune ever send us fair winds and following seas!*

"Well, that's awful," I said.

The pert receptionist thought I was talking to her, and called out that Neil would be down any minute. I thanked her, and squinted at the little boat. There was a plaque:

35th Annual Spiritsail Invitational
Winner, First Place: ANN MARIE
Skipper: ARNOLD SPITZ

"Huh," I said.

Behind the model was a glossy photograph of Arnie outside the St. Francis Yacht Club. He was holding a huge silver trophy and wearing white shorts and a cable sweater, boat shoes and a shit-eating grin. A group of half a dozen middle-aged men backed him. The caption indicated they were the board of directors for Siloam Biologic.

One man in that group stood out. He was square-built, with hair the color of ash and a mustache that matched. He had a face like a dead lawn.

I'd seen him before.

"Dr. Teska?"

Neil Dupree approached, cowed and miserable. I pointed at the figure in the picture. "Who is this man?" I demanded.

Neil was taken aback. "I…uh… I don't know, Dr. Teska."

"Take a close look."

He did. He repeated that he didn't know the man. The receptionist was on the phone but watching us. Neil smiled and nodded to her, then drew closer to me at the display cabinet and moved his finger till its shadow fell on Arnie. "This guy, though." He tapped the glass. "That's the investor I told you about. The one who got Rebecca canned."

"The man who came into your meeting with grocery bags full of cash?"

Neil's eyes skittered to the receptionist. "Yes," he said, sotto voce. I allowed him to steer me toward the chairs in the farthest corner of the lobby but cut him off before he could start protesting his innocence again.

"You were helping Rebecca get direct access to her Tech-Folio investment account so she could funnel money to her family in the Philippines. Was that stolen money?"

Pure panic flashed right through him. He went bone white and twitchy, and stammered no a couple of times. "It was hers…her own money—and her idea. She'd been sending it home for years, and figured this way it would be easier, and avoid the wire transfer fees. There was nothing illegal about it…"

"Her own money."

"I swear."

"Seems reasonable. It got Rebecca fired, though."

"I…" Neil's Siloam Biologic polo shirt puckered as he bent his head toward his belly and crumpled tighter into the chair. "It was important to her. Real important. If anyone finds out I helped her…"

I affected the compassionate tone I employ when delivering bad news to families. "All you were doing was helping Rebecca navigate past the firewall because she didn't have the computer skills to do it. You were doing a favor for a friend, a friend who was supporting her family overseas."

"That's right…"

"Your girlfriend."

His skittish eyes met mine—mine, warm and liquid with sympathy.

"Back then. But—you've got to believe me—I had nothing to do with…"

"With her death?"

He nodded.

"I do believe you, Neil. I know you didn't."

I rose from the chair, offered my hand, and assured Neil Dupree that the police wouldn't be bothering him at work again. He leaped up and shook gratefully, then left the lobby in a hot hurry—ignoring the receptionist and vanishing into the elevator without so much as a glance back.

The clock on the fancy espresso machine read 5:47. I needed a caffeine fix before heading back to work, so I grabbed a to-go cup and started pushing buttons. My back was to the Siloam Biologic entrance when I heard him come through it.

"Well, well! Look who's working late…"

"Mr. Spitz. Long time no see."

Arnie Spitz was pulling a small Rollaboard bag behind him and striding toward the receptionist. "I've been busy—that's good news, in my trade. A little bit here, a little bit there."

"I'll bet."

"I'm glad I made it here in time to catch you…"

He was leaning across the reception desk. The receptionist's back was straight and her tone was arch. "Mr. Anson asked me to wait for your arrival and welcome you back."

"And I feel welcomed. Tell Mark I'm here and then feel free to head home. Or wherever it is you're off to…?"

"Thank you, Mr. Spitz," the receptionist said. "I'll have to ask you to sign out now, Ms. Teska…"

The shock followed Arnie's gaze as it flew in to meet mine, but it flashed away just as quick and was replaced with a facsimile of delight. He asked the receptionist to tell Mr. Anson he would be up in a few minutes.

"Another happy surprise!" Arnie crossed the lobby, beaming like I was the fulfillment of his waking dreams—before he switched gears, to penitence. "I've been meaning to call you. I must apologize for my boorish behavior the other night at Sobakasu. I was drunk. I always forget how deceptively powerful those soju cocktails are—"

"How much cash you got in the bag there, Arnie?"

His smile wobbled but didn't fall. He looked over his shoulder, and we both waited for the receptionist to gather her purse and leave.

"Two hundred forty thousand dollars," he said finally. "Seed capital for an exciting new assay Siloam is developing. What's your reason for being here?"

"Tell me why you ordered Rebecca Corchero fired."

The smile slipped another notch. "I didn't. And that's a Human Resources matter. You know I can't discuss it."

"You pressured the CFO Mark Anson to fire her because she was taking advantage of her computer access here at Siloam to send money to her family in the Philippines. She was using TechFolio like a bank. So what?"

"We're not a bank."

"It was her own money—"

"It was a violation of her employment contract. As I've already explained to you, our business model is predicated on strict client and investor confidentiality."

"Especially for investors like Hector Marroquin."

"Who...?"

I turned to the display case, with its model boat. "Your friend. On the Siloam board of directors. You told me you had no involvement with the owner of the *Ann Marie* apart from a mutual interest in yachting. That was a lie."

I tapped my finger on the picture, under the face I had seen in news reports about Stone's RICO testimony. "Hector Marroquin is your friend with the boat. He's on trial in federal court right now for drug trafficking and conspiracy. I'll bet he's a heavy investor in TechFolio, too, isn't he. Did you know that your friend and backer there was involved in Rebecca Corchero's murder?"

Still Arnie said nothing. The Rollaboard shifted an inch as he tightened his grip on its handle; other than that, he was still as a stump.

I pressed on. "Emilio Viscaya. That name ring a bell? Viscaya killed Rebecca, and he didn't act alone. He reports to Hector Marroquin. Rebecca worked for you and had access to your precious client list, with its...how did you describe it the other night...? Its unassailable anonymity. Don't try to tell me you don't know anything about why they killed Rebecca."

Arnie didn't even blink. The only indication he was alive was in the wings of his nostrils. They flared with each breath.

"That two hundred forty K you have there isn't seed capital for some pharma breakthrough here at Siloam. It's Marroquin's dirty cash, and you're using this company and a bunch of others to launder it for him. That's what's propping up your crooked bitcoin scheme. And Rebecca got in past your firewall and figured it out. Did you tell Marroquin? Is that why she's dead?"

Arnie had a boyish face. It's one of the things I had liked about him. Now it belonged to a frightened boy.

"I have people waiting for me. If you have any further questions, Dr. Teska, you're going to have to talk to my attorney."

"Let me guess—Jackson Heffernan."

There were footsteps. A door opened at the far end of the lobby, and a security guard came through it.

Arnie drew himself up and said, "See this woman out right now."

The security guard started our way. Arnie Spitz showed me his back and went to the elevator. It opened right up for him.

"This way, miss."

The security guard was holding open the door to Brannan Street. The stink and noise of rush hour traffic greeted me as I went through it. The guard locked it as soon as I was clear of the threshold. Too late, I looked back. My coffee was still in the fancy machine's tray, going cold.

The sun was lowering behind me as I hiked back to the Hall. I had to get home to Bea before she tore up Mahoney Brothers #45 again, but I needed to do one other thing first. I needed to talk to Michael Stone.

I avoided the loading dock and used the main entrance to the Office of Chief Medical Examiner. The public counter was empty, so I unlocked the heavy door myself and went through to the Ops Shop. Their atrocious coffee was on the warmer, but no one was in. The chalk on the big board told me why: *2578 Reilly 3578 McD/ 801 hang 42 DeSoto*. The investigators were at a suicide scene.

The fluorescent bulbs in the main corridor had gone sickly and strobing—but a bright light shined from the deputy chief's office. The door was open a crack. I rapped on it.

"Dr. Stone...?"

Mike Stone didn't kill Rebecca—but I was more sure than ever that she was murdered. She had been using Arnie Spitz's tech fund as a glorified wire-transfer service to send her own money home to the Philippines. I had seen those books on Rebecca's shelf, all about online investment, and I knew from the windows still open on her laptop that she had been exploring some pretty sketchy bitcoin websites on the night she died. Her roommate Melodie said Rebecca was obsessed with cybercurrency get-rich-quick schemes. Once Neil Dupree had helped her get past the firewall at Siloam and into TechFolio, she might have grown curious. She might have gone exploring, and found Arnie Spitz and Hector Marroquin's money-laundering operation. That was a dangerous place to be. If Mike and I went to Howe together and convinced him that Marroquin might have sent Emilio Viscaya after Rebecca, we could convince the chief to file her manner of death as homicide and kick it up to the feds...

I knocked harder. The door creaked wider. I pushed it open. "Mike?"

He wasn't there. On his desk sat a pile of manila evidence envelopes, torn open and scattered. I spotted my own signature on one, with the description of materials *Injection drug kit box*. It was from one of those old cases I'd discovered on the first day of work, when I'd picked the lock on the cabinet in my new office.

A shadow fell across the desk. Michael Stone stood in the doorway. The cuff buttons were unfastened on his rumpled shirt and his tie was loose. In his hands were more evidence envelopes.

"What are you doing here, Jessie?" The question wasn't posed in anger. It was one more hassle.

"I came... I came to talk to you about Rebecca Corchero."

"There's nothing to talk about. Get out of my office."

"Mike. I know you didn't kill her—"

"Thanks very much."

"I know who did."

That got his attention. He dumped the evidence envelopes on a corner table and closed the office door.

"Who. Tell me."

"You don't believe it was an accident, either—"

"Tell me."

"You know Howe has signed that case out—? As an accident. He took it out of my hands."

"Who killed Rebecca?"

"His name is Emilio Viscaya. He's dead."

"Dead, how?"

"Ligature strangulation, postmortem decapitation and mutilation of the fingertips, and dumped in the bay."

Suddenly Stone got a lot less tired. "Like Robert Falmouth."

"Exactly like Robert Falmouth. Mike, this Emilio Viscaya didn't just murder Rebecca—he was the man with the gun who tried to murder *me* in the morgue on Friday night. And he works for Hector Marroquin. I think Marroquin had Falmouth killed the same way, and I think you blew your testimony in the RICO trial to protect him. Tell me why."

Stone dropped into his office chair and stared at a corner.

I said, "You knew Emilio Viscaya."

"No."

"But he knew you."

"He didn't shoot me."

"Because he knew who you are."

Stone shrugged.

"You realize that by inserting reasonable doubt into Marroquin's trial in the Falmouth murder, you're covering for Rebecca's killer, right? I think Marroquin sent Viscaya to kill me, too, and I think you know why. Tell me."

I jumped at his laugh. It was the only answer he gave. He rose and went to the side table and started ripping open the evidence pouches.

"Mike. Why?"

"I told you to leave." He shook an envelope, and out fell a used syringe and a couple of empty vials.

"Rebecca hacked into the computer system at work and discovered the details of Hector Marroquin's dirty business, didn't she? So Marroquin sent Emilio Viscaya to kill her. Is that it?"

Stone said nothing. He tore open another envelope and up-ended it: a color-whorled glass pipe.

"The only link I can make between me and Viscaya is that he killed Rebecca Corchero and I autopsied her—and I only figured that out *today!* So why come after me?"

Stone opened one last envelope and produced a small baggie of what looked like marijuana. Then he pulled out a shredder.

"Mike. These people are laundering money through Si-loam Biologic, the company Rebecca used to work for. Did she ever talk to you about Siloam? About Arnie Spitz? Was she mixed up with—"

"No!" An angry spark came off Michael Stone, but faded fast. "That's not what got her killed. Rebecca's death was not her fault. It was mine."

I took a step backward.

"It isn't what you think," he said, and paused to feed an envelope into the shredder. The din of it filled the office. "I didn't kill Becca. She was my great love." He glanced over at me, sheepish. "Foolish, I know—but true. She was my one great love."

Stone fed the rest of the evidence envelopes into the shred-der. He crossed the room and opened a wall cabinet beside his mussed-up cot. He placed the one-hit pipe and the bag-gie of pot inside it.

"Mike. What are you doing?"

Stone ignored me. He gathered the empty glass vials and the hypodermic needle and opened a desk drawer. Inside I could see another needle—full of clear fluid, the plunger ex-tended—plus a glassine bag of white powder and a scorched spoon. Stone closed the drawer and settled into his desk chair with a weary grunt.

"You didn't convince Howe that this guy killed Rebecca," he said. "Howe thinks she was a junkie and overdosed all by her lonesome, right?"

"Yes, but—"

"But nothing. Leave it alone."

"Viscaya murdered her!"

"Let's say you're right. Viscaya killed Rebecca and someone else killed Viscaya—and did you a favor, as long as Rebecca's death stays an accident. The case is closed. You can't overrule old Jimmy Howe and you can't go over his head—there's nowhere to go. No one will listen to you."

"The DA—"

"Won't do a damned thing with a case the chief medical examiner has ruled an accidental drug overdose, no matter how hard you shake your fists, Doctor."

"But who killed Viscaya?"

Stone said nothing. He was looking off. He was somewhere else.

"You *know*. You know, Mike, don't you. Tell me."

"What good would it do?"

I finally lost my shit. I slammed my open palm on his desk, then slammed it again, harder.

"You *tell me!*"

I put my bruised face in Mike Stone's and stayed there until his bent smile of defeat came back, and he shrugged.

"It's your funeral."

Dr. Michael Stone had done consult cases for Jackson Heffernan for years. He was good to Jack—and Jack was good to him, to the tune of eight hundred dollars an hour.

"Eight hundred an hour, Jessie. Think about that."

I didn't have to think long, not with two hundred thousand dollars of loan debt hanging over my own head.

"That...sounds high."

"It is high. I'm the golden goose, remember."

Usually the cases Stone did for Heffernan's firm were ordinary consults: malpractice, insurance actions, lawsuits. He would review documents about a death, state his medical opinion, walk away richer.

"Heffernan hardly ever lost when he had me on board. He didn't even have to go to court. One look at my report and the other side would fold and settle. Except for this one case. It was a San Francisco autopsy I caught about a year and a half ago, an African American male, midtwenties, shot once at close range in broad daylight. Straightforward findings— bullet went right through the basal ganglia. Entrance wound with soot in the hair on the back of his head, exit with beveling in his forehead."

That detail triggered my memory. "You testified in the RICO trial on this case."

Stone got defensive. "I didn't do anything wrong. It wasn't a consult—I wasn't working it for Jack Heffernan, okay? I was the doctor of record. I did the forensic autopsy, I filed the death certificate, and I got subpoenaed by the federal prosecutor."

That was the afternoon Stone had spent on a hallway bench at the federal courthouse, waiting to take the stand in the RICO trial. Jackson Heffernan appeared next to him on the bench. Heffernan was part of the defense team. This thing was a clear-cut matter of self-defense in the face of imminent lethal harm, Jack explained. It wasn't a drug-gang execution—it was the unfortunate outcome of a confrontation, a face-off between two armed men. The decedent threatened the defendant and displayed a pistol. When he reached for it, the defendant outdrew him and shot the decedent at close range in the forehead.

"That's what Jack said—that was the defense theory of the case," Stone said. "No, he didn't, I told him. The soot and stippling were on the back of the decedent's head. It was a back-to-front trajectory. But Jack knows his stuff. There was some dirt on the decedent's forehead, probably off the sidewalk where he landed. Jack told me I was going to testify that this crud was actually gunshot residue, and that the fine black powder on the *back* of his head was dirt. Reverse the direction of the bullet, and it's self-defense."

"But that's ridiculous! What about the beveling in the skull? Did you reapproximate the edges on the exit?"

"Yes and yes. You're right. It's ridiculous. To you. To me. But to a jury? Heffernan was betting they could get away with it, as long as the medical examiner said so. I told him I wouldn't do it. I *couldn't!* It was impossible…"

Heffernan warned Stone there would be repercussions if he failed to produce the right result. Between you and me, Heffernan told him, these clients are not the sort of people who fuck around. It's very important to them that this defendant not go to jail.

"The client. The client was Hector Marroquin," I said. "The defendant worked for him?"

Stone nodded. "Jack didn't say as much, of course. But he had this worried look. What was it he said? 'The consequences will be immediate and severe, Mickey.' That's what he told me, to my face, sitting there outside the courtroom before I went in to take the oath and testify. The son of a bitch."

Dr. Michael Stone sat at his desk and shook his head. "It was impossible. That I would mistake dirt from a San Francisco sidewalk for gunpowder? Impossible."

I agreed—but I wondered if, for the right price and given

a little more wiggle room, Stone would have found a way to go along with Jackson Heffernan's plan.

"That was when the paralegal came out and told me I was excused. They weren't finished with the other witness, and it was four thirty. Court was going to adjourn. I'd have to come back." Mike Stone had tears in his eyes. "That was Friday, so the next court day was Monday. They killed Rebecca on Saturday, the ignorant fucks. They didn't know I wouldn't get the news."

"Because we don't work weekends—and *I* caught the Corchero case on Monday."

He nodded. "I went straight to the courthouse on Monday morning to take the stand, without coming into the office."

"So you testified to your true findings—gunshot wound, close range, back-to-front trajectory."

"Routine, on both direct and cross. Nobody approached me, nobody threatened me. The defendant, this kid—he didn't even look at me. Neither did Hector Marroquin." The tears fell on Michael Stone's cheeks. "He looked *bored*..."

"The first you knew about Rebecca was when I knocked on your door asking you about it."

"Yeah."

"And that's the first you knew she was pregnant?"

Stone wiped his tears. More of them welled in his eyes, but now those eyes were ablaze.

"Why'd you have to go and stir things up?"

I felt the blaze behind my own eyes.

"Go ahead—shoot the messenger, Mike! There was a fetus! Until you flushed it, that is."

"Says you."

"Bet your ass I do! I know I didn't lose that specimen, and you have the keys to the morgue cold room, too."

"You didn't convince Jimmy Howe of that, though, did you?"

"You could fess up."

"I won't."

"You destroyed that fetus and you made sure Rebecca's body was destroyed, too."

"I meant what I told you. Cremation was the best option for the Corchero family."

"You knew it was a homicide, so you destroyed the evidence. Then you misdirected me to take a look at Neil Dupree as the mystery boyfriend, and when that didn't pan out—"

"You're not a goddamned cop! You didn't have to go interrogate—"

"—when that didn't pan out, you pressured me—hell, you *threatened* me—to put the case to bed as an accident, just to cover your own ass!"

The flame in his eye was gone, and so were the tears. Left behind there was nothing.

"Want to know what happened when I got home that Monday night, Jessie? First I called the Philippines, to break the news to the Corcheros. They didn't take it well. Then I get an incoming call. It was Jack Heffernan. He doesn't mention my testimony in the shooting case, oh no. He asks me how everything's going in the morgue. He's been reading in the papers about this rash of overdose deaths. Seems there's a powerful batch of heroin laced with fentanyl going around and it's killing a lot of naive users, especially young women. He's calling me because he's worried about my daughter, my Callie. There's drugs in schools nowadays, he says. You gotta be careful. Then he says he's gotta run, and he hangs up."

"Jesus…"

"Think about that a minute."

"But why…why Rebecca Corchero?"

"Rebecca and I had kept our secret—carefully. So I thought. But Marroquin and his goons found out about us. Nobody else knew what Rebecca's death would mean to me. Nobody but me and them, that is. I'd already said no to these people one time. They don't threaten twice. Jack was passing on the message that my daughter was next on their list if I…"

He trailed off and looked down at his desk.

"Jesus," I said again as another piece fell into place. "When you got called to testify again in the RICO trial—on the Falmouth case—you knew Rebecca had been killed to influence you. Marroquin was behind Falmouth's death, too. That's why you took a dive and said the case was undetermined."

"Fat lot of good that did. Howe came in to undermine me the next day. That case is up for verdict pretty soon. If Jack's clients don't like the result, what will they do then?"

Stone picked up a disposable lighter from the pile of old evidence, and flicked it a couple of times. "I got Becca killed and I've lost everything—my reputation, Howe's trust, my marriage. My daughter hates my guts, and now these monsters will go after her to get to me."

"Mike. You can't let this stand. You can't let them get away with it."

"Nothing I can do."

"Go to the police!"

He bit off a dry piece of a laugh. Then he started rolling his left sleeve up, way up.

"Go to Howe! Tell him!"

"And bury my daughter? I won't do it. What do you want? Justice for Rebecca? Her troubles are over."

"Oh, Mike, you are so full of it! I don't even buy your 'great love of my life' bullshit… You were feuding with your wife and wanted a little something on the side, and you got it—with the nanny. But once the nanny got pregnant and died? Well, then she's pregnant *forever*, isn't she, Mike? Pregnant forever with your child. No way around that. And you know what's worse? I think Rebecca Corchero was truly in love with you. I think she bought your line."

He sneered. "Your expert opinion?"

"What did you say—?"

"You heard me."

He opened his desk drawer. He pulled out a short length of surgical tubing and started wrapping it around his upper left biceps.

"Mike, what—"

"You better get out now, Jessie."

He lifted the full syringe from the desk drawer.

"This is that batch from the mule case. I didn't cook up enough for it to be clearly intentional, but I did add a good-size dose of potassium chloride to make sure."

He flexed a fist and his veins bulged under the switchyard of blood-donation scars he had collected so proudly all his adult life.

"You know what gave me the idea? When Howe told me you'd accused me of stealing that missing bindle, the one I took straight to the police lab for testing. It made me think of the broken bindle in our tox lab. Plenty of Soul Sister left in it. It's back there now, minus this little hit here. One more secret between you and me, Jessie."

"Wait! I will back you up, Mike… The two of us going to Howe—he can't ignore that. Otherwise, Heffernan just keeps doing what he does—"

"He'll do that anyway, and I'm not taking any more chances with my daughter's life. This is the way they do business. They're using Callie as leverage against me. Well, with me gone, there's going to be no point in going after her."

Michael Stone held the syringe upright and flicked it with his fingernail.

"And chew on this, Dr. Teska: If you tell anyone else what I've told you here tonight, *you'll* become a liability to these people. Heffernan will see to it that someone comes gunning for you again. Like I said—it's your funeral."

He primed the syringe. A thin stream arced out of the hypodermic needle.

"Becca died in an accidental overdose and so will I. Between the potassium and the fentanyl, no amount of naloxone and CPR is going to bring me back. By the time you get a dispatcher on the phone, I'll be brain dead."

He slapped his arm with his fingers.

"So leave now—right now. Lock the door behind you, and let me go out as an accident. There's plenty of paraphernalia around to demonstrate chronic use. Howe will turf the autopsy to San Mateo anyhow, so you or Ted won't have to do it."

"Mike, wait!"

He put the needle in his arm. He was careful and steady about it.

"Go home, Jessie," Mike Stone said, and pressed the plunger.

He gasped. His gaze came up to meet mine. His eyes rolled up and his head tipped and the tone went out of his muscles. I felt the bile rise in my throat as Mike crumpled at his desk. The empty syringe clattered to the floor.

I bolted out of the deputy chief's office, shouting for help. The Ops Shop was still empty. I ran past the tox lab, through the locker rooms, to the autopsy suite. I was alone with the cadavers.

I ran back to the office. Mike wasn't breathing. I didn't waste time checking for a pulse—if what he'd said about potassium in the hot shot was true, then he wouldn't have one.

I yanked up the receiver on his office phone and punched the keys.

"Nine-one-one. What is your emergency?"

My mouth opened but nothing came out.

Mike was right. Rebecca's body was burned to ash and the blood evidence on the gecko was destroyed in a bucket of bleach. Now he was dead of the same heroin—? Dr. Howe would say they were shooting it up together the night Rebecca died. He would say that Stone was a secret junkie who had introduced his mistress to his favorite high. Howe would say it had killed both of them, separately—in tragic accidents.

"What is your emergency...?"

Rebecca's killer was dead, and there was no case for the DA to pursue. Michael Stone had died by his own hand, but Howe would make sure his manner of death was ruled an accident. A valued right-hand man succumbing to the demons of drug addiction makes for a better story than the same man driven to suicide after his mistress is murdered in a criminal scheme to compel him to perjury. All Stone's old cases would be compromised. Howe wouldn't let that happen. And if I fought him, he would win.

"Nine-one-one. What is your—"

I hung up the phone and took one last look at the tableau: Michael Stone's dead body at his desk, no sign of a struggle, drug paraphernalia present, multiple needle track marks. His tox would come back positive for heroin and fentanyl, but no one would ever know about the potassium hot shot. Dying cells release potassium into the blood; it's a natural part of the process of decomposition. The little bit extra in that syringe would just add to it undetectably.

I went to the door. I pressed the lock button on the inside, then closed it behind me. I walked down the wood-paneled hallway and out through the sally port and the electric double doors to the loading dock, to my parked car.

Late-summer evening. Despite the fog, it was still plenty light out. I was glad it was still light.

PART THREE

THE HALL OF JUSTICE

MARCH

The elevator door on the seventh floor opened onto a shallow cage. I stepped into it and the doors slid shut behind me.

It was only my second time visiting the San Francisco County Jail. The jail occupied a separate, more modern wing of the Hall of Justice, all gray steel and glass in swooping curves like a wave pool turned sideways. Under my arm I carried the Emilio Viscaya file, including scene and autopsy photos. For this occasion I wore my one and only white lab coat. On the other side of the cage a thick San Francisco sheriff's deputy strained the buttons on his uniform. Anup Banerjee stood behind him. I flipped my badge wallet open. The deputy inspected it and opened my cage.

"May I?" Anup asked. I handed him the badge. He ran his brown fingers over its gold surface and smiled. "Congratulations, Deputy Chief Teska," he said.

"Don't," I groaned. "Please. It's an interim appointment anyways."

"Still. Word around my office is that you're doing a great

job under extremely shorthanded circumstances. How long's it been—six months?"

"Seven. Just me and Ted cutting all cases. Yeah, it's been crazy. A lot of overtime."

"Why hasn't Howe hired a new doctor?"

"Ask Howe."

The jail deputy handed me a VISITOR sticker, and I plastered it opposite my lab coat's blue embroidered JESSIE TESKA, MD.

"Losing Michael Stone was a tragedy and a great loss to the city," Anup said. "He was a good doctor."

"He was a great doctor."

I didn't like talking about it. Dr. Howe had appointed me interim deputy chief medical examiner before Mike's body was in the ground. Ted Nguyen had seniority on me, but there was no way in hell he was going to take the job, not with the teaching mandate and the expectation that the deputy chief take the high-profile cases. So now it was my circus. My monkeys.

Anup had grown his hair since I'd last seen him. It was wavy and rich, and still had that subtle scent of coconut. A forelock fell across his right eye, and I almost reached out to brush it back.

"Why'd you want to meet up here?" I asked him.

"I need you to talk to a prisoner. Juan Viscaya."

"Viscaya…?"

"Emilio's brother. Fresno PD picked him up on an old warrant, and San Francisco brought him in for questioning on that drug mule case in the Tenderloin."

"Graciela Natividad."

"You remember it. His prints and his brother's were in the hotel room. When Juan's lawyer told him he could be charged under the felony murder rule in Graciela's death—along with drug and human trafficking and conspiracy—his lawyer sent word that Juan can give us Joe Azarola on the Natividad case. But that's *all* he'll say until you talk to him about his brother's death."

I held up the case folder. "That's why you wanted me to bring the autopsy report? I gotta warn you—this material is pretty bad. Pictures like these…there's a good reason I don't show them to family members of decedents."

"Jessie," Anup Banerjee said as the deputy ushered us across the jail foyer, "no matter what he gives us on Azarola, I'll still be charging Juan Viscaya on mutilation of a corpse. Don't forget what he and his brother did to Graciela in that hotel room. This kid has seen—and done—bad things."

The deputy unlocked an armored door and led us down a concrete passage. Men in orange pants and sweatshirts watched us from a procession of cells. We entered a room at the end of the cell block. A man in a cheap lawyer suit with a visitor badge slouched against a wall. Another sheriff's deputy stood erect nearest the doorway.

Seated at a table was the prisoner, Juan Viscaya. He shared his dead brother's strange, pale yellow-green eyes, but showed none of his menace. He was clean-shaven and crew-cut, with a tattoo peeking out of his collar. No crow's-feet—I reckoned he was barely twenty. He looked anxious, out of his depth.

There weren't many preliminaries. Juan asked me if I was the doctor who did the autopsy on Emilio. I said I was. He asked if those were the photos. I said yes—and then I gave him my spiel about how bad an idea it was for him to look at them. Once seen, they wouldn't be forgotten. They would be the last image he'd have of his brother.

"Let me see them," he said quietly. Juan had that flat Californian accent, the lazy vowels and earnest consonants. He sounded like a lot of the medical students who rounded at the morgue.

I spread the pictures across the table and started telling him what they showed. The lawyer coughed and turned away. The deputy guarding us craned in curiosity. Juan was silent. He focused all of his attention on the images. He asked me why Emilio's hands were so fucked up. I told him someone had cut the fingertips off after his brother's death, probably in an attempt to disguise his identity.

He looked up at me. "Where's his head?"

"It wasn't recovered with the body. Based on the nature of the wound, I'm certain it was removed after he died."

"Yeah."

Juan Viscaya lifted a picture out of the pile and asked me what it was. I told him it was a chemical burn to his brother's right forearm, and that it, too, happened after he was dead.

"They burned off the tat so they could hide what they done, like with the head and fingers, right?"

"I think so, yes."

He pulled up the right sleeve of his orange prison sweat-shirt to show me a tattoo: a rose and a pair of dice, and the words *RIP Paquito 12.20.13.*

"Our brother Francisco. He had a heart problem, born with it. He was six when he passed."

"I'm sorry," I said.

Juan Viscaya nodded and rolled his sleeve back down.

He turned to Anup. "Okay, you were telling the truth. So what do we do now?"

Anup huddled with Juan's lawyer for a moment. They came to a murmured agreement; then Anup said, "Tell me what happened on July first of last year, the night you ended up at the Hotel Somerville with Graciela Natividad."

Juan had his eyes on the pictures of his brother's grotesque remains again. I started to gather them up, back into my folder.

His hand shot toward mine but stopped just before we touched, and the guard ticked closer to the table.

"No," said Juan softly. "Leave them there."

I did.

Juan turned back to Anup and said, "I didn't know her name till after."

Anup leaned against the wall and listened. His expression was serious and attentive, without a hint of hostility or skepticism.

Joe Azarola picked up Juan and Emilio at their house sometime in the evening of July 1. A girl was in the car with him, dressed in a short pink skirt and white top and fuck-me boots. She spoke Spanish. Azarola was kind to her, accommodating. He didn't use her name; he addressed her as *cariña*.

"That was the only time I saw her smile, when Joe called her *cariña*."

They went to the Hotel Somerville, where Azarola dropped off Emilio and the girl. He and Juan went to the KFC on Polk and loaded up on fried chicken, and to the Walgreens on Van Ness for a box of laxatives.

"What time was that?" Anup asked.

Juan shrugged. "Seven, seven fifteen."

I caught Anup's eye. That's when the video surveillance camera over the hotel parking lot picked up Joe Azarola and the man with the white plastic bags, parting ways near the corner of Geary and Polk. That was Juan with the takeout. He was telling the truth.

Juan went up to the hotel room. He and Emilio and the girl passed the time chatting about pop music. She looked uncomfortable. She didn't feel well. She wanted to get the job over with.

"So we gave her the Ex-Lax and we all ate some chicken. We tried to get her to eat more of it before it got cold, but she said she couldn't. Joe kept texting us. He wanted to know what was taking so long."

"Besides texting, did he call you?" I asked.

"Only once."

"When?"

"I dunno. It was just getting dark."

That jibed with the video, too: Azarola stepped outside the Café Oui-Fi right after sunset to make his phone call, when he looked up into the trees that weren't there. Up at the Hotel Somerville.

"Everything was cool until a little after nine. All of a sudden the girl stands up and says she's gonna puke, and she starts toward the bathroom. So me and Emilio get up to help her, because—well, you know, we gotta...collect the stuff. But she don't make it to the bathroom. She just drops. We pull her over to the bed and put her down on it. She's all pale and sweaty, and there's this bubbly shit coming out of her mouth and nose."

The brothers slapped Graciela Natvidad on the face and threw cold water on her, but she was dead.

The condoms full of acetylfentanyl-laced heroin were still inside her body.

Emilio called Joe Azarola, argued with him briefly, and Azarola hung up on him. Azarola told Emilio he'd run into some trouble himself and couldn't come bail them out.

"He told my brother we had to cut her open and get the stuff out of her ourselves. Start from the bottom and go up, he said."

So they did. The Viscaya brothers donned gloves and opened their knives, and cut into Graciela Natividad's dead body.

"We...there was a lot of blood. It got all over the bed, and we were trying not to get any on us. Her insides were all slippery, and we...couldn't see what we were doing. We moved her to the floor, but that didn't help. Emilio kept cutting and cutting, but it seemed like there was just more and more guts in there…"

Juan didn't look so good. His lawyer asked him if he needed a glass of water. He shook his head.

The brothers hacked away at the dead teenage girl for ten minutes before they noticed the police cars. Their hotel window faced Polk Street, and there was a lot of flashing blue down there. When they saw the yellow tape go up, cordoning off the whole corner behind the hotel, they panicked.

"We had to get out of there. We weren't going to get the packages, no way we could do it. I mean…it wasn't just the blood. There was *shit* all over the place, and this…yellow stuff that came out whenever we cut into her… I was trying not to puke. Emilio, too. He told me to clean up, we were getting the fuck out of there."

The two men washed as best they could and took the stairs down to the hotel lobby. They took a left on Geary—away from the police cordon and news vans around the Café Oui-Fi—and just kept walking.

Juan said he sure would like that glass of water now, and the guard gave it to him.

"What time was that, when you left the hotel?" Anup asked.

"Between nine thirty and ten."

"Did Azarola say why he didn't come upstairs with you and Emilio in the first place?" I asked.

"Yeah. The hotel has shitty internet. He's always on his laptop working, and that coffee shop's got internet."

"Working on what?"

"He didn't say."

Juan Viscaya looked at Anup again.

"You'll have to testify to all of this in court," Anup told him.

"I want a deal and protection."

"We can do that. What else can you give us?"

"You tell me."

"I want everything you know about Josu Azarola's role in the cartel."

"Wait a second, Anup," said the defense lawyer. "That's federal. The RICO action is outside the scope of our—"

"Hey," said Juan Viscaya quietly but not gently. He tapped a finger on the pictures from my case file. "This is my brother. They did this to my *brother*."

The lawyer said nothing. Juan sat still for a moment.

"I can tell you about the Chinese girl."

"Who…?"

"The one Joe shot up with Soul Sister."

My heart beat faster. Out of the corner of my eye I could see Anup go a little stiff, but he didn't change his expression or his relaxed tone of voice.

"Okay. What about the Chinese girl?"

Emilio and Juan and Azarola all lay low after the snafu with the drug mule. Joe Azarola was wanted for murder in the shooting at the café, and the Viscaya brothers weren't expecting to get any work for a while, not after what happened in the Hotel Somerville. But then they got a visit from Azarola.

"It was a Friday night, late. Joe came by and told me and Emilio he had a job for us—our chance to make up for the thing at the hotel."

The next night the three men sat in a car in the fog, outside a house in the Sunset District. Azarola had a plan, but had to wait until the girl was alone. They got their chance when her roommate left the house and drove off.

"How'd you know that was the only roommate?" I asked.

"Joe checked the place out on Friday before he came to see us."

"Okay," Anup said. "What happened next?"

"We waited a few minutes. Then Joe and Emilio went up

the stairs. I was the lookout. There was a car in the driveway and Joe told me to try rocking it, to set off the alarm—"

"Tell me the make and color of the car," I said.

"Blue WRX."

Rebecca's Subaru.

"Okay. So the alarm goes off..."

"Yeah. The alarm is going, and Joe starts ringing the doorbell. The inside door opens, and I hear a girl ask what's going on."

Joe Azarola tells the girl on the other side of the security gate that he and his buddy were walking down to the N-Judah train when they saw someone break into the blue car in the driveway. There's glass all over the place, he says. That story gets the girl to unlock the gate. As soon as she does, Azarola swings it wide and he and Emilio push their way in. They catch her off balance. They don't even have to rush her. All they do is keep walking right into her house, talking excitedly about three black teenagers they saw running down the hill with something in their arms...

I pictured the divot in the wall behind the doorknob, the cracked lath and crumbled plaster in Rebecca and Melodie's entryway.

"This is all what Emilio told me *after*, okay?" said Juan, those yellow eyes of his shooting back and forth between Anup Banerjee and the public defender. "I was outside the whole time. I never laid a hand on that girl."

"All right," said Anup.

"So Emilio told me they got her into a chair and Joe shot her up—to make it look like she was a junkie."

"But she fought them," I said.

"Emilio said he had to lean on her to keep her still, and it took Joe a long time to get the needle in her arm. They put a pillow over her face to shut her up. I didn't hear nothing from outside and nobody came by."

"That's all?" Anup said.

"Yeah. Joe waited a couple minutes and made sure she was done for real. Then they came out the door and shut the gate and we left."

"Did your brother tell you why they killed this woman?"

"My brother didn't kill nobody."

"Did Joe Azarola tell you why *he* killed this woman?"

"No."

"Did your brother tell you anything else about what happened that you haven't told me?"

"No."

"Our deal hinges on my trusting that you're telling me everything you can tell me, Mr. Viscaya."

"I know how it works."

"Okay," said Anup.

I was sick to my stomach. Rebecca Corchero's torn frenulum wasn't from a trip and fall—it was from a pillow smothering. Same with her petechiae. The broken fingernail and the abrasions on her right arm were restraint injuries. The big bruise in the crook of her left elbow wasn't a sign of a rookie needle stick—it was part of a struggle during an intentional poisoning. A homicide.

"Are we done?" said the defense attorney.

Anup paced across the interview room.

"What about your brother's death? Was Azarola involved?"

Juan shrugged.

"Tell me what you know."

Juan looked at me, then back at Anup.

"Not with her here."

"What?"

"You heard me."

"Okay," said the defense attorney. "Doctor, if you wouldn't mind—"

"No," said Anup. "You don't set the terms here, Mr. Vis-caya. The doctor stays and you talk or *I* go." He was pointing at the door. "And if I go, the deal is off."

"Hold on!" said Juan's lawyer. All eyes went to him. "Juan, you're not going to say anything about anybody but Joe Az-arola. That includes your brother."

"My brother's dead," Juan said. Then, to my surprise, he turned to me.

"Look, it was his idea, not mine."

"Juan, I'm advising you to stop—"

"You were in the car with him, weren't you?" I said. "The Dodge Charger."

Juan Viscaya turned and addressed Anup Banerjee. "I was only along for the ride. I didn't know what was going on." He swiveled back to me. "My brother thought you were a problem. He thought it would look good if he took care of it himself."

"How was I a problem?"

"After Joe got picked up on that thing in the coffee shop, these two cops came in to meet with him and his lawyer. They told Joe a coroner had connected him to the job we did at the hotel. Scientific proof, they said—this coroner went through some video from outside the coffee shop and measured Joe's limp, and ID'd him that way. Joe got word to Emilio that the two of us better get out of town, just in case they had me on camera, too."

"How'd he get word to Emilio?"

"He sent a message."

"How?"

"How d'you think?" Juan growled. "He was in jail."

Heffernan. The cops must have been Keith Jones and Dan-iel Ramirez, and the lawyer in the room was Jackson Heffer-nan. Those two dipshit cops had invented a tale of my magical forensic powers so they could shake down Joe Azarola, and Heffernan passed the word to Emilio Viscaya.

"I wanted to head straight to Fresno," Juan continued. "We could get some work there, no big deal. Emilio said he needed to take care of the problem first. He was convinced this coroner—you—could ID both of us, too. That's why we followed you. But you got away."

Juan smiled. A rather sweet, apologetic smile. It sent a chill right down the length of my spine.

"I didn't want no part of it after that. Emilio...well, I don't know what my brother did. A couple of nights later, he comes home with a broken nose and his eyes all swollen, and he can hardly walk. He's *bugging*. He made a phone call, and when he got off he gave me the keys to the Charger and told me to drive it to Fresno and get rid of it. He said he had something else to do, and then he'd meet me down there."

"Who was on that phone call?"

Juan just shook his head. I stayed locked on him.

"Whoever it was on the other end of that phone call, that's who had your brother killed, Juan. You know that, right?"

"All I know is I left for Fresno and I never saw my brother again until now." He looked down at the pictures one more time, then gathered them up neatly and stacked them on top of my file folder.

"They killed your brother," I said. "Why'd they do it?"

Juan Viscaya looked at me in puzzlement, like the question answered itself.

"He fucked up."

Anup Banerjee leaned against the peeling pillar of a disused car wash and loosened his tie.

We were down the street from the jail and around the corner from the OCME, heading to our respective cars. It was sunny out and gusty, the stink of the Bay Bridge viaduct sweeping down on us.

"...because Joe Azarola was the head of the conspiracy, but he wasn't in the room—he was across the street in the café when she died." Anup was explaining why Juan Viscaya's testimony in the Graciela Natividad case would be so important to the district attorney. "This way we can squeeze Azarola with felony murder. Between the mule's death and the Chen shooting, we might be able to flip him, get him to give us bigger fish."

I was skeptical. "Azarola won't talk. He'd get capped if he did. Look what they did to Emilio Viscaya, and all Emilio did was screw up trying to kill *me*. It wasn't Heffernan or Marroquin who sent him after me—Emilio came up with that dim bulb idea all by himself. That's why he finally quit and bugged out after Mike Stone came into the Ops Shop. Emilio recognized Mike from the RICO trial or something, and must have known Mike's connection to Marroquin—through Heffernan, that is. These guys, Azarola and Arnie, Mike Stone and Jackson Heffernan and the Viscaya brothers—for Christ's sake, they're all...subcontractors."

Anup smirked. "I still can't believe you called his bluff with an empty shotgun. I would have passed out. With a loaded shotgun maybe I'd have some balls, but empty?"

"Don't remind me."

He stopped smirking.

"Sorry," I said. "I try not to think about it."

I sidled up next to him. The post was narrow. Our shoulders pressed together.

"Ever heard of Holi?" Anup said.

"Think the rain'll ruin the rhubarb?"

"It's a spring holiday for us."

"Lawyers?"

"Hindus."

"No, never heard of it."

"It's coming up. Holi revolves around the usual springtime themes—the triumph of light over darkness, good over evil, justice over wickedness."

"Okay."

"But it's cyclical. The joy doesn't last. Darkness returns and evil triumphs. Sometimes."

He drew a figure eight in the dust with his toe.

"What are you going to do about the Corchero homicide?" I asked.

"Nothing."

"Joe Azarola murdered her."

"And there's not a thing we can do about it. Either of us. Your boss filed her death as an accident. My boss won't proceed with that case based on anything Juan just told us."

"Why the hell not?"

"It's all hearsay. If it were testimony against Juan's own interest I could use it—but he wasn't in the room when they killed her. He's relying on what Emilio told him, and Emilio can't testify."

He dug the figure eight deeper. The gray dust turned to sand. I wondered if all of San Francisco was built on sand.

"We don't work in a justice system, Jessie. It's a legal system. We take what we can get."

"Or what our bosses want to give us."

"Well."

He turned to face me.

"Think of it this way. Before you found those pieces of computer chip in Lumpy Chen's body, I had a so-so case against Joe Azarola. I might have settled for manslaughter. I mean—the guy did get robbed."

I scoffed.

"I'm serious. I could have got a solid felony manslaughter out of what I had. Once you gave me the computer evidence, though—that brought my demand up to murder two. Heffernan was apoplectic. Well, now he's screwed even worse. *Now* we can squeeze Azarola with felony murder in the Graciela Natividad case. Murder one and felony murder on two separate cases, plus kidnap, drugs, conspiracy…? Azarola just might decide to work with us."

"And do what?"

"Give us Hector Marroquin."

"No way. Heffernan will make sure Azarola won't deal."

"We'll see."

"What about the evidence I gave you on that thumb drive? Connect Arnie Spitz with Joe Azarola, and you don't need to flip him."

Anup's eyes narrowed in anger. "The feds don't want it."

I grunted. "Can't say I'm surprised."

"I was. They say it's not evidence, it's stolen intellectual property. That's a specious argument—they could get a warrant and a cybersquad and open up the path your informant already blazed. Are you sure you won't tell me who got that data? If I could—"

"Confidential informant. You know how that works."

He sighed. "I tried, Jessie. Believe me. I kept bumping that damn data drive up the chain of command, but everyone who looked at it dropped the thing like a hot rock. From what I could see myself, Spitz's client base doesn't just include anonymous drug dealers—there are some very well-connected tech industry players in there. Political donors. We would need something much more damning before any elected official in this city is going to go after them."

"More damning—!"

"Come back to me with some kiddie porn, and we'll talk."

"That's not funny."

"No," Anup said, "it isn't."

He shifted away from the pillar, taking in the view of the rusty guts of a deceased car wash.

"Nothing's going to change."

He was right, of course. Look at Stone's death. Dr. Howe went into crisis mode and called the coroner in neighboring San Mateo County, just like Stone predicted he would. San Mateo sent their own team to work the scene. They found a dead man with multiple track marks and a syringe, illicit drugs and paraphernalia among his personal effects, and no sign of a struggle. They transported the body to their morgue for an autopsy.

Half-assed scene investigation. Stone would have been appalled. I smiled.

"What's funny?" said Anup.

"Nothing at all."

When the rush tox came in, the San Mateo coroner shared the results with Dr. Howe. Howe pointed out that the mix of heroin and acetylfentanyl in Michael Stone's blood was chemically identical to the toxicology results from his mistress, who had died in an accidental overdose a couple of weeks before. The San Mateo County Coroner determined that Dr. Michael Stone's death was likewise an accident. It took them barely two weeks.

Our mayor made a statement, with Dr. Howe by her side at the podium. The immense loss to Michael Stone's family, his coworkers, the city. The scourge of illicit drugs, especially the unchecked spread of fentanyl and its derivatives. Stone was a victim. Rebecca was a victim. It was all senseless. A better story that way.

"Anup." I looked up at the Hall—I couldn't look him in the eye. "Rebecca Corchero wasn't just any case for me. I thought… When I found that scar on Emilio Viscaya's arm, I thought I'd found her killer. You see? Even if Howe wouldn't back me up, even if he wouldn't rule it a homicide, at least I'd found her killer—and he was dead. So that was okay, in a way, right?"

"Justice."

"Of a sort. But now…!"

"Emilio Viscaya didn't kill Rebecca Corchero. He was an accessory. Joe Azarola pushed the plunger."

I faced him. I nodded.

"Believe me, Jessie. We're going to get Azarola."

"You're going to *use* Azarola."

"And we're going to get him. Azarola was following orders from Hector Marroquin when he killed Rebecca. We'll pit them against each other. This time Jackson Heffernan won't be able to do a damned thing to stop it."

"Not good enough. It's not…"

Anup put his arm around my shoulders. "It's okay," he said. "I know."

"No, you *don't* know!" I shrugged him off and stood.

"What don't I know?"

"About Rebecca! It's… Oh, never mind."

I started walking along the razor-wire fences toward the OCME loading dock and my car.

"It's not just Rebecca," Anup called out. "I said I *know* and I mean it. I said it's okay and I mean it, Jessie."

I waved vaguely without turning around.

"I know about Cat."

I stopped. I heard the scratch of soles on dirt. Anup came up right behind me.

"I always background check my witnesses, Doctor."

I waited. I had nothing to say until I knew if he was bluffing.

"Stop it," Anup said, and stepped around in front of me. "You didn't do anything wrong."

"You don't know."

"I do. On May eighth of last year you did an autopsy on a Los Angeles woman named Mary Catherine Walsh. You determined her death was suicide by intoxication of the prescription painkiller OxyContin. It was a straightforward case. Stop punishing yourself."

"She was—"

"Pregnant. Twelve weeks. Same as Rebecca Corchero. And you blame yourself for her suicide because you were sleeping with her husband. I know. I don't care." Anup was drilling with those big frank eyes of his. "His name is Finbar Taylor. He's a cop, a detective in the LAPD—"

I couldn't help smiling. "Barry. Finbar's a ridiculous name, he never uses it."

"Okay. Mary Catherine didn't use her name, either. She hated the old-lady name Mary and went by—"

"Cat. She went by Cat."

He nodded grimly. "And kept her maiden name. Cat Taylor came into the morgue as Mary Walsh. That's why, when you did the autopsy, you didn't know…who she was."

I searched Anup's face for the disgust that had to be there. I couldn't find it.

"That's…a nightmare. I can't imagine. But I can understand why you left Los Angeles. I talked to Dr. Kashiman—"

"No!"

"Of course I did!" He looked offended. "You're my witness! I'll bet Heffernan backgrounded you, too."

"Oh God." I slumped to sit on a dirty electrical box at the edge of the car wash. "Oh, *boz.e mój.*"

Anup sat down beside me and put a hand on mine.

"Stop it. Please. Jessie, do you want to know what Dr. Kashiman said about you? He told me that your last day was a bad day, but it was the only bad day. He said you were the best young doctor he has ever trained. And you know what he did at the end of our conversation? He congratulated me. He congratulated me as a court officer in San Francisco who could consult with Dr. Jessie Teska whenever I needed to. He regretted having lost you."

"That's...kind of him."

"No, it isn't—it's the truth. I have no doubt he's right. None."

"Yeah? I left Emil Kashiman for Michael Stone. Look where that got me."

"Dr. Kashiman didn't want to let you go."

"No, he didn't. Neither did Barry. But there was no way I could stay in Los Angeles after I did that autopsy. Cat Taylor and her baby... *Barry's* baby? There was no way."

We sat in silence for a good long while after that. Anup took his hand off mine, but then I grabbed it and laced my fingers through his and gripped. A little too hard, maybe. I have trouble calibrating sometimes.

"Barry was going to leave her. So he said. We had plans. He made promises to me, and I believed him. But Barry's private, the way some cops are—no social media, none of that. I didn't know what...what his wife looked like. All I knew was that she was called Cat. So when I read what she wrote about us, the three of us, in that suicide note...when I realized who the dead woman on my table was, that she got pregnant right around the time Barry and I started seeing each other…and that Barry would have been a father if she hadn't…"

I couldn't look at him. I turned my head away and loosed my grip on his hand. But Anup wouldn't let it go, and I felt him lean closer. I felt his words on the small hairs of my neck when he said quietly, "You aren't responsible for the things other people do to themselves."

"I'm responsible for what I do to them, though."

"Yes. But you're not alone. We make our choices and we hurt people and we regret it."

"You don't know."

"Maybe not… But you don't know what *I* know, either— and I *know* that you don't know what I don't know, so you don't know what I *might* know about what you don't know."

I turned back to him. He was trying very hard to look deadly serious. He was failing around the corners of his eyes and in the purse of his lips.

"You're an asshole."

"Always go with your first impression."

A truck shuddered as it engine-braked on the freeway over our heads. Anup let me sit with him and not talk. It felt good.

"Poor stupid Lumpy Chen," I said at last. "We can blame him."

"What do you mean?"

"He jacked the wrong guy. That's all. If he hadn't made that one bad split-second decision to grab Joe Azarola's laptop at the Café Oui-Fi, none of this would have happened. Well, *some* of it would have happened. But Azarola and the moron Viscaya brothers could have completed their mule job and no one would have been the wiser."

"Maybe. But Graciela Natividad would still be dead."

"And Rebecca Corchero. But it was the Chen case that led us to her killers."

"So…thanks, Lumpy Chen?"

"More bad choices."

"Best not overthink it."

A flock of tropical green birds tore over our heads, chattering. They made a coordinated landing in a tree across Harrison Street and kept up their racket. We watched a feral cat claw his forepaws into the tree's base, thinking about making a go.

"Is there a meal?"

"What?"

"This cheery springtime festival of yours. I don't trust any holiday that doesn't have a special meal attached."

"Oh. No… No special meal at Holi—but something much better."

"Nothing's better than a good meal."

"How about a giant wet color dance?"

"You have my attention."

Anup described the crowds on the streets in India, people running around and throwing brightly colored powder on one another, usually in the rain. If there was no rain, there were squirt guns. By the end of the day, everyone—rich and poor, young and old—is splashed in a messy rainbow of pigment.

"That sounds absolutely delightful."

"It really is."

"Makes me wish I were in India."

"Oh, you don't have to go to India. We do it here, too. There's a Holi festival down the Peninsula this weekend. I'm going on Saturday."

He wound out a sly smile.

"Come with me."

I sighed. "Anup, I…"

"Did I tell you I quit?"

"You…*what?*"

"I've given four weeks' notice at the DA's office. It means

a pay cut, but I'm taking a job with the state as an appellate attorney. I love this city—I really do—but I'm sick and tired of watching powerful people get away with the things they get away with here."

"Working for the state is better?"

"I'm going to find out."

"Well…!" I forced a cheery face. "Good luck in Sacramento…"

The sly smile came back, wider.

"I'm not going anywhere. My new job is with the First District Court of Appeal—at 350 McAllister Street."

"In San Francisco?"

"Across from City Hall. I'll be reviewing appellate briefs—criminal, civil, juvenile. That includes appeals for factual innocence in light of new evidence."

"Like that letter on your wall—"

"Daryl Harrick. Yes."

"Old cases."

He nodded.

"Not a lot of need for a state's attorney to consult the San Francisco city medical examiner in that branch of law, is there?"

"Not a lot. Hardly any."

"Then we couldn't really be considered colleagues anymore, you and I."

"No, Doctor. We aren't colleagues anymore."

Anup was grinning.

I found that I was, too.

"So," I said. "This colorful festival you're going to, on Saturday."

"Holi."

"Right. If there's no meal, what do you do after you get home, all dyed up?"

"We eat sweets. We're big on sweets."

"Ooh! What else?"

Anup was nonplussed. Maybe he'd never really given it much thought.

"Well...nothing. Take a shower, of course. And usually I'm pretty tired after all that running around and dancing. So I take a shower and go to bed. That's all."

I tried to pack away my grin. I was picturing the shower stall in Anup Banerjee's apartment, with two pairs of feet and a whole lot of color swirling around the drain.

"Thank you, Anup," I said. "I would love to join you..."

My Beemer was parked in the shadow of the Hall of Justice, not far from the spot Rebecca Corchero gave me on my first day of work. I unlocked the door and settled into the driver's seat. I started the engine but left it in Park.

I pulled out my phone. I went to the saved voice mails and scrolled to the bottom.

From: Barry Taylor.

I pressed my thumb onto the red-lettered word.

Delete this message? a dialogue box asked. *This action cannot be undone.*

I know.

Yes.

ACKNOWLEDGMENTS

Our deepest gratitude goes to Tom Mitchell, Rita Mitchell, and Rutka Messinger; our agent and fairy godmother, Jessica Papin, and to John Glynn, Peter Joseph, Roxanne Jones, Cathy Joyce, Sean Kapitain, Mary Sheldon and Eden Church, and the entire crew at Hanover Square Press.

Many thanks to our beta readers, Neal Baronian, Liz Ehr, Michael Ehr, Dr. Hadas Gips, Andrew Gould, Jesika Grubaugh, Ron Santoro, CFX, Sarah Lansdale Stevenson, and Judith Michelle Williams, Ph.D.

Additional thanks to Mary Jo Mitchell Angersbach, for fashion; Howard J. Baum, Ph.D., for toxicology; John R. Briley for instruction in the art of dialogue; Caroline Cargado for Filipino culture; Todd Michael Day for East Lynn bona fides; Dr. Jon Ford Finks for clinical and emergency medicine; Nina Fiore for ME office logistics; Liam Ford and Ann Weiler for journalism; David Fox, Jon Hill, Cristin Pescosolido, and José Quinteiro for IT help; Kelly "Gouldilocks" Gould for makeup and hair; Dr. Juan Jaime Guzman and Martin Villa for American Spanish slang; Christine Lukacs for the Beemer; Officer

Francisco Morrow for police procedure; Izabela Pań ków-Mai for all things Polish; Asit Panwalla and Laurel Thompson for lawyer (not legal!) advice; and Chris Passanisi for Rebecca's RN without bedpans.

Finally, we extend our bottomless gratitude to Catherine Ehr for being our cheerleader, sounding board, and friend—and to Dina, Leah, Anna, and Daniel for their love and support, and for putting up with everything.

ABOUT THE AUTHORS

Judy Melinek and T.J. Mitchell are the *New York Times* best-selling coauthors of *Working Stiff: Two Years, 262 Bodies, and the Making of a Medical Examiner*. Dr. Melinek was an assistant medical examiner in San Francisco for nine years and today works as a forensic pathologist and as CEO of PathologyExpert Inc. T.J. Mitchell, her husband, is a writer with an English degree from Harvard, and worked in the film industry before becoming a full-time stay-at-home dad to their children. *First Cut* is their debut novel.

Read on for an excerpt from the next Dr. Jessie Teska mystery,
Aftershock, *coming February 1, 2021.*

CHAPTER ONE

A steel band cover of "Don't Fear the Reaper" makes for a lousy way to lurch awake. Couple of months back, some clown of a coworker got ahold of my cell phone while I was busy in the autopsy suite, and reprogrammed the ringtone for incoming calls from the Medical Examiner Operations and Investigation Dispatch Communications Center. I keep forgetting to fix it.

I reached across my bedmate to the only table in the tiny room and managed to squelch it before the plinking got past five or six bars, but that was more than enough to wake him.

"Time is it?" Anup slurred.

"Four thirty."

"God, Jessie," he said, and pulled a pillow over his head. I planted a nice warm kiss on the back of his neck.

Donna Griello from the night shift was on the phone. "Good morning, Dr. Teska," she said.

"Okay, Donna," I whispered. "What do we got and where are we going?"

I didn't need the GPS navigation from my one extravagance in this world, the BMW 235i that I had brought along when I moved from Los Angeles to San Francisco, because muscle memory took me there. The death scene was right on my old commute—a straight shot from the Outer Richmond District, along the edge of Golden Gate Park, then the wiggle down to SoMa, the broad, flat neighborhood south of Market Street. The blue lights were flashing on the corner of Sixth Street and Folsom, just a couple of blocks shy of the Hall of Justice. I had performed autopsies in the bowels of the Hall for just over a year until the boss, Chief Medical Examiner Dr. James Howe, had the whole operation moved to his purpose-built dream morgue, way out in Hunters Point. Along the way, Howe made me his deputy chief. The promotion came with a raise, an office, and a ficus, but I hadn't sought it and it wasn't welcome—I was only a year and change on the job and didn't have the experience to be deputy chief in a big city. Howe needed someone to do it, though. So the gold badge and all its headaches went to me.

The death scene address Donna had given me over the phone was a construction site. From the outside, I couldn't tell how big. They'd built a temporary sidewalk covered in plywood, and posted an artist's rendition of a gleaming glass tower, crusted in niches and crenellations and funky angles, dubbed *SoMa Centre*.

I double-parked behind a police car and walked the plankway between a blind fence and a line of pickup trucks with union bumper stickers. The men in them eyed me with either suspicion or practiced blankness while they waited for their job site to re-open. A beat cop kept vigil at the head of the line. He took my name and badge number, logged me in, and lifted the yellow tape. He pointed to a wooden crate. It was full of construction hard hats.

"Mandatory," he said.

"You aren't wearing one," I griped.

"I'm not going in there, either."

"Good for you. Give me a light over here."

I sorted through the helmets under the cop's flashlight beam. Sizes large, extra large, medium. I am a woman, five feet five inches, a hundred thirty-four pounds, and not especially husky of skull. I certainly wasn't husky enough to fill out a helmet spec'd for your average male ironworker, which seemed to be all that was on offer.

I tried out a medium. Even when I cinched the plastic headband all the way, the hard hat swallowed my sorry little blond noggin.

"Yeah, laugh it up, Officer," I said, while he did.

"Sorry, Doc. You look like a kid playing soldier!"

"Laugh it up," I said again, because I wasn't equipped, at that hour, to be clever.

Not all the workers were stuck outside in their pickups. A few men in hard hats stood around, waiting for work to get going. They shied away from me, in my MEDICAL EXAMINER windbreaker, polyester slacks, and sensible shoes, like I was the angel of death collecting on a debt.

I found Donna. She's hard to miss: more than six feet tall, eyes and beak like a hawk. Her hard hat fit just fine. She was leaning against the medical examiner removals van with Cameron Blake, her partner 2578—our bureaucratic shorthand for death scene investigators—on the night shift. Cam is round-faced and ruddy, half a foot shorter than Donna but just as brawny. He greeted me.

"Any coffee?" I said.

"The site superintendent says it's brewing. First shift is just getting here. That's how come they found the body. You want to talk to him?"

"The body?"

"The superintendent."

"Let's find out what the dead guy has to say first."

Donna chuckled in a dark way. "Just you wait and see, Doc."

The pair of 2578s led me across the construction site by flashlight. Work lights were coming on, but they left big dark gaps.

"Who found the body?"

Donna consulted her clipboard. "Dispatch says a worker named Samuel Urias, opening up after the night shift."

The construction site by flashlight was a spooky place, even by my standards. Dirty yellow machines loomed in the beams, and plastic sheeting fluttered from the shadows. Our feet crunched on gravel, then whispered over packed dirt. The only thing that was well lit was a mobile office trailer, on a rise to our left, surrounded by silhouettes in hard hats.

Donna led us toward a detached flatbed trailer, parked with its landing-gear feet pressing into the dirt. It was loaded with long metal pipes, six or eight inches in diameter, in bundles of twenty or so. The bundles were bound together with tight black bands at either end and had been stacked four high on the flatbed. One of the bands securing the top bundle had snapped. It waved drunkenly in the air—and half a dozen pipes lay tumbled in the dirt.

Underneath them was a body.

It was a man. He was on his back. His head and shoulders were crushed under the pipes. He wore a business suit and black wingtip shoes, the left one coming off at the heel. His arms were flung out. I determined his race to be white from his hands, which offered the only visible skin. They were clean and uncalloused, fingernails manicured, wedding band on the left ring finger, a college ring on the right.

I shined my flashlight at the pipes. They had done a job on him. We walked around the body, looking for a pool of blood. There wasn't one.

When I pointed this out, Donna elbowed Cameron and smirked. He scowled back.

"What?" I said.

"I noticed that too," Donna said. "Cam thinks it's no big deal."

"Can we just get this guy out of here?" Cameron said. "The superintendent is antsy. He's worried about press, and I don't blame him."

I crouched to take a closer look at that left shoe. The leather above the heel was badly scuffed. Same for the right one. The dead man's pricy wool dress pants were torn at the hems. My flashlight picked up a faint trail in the dirt running away from his feet. I warned the 2578s to watch their step until the police crime scene unit had photographed the area.

"What—?" said Cam. "CSI isn't here. This is an accident scene."

"Get them. This is a suspicious death."

"Oh, come on…"

"It's fishy." I pointed my flashlight around. "Where's all the blood from that crush injury? There's drag marks and damage to the clothing to match. Soft hands, expensive suit. Where's his hard hat?"

"Maybe it's under the pipes."

"Maybe. But does this guy look like he belongs on a construction site, after hours? No way I'm assuming this was an accident."

"Told you it was staged," Donna said to Cam.

"Whatever," he muttered back. He pulled out his phone,

said good morning to the police dispatcher, and asked for the crime scene unit.

The sky was lightening behind the downtown towers a few blocks away, and more construction workers were starting to trickle in. "We need a perimeter," I said. "And I want to talk to the man who found the body. Do we have a presumptive ID?"

"We found this just like you see it, and didn't run his pockets yet," Donna said.

"Let's wait till crime scene documents everything before we touch him."

Donna smiled. "Because this is fishy, right?"

I couldn't help smiling back. "You won the bet. Leave Cam alone." I started toward the lit-up office trailer.

"Where you going?" Donna said.

"Coffee."

A figure in the small crowd huddling at the trailer saw me coming and met me halfway. He was a late middle-aged white man with a gray mustache, dressed like a soccer dad in blue jeans and a collared shirt. No tie, no jacket, heavy work boots. He had a fancy hard hat. It said SITE SUPER.

"Where's the hearse?" the construction superintendent demanded.

I introduced myself and told him we were waiting for the police crime scene unit to arrive and document the scene.

"How long will that take?"

Fuck if I know, I thought. "It could be a while," I said.

"What's a while? We have work to do here."

Bałwan. I grew up outside of Boston, but Polish is my first language. Sort of. My mother is from Poland and my father is a son of a bitch. *Mamusia* taught me and my brother Tomasz the mother tongue—which Dad doesn't speak—and the three of us stuck with it inside the four walls of our three-decker flat on

Pinkham Street in East Lynn. *Mamusia* said it was to preserve our heritage. It was also useful for hiding things from the old man.

Polish has a lot of terms for a son of a bitch. *Bałwan* was *Mamusia's* word for her husband Arthur Teska on a good day. If he had been drinking, he was a *sukinsyn*. So far, the site superintendent was turning out to be a *bałwan*, but the day was young.

"First the police will do their job, then my colleagues and I will do our job, and then you can get back to yours."

"But the police are already here, and they aren't doing anything!"

"We're waiting for the homicide division."

The superintendent went pale and stammery. "Homicide—? But this isn't... This is..."

"This is a death scene. It might be a crime scene. That's for the police to determine before I can continue my investigation as the medical examiner, and certainly before we can remove or even touch that body."

The superintendent said nothing. He dug into his pocket for a phone and walked away, dialing. Not an unusual reaction. People freak out when they hear homicide is coming.

I dug a hand under the wobbly hard hat to scratch my scalp. It was Anup's damn shampoo. I had been dating Anup Banerjee for seven, almost eight months. I live in a rental, a tiny back-garden cottage in the Richmond District, half a mile from the continent's Pacific edge. *Cottage* does the place too much justice—it's a converted San Francisco cable car called Mahoney Brothers #45. It was abandoned in the sand dunes at the end of the line after it had outlived its usefulness, until someone jacked the thing up, built a foundation under it, and added box wings for a bedroom and a kitchen and a water closet. Mahoney Brothers #45 covers 372 square feet of the most expensive real estate in the country. Back when I had lived in it alone with my beagle, Bea, it was my very own cozy paradise.

Anup and I were not quite living together, but he had started spending most nights in Mahoney Brothers #45, and the place is no cozy paradise for two grown adults and a demanding dog. It's more like sharing a Winnebago. I am not a domestic goddess. Anup is a lawyer by training and a fastidious, detail-oriented person by inclination. I ran out of shampoo; he got more. But it had turned out to be some awful stuff that only a man would buy, and it made my scalp itch.

I scratched at it. Then I headed up to the over-lit trailer to scare up some coffee.

I couldn't juggle three cups, so I shanghaied one of the beat cops into helping. He told me that press and camera trucks were already arriving at the gate.

"And our LT wants us to wrap things up here. The captain's already riding his ass. That means someone with pull called the captain."

I didn't have the heart to tell him it was a complicated and hazardous crime scene, and we'd likely be holding vigil over that body for hours to come.

Cam and Donna and I sipped our coffees and waited for the crime scene unit. They didn't take long. They rearranged our perimeter. They took pictures. We stayed out of the way.

I was about to mosey up to the trailer for a refill when Cam nudged me and pointed his chin toward the entry gate. A black man in a blue suit was swapping a fedora for a hard hat. Even at a distance in the dismal predawn light, I could pick out that mustache of his. It scowled.

"*Zasrane to życie,*" I muttered. My shit luck. It would appear that the homicide detective assigned to this case was going to be Keith Jones.

Inspector Jones and I had a history, and not a happy one. The year before, we'd done a case together, a drug overdose that he and his partner wanted to call an accident. I disagreed and tried to certify it as a homicide—but I was overruled by Dr. Howe, my boss. Jones had never forgiven me for putting them through a pile of work over a stupid OD just because I had decided it had to be a murder.

"Dr. Jessie Teska," he said. "On a construction site. So I'm gonna guess I'm out here wasting my time with another accident."

The crime scene photographer's camera flashed, illuminating the dead man and the pile of pipes across his head and shoulders. Jones nodded thoughtfully. "Will you look at that," he said.

I bit my tongue. "Hello, Keith."

"Why are we here?"

"It's a suspicious death."

"What's suspicious about a load of pipe falling off a truck?"

I ran through my initial findings for him: the decedent's inappropriate attire, damage to the heels of his shoes and pant hems, drag marks in the dirt, the lack of evident bleeding.

"So what? Maybe he got drunk and tripped and tore his pants. Maybe the blood's under those pipes."

"Maybe the scene's been tampered with. Maybe it's a homicide dressed like an accident."

"Who is he, anyhow?"

"We'll try to get a presumptive ID when crime scene clears us to handle the body."

"So you don't know. Witnesses?"

"No. One of the workers found him when they opened up the site this morning."

"You spoke to this worker?"

"I figured you'd want to."

"That's what you figured, huh, Doctor. Did you figure maybe he could give you a presumptive ID on this dead person? Get us started, at least?"

Again I bit my tongue. I didn't like being dressed down by Jones, especially in front of the 2578s and the precinct cops, but nothing good would come from calling him out. By luck of the draw, it was a case we had to investigate together.

Jones sighed and massaged his boxy eyebrows. "Okay, then, Deputy Chief Teska. You've got the whole circus rolling in, and it's going to be here for hours. Let's see what's what." He headed off toward the lit-up office trailer.

I rejoined Cameron and Donna, who were studiously pretending to ignore us by watching the crime scene unit photograph the death scene.

"How are we going to get those pipes off the body?" I wondered.

"Can't be that hard," Cam said. "I'll go talk to the superintendent."

The pallid sky brightened a little, and I could hear the growl of rush hour rising on all sides of the future home of SoMa Centre. I checked my phone. It was 7:05. Anup would be getting up soon. He'd take Bea out. He had no problem with the dog. I'm her alpha for sure, but Anup is a runner and Bea enjoys chasing him around Golden Gate Park. I thought about calling him, but decided it was better to let him enjoy his last few minutes of sleep. Anup had a nice desk job at the First District Court of Appeal. Never did he have to roll out of bed at 4:30 to sit around a construction site and watch cops take pictures of a mangled corpse.

Lucky him.

Cam returned. Behind him, the site superintendent had picked two men out of the crowd by the trailer and marched them over to a giant front loader.

"We have an issue," Cam said. Apparently, those two were the only workers on hand qualified to operate the equipment that would safely lift the pipes off our dead guy—and they refused to do it. They wanted nothing at all to do with dead bodies, especially if the police were involved. The superintendent was threatening to fire them both if one of them didn't shift those damn pipes.

A ripple went through the crowd of hardhats watching the confrontation, and they turned in unison toward a wiry, sharp-angled man approaching from the entrance gate. The way he stalked across the construction site told everyone he was not playing games. He went straight up to the superintendent, and the two of them got to shouting, nose to nose, like they'd had practice at it.

Homicide Inspector Jones intervened. He brandished his pad and pen, introduced himself, and asked the men to give him their names, addresses, and phone numbers.

"How come?" said the wiry man. "We didn't do nothing."

"I'm not saying you did, okay?" Jones assured him in a soft-glove way. It's just that this is a crime scene here, and we need to document everyone who has been on it."

"You can't detain nobody that's not under arrest!" the man shouted, and repeated the message in Spanish to the crowd of hardhats.

"Hold on, now," said Jones, still softly. "We can't allow any of you people to leave this crime scene until we document who you are and how to reach you. All of you." He gestured to one of the precinct cops, who said something into his shoulder mic. Uniforms materialized from all around, and surrounded the crowd of hardhats.

The wiry man said, "Is anyone here under arrest?"

"Nobody's under arrest. There's been a death at your workplace, and there will be an investigation. We just need to see your IDs, and then anyone who wants to leave can go."

"These men were not even here last night."

"Until we get everyone's information, no one is leaving."

I felt Cam, next to me, tense up. He's a crime scene veteran. His instincts are worth paying attention to.

The wiry man tried to stare down Keith Jones. Jones didn't blink. Nobody in the crowd moved a muscle.

Then the wiry man nodded and pulled out his wallet, and we all unclenched. "I would like your business card, please, Detective," he said. "My name is Samuel Urias, and I am the union steward on this job."

I cast an eye to Donna and she nodded. Samuel Urias was the man who had called 911 to report the dead body.

Urias said something to the two men behind him, and without a word they produced their IDs, too. Jones handed out his card. "Mr. Urias," he said, "we can't determine what happened here to cause this death until we get those pipes lifted. Will one of these machine operators be willing to help?"

"No," Urias said, without bothering to ask the workers. "They're not doing it. But I am certified on this equipment. I will move the pipes."

Urias started off toward the giant front loader, and over his shoulder he said, "Clear the area."

Jones let a deadly smile slip past his mustache. Then he said to the nearest uniform cop, "You heard the man. Safety first."

Samuel Urias took his sweet time moving those pipes off our corpse. He did a thorough walkaround inspection of the front loader. Then he powered it up, fiddled with the coupling on its talon-like grabber arm, and did another walkaround.

Donna yawned. Cam worried out loud about press helicopters being bound to appear, now that there was daylight. One of the beat cops reported to Jones that a clot of trucks trying to get onto the site had gummed up the intersections across Sixth Street for blocks in all directions. That gridlock was spreading to the Central Freeway off-ramp, which was, in turn, backing up the Bay Bridge.

"You know who lives in these condos?" Cam murmured. "Tech bros. The Google bus can't get down Eighth Street, that's a class-A clusterfuck."

"DEFCON 1," Donna agreed.

I scoffed at the pair of them. "Come on. It's traffic. There's traffic every day. Big deal."

"Just you wait and see," Donna said for the second time that morning. Her boardwalk soothsayer routine was starting to grate on me.

The site superintendent complained that the duty contractor should be here managing this emergency, but that he wasn't answering his phone.

"Maybe that's him under the pipes," Donna said to Cam.

"Not in that suit. Or those shoes."

It was getting near 8:30 by the time Urias finally swung the arm of the heavy machine up in the air, opened the grabber, and lowered it slowly onto our death scene. The grabber's tines closed around the pipes and they clattered. The truck roared. It lifted the metal pipes, pivoted them well away from the body, and dropped them in the dust beyond the flatbed trailer.

Jones lifted the police tape to approach the body, then jumped clear out of his shoes at a deafening blast from the front loader's air horn. Up in its cab Urias was wagging his finger wildly. He swung the grabber arm away to the far side of the machine, lowered it to the ground, and killed the engine.

"Okay," Urias hollered. "Clear!"

It's not easy to rile a big-city police detective, but at that moment Homicide Inspector Keith Jones looked like he had developed a burning desire to rip off Samuel Urias's head and shit down his neck.

We followed Jones under the tape to get a clear look at the body. The head, neck, and upper rib cage had been obliterated. I'd never seen a worse case of disfigurement, except maybe in one or two bodies that had been left to decompose in the open, where animals had gotten to them. A case from the year before, involving a coyote in the woods near the Lincoln Park Golf Course, came vividly to mind. This pulpy slew leaking into a business suit was even less recognizable as a human body. Brain matter was smeared into the dirt, and hairy chunks of skull had been scattered like pottery shards. The crushed area was pink in places, red in places, but mostly just kind of tan colored.

Donna was seeing what I was seeing, and shaking her head. "That ain't right."

"Well," I replied, "it's interesting."

"What about it?" said Inspector Jones.

"I'm concerned that we're not seeing a giant puddle of blood here. I would expect much more bleeding from such a violent crush injury. Practically all the man's pressurized blood should have gushed out of those ruptured neck vessels."

"So where is it?"

"I can't tell you that until I perform the full autopsy. But just on first impression, this looks like postmortem injury to me."

I didn't have to explain to the homicide detective what that meant. "You think this is a homicide staged to look like an accident."

"I think the visible evidence indicates that this man was already dead when those pipes came down on him. Let's see what else we can determine right now."

"Uh-huh," said Jones with zero percent conviction.

The beat cops tried to keep the construction workers from crowding the tape cordon, but it was no use. We had an audience. The crew from CSI moved back in to take more pictures, then gave us the go-ahead to handle the body.

"'Bout time," Cam grumbled.

"Chill, big guy," one of the crime scene cops snapped back. Cam didn't like that.

Identification is our first job and top priority. We went straight for the dead man's pockets and found a wallet. It had a California driver's license under the name Leopold Haring, address in San Francisco on Castenada Avenue.

"Forest Hill," Cam said. "Money."

Jones peered at the picture on the driver's license, then at the pulp piled on the end of the man's shoulders, and grunted. I manipulated an arm. The body was in full rigor mortis. That meant, I told Jones, he'd been dead at least six hours. Three a.m., maybe two a.m. at the earliest for a ballpark time of death.

"But," I reminded him, "that's the outside window. It could be a lot earlier."

"Can't you narrow that down?"

"Let's do a body temperature," I said to Cam.

We put the wallet back in Leopold Haring's pocket where we'd found it, and Cameron yanked down the trousers. It required some effort thanks to the rigor mortis. He inserted a thermometer into the cadaver's rectum and told Donna it came to 80 Fahrenheit. She wrote that down, consulted an outdoor thermometer she kept in her death scene kit, and told me the ambient temperature was 54. I looked at the time and did the math.

"He probably died between six and ten last night."

"That's the best you can tell?"

"Yes. And I might be wrong."

"You guys always say that."

"We mean it. Time of death estimation is unreliable. It depends on too many variables…"

"Okay," the detective said. I recalled from working with him before that he said okay a lot, but usually didn't mean it.

"Detective!" someone yelled from behind the cordon line. It was the superintendent, cell phone still on his ear. "Do we know who it is?"

Jones wasn't about to shout the dead man's name into the crowd, so he gestured the superintendent over. I watched Jones read the name off his notebook. The superintendent's jaw fell open. He bobbled the cell phone, dropped it in the dirt, and scrambled to pick it up. He stared at the shattered corpse in disbelief. Then he dusted off the phone and walked away, dialing frantically.

"Hey!" the detective called out, irked. "You know this guy?"

"Google it," the superintendent said, and disappeared into the crowd of hardhats.

"Goddamn people," said Jones, and stalked after him.

Donna already had her smartphone in hand and was typing. Cam and I huddled with her.

Leopold Andreas Haring, 52, born in Austria, immigrated in 1989 as a graduate student in architecture at the University of Pennsylvania.

"Oh, man," said Cameron.

Leopold Haring was one of the most famous and acclaimed architects in the world, known for a boldness of vision coupled with a towering intellect, said the one article. "'Haring's work unites a classical rigor of form with a disciplined attention to, and intention of, function as the *sine qua non* of a building,'" Donna read. "'His use of materials has proven famously visionary, yet has always been coupled with a miraculous lack of pretension…'"

"Enough," said Cam.

"Wait, you gotta hear this one. 'He is our great cityscape cubist, the Picasso of the building arts.'"

"Donna," said Cam, "our shift ended half an hour ago. Can we get the pouch and gurney, please, before we end up on the news? I don't like being on the news."

"Fine, fine." She produced a white sheet, which she draped carefully over the acclaimed architect's mortal remains, and the two of them trekked back to the van.

I scanned the crowd of hardhats for Jones, but didn't see him. My cell phone rang. It was the boss, Chief Medical Examiner Dr. James Howe.

"Jessie…?" He sounded faint and far away.

"Dr. Howe," I hollered, and stuck a finger in my left ear. The morning shift had been standing around with nothing to do for more than three hours, and had apparently decided to fire up every heavy vehicle on the lot in preparation for the moment we allowed them to start work. I started walking and talking, searching for a quiet spot.

"What the hell is going on up there?" Dr. Howe said. "I've got everyone from the highway patrol to the mayor on my ass about your death scene. They're saying you've locked it all down…?"

"Yeah, it's not looking like an accident over here…"

"What do you mean? It's a construction site with a fatal crush injury, right?"

"Not exactly. The injuries all look postmortem. It turned into a suspicious death pretty quick, so I had to call in CSI…"

I finally found a sheltered spot, a section of unfussy concrete foundation behind a chain-link gate. It was below grade and dark, but good and quiet.

"We just got access to the body a minute ago," I told Dr. Howe. "We also just got a presumptive ID, but that's another complication."

"Why?"

"Now it's suspicious *and* high-profile. The driver's license in his pocket belongs to a Leopold Haring. Apparently he's a famous—"

"Oh sweet Jesus."

"You've heard of him."

"Get that body into the truck and out of there before the press shows up, Dr. Teska! What happened to him?"

I described the circumstances as we had found them, and what we had gone through to extricate the body. Dr. Howe didn't like the story—especially once he reckoned how many scene spectators there were among the hardhats, and how many of them might have been sneaking cell phone pictures. I issued the soothing assurances I'd perfected in my short career under short-tempered boss men. I was good at it, and it worked. Dr. Howe let me go.

I climbed back up to the cordon line. Donna and Cam had staged their gurney and were laying out a body pouch next to Mr. Haring.

"Hang on," I said. "Let's get some pictures of the damage to the trouser hem and the shoes, while we still have them in situ with the drag marks in the dirt."

"*If* those are drag marks," Cam groused.

"That's why I want to document them, Cam. If."

Donna lifted the sheet off the body and set it aside, and Cam summoned the CSI photographer to take some close-ups of the ripped fabric and scuffed leather, the socks balled down, and pale pink abrasions on both Achilles' heels.

"Those look postmortem, too," I started to say—but was cut off by an anguished cry from behind us.

"Oh my God! Oh my God! What..."

It was a lanky man, well dressed, middle-aged, with silver hair. His face had gone as white as the morgue sheet.

"Is that...is that Leo?"

"That's what we need you to tell us, Mr. Symond." That was Jones. He was standing on one side of the pale man. The site superintendent stood on the other.

"Do you recognize him, Mr. Symond?" Jones said. "I mean, anything among his effects, maybe?"

"His head...what happened to his head? Oh God... Leo..."

Jones put a hand on the man's shoulder. "Take all the time you need."

The superintendent cleared his throat and turned away. "I'll be in my office, Jeff," he said, and strode briskly toward the trailer.

"Oh God..." the pale man—a Mr. Jeff Symond, evidently—said again. "That's his suit. It looks like his shoes. Is he wearing a U-Penn ring?"

Jones turned his flat gaze to me. I lifted the dead man's hand and examined the college ring.

"Yes."

"What year, Mr. Symond?" asked Jones gently.

"Nineteen ninety-one."

They both looked to me. I nodded.

Jeff Symond's mouth hung open. His breathing was shallow, eyes glassy. He swiveled suddenly, stumbled, and vomited into the dirt under the police cordon tape.

Cameron muttered, "That's another DNA profile to rule out," and Donna stifled a snicker. I glared daggers and ordered them to get going with collecting the remains.

Symond wiped his mouth with a handkerchief, his back still turned. I went to him, asked if he was dizzy. He shook his head. I waved over a patrol cop.

"Take Mr. Symond up to the trailer and get him a chair and a glass of water, okay?"

They started off, carefully. Symond did not look back.

"Can I talk to you, Keith," I said to Jones, and walked away from the cordon. He followed.

"What the hell is wrong with you?" I spat, too loud, and turned the heads on a couple of nearby beat cops. I tamped down my temper and dropped into a church whisper. "You don't bring a civilian to a crime scene! What were you thinking—?"

"What's wrong with *me*? You're forgetting this is my scene." He kept his body language lax for the benefit of the uniforms and hardhats craning to eavesdrop, but the anger in his voice matched mine. "This guy shows up at the gate, says he's the decedent's business partner. Apparently the superintendent called him, asked him to get down here. He demands—*demands*—to see the scene of the accident. He wants to see how it happened."

"Accident—?"

"Yeah, accident. To me this looks like an industrial accident. You say different, based, as far as I can tell, on intuition about the blood spatter. Okay. Maybe you're right—we'll all find out sooner or later. But you've been *way* wrong, calling accidents homicides before, and I'm not taking any chances with your work, Doctor."

"That is not fair."

"Maybe not. Like I said, we'll all find out sooner or later. This Mr. Jeffrey Symond is the partner of the man who holds the presumptive ID for our corpse over there. I figured he could tell us something about the pipes and how they fell, maybe. Or at least he could confirm the ID—"

"On a guy with no fucking face? Give me a break, Keith. You and I both know we're going to get fingerprints off that body as soon as we get it back to the morgue, and those prints will match the DMV database for our presumptive. The ID will be solid. You didn't have to drag that poor man over here. It's unprofessional and sadistic."

"Sadistic—?" Keith Jones was losing his struggle to keep his body language from matching his words, and the hardhats were starting to notice. "*Sadistic* is leaving that dead man out there for, what—? Four hours now? Why don't you do your job and get the body out of here."

"Your crime scene, Inspector, but my body. You know that. The body and everything on it is my jurisdiction."

"So why don't you go look after it."

"So why don't *you* go—"

He turned his back and I stopped myself, which was just as well. He walked away.

Donna and Cam had slid the body onto the white sheet, scooping up the mess that remained of the man's head and shoulders, along with some bloody dirt and rubble. They tied the ends of the sheet into knots like a shroud, then lifted it up and placed it in the body pouch, which in turn went onto the gurney.

I told them to take it back to the morgue without me. "It's too late to start the autopsy today. Print and weigh him and hold him over for tomorrow in the cooler."

The 2578s calculated overtime while they pushed the gurney across the dirt lot to their truck. I covered a yawn and rubbed my face. If Mr. Jeffrey Symond was still recuperating in the office trailer, I figured I might as well go talk to him and see what he could tell me about the late Leopold Haring.

I opened the flimsy door to find Mr. Symond propped on a folding chair in a corner, drinking water from a paper cup. He looked badly shaken, but not on the verge of puking again. I got him a refill of water. He thanked me, absently.

I introduced myself. Jeffrey Symond did the same. I asked him how he knew the decedent.

"I'm his business partner," he said. "Twenty years. More than that. This project is one of ours—his design, his blueprints. I do operations and permits, pitching new clients, the business end. Leo is the creative one."

He sighed in the desperate way some men do to keep from crying.

"Mr. Symond," I said, "I'm very sorry you went through that. No one should have to see a friend in that state."

His eyes had a plea in them. I knew what was coming next. It was the vanguard of the denial phase.

"Are you sure that's him?"

"The driver's license he was carrying says it is, and the college ring you asked about substantiates that. We'll know for sure in a few hours, when we compare his fingerprints to the database at the Department of Motor Vehicles."

"Oh," he said, despondent again. "Right."

"He wears a wedding ring. Is he married?"

"Yes. Natalie. Natalie Haring." I wrote it down, and asked him for Mrs. Haring's phone number and address. He knew both from memory. "We all work together," he said. "We have a company. Natalie and Leo and myself."

"Does Mrs. Haring know yet?"

"I haven't spoken to her…"

"I'm going to ask you not to, then. Our office will provide notification once the fingerprints come back and it's official, which should be in the next couple of hours. Okay?"

"Okay."

I gave Jeffrey Symond a moment to fiddle with his paper cup, then I continued.

"Did Leo use drugs or alcohol?"

"He drank. Not a lot."

"No history of substance abuse that you know of?"

"No drugs, and I can't remember the last time I saw him drunk, or even tipsy."

"Was he on any medications? And do you know if he has any medical history?"

"I don't know. You'd have to ask Natalie."

"Okay. When did you last see Mr. Haring?"

"Yesterday around six."

"In the evening, you mean?"

"Yes."

"Where?"

"At our office. Natalie and I were both there, expecting him to be working with us. When he finally showed up, he was agitated—he'd been in a fight with his son."

"What's his name and age, the son?"

"Oskar. He's twenty-three."

"Natalie is his mother?" I asked.

"Yes."

"But Oskar wasn't there, at the office."

"No."

"Did Mr. Haring say what the fight was about?"

"No," Symond said. "But he did say he was planning on coming down here, to the SoMa Centre site."

"What for?"

"I don't know exactly. He had a lot of complaints about the way they were doing this job."

"What was going on?"

"Leo kept telling me the contractors were cutting corners. Materials, even methods. He was worried about it. You heard of the Leaning Tower of Pine Street?"

I nodded. The Leaning Tower was infamous. One of the city's tallest new skyscrapers, right downtown, had been built with the wrong sort of foundation or something, and had started listing to one side. Pipes ruptured, electrical wires snapped, and windows were cracking—one had even popped out and crashed to the street below. No one knew what was going to happen to that building. Hundreds of people—very rich people—had already invested in luxury condos there. They were bleeding untold millions of dollars in lost real estate value. Demolishing the building was out of the question and repairing it was impossible. Years in the planning and construction, and it had yielded nothing but decades of finger-pointing and lawsuits for everyone involved.

"The Leaning Tower is every architect's worst nightmare," Symond said. "Something like that happens, it ruins your life. So Leo was worried about the foundation work on this place, on SoMa Centre."

"Is that why he came down here last night?"

"He didn't say as much, so I don't know."

Jeffrey Symond looked around the superintendent's trailer, as if noticing for the first time where he was. There was a poster of the artist's rendering. He rose and went over, contemplated it.

"They're trying to keep too fast a pace on this thing," he said. "I'm not surprised there was a fatal accident. I'm just surprised it was Leo."

He moved to look out the trailer's little window. Jones must've allowed the site opened up for work, because there was a lot more action—voices shouting commands, workers hustling around, machinery belching smoke and hauling off. The death scene cordon was still in place, but someone had shifted the fallen pipes farther off. A man in a hard hat stood over them with a hose, rinsing them down. He was washing bloody bits of Leopold Haring into the dirt.